ChangelingPress.com

Passionate Prisoners

Angela Knight

Passionate Prisoners
Angela Knight

ISBN: 978-1-60521-808-3

Publisher:
Changeling Press LLC
315 N. Centre St.
Martinsburg, WV 25404
ChangelingPress.com

Printed in the U.S.A.

Editor: Karen Williams
Cover Artist: Angela Knight

The individual stories in this anthology have been previously released in E-Book format.

Table of Contents

Roarke's Prisoner
Angela Knight

Starship captain Elise Morrell remembers the eager animal submission she'd known at Captain Michael Roarke's ruthless hands.

She's determined not to become his toy again, but she has no idea of the delights he's got in store.

Chapter One

Captain Elise Morrell sat at her command center and wondered if she'd feel something beyond this numb defeat when the ship's engines exploded. She doubted it. Roarke's next blast would drown her star frigate in nuclear fire so fast none of them would even have time to feel the heat.

At the five horseshoe-shaped stations that surrounded her own, her bridge staff sat with bent heads and white faces, staring down at disastrous readouts as their hands darted over the controls. Vidscreens surrounded them with images of the chaos on the ship's lower decks as her people struggled to save the *Star Raker*, while on the primary screen ahead of them, the *Liberator* cruised through space, waiting for Roarke's order to destroy them.

Her private communications unit beeped, and Elise looked down at the vid inset in her station just as Henry Voronnin's face popped into view. Her second in command must have finally gotten a chance to report in. Elise had sent him down to lead the damage control teams, and she knew he had his hands full.

"How bad is it, Henry?" she asked.

He rubbed a big hand over his head, leaving a streak of soot on the hairless pink dome. Dark shapes raced around in the smoke behind him, training hand foamers at the tongues of flame licking up from equipment panels. "Well," Henry said, "we haven't blown up yet."

She winced. "I'd hoped the sensors were exaggerating."

"They weren't. That last shot turned the drive room into an inferno. We lost the entire engineering crew, not to mention the engines themselves."

Ignoring a stab of agony at the thought of those deaths, Elise set her jaw. "Which means no weapons and no defense screens."

He nodded, his broad, meaty face grim. "We're at that sonofabitch's mercy -- and I haven't noticed that he's got any."

"Any hull breeches?"

"One, but the emergency systems sealed it. We've still got the battery backups, so we won't start sucking CO2 for at least a couple of days."

Assuming Roarke doesn't blow us to plasma first. She didn't voice the thought.

Henry paused, staring into her face. "You did everything you could, Captain. The *Liberator*'s four times the size of the *Raker*, and it's got six times the firepower. Once Roarke caught us, it was over."

There was no response she could -- or would -- make to that. "Get that fire out, Henry."

"Aye, aye." He paused. "Good luck, Captain."

The vid went black. Elise lifted her head and looked at the central screen and the armored shark that was the *Liberator*, cruising through space a hundred kilometers away. The Rebellion dreadnought bristled with sensor dishes, beamer projectors, and D-screen generators -- devices normally recessed into the hull to survive the stress of Superlight travel, now extended for battle. It was fully as lethal as it looked; the *Liberator* had already captured or destroyed every other Coalition ship assigned to this sector. Only the *Raker* had managed to elude its lethal pursuit, though she knew Roarke had been hunting them for the past year.

Now all they could do was wait for him to finish them off.

Unless she was willing to beg. Roarke would like that. He might even like it enough to spare the *Raker*.

As Elise considered that dubious hope, her communications officer spun his chair toward her. His young face was too pale, and his eyes were wide, though she could see how hard he was fighting his fear. "Captain, I'm getting a call from the *Liberator*."

God, this would be humiliating, but she was going to save her crew if she had to grovel to do it. "Put him on."

Michael Roarke filled the forward screen, the blue and gray uniform of the Rebellion Starforce stretching across his muscled torso. Even Elise had to admit he was a handsome bastard, with broad, angular cheekbones and an aggressive chin. The bridge of his nose was narrow, yet the nostrils flared, a combination that gave him a faintly wolfish appearance enhanced by the pelt-short cut of his hair. His eyes were black, intelligent and wary, deep-set under thick dark brows. In contrast to those cool lupine features, his mouth was blatantly erotic, with lips that were every bit as hot, soft, and skilled as they looked.

Best not to think about that.

"I've been evaluating our options, Captain Morrell," Roarke told her, his voice rich and faintly British.

Elise leaned back and crossed her legs, lifting an inquiring eyebrow. Her heart was pounding. "That's kind of you, Captain Roarke," she said, too sweetly. "And what are your conclusions?"

He smiled like a courtly wolf. "You can surrender, or I can blow you to hell."

Oh, he was going to be a son of a bitch to deal with. But then, he always had been. "Providing you allow my people to --"

"No," Roarke interrupted, his tone flat, almost brutal. "The only thing I'm going to accept is your unconditional surrender."

She was willing to surrender, but not unconditionally. Not to a commander with his reputation. "You're not going to get it."

"Captain, you are not in a position to refuse." His grin was nothing short of feral.

Elise displayed her own teeth. "My engines may not be up to generating D-shields, but they'd make a very pretty fire ball."

Roarke's amusement vanished, wiped clean from his handsome face. Then he smiled and lifted a brow. "Nice try, Captain, but suicide isn't your style. Particularly not when you'd be taking your crew along for the ride."

"At least engine implosion is quick and clean. I'm not so sure about whatever you've got in mind."

"Unlike the Coalition, the Rebellion doesn't abuse prisoners of war."

"So your propaganda says."

"I've sampled the Coalition's hospitality, Captain. Believe me, ours is preferable."

"And you'd know, wouldn't you?" She shot him a grin of pure malice. "Such a shame you escaped."

His fine upper lip curled into a snarl. "But you won't."

"You don't have me yet."

Roarke's grin was slow and malicious. "Don't I?" He stopped and stared into her face, as if reading her determination, gauging her strength of will. Caution flickered into his eyes. When he spoke again, his voice was as coolly businesslike as a banker's. "I swear to you on my honor as an officer that your people will not be harmed -- unless they attempt escape."

"We wouldn't dream of it." Elise felt a knot of fear unwind in her belly. If Roarke promised her crew's safety, they were safe.

At her implied surrender, there was a faint but visible loosening in the set of his shoulders. "And I believe you," Roarke said, his tone silken. "After all, I've seen how very loyal and obedient the *Raker* crew is."

She inclined her head. "Thank you."

"Which is why you're going to serve as my hostage."

"I beg your pardon?"

Roarke leaned an elbow on the arm of his command seat. His biceps strained his sleeve. "You heard me. With you as a hostage, I won't have to deal with any heroics from your crew."

Elise stared at him, remembering the last time she'd been at his mercy.

His fingers brushing paths of fire across her bare, aching breasts.

He gave her a silky smile. "Do you accept?"

His skillful mouth sucking, biting gently, the thick ridge of his erection pressing into her belly.

If she became his personal captive, he'd plunge her back into that eager animal submission she'd known on Tyus. And she was damned if she'd let him turn her into his toy again.

But -- there was the crew to think of. Henry, Amanda Yancey, Don Hart, Dr. Rodriguez, all the others who wouldn't be here if not for Elise Morrell and a Coalition admiral with a political agenda and an ugly grudge. She couldn't let them die, not even to save herself from Michael Roarke.

"I accept your terms." The words tasted like acid in her mouth.

"Very good. Prepare to be boarded. I'll expect to see you waiting for me at the *Raker*'s primary airlock."

He didn't bother hiding the menace as he added, "Alone and unarmed."

* * *

She'd agreed.

Roarke felt the muscles in his neck unlock for the first time since he'd gotten the anonymous communiqué revealing where the *Star Raker* would emerge from Superlight. It had been far too close.

Standing, he nodded to his second in command. Knowing Roarke's plan as well as he did, Hendricks moved to take the command station as he headed for the bridge hatchway and the docking bay where his troopship waited. As he passed, Yolanda Boniface fell in beside him, the top of her head barely reaching his shoulders.

The instant the bridge hatch closed, the little engineer flashed him a wicked grin. Her dark, Asian eyes glittered with unholy amusement. "Scared the shit out of you, didn't she?"

Roarke turned his head to stare at her. Anyone but Yo would have backed up a pace. "I beg your pardon?"

"Save that look for someone who hasn't known you for seventeen years," she told him. "You handled the *Raker* like a glass eggshell trying to take Morrell alive, and then she threatened to blow it up herself. She really had you going."

"Of course not," Roarke lied. "I knew she wouldn't suicide."

"Uh huh. So tell me. Now that you've got her, what are you going to do with her?"

A deeply sensual memory flashed through his mind -- the way Elise's sex had felt, tight and slick around his probing fingers. He forced the thought away. He wasn't going to lose control this time. "I have no idea."

Yolanda looked at him, one brow lifting. "Uh huh."

* * *

"You do realize somebody betrayed us," Henry told Elise as they stood waiting in front of the main hatch to the docking bay. Roarke's troopship would be arriving at any moment.

"It is pretty obvious." Behind her back, Elise's fists clenched. "Roarke should have had no idea where we'd emerge from Superlight, but he was there waiting for us. Somebody told him where we'd be."

"You think it was Price?"

Lieutenant Gloria Price was the *Raker*'s morale officer, but she was also a spy for Admiral Frank Scordillis, Elise's superior in the Coalition Stellar Service. And Scordillis was gunning for Elise. "I doubt it," she said finally. "I've been monitoring her communication traffic for some time. Can't read the communiques themselves, but I know the destinations, and nothing went to Roarke."

Henry's lip curled. "If it wasn't Price, Scordillis did it himself."

"Probably."

He swore.

"My thoughts exactly." Elise grimaced. "You know, my father warned me months ago something like this might happen. I should have had the sense to resign before they sacrificed the *Raker* to get to me."

"It's not your fault." Henry swiped a big hand over the smooth dome of his head in a gesture of frustration. "Who'd have thought they'd throw us to the wolves just because your father's big in the Reform Party?"

"He's not just big, Henry," Elise said drily. "He

just may be the next president of the Coalition."

"*If* the Reformists can get control away from the military. And that's a very big 'if.'"

"Which gets even bigger if Roarke kills me." Catching his questioning look, she explained, "Dad advocates letting the Rebellion Worlds have independence. If a rebel kills me, the military could use it to discredit him."

"I'm beginning to think the goddamned Rebels have a point."

"Commander, lower your voice," Elise snapped, then added more lightly, "My father would tell you the best way to change the system is from the inside. Why do you think I'm still in the CSS?"

"I don't know, Captain, why *are* you still in the CSS?" a female voice cut in.

Elise and Henry turned to watch as Gloria Price sauntered up the hall to join them. Her blonde hair foamed in gleaming curls around the shoulders of her stark black uniform, and her tall boots shone. There was an expression of malicious amusement on her elegantly boned face. But then, there usually was; as Scordillis' pet, she thought she was untouchable. "I understand you'll be playing hostage to Captain Roarke," Price said. "That should be interesting. Particularly considering he's not very fond of the Coalition Stellar Service."

"If he was, he wouldn't be a rebel, would he?" Elise growled. She'd put up with the blonde's games for the past few months because she knew Price was under Scordillis' protection, but that was before the admiral had betrayed them all. Now she was seriously considering throwing the little twit in the brig.

"True, but there's more to it than that." Price sent her a sly smile, completely oblivious to the danger.

"You do know Roarke once spent two months in the CSS prison camp on Elba? I understand one of the intelligence agents there tortured him with a neurowhip until Roarke finally murdered him and escaped." Her full lips curved. "You know, they never did find that whip."

"You've got far more to worry about than the captain, Price." Henry taunted. "Everybody on this ship knows you're working for CSSIntel. You'd better pray nobody lets that little fact slip to our captor -- or you just may find out if he's got that neurowhip the hard way."

Before he could add anything more, Elise cut him off. "That's enough, Commander. If I want the lieutenant disciplined, I don't need Michael Roarke to do it for me." She glanced coolly at Price. "Dismissed."

Even Scordillis' spy knew better than to buck her when she used that tone. "Aye, aye, Captain." She pivoted on her heel with a military snap and retreated.

They watched her go. "Henry, I want you to do something for me," Elise said softly.

"Shoot Price?"

"Tempting, but no." Her brief grin disappeared. "Save my ship. If you see a chance to escape, do it. If you've got to leave me behind, do it. That's an order."

He swiveled to face her, thick brows flying toward his non-existent hairline. "You don't seriously expect me to abandon you?"

Elise let her gaze chill. "Expect you? By God, I'm *ordering* you to. The *Raker*'s your first and only consideration."

"And what's Roarke going to do to you in the meantime? Remember Tyus? By the time you got away from him, he had you half-naked."

"He won't molest me, Henry, if that's what you're

worried about." She gave him a reassuring smile, but it felt thin and tight. "Roarke's not the type to bother; he already thinks he's irresistible."

Henry just looked at her, his opinion of that statement clear in his eyes.

A soft, warning chime interrupted before she could make another attempt to convince him -- and herself. Turning, Elise looked over her shoulder at the airlock hatch. The vid screen set in the wall above it revealed an image of a blocky troop transport finishing its docking procedure. "I've got to go."

"Captain --" He broke off and sighed, giving the sailor's traditional blessing. "Fair winds, Elise."

"Thanks, Henry." She hit the key panel, waited barely long enough for the airlock to open, then ducked through. Before the hatch closed again, she looked back at him. "Get my people out alive, Commander. That's an order."

The airlock rolled closed with a hollow, lonely *thud*.

Walking out onto the cargo deck, Elise listened to the echoing thrum of the *Raker*'s engines and the *bang* and *clank* of the troopship settling in. She picked a spot to wait and fell into parade rest, resisting an impulse to dry her damp palms on the fine fabric of her dress trousers.

She hadn't seen Roarke in a year.

Oh, there'd been plenty of encounters since then, but all of them had been over the bridge vidscreen during some military game of cat and mouse. Yet even then, with kilometers of space between them, she'd always been too aware of him, the memory of their first meeting vivid in her mind.

Looking back on it, Elise suspected that particular disaster had been another of Admiral Scordillis' attempts to set her up. A ship's captain had no business playing spy, yet Scordillis had sent her and Henry Voronnin to the planet Tyus with orders to pose as pirates with a captured cargo to sell. They were supposed to discover who was smuggling supplies to the rebels.

She'd met Roarke in a bar there, of all places. He'd been trying to buy ship's stores for the *Liberator*, and someone had directed him to her. At the time, they hadn't met in battle and Elise was new to the sector, so he'd had no idea who she was.

It had gone well at first. She'd even been attracted to him; Roarke was witty and intelligent, not to mention handsome enough to tempt a neophyte spy to forget her common sense. In fact, when he invited her for a walk on the beach, she'd almost accepted. But in the end, Elise decided not to take the risk, just as Roarke turned down her deliberately exorbitant price for a cargo she didn't even have.

Still, it had been that invitation that had given her the idea for a moonlight swim late that night. After calling Henry to tell him where she was headed, Elise put on a stringsuit and went down to the beach behind their hotel.

Battling ocean swells for a brisk hour burned away the last of her adrenaline; by the time she emerged from the water, she was nicely tired. Elise dried herself off and wrapped her body in the thick, warm robe she'd brought along. Savoring the glow of heated muscles and pleasant exhaustion, she bent, meaning to pick up the sheathed knife she'd left wrapped in a towel. She was, after all, still in enemy territory.

Elise pulled up short as the wet fabric of her stringsuit dug into her skin. The outfit was nothing more than a set of fine cords which looped around her neck, wove together at strategic points as they descended, and dipped between her thighs to come up behind and tie at the waist. And at the moment the suit seemed to be chafing each and every one of those strategic points. Reaching past the lapels of her robe, she adjusted it to lie where it was supposed to.

"Lisa Morrow?"

She turned, a smile forming at the sound of Roarke's voice -- a smile that froze across her teeth as she came completely around.

He was holding a beamer pointed between her breasts, the red glow of its charge burning deep in the weapon's dark barrel.

"You told me you were Lisa Morrow," Roarke said, his deep voice sounding almost metallically chill. "But that's not really your name, is it?"

"What else would it be?" The knife still lay wrapped in the towel at her feet. If she could get to it… Casually, she started to bend over.

"Captain Elise Morrell of the CSS frigate *Star Raker*. And leave the blade where it is, Captain. I'd hate to shoot you."

"I'd hate to be shot," Elise said easily, though her stomach was twisting with the sick realization that everything had just gone straight to hell. "You think *I'm* CSS?" She shook her head in carefully feigned astonishment. "Captain, I hate those bastards. No way would I work for them."

"So you said -- just a bit too loudly." Roarke began to circle around her, keeping his weapon aimed between her breasts as she pivoted with him. "Oh, you're a good actress; you sounded damn convincing talking about the way they'd screwed you. And that's what made me wonder, because no real rebel would tell a stranger that much." He smiled mockingly. "I don't know if you've heard, but Tyus is crawling with spies."

She tried out an apologetic smile. "I suppose I should be more discreet, but is that really a reason to kill me?"

He snorted. "Give it up, Morrell. I got an anonymous tip half an hour ago telling me exactly who you are. I checked it out with Starforce, and they confirm." The black eyes chilled. "But even so, I don't intend to kill you unless you give me no choice. Lie down on the ground. Kick the knife away first."

Elise shrugged and started to obey, but just at that moment gust of wind grabbed at her robe, dragging it open to reveal her stringsuit-clad body and its nearly naked curves. Roarke's eyes widened.

She knew an opening when she saw one.

Pivoting her body into a hard, tight kick, she struck his wrist so hard his beamer spun out of his hand. Elise reversed direction, meaning to plow her foot into his jaw on the return stroke, but Roarke wasn't caught napping twice. He grabbed her ankle and jerked, dumping her on her backside in the sand. Even as he pounced on her, she was launching another attack, punching her palm upward in a strike calculated to drive the bones of his nose into his brain. He jerked his head aside, turning what would have been a lethal blow into one that did nothing more than bloody his mouth. She pulled back for another shot, but he grabbed her hands in both fists and pinned them to the ground. "Surrender, Captain," he grunted. "You don't want to go one-on-one with me."

"I could say the same to you," Elise growled, fighting to brace a foot against his body and kick him away. As she surged against him, she breathed in his scent; a faint tang of male sweat, a hint of something woodsy that must have been his soap, the trace of Scotch on his breath. She ignored it and tried even harder for the throw, but Roarke applied a counter pressure and kept her down, mashing her breasts into the hard wall of his chest, his powerful thighs imprisoning hers between them.

God, he was strong. Even worse, he had the combat skills to match. There was a host of techniques she knew to flip him clear or strike sensitive nerve groups; punches that could have incapacitated him, kicks that could cripple, but he countered every move she made. With a growl of rage, Elise realized that infuriating male body would prevail; she was just wasting strength she might be able use to escape later. She had no choice but to submit and watch for her chance. Sooner or later his guard would drop.

Feeling her go limp, Roarke nodded in satisfaction. "That's better." He pulled back slightly. "You..." His eyes widened.

Following the path of his gaze, Elise gasped.

Her stringsuit had slipped aside in the struggle, revealing the thrust of one nipple. Something about the way the cords pressed against the hard little nub made her breast look more erotically naked than it would have if she'd been nude.

Instinctively, Elise looked up at her captor, who stared back at her with a sort of disgruntled arousal. He liked what he saw, she realized, but he didn't like liking what he saw.

"At least let me belt my robe closed," she snapped.

To her surprise, Roarke released her hands and sat back on his heels, still straddling her. Which was when she realized that he had a massive erection.

Without thinking twice, Elise plowed a punch right at that very prominent target.

With a roar of raw fury, Roarke caught her fist just before it struck. He fell on her like the wrath of God, crushing her into the sand, pinning her arms and legs in a wide spread eagle under his powerful body.

Looking up into the rage in his black eyes, Elise felt her mouth go dry. She forced herself to shrug. "I couldn't help myself."

A slow, very nasty grin spread across his mouth. "Neither can I."

Roarke's head dipped. She knew at once what he was going to do, but there was absolutely no way she could stop him. His biceps working against the side of her head as he controlled her struggles, he parted his lips and took her bare nipple into his mouth. Instantly the pink bud hardened. Pleasure zinged through her.

Looking up to gauge her reaction, Roarke smiled around the sensitive flesh. His tongue pressed it against his teeth, then began to swirl a hot, wet dance around it.

"You've made your point." Elise fought to ignore the tingling rush of delight roaring through her nerve endings. "Now get off me!"

"When you leave your toys out," he rumbled, "you shouldn't be surprised if somebody wants to play with them." He went back to teasing the captive nipple.

He had a very wicked tongue. She drew in a hard breath. "Arrest me if you're going to. Hell, kill me if you're going to. But *stop* that!"

"Not on your life."

"I could have you jailed for assault!"

"Oh, I know. I just don't care." Roarke drew the nipple deeply into his mouth as, with a single rough pull, he jerked that side of the string suit all the way off her right breast. She cursed him, then broke off when she realized her voice sounded like a croon.

Injecting some steel in her tone, she growled, "Let me go, Roarke. Now."

He looked up at her. Her nipple felt suddenly cold without his hot mouth around it. "I've wanted to get you in this position all evening, Captain. I'm not stopping until I'm finished." Still watching her, Roarke nipped the pouting pink tip. She strangled a moan. He whispered, "And that won't be for hours yet." Grabbing the other side of the stringsuit, he freed her left breast with a hard jerk.

Then, like the wolf he resembled, Roarke began a leisurely feast, biting, sucking, licking at her erect nipples, sending a barrage of delight roaring along her nerves that ripped every thought of protest out of her head. His free hand worked whichever breast his mouth did not, squeezing and stroking, knowing just the touch, just the rhythm, to waken her hunger and twist it tight.

Dimly she realized he'd transferred both her hands to one of his. She knew she should pull free, but she didn't even have the strength to try. It was as though he were suckling away her will to resist with each tug of that wicked mouth. Until nothing else mattered, not rank, not enmity, not fear. Nothing but her need to feel him touching her.

Elise threw back her head at the storm of sensation, pressing her face against the hard bulge of his biceps. Barely aware of what she did, she opened her mouth and bit into the firm muscle. He tasted of desire and male sweat. Roarke growled, squeezing her breast between his long fingers before releasing it to continue his seductive explorations.

His hips rocked against hers. He was massively hard in a long thick ridge that pressed against her belly, scalding her with the need to feel him naked and strong in the cradle of her body.

She had to stop this, Elise told herself, but the thought was vague, powerless against the desire Roarke was building so skillfully.

He shifted over her, and his clever fingers moved down the V of bare skin revealed by her stringsuit, then wormed their way under the tightly woven cords that concealed her sex.

"Roarke," she moaned.

"Shhh," he whispered. "Let me touch you. Let me make you burn." His fingers found her, stirred the fine down at the juncture of her sex. "So soft," he crooned.

He discovered her clit, brushed it with a feather touch. She caught her breath as rapture seared her.

Elise was still reeling when he slid a big finger deep inside her. "Wet and hot and tight," Roarke murmured, "You want me as much as I want you. And God, how I want you."

He plunged two stiffened fingers into her. She cried out.

"It's good, isn't it? And it's going to get even better." Slowly, seductively, he pumped, until she could almost feel them locked together, his body bucking against hers, plunging so very, very deep.

Abruptly Roarke pulled away, his expression nakedly feral. "We can't finish this here; it's not secure. I'm taking you back to my ship." As if unable to resist, he ground his hardness into the notch of her thighs. His eyes closing, he murmured, "Then, in a day or so, when we're finally done, you're going to tell me where you left the *Star Raker*."

Elise blinked, feeling stunned and stupid, still in the grip of his spell. But even dazed as she was, she knew there was danger here. Danger to her ship.

Grabbing both her wrists, Roarke hauled her up off the sand as he bent at the waist. She realized he was about to throw her over his shoulder.

He was going to make her tell him where the *Raker* was. And against that dreadnought of his, her people wouldn't have a prayer in hell.

A wave of adrenaline drowned the erotic fire he'd so carefully built, leaving Elise cold and aware. "No," she whispered. "No, goddamn you, you're not getting my ship!"

With every ounce of her strength, Elise smashed a knee into his groin. Caught off-guard, Roarke roared in pain and dropped her. She rolled across the sand, sprang to her feet, and ran like hell. The sea breeze felt cold on her naked breasts, still wet from Roarke's sensual feast.

"Damn it, come back here!" He lunged, grabbing for her. Half-crippled as he was, he missed.

Elise scrambled down the beach kicking up sprays of sand. She couldn't afford to let him put his hands on her again. She rounded a dune …

And ran right into Henry Voronnin on the other side.

"Captain!" Henry said, startled. His eyes fell on her naked chest. "*Captain*!"

"Elise!"

Roarke, bulling his way around the dune after her, spotted Henry and drew back a fist. Before he could strike, Henry plowed a foot into the side of his knee. It buckled under him with an audible *snap*. He hit the sand swearing.

A snarl on his face, Voronnin reached for him.

"Come on, Henry!" Elise yelled.

"We can take him hostage!"

"The Rebellion gives their people com implants!

We'd never get off the planet with him. Besides, his knee is broken," she told him, taking in Roarke's bloodless face with practiced eyes. "He's not going anywhere but to a medic. Let's get out of here before somebody comes!"

Grumbling, Henry turned and followed as Elise broke into a run.

Behind her, she could hear Roarke's deep-throated bellow of fury, "We're not finished, Elise!"

They'd run like hell back to the hopper. Roarke hadn't stayed down long; they'd barely taken off when they picked up the *Liberator*'s sensor signature roaring in pursuit. It had taken them another three days of hiding and evasive maneuvers to make it back to the *Raker*, with Roarke hunting them the whole time.

But even as they made good their escape, Elise had known he was right: he wasn't through with her.

* * *

A year later, Roarke chased her down, defeated her in battle, and forced her to surrender to his overwhelming strength of arms. Now he was about to board her ship and take her hostage. The exterior airlock opened, revealing ranks of mammoth armored shapes, beamer rifles held at ready: the boarding party.

Watching them advance, Elise swallowed, wondering which jointed gray suit held her enemy. And whether he intended to take up where he'd left off.

Chapter Two

When Roarke and his boarding party marched onto the frigate's cargo deck, he found Elise standing at parade rest, proud in her black dress uniform with its silver piping, tall dress boots emphasizing the delicious length of her legs. She wore her blonde hair arranged in a businesslike bun that would have looked ridiculously prim on any other woman, yet the regal tilt of her chin turned it into a crown. Still, queenly as she was, he was surprised by how small she looked. Almost defenseless.

Then again, he was used to seeing her on his bridge vid screen, larger than life, playing out one of her elaborate combat strategies. But not this time. This time he had her. At last.

Roarke stopped a pace away from her, flanked by his fifty armored troopers. Keying his suit face plate open, he said, "It's a genuine pleasure, Captain Morrell." He could feel his lips curving into a grin he knew revealed too much.

Elise looked at him with those slanting go-to-hell green eyes. "I'm afraid I can't say the same, Captain Roarke."

"I know." He paused to drag the grin into a more professional expression. "Have you prepared any interesting surprises for us, Captain?"

She lifted a brow. "Why don't you see for yourself?"

"I do believe I will." With a nod and a gesture, Roarke sent his troopers fanning out, their beamer rifles held at ready, to search the area for snipers. Snipers who would be damn sorry to be found, considering that the armor made each trooper not only virtually invulnerable, but ten times stronger than anything human.

Roarke unslung his own rifle, pointed it at her, and said mildly, "I certainly hope they don't find anyone."

Elise gave the weapon a contemptuous glance, then ignored it.

God, she was something. Even watching her over a rifle sight, he felt the effect of her body on his -- the long, sleek legs and narrow waist, the curve of her hips, breasts swelling and lush even in a uniform designed to minimize them. His mouth went dry as he remembered what those gorgeous breasts looked like bare, the nipples stiff and wet from his mouth. God, he loved her breasts.

Roarke gritted his teeth and banished that treacherous memory. She had a way of sending his professionalism right out the airlock -- and he could swear she did it deliberately. Elise Morrell was a deadly little mantrap baited with lush tits and long legs. And he, God help him, tumbled right in every time.

Her face made the whole deception work. Knowing what an indomitable warrior she was, Roarke would have expected sharp, classic features, beautiful but cold. Instead, there was an elfin delicacy about her. Her cheekbones and chin were softly rounded, her nose pert, her eyes wide and leaf-green. And her mouth -- God, her mouth. With those wide, seductive pink lips that threatened and taunted and curled into dangerous grins. He had a recurring fantasy of sliding his aching hard-on into that mouth.

It irritated him.

Here they were, aboard an enemy vessel crawling with cornered Coalition forces, and he was focusing on Elise Morrell and his own lust. He was a captain of a ship at war, damn it. He couldn't afford this kind of distraction. He knew the price of failure too well.

Besides, she was a Coalition officer, for God's sake. She should disgust him.

He desperately wished she disgusted him.

Through the communications implant behind his left ear, he heard the boarding party begin to call in. "Clear, captain."

"Looks good here."

"Doesn't seem to be anybody around."

Roarke waited for the last of them to confirm it, but even when confirmation came, he didn't relax. Staging an ambush in the cargo bay was the obvious thing to do. Elise never did the obvious. The ambush would come from the direction he least expected.

"All right," he said at last, "Assume your assigned positions and stay alert."

Slinging the rifle back across his shoulder, Roarke removed his helmet, pulled off his bulky gauntlets and handed them to the yeoman who stood a discreet distance away. Finally he turned to Elise. "Lace your fingers on top of your head and spread your feet apart."

She looked up at him, green eyes narrow and hard. Just when he was wondering if he had to force her, she lifted her hands and obeyed. He stepped closer, acutely aware of how small she seemed against his armored body. The perception sent another unprofessional surge of lust through him.

Careful not to linger, Roarke searched her for weapons, skimming his hands along the fine muscles of her arms, the narrow waist, the sweet rounded curve of her rump. And down those long, long legs that seemed to make up most of her body.

Which was when he realized he should have

ordered someone else to conduct the search. Yolanda Boniface, for one, wouldn't have gotten a hard-on.

Erection or no, it took him just less than sixty seconds to find the knife tucked in her dress boot. Raising a brow, Roarke stared up at her as he drew the six-inch stiletto from its sheath. Elise shrugged. "Just checking to see if you're awake."

"I'm awake," he said drily. Handing the knife to the yeoman, he reached into one of the belt pouches on his armor and drew out a pair of neurocuffs. Though they looked like thin silver bangles, each generated a neural field that locked the prisoner's muscles, immobilizing his arms in place. Because the captive's own strength held him, the delicate shackles were impossible to break.

Roarke should know. He'd once tried desperately to break a set just like them.

Elise paled, then hid her fear and curled her lip. "What's the matter, Captain? Afraid you can't handle me even with boarding armor and a hundred-pound advantage?"

"No, I'm making damn sure your crew grasps your situation," he snapped. "I didn't tell you to take your hands down, Captain. Lace them on top of your head."

Moving stiffly, Elise obeyed as he stepped behind her. Catching one slender wrist, he pulled it around to the small of her back and locked it in a neurocuff, then captured the other wrist and manacled it to the first. Instantly, her arms went rigid as the field kicked in, paralyzing them. Grimacing in distaste -- he knew too well how it felt when the 'cuffs locked down -- Roarke moved in front of her.

And was suddenly, intensely aware of the way her captive wrists arched her spine, thrusting her breasts outward. An image popped into his mind: Elise, lying naked on his bed, her arms 'cuffed under her, her stiff pink nipples pointed at the ceiling. Inviting his hands, his mouth, the lust that had been scalding him for months.

Cut it out, you lecherous bastard.

Disgusted with himself, he keyed his radio implant with a flex of his jaw muscles. "People, please be aware that we're in a very hazardous situation here. Captain Morrell has probably instructed her crew to disregard her safety. I'm assuming they'll be reluctant to endanger her once we parade her by in neurocuffs, but I could be wrong. Stay alert."

He thought he heard her growl.

Taking Elise's arm, Roarke guided her toward the hatch, his eyes sternly directed away from her lushly jutting breasts.

* * *

The next three hours were some of the darkest in Elise's life as she marched through her own ship surrounded by armored invaders. She could only watch as Roarke deployed his troopers to herd her crew into their quarters and take control of the posts they were forced to leave. Despite her helpless rage, she focused on every move he made, every order he gave, hoping for a mistake, an overlooked opening she could use to free her ship.

Nothing. Elise wanted to howl in frustration.

But the worst moment was when Roarke strode onto the *Raker*'s bridge and ordered his remaining troops to systemically search the bridge crew. When he was satisfied that no one had managed to stash away any weapons, he sent her staff off under guard. Until finally he and Elise were the only ones left on the bridge.

She tensed, but Roarke ignored her, busy directing the boarding parties through his implant. Elise had nothing to do but sit down in a bridge chair and hatch far-fetched escape plans.

She was beginning to wish she'd blown up the ship.

By the time Roarke stood up almost two hours later and reached for the seal of his boarding armor, she was actually relieved. Finally, a diversion from her own spiraling desperation, even if it meant fighting another losing battle with Roarke.

He caught the expression in her eyes and paused. A wry grin twisted his mouth. "No, I'm not getting ready to attack you, I've just got to get out of this suit. I'm drowning in my own sweat."

She shrugged. "Whatever you say."

Roarke eyed her, his grin going wicked. "Ah, if only you meant that." With a flourish, he hit a button. The armor's chest plate split open with a pneumatic *hiss*, and he quickly wrestled his way out of it. The thin, sleeveless skinsuit he wore underneath was wet with sweat, and his short black hair was slicked tightly to his elegant skull. Apparently the coolant systems in Rebellion armor worked as poorly as that in the Coalition's version.

Unfortunately for Elise's peace of mind, the result of that poor design left the skinsuit practically transparent. The thin, damp fabric hugged Roarke's broad torso, displaying his body to her reluctantly enthralled gaze. Chest, arms, ribs, belly -- it seemed every inch of him was covered with rippled plates of muscle. Roarke looked armored even when practically naked.

Throwing back his head, he sighed, the cords of his strong neck flaring. "God, that cool air feels good."

Bending over, he went to work on the bottom half of his armor, his big hands brisk and competent on the catches. Hard muscle shifted in his tight, masculine rump, and his thighs bunched as he pulled his legs clear and turned toward her. Elise's eyes widened.

The skinsuit cupped his genitals as though presenting them for her approval. And there was a lot to approve of. Elise swallowed, remembering how he'd felt in full erection, rocking seductively between her legs.

She really had no business being intrigued.

* * *

It was going far more smoothly than Roarke had any right to expect. Evidently his ploy had worked; the knowledge that Elise was within his armored reach dampened her crew's interest in rebellion. At last report, they were all safely locked in their quarters and under guard.

Which left him entirely too much time to think about the captive sitting bound and helpless a few feet away. His lovely enemy, defeated at last, looking like the recurring erotic fantasy he'd been having since Tyus -- and playing merry hell with his self-control. The situation was just too damn tempting: a beautiful CSS captain at his mercy, just as he'd been a prisoner of the Coalition. Though, of course, he had no intention of mistreating her, the possibilities inherent in holding her captive were so lush and dark they'd been haunting his dreams for months.

It didn't help that he'd had to work his ass off to capture her. In the two years since his escape from CSS custody, Roarke had defeated far more powerful ships than the *Star Raker*. When they'd begun this running war a year ago, he'd expected to make Elise Morrell his prisoner within the month.

Unfortunately for his frustration level, Elise turned out to be an elusive opponent, staying one jump ahead of him no matter what he did. He had to admit she was better than any CSS dreadnought captain he'd ever fought; if she'd had a ship equal to his, she would have been a major threat. But luckily all she'd had was the underpowered, under-armed *Star Raker*, and now Elise sat on her own bridge in neurocuffs.

And there wasn't a damn thing to stop Roarke from feeding the hunger that had tormented him for so long. The *Raker*'s crew was safely locked away, and damage control parties were hard at work making sure he had nothing else to worry about. And he was alone with Elise.

Elise, her slim body deliciously nude, stretched out and cuffed in his bunk.

This is damned unprofessional.

Elise on her hands and knees, ready to be mounted.

He was getting hard.

But a captain in the Rebellion Starforce did not sexually abuse his female prisoners, no matter how beautiful or how tempting. It was dishonorable.

Now, if he'd been a Coalition captain, and she a captured rebel…

He'd go to her, and he'd peel her out of that pretty dress uniform, and he'd force her to her knees. He'd make her open that soft, beautiful mouth. She'd use her tongue as he commanded, licking slowly at the erection he could feel swelling his skinsuit.

But he was a Rebellion captain, and he was supposed to treat his captives with mercy. Even Coalition captives.

Even when the Coalition had been merciless to him.

The memory of his captivity rose up in a dark,

choking wave, as it so often did when he was tired or distracted. But this time, Roarke let himself remember it, knowing it would kill his arousal if anything could: Amin Nygaard's thick, wet smile as the little bastard used the neurowhip, creating agonizing sensory illusions with every touch of the device. Skin being flayed slowly away, bones shattering, muscle ripping, eyes torn from sockets; the injuries themselves may have been illusion, but the pain was real. As real as his screams.

As real as Nygaard's blood on his hands.

Roarke realized he was staring at Elise again. She sat quietly in her seat, helpless, her high, round breasts tempting in that hated black uniform of hers.

That Coalition uniform.

She hadn't been there, he told himself. She'd had nothing to do with what Nygaard did to him on Elba.

But she was one of them. By donning that uniform, Elise had announced her belief in CSS policies, her willingness to defend them with her life and her honor.

Roarke started for her, intensely aware of his cock, of the cruel hunger roaring through him. He knew he shouldn't go anywhere near her when he was in the demon grip of Nygaard's memory. But he really didn't give a damn.

* * *

Elise was intensely aware of Roarke's swift, silent approach, but she fought to ignore it. She was damned if she'd show him any fear.

He stopped. The nape of her neck prickled. It took every bit of self-control she had not to spin in her chair to face him.

"How are your arms?" Roarke demanded, the question sounding almost reluctant. "You've been bound a long time."

She shrugged. "Numb."

He dropped to one knee behind her so suddenly she jumped. "Don't give me that look, I'm just decreasing the setting," he told her gruffly as she shot him a wary backward glance.

Elise eyed him, wondering if that really was a flicker of guilt on his face.

He worked over the cuffs in silence for a moment. Finally she heard a *click,* and some of the tension left her muscles. Feeling raced back on a river of pins and needles. She tried to pull her wrists apart. They still wouldn't budge.

Roarke's big hands closed over her arms and began to rub.

What now? "Captain Roarke…"

"I once spent a very unpleasant twenty-four hours in neurocuffs. Believe me, you'll thank me for this later."

"Somehow I doubt that, since you're the one who put me in the 'cuffs to begin with."

He laughed softly. "You've got a point."

"In any case," Elise continued firmly, wanting to get his hands off her, "I think I can withstand the pain."

"True," Roarke said, his strong hands rubbing and pulling, "but there's no point. Your suffering is the last thing I've got in mind."

She gritted her teeth. "Your hospitality is dazzling."

"Oh, it's my pleasure," he purred.

Finally he released her arms and stood. Before Elise could relax, he reached into the neat bun on top of her head.

"What are you doing now?"

"I want to see it down." Roarke found the clasp

and opened it with easy skill. Her hair collapsed around her face in a cascade of cool blonde silk. He caught it in both hands with a rumbling croon of delight. Slowly, he drew his fingers through it, stroking, still making that guttural male sound in the depths of his throat.

Taking his pleasure the way he always did, Elise thought -- without asking. Yet somehow she couldn't bring herself to protest. Each time Roarke's fingers moved, they brushed against her body, her neck, her head, the side of her face, in a constant, sensuous caress. The prickle returned to her nape, but this time from pleasure rather than fear.

"It's so soft. So fine." His tone deepened into a rumble. "Like the down between your thighs."

"Captain…" She winced as her voice cracked.

"Surely you were expecting this."

"Barbaric behavior? I suppose I certainly should have."

"No -- defeat." Lazily, Roarke caught up a handful of her hair and bent close to inhale the scent. His cheek brushed hers. She tensed. "You must have realized how thoroughly I had you outgunned."

Elise twisted her head, trying to draw her hair free from his grasp. He tightened his grip, not cruelly, but leaving her no doubt that he was in control. Slipping his free hand past her hair, he stroked the vulnerable length of her neck, the line of her jaw. His fingers felt warm, slightly rough. "Once I cornered you," Roarke continued softly, "it was a simple matter to strip away your defenses and render you helpless." Putting his mouth against her ear, he whispered, menace lacing his tone, "Then it was easy to… penetrate."

To Elise's horror, she felt arousal tighten low in her belly. Ignoring it, she demanded bluntly, "Are you planning to rape me, Captain Roarke?"

"Why, no, Captain Morrell. What I'm planning" --his hot tongue flicked out and swirled around her earlobe --"is a ruthless" -- Roarke closed his teeth over the sensitive flesh in a gentle bite --"seduction."

His hand dropped smoothly to brush the tip of her breast. Even through the tough fabric of her uniform, she felt the sensuous temptation. Her nipple drew tight and eager.

"You're splitting verbal hairs, Roarke. You may get a response out of my body, but I'm still saying no. And that makes this rape." Her breasts were aching.

"Hmmmm. You have a point." He lifted his hand to touch the center of her throat at the top of her high uniform collar, then slowly ran his fingers downward between her breasts, along her tensed abdomen, right to the top of her pubic bone. As he triggered the invisible closure, her uniform split open with a whisper. "I suppose," Roarke purred, his hot gaze directed down at the arrow of naked white skin, "I'll just have to get used to being a rapist."

"If you think I'm just going to submit, you're greatly mistaken." Elise hoped he missed the husky note in her voice.

"No, you're hardly submissive, are you?" Moving in front of her, he took her shoulders in his powerful hands and lifted her straight up off the chair, then turned her around and gently, relentlessly forced her to kneel in the seat, half bending over the back. "In fact, I'm waiting for you to kick me in the teeth at any moment."

"What the hell are you doing now?" She wet her lips.

To her outrage, his teeth nipped her bottom. "Worshiping your magnificent ass." Taking it between his hands, he squeezed her cheeks, caressed the firm, muscled flesh with strong, possessive circular strokes.

"And I'm going to report *your* magnificent ass," Elise gritted. "I suspect the Rebellion high command would frown on this." She kicked back at him, but he grabbed her ankle in an iron clasp before her foot could connect.

"No doubt," he said coolly, releasing her leg, "But considering the length of time I spent being tortured by the CSS, I think they'll be more understanding than usual. And if not, I really don't give a damn."

"Is that what this is about? Vengeance?" Warily, Elise looked back over her shoulder at him.

"Wondering what nasty perversion I have in mind?" He dragged her back until his erection pressed against her bottom. "Don't bother. I've already had my revenge; I killed that sadistic CSSIntel bastard when I escaped. No, this is about pleasure. Mine" -- he rolled his hips --"and yours."

Despite herself, she felt a tingle of building arousal, a shameful, reluctant anticipation. He felt so… thick. She had a sudden, intense memory of his powerful body pinning her, his mouth suckling at her nipples as his fingers dipped into her wet core.

This time he wouldn't stop.

This time she'd get to have it all.

But she shouldn't *want* it.

He leaned closer, draping himself over her so he could reach into her open uniform. Tugging back one edge of her tunic, he liberated her right breast. She felt it thrust out into the cool bridge air, its nipple hard, shamelessly eager for his fingers. And he gave them to her, cupping her in delicious warmth before catching the stiff tip to pull and roll until Elise could no longer hold back a moan.

"You see?" Roarke murmured. "Pleasure. And you can blame it all on me. You're neurocuffed and defenseless, and I'm the nasty, dishonorable son-of-a-bitch rebel captain taking advantage of the situation to feed his own lusts. You can let yourself enjoy every luscious second."

She licked her lips. "What makes you think I'm enjoying this?"

Leaning into her from behind, his strong thighs snuggling against hers, he reached one hand down her uniform trousers and between her legs. A finger slipped easily into her in a long, slick glide. "Why, nothing, Captain. It's obvious you don't care for my advances." The finger withdrew, then slid deep again. It was all she could do not to moan. "You're completely… cold to me."

A second finger joined the first, and he burrowed in and out of her until she shuddered. At the same time, his other hand resumed its torment of her breast. 'Cuffed, Elise could only rest her chin on the back of the chair and try not to moan as Roarke rolled his hips against her bottom.

"God, you're making me hot," he rumbled in her ear, using his thumb to stroke her erect clit. "Bound and bent over, ready to be mounted. And so creamy. This arouses you as much as it does me, you're just too stubborn to admit it. You'd rather deny both of us because I had the gall to defeat you in battle."

Elise sucked in a deep breath that almost became a whimper before she could stop it. She did desire him. Humiliating, but there it was. And why shouldn't she? His body was big and powerfully built, with strong, broad hands. He had a face as handsome as an ancient god's and wicked black eyes that knew entirely too much and promised even more, and a mouth that wove spells of sin and carnal pleasure. He was every dark fantasy she'd ever had.

But he'd blown the *Star Raker* halfway to hell, and he was going to put her and her crew in a Rebellion prison camp.

And he was not, damn him, going to win this one too.

She turned to give him a chill glare over her shoulder despite the pleasure he was wringing from her wet, ready flesh. "If you're going to rape me, do it and get it over with."

"Oh, I *am* tempted, Elise. I want to strip you out of that ugly black uniform, bend you over your own captain's chair, and make you come so hard my engineering crew will hear you scream six decks down." Roarke's eyes narrowed. "And why not? Hell, if you want to play martyr, who am I to refuse?" With a quick pass of his fingers, he resealed her uniform, straightened off her, and padded toward his armor.

She twisted away from the seat back and struggled awkwardly to her feet, though her hands were 'cuffed behind her. Hoping her treacherously weak knees wouldn't dump her to the floor, Elise demanded, "What are you doing now?"

"Getting dressed." He shot her a nasty grin as he reached for the chest plate. "It's a delicious idea, but I suppose it would be tacky to actually screw you on your own bridge."

She set her teeth. "You suppose right."

"And your being paraded through the corridors by a half-naked rebel captain would make the situation a little too obvious to the crew. After all, we wouldn't want to set a bad example." Flexing his broad shoulders, Roarke picked up the heavy torso armor and shrugged into it like a coat. "But since you're so determined to be victimized, I'll just have to cooperate -- discreetly."

"Do you think this is some kind of kinky game to me?" Elise demanded, trying to ignore the erotic play of muscle as he suited up. "Yes, I'll admit you arouse me. You're a skilled lover. You could probably wring a response out of a neutronium bulkhead. But no matter what you do to my body, I won't willingly sleep with you. And if you force me, I will fight. I may not win, but you won't get any enjoyment out of it."

Roarke looked into her eyes, his own hard, level. "I'm aware of that, Elise. I've met you in combat often enough to know you're not the type to make it easy." Moving to tower over her in his armor, he flexed a gauntleted hand. "Fortunately, that's not a problem. With the suit, I don't have to hurt you to subdue you."

She glared up at him bitterly. "You're not going to leave me any dignity at all, are you?"

"Not if you refuse to give us both what we need, just to soothe your stiff pride."

"Why not? You've got a stiffness of your own you seem obsessed with."

He laughed. "Touche'." Reaching out, Roarke took her arm. "Now that you mention it, I think it's time we got started on that problem."

Elise growled, but she knew better than to attempt hand-to-hand combat with a man in armor.

Once again, Roarke held all the cards.

Chapter Three

Lifting her chin, Elise allowed Roarke to guide her to the bridge doors and out into the corridor. Glancing at his face, she saw he was watching her, his gaze hungrily flicking from her eyes to her mouth to the thrust of her breasts and back again. She felt her nipples tingle and harden.

Quickly redirecting her own gaze, Elise swore silently. How did he keep doing this to her? The man was her worst enemy, an arrogant rebel taking advantage of her status as his hostage. She was going to file a complaint with his Rebellion superiors. She was going to kick him in the balls the minute she saw an opening. She…

That pointed tongue flicking out to swirl around her hot, wet nipple. His mouth descending, engulfing the stiff peak, sucking, biting, pulling, until pleasure roared through her, drowning duty and honor and even self-preservation in a bright red flood of delight and desire.

She shook her head hard, infuriated. The bastard had the ability to seduce her even inside the privacy of her own mind.

It was embarrassing.

Stiffening her spine, she marched around the corner and down the corridor toward the door of her quarters. Jerking against Roarke's light hold, she managed to break it as she snarled at the key plate, "Captain Elise Morrell. Admit me." The door opened. She stalked through without looking back.

Taking a deep breath, Elise paused to regain control of her anger, aware of Roarke moving in behind her as the door slid closed again.

His gauntleted hands caught her arms and quickly disengaged the muscle lock on her neurocuffs. Elise jerked and started to whirl, but it was too late.

Dragging her arms over her head, Roarke clasped her wrists together to reengage the 'cuffs, then scooped her up and dumped her on her back on the wide captain's bunk.

"What the hell?" Instinctively she tried to launch a punch at him, but her arms, locked in the neurocuffs, were pointed stiffly at the headboard.

"I'm not going to fight you, Elise," Roarke told her. "I won't hurt you even to soothe your pride. But I am going to take you. And if that means putting you in shackles, I'll do it." He reached down with one of those huge gauntlets, grabbed a fistful of her jacket, and ripped. The tough cloth shredded like rice paper, and the entire coat came off in his hand.

Elise stared at the ripped fabric in wordless shock. "Bastard!"

"I've always hated this thing," Roarke told her, wicked laughter in his voice, as he reached down to grab another handful of cloth.

"That was my best dress uniform!" She aimed a kick at his head as he finished off her jacket.

"But black and silver is such a pretentious combination." He caught her booted foot in one hand, grabbed her pants leg in the other, and jerked. It split open, baring the length of her leg right up to her crotch. She slammed another kick into his ribs and winced as her heel glanced off the armor. Calmly, he pulled off her boots. "Besides, ripping the victim's clothes off is half the fun."

Reaching into one of the pouches on his equipment belt, he pulled out a slightly bigger version of the neurocuffs and snapped one around her bare ankle. Elise tried for another kick but it was too late; he'd already activated it. Her entire leg went stiff and unresponsive.

"Roarke, I'm warning you," she snarled, "if you do this to me, I'm going to slit your throat!"

"Then I'll just have to keep you in bondage, won't I?" he taunted, as he stripped away the rags of her trousers and imprisoned the other leg in the second neuroshackle. Taking each ankle in hand, he positioned her with her legs wide apart in the air. "Not that I need an excuse."

Elise desperately wanted to change her shamefully open position, but she couldn't even twitch. She was immobilized -- and completely naked except for a few scraps of black. "This is ridiculous."

"Not at all. You look like my favorite wet dream." Roarke's grin was astonishingly boyish, considering he'd just ruthlessly ripped her clothes off and bound her for forced sex.

"One of these days, Michael Roarke," she spat, "you're going to find out how *you* like it in shackles..."

His humor vanished as if cut off with a switch. "I already know the answer to that one. And an intelligent woman would not bring back that particular set of memories when she was naked, shackled, and spread wide."

Seeing the sudden cruel black glitter in his eyes, Elise winced. He had a point. "Then I'll just have to settle for reporting you," she growled anyway, refusing to back down. "Your Starforce will bust your ass back to ensign."

He ignored that, busy with getting himself out of his armor. This time though, he didn't stop with the skinsuit, shucking his broad body out of it with as much ruthlessness as he'd ripped away her own uniform. He actually looked bigger without it, as though the suit had camouflaged his size.

Elise caught her breath at the width of his

powerful chest, with its thick masculine pelt that flared from nipple to nipple in a broad cloud. Unconsciously her eyes tracked that pattern of soft hair, watching as it narrowed into a band to flow down over his hard, rippled belly. And down even further, pointing the way like a slim finger.

With a sinuous roll of his hips, Roarke freed his sex. It sprang outward, surrounded by the soft ruff. Elise blinked. His cock was bigger than she'd expected, even after feeling it through his clothes. The long shaft with its prominent veins looked almost too thick for its head, which was easily the size of a plum. It was also stone hard. That same obvious arousal pulled his furry dark balls tight, taut and full.

Roarke stood framed between her raised, spread legs like a stallion about to mount a mare, erection jutting, his hungry jet eyes locked on her face. His nostrils flared; Elise wondered whether he could actually smell the heat she felt trickling into her sexual core.

"Now lie to me," he rumbled, cutting the heavy, erotic silence. "Tell me again how you don't want me. Lie and call me a rapist. Or be honest with both of us and ask for my hands on you."

"You're an arrogant, egotistical bastard," Elise told him, her low voice too husky to be convincing. "And I'm not going to give you the satisfaction."

Roarke smiled slowly. "You will." He reached out and caught her ankle as he slid a knee onto the bed. Slowly, watching her face the whole time, he leaned forward and parted his lips. His pointed tongue reached out, found a quivering tendon, and began to trace a wet, hot trail downward.

Elise bit back a moan and closed her eyes, unable to withstand the combined raw eroticism of his hot stare and the feeling of him tasting her skin like a predator. She knew she should say something, make another pointless protest, yet the heavy mood of sensuality radiating from him was as good as a gag.

* * *

Roarke watched her, an urgent pulse pounding through his cock. Tatters of Coalition uniform lay on her skin like leaves, starkly black against her pale skin. She looked deliciously sensual, her breasts swelling, nipples stiff and dark, her hair a soft pale cloud around her flushed face. Her legs, wide apart in the air, revealed the pink petals of her sex, parted as though eager for his probing tongue and hungry prick. It was all he could do not to fall on her like the rapist she'd accused him of being.

But that wouldn't be good enough, Roarke told himself, clinging to the last shreds of his self-control. If he took her like that, so quickly, so selfishly, she could dismiss the experience -- even if he wrung from her the climaxes he intended. He wanted something more. He wanted to brand himself on her senses, force her to admit she was as helpless in the face of this obsession as he was. He had to be something more to her than an enemy, more than a rapist. Why that was so important, he didn't know -- and didn't particularly care. She was still going to submit to him, to his mouth and his hands and his cock. And he'd reward her with every jolt of pleasure he could wring out of her body.

That would be enough. It would have to be.

Roarke drew in a deep breath, drinking her scent as he grazed his lips down the long, curving sweep of her calf. Her skin felt silken against his mouth. Discovering a sensitive spot behind her knee, he hesitated, biting gently at the muscle swelling there. Elise caught her breath. Roarke smiled and kept going, letting his hands explore the fine weave of tendon and muscle and bone in her strong thighs.

A trace of musk and salt teased his nostrils, and he inhaled deeply, savoring the evidence of Elise's growing arousal. He moved closer, edging his head between her legs, looking at the petals of her sex, half concealed by her soft bush. Lifting a hand, he stirred through the fine blonde hair with one finger, tracing the line between her delicate lips, careful not to push inside. *Not yet, not yet.*

"Pretty Elise," he murmured, drifting his finger along her mound, just brushing. "Do you know your danger, I wonder?"

Elise made a faint sound, not quite a gasp.

"Oh, maybe you think you do." Another brush of his fingertip, exploring the delicate textures of vulnerable female flesh and silken hair. "Maybe you're expecting me to fuck you like a pirate, brutally, not caring if I hurt you, out of revenge or selfishness or simple cruelty. But that's not the danger at all." He leaned closer, drinking the rich, sexual smell of her. "No, the danger is that now that I've finally caught you, I may never let you go."

She whimpered. Roarke smiled and dipped his head.

* * *

She ought to make a comeback to that, Elise thought, feeling the muscles of her belly lace as she stared down at the crown of his dark head. She shouldn't let him think he was getting to her. But Roarke's warm breath was gusting gently over her sex, and anticipation had stripped away any interest Elise had ever had in repartee. If he was trying to drive her mad, he was doing a good job.

Lick.

A single pass of his tongue along the edge of her outer lips, nothing more than a tantalizing promise. Roarke nuzzled closer and breathed deeply, blowing across her damp flesh. Then that long, lush tongue touched her again, pushing delicately inside to start slipping in and out, leaving wet, burning trails behind, lighting up her nervous system with starbursts of pleasure. He edged closer. She could feel his warm, muscled shoulders pressing against her legs, the brush of his short-cropped hair against her inner thighs in a silken caress.

Instinctively Elise tried to bring her hands down to cover her sensitive, vulnerable sex, but her arms, locked in the neurocuffs, didn't even twitch. She could do nothing at all. And he could do everything.

He'd found her clit. His tongue circled it with wet, hot flicks, then slowed for a leisurely sampling swirl. His teeth closed in a gentle almost-bite, followed by another flick of that skillful tongue. His lips closed to suck briefly, then opened again for another swirling assault. She realized she was moaning and tried to stop.

A gentle bite.

Elise whimpered. Her hips began to flex. Pleasure curled in tight corkscrews in her belly.

He reached up, brushing along her sides to find her breasts. Rough fingers caught her nipples to gently pinch and roll the hard, tingling tips. "Feeling abused yet, Elise?" Roarke rumbled, only his eyes visible as he looked up at her from between her legs. "Wondering what nasty revenge I've got in mind?"

"Bastard!" she gasped, unable to think of any other word.

"Of course. Are you thinking about what it's going to feel like when I slide inside?" He lifted his head, extending a pointed tongue. Licking slowly, he watched her, then paused. Her thighs twitched. "I'm hard and hungry, Elise. And soon, very soon, I'm going to take it all."

He went on licking, circling his tongue around her clit in slow, lazy strokes. The air filled with the liquid sound of it, with the smell of salt and sex as her arousal climbed, whipped hot by every flick of that clever tongue. She fought her need to writhe, trying to preserve some rag of self-control.

She lost it by inches. First with tiny hunches of her hips against his dancing tongue. Then with full thrusts until she was grinding, half-maddened. Her pleasure spiraled, up and up until... *Oh, God*!

Sweet God, Elise wanted him. Wanted everything he'd been threatening her with. She wanted to feel his massively powerful body pressing heavily onto hers, that long, thick erection digging into her hungry core. "Roarke..." she groaned, and swallowed.

He was sucking carefully on her clit now, his tongue flicking. Elise felt a burning pulse begin as her thighs started to twitch. She rolled her head back into the pillow, feeling it come.

Roarke stopped, though his strong fingers continued to pluck and play at her nipples.

"No! Roarke, please," she gasped, pride forgotten.

"Please what?" he rumbled. And licked.

"Please," she whimpered. "I need..."

He sucked, his mouth drawing at her needy flesh. She quivered. Lifting his head, Roarke pressed his cheek against the inside of her thigh and looked at her. "What do you need?"

"You... *Ah*! I need... you."

"You need me to do what?" He twisted one nipple with exquisite care.

"I need you to… take me. Ride me. God, Roarke, please!"

"But I defeated you, Elise. I ran down your poor little ship with my big, ugly dreadnought and beat the hell out of it. And then I took you hostage and stripped you naked and bound you like a pleasure slave. Are you sure you want *me*?"

"*Yes*!" It was a scream.

"Then *take* me." In a single, violent gesture that shouted of snapped self-control, Roarke heaved his big body upward. Hunger drew his features sharp as he reared back on his knees and took his thick cock in hand. He moved between her legs, braced a muscled arm beside her hip. Aimed himself. And thrust.

Elise threw back her head and screamed at the sheer animal pleasure of it, at the shattering sensation of that huge cock ramming into her, giving her just what she so desperately needed.

"Yes!" Roarke growled, coming fully down over her, staring into her face. "That's it, Elise. That's what I want from you. That's what I'm going to take." He began to thrust, his powerful hips working as he stroked between her wet, clamping walls. She writhed under him, feeling the soft hair of his chest brushing her nipples, his hard belly rolling against hers as he rocked.

"God, Roarke," Elise moaned, "I've never felt…" The pleasure was building with every strong thrust, searing her core, winding her tighter and tighter until it seemed she was going to explode. Desperately she hunched up against him, wishing she could wrap her legs around his hips and drag him even deeper.

Roarke pounded into her, circling his hips as he plunged until his sweat splattered her skin. His teeth clenched. His bunching shoulders blocked the light.

Elise writhed, unable to bear the strength of the pleasure drilling into her core. "Roarke!" she screamed, and convulsed as her mind flew apart in a silent, glorious detonation.

* * *

For a long moment Roarke lay over Elise, loving the way her full breasts pressed into his chest. Opening one eye, he saw the sweetly curved columns of her legs pointing into the air. "Inconsiderate bastard," Roarke muttered at himself, remembering that she was still neurocuffed. Sighing, he reluctantly dragged himself off her tempting body and up onto his knees.

Taking the 'cuffs from her ankles, Roarke eased her long legs to the bunk. The muscles were still quivering and jumping under her dewy skin, and he bent to massage them, savoring the silky feel of her calves and thighs under his hands. Even after the heated passion of the past hour, he felt a slow, warm tide of arousal. He was tempted to start again, but he knew it would probably make her sore after all they'd already done, so he hastily backed away to take care of the neurocuffs on the wrists, still stretched over her head.

Elise whimpered at the sudden freedom and stirred, a frown forming between her brows. Quickly, in case she should decide to get up, Roarke lay back down and lifted her sated body to drape it over his own. "Roarke," she murmured huskily, trying to pull back from him.

He twined his arms around her drowsy nakedness and pulled her close. "Shhhh. It's been a long day. Sleep."

Elise made a grumbling sound and subsided. He knew that capitulation was a measure of both her satisfaction and her exhaustion, and grinned a little wolfishly. Poor baby. He'd worn her out.

Her hair tumbled over the back of his hand. Roarke reached up and stroked his fingers through it. It felt slightly damp, tangled, fine as strands of starsilk. She lay over him completely and deliciously limp, a sweet, intensely female weight. Roarke took her chin and tilted her head up. Her lips pouted, parted and rosy. Unable to resist, he bent his head and took them, brushing their moist, soft velvet with his mouth. He slipped his tongue inside to explore the slick surfaces of her teeth. She moaned, a muffled sound of pleasure and desire.

Roarke's arms tightened, pulling her close even as he drew away from those tempting lips. He wondered if she'd let him kiss her like that when she was awake. Afraid he knew the answer, he frowned.

Her breathing was deepened into sleep, puffing warmly across his left nipple. Roarke forgot the moment's uncertainty and sighed. He went to sleep more at peace than he'd been since the day he'd been captured.

* * *

Elise woke to the feel of Roarke's muscled chest pillowing her head and his hot erection pressing into her belly. She blinked her eyes, surprised at the heat that flooded her.

"You're awake." Arousal roughened his voice to a husky velvet drawl. With a twist of his powerful body, Roarke rolled her under him. She blinked as he loomed above her, staring down into her face. Yet the urgent lust she'd come to expect was absent from his eyes, replaced by something else, something… warmer.

Tenderness?

Lifting a hand, Roarke drew it gently through her hair, combing the pale strands back onto the pillow.

His absorbed gaze flicked over the tangled silken mass, then came to rest again on her face. Slowly he lowered his head and kissed her, a deep, languorous tasting. Surprised at the softness of his mouth, Elise parted her lips. His tongue swept in to swirl around hers.

Within her something slowly dissolved, a bitter ice chip of rage and hate melting beneath his surprising warmth.

Leaving her vulnerable.

Elise stiffened. She couldn't afford this. Not now. Not here, with her ship and her crew and herself in his control. She had to stop. She wrenched her head away, wincing at the sting as his teeth accidentally scraped her lip.

Roarke drew back and studied her, puzzlement at her withdrawal evident on his face. "What?"

"Don't you think you've proven your point?"

Without moving, he seemed to pull away. "And which point is that?"

"That you could seduce me." She steeled herself.

"Ah, I see." His smile was very male. "Your pride again. You just can't allow yourself to enjoy the moment."

His amusement stung, so she set out to sting back. "Oh, I did. But now the moment's past."

Roarke arched a dark, brow, his expression taking on a predatory cast. "Is it?"

"Yes," Elise told him, forcing icy dispassion into her tone. God help her if he started on her again. She'd never be able to resist him now that she knew what he was capable of doing to her. "Don't get me wrong, you were skillful. In fact, I think you're the best I've ever had. You seduced me with ease."

The lids lowered over those dark, hot eyes. "Darling, I didn't just seduce you. I made you beg."

"But I've had a bitch of a day," she continued, though she could feel a blush heating her cheeks, "and I need to get some sleep. If it's not too much to ask."

With an abruptness that startled her, Roarke sat up, his strong hands grabbing her hips to flip her over on her belly. Before she could think to struggle, Elise found herself up on her knees, her bottom in the air, the hot head of his erection brushing her rump. His voice laced with humor and erotic menace, Roarke purred, "And what if it is too much to ask?"

She couldn't show him any sign of reaction. "Unfortunately, I'm afraid I'm far too tired to do you justice." Looking over her shoulder at him, Elise gave him a distant smile. "Perhaps later."

Not at all offended, Roarke slowly rolled his hips against hers. "I could change your mind…"

She kept her gaze steady, cool, disinterested. It took entirely too much work. He stared back for so long she could feel her palms begin to sweat. Then, casually, he broke the moment, his lips pulling into a wry twist. "But unfortunately, I've got duties I need to attend to. So you're off the… hook, as it were." Releasing her, Roarke rolled off the bed, then turned to quirk a brow at her. "For the time being."

Elise watched as he sauntered into the head for a quick shower, anything but the picture of a rejected and sexually frustrated male. He hadn't bought the act.

Damn it. What was she going to do when he got off shift?

* * *

Roarke stepped under the stinging ice cold spray from the dozen tiny shower nozzles. God, that woman was stubborn. *What did you expect, you dumb bastard*? He endured the water pounding the length of his cock, instantly killing his erection. *You put her in neurocuffs, ripped her clothes off and screwed her. Was she supposed to roll over, smile sweetly, and swear her undying love? Maybe even admit last night meant as much to her as it did to you?*

And just what *had* last night meant to him? Hell, he had no idea. Punching the soap dispenser, he let a handful pour into his palm, then scrubbed his hair brutally. The whole obsession with Elise had begun so simply, touched off by the encounter on Tyus. Nothing but a recurring dark, kinky fantasy of seducing the enemy ice queen and making her beg. Typical male bullshit, raw ego at work. But she'd been more of a challenge than expected in her ridiculous little ship, more clever, more elusive. He'd become intrigued.

In time, he'd become a lot more than intrigued -- he'd become fascinated, obsessed, determined to have her. Until finally it wasn't a game anymore. He'd even begun to dream of her more often than he did Amin Nygaard. Dreams that were, God knew, a definite improvement over his usual torture-inspired nightmares.

And then there was last night. He'd seduced her just as he'd planned since those first two-dimensional male fantasies. And it had been the best sex he'd had in his life. He'd held her while she slept, woke with her in his arms. And she'd felt… precious.

Roarke considered the idea uneasily. It almost sounded as though she meant something to him, something more than a military victory that had morphed into a kinky bondage fantasy.

Jesus. Was he falling in love with Elise Morrell? God, he hoped not. Conducting a romance with an enemy captain -- particularly one on her way to a prison camp -- was flatly impossible. Especially considering this particular captain was proud as a Deltan aristocrat and about as flexible as neutronium plate. Surely he wasn't that stupid.

But God, she'd felt so good lying in his arms this morning, warm and soft and sleeping, her long legs tangled with his... At that last thought, Roarke groaned, leaning his head back until cold water pounded his face. There was no doubt about it. He was screwed.

* * *

Roarke emerged from the head and prowled, magnificently naked, to his armor. Elise watched him dress, scanning his hard, angular features for any hint of emotion. This time she couldn't seem to read him.

Suited up, Roarke walked to the computer pad set into the wall and keyed it on. "Captain Morrell is not permitted to leave her quarters." The pad beeped twice, acknowledging his orders. Elise knew he'd already had his computer expert reprogram the ship's network so that it would no longer accept the commands of any *Raker* crew member -- especially her. Now not even the door would open.

He turned toward her. "I'll have somebody bring you something to eat. What do you want?"

"I'm not hungry."

Roarke hesitated, then shrugged. "Suit yourself." With that, he strode to the door and out into the corridor. Watching the door slide closed behind him, Elise fought a wave of depression she didn't even try to understand. She'd gotten what she'd wanted; he'd left her without another mind-bending dose of his sensual attention.

It didn't matter anyway. Fighting the mood, she stood up went to one of the closets set into the wall. Digging through it, Elise finally found what she was looking for: a thick white robe. She slid her arms into it, wincing a little at the soreness of her muscles, and tied the belt around her waist. Walking into the head, she paused, catching sight of her mussed hair in the mirror, and picked up a brush. Mechanically, Elise began to stroke it through the blonde tangle until she'd tamed it smooth.

God, she was depressed. If this was the price of fantastic sex, next time she'd pass. And she looked like hell. Her lips were swollen, and her eyes looked dazed.

Forget it. She had work to do. Turning, Elise walked through the head doorway into the office that lay beyond it. Dominating the room was her horseshoe-shaped private control center, with its inset vid screens and instrument panels. She sat down in the thickly padded cream chair and placed her palm on the ident plate. "Captain Elise Morrell. Access."

"Access denied under the authority of Captain Michael Roarke," the computer told her.

Elise leaned back in her chair and closed her eyes. "Override code Ragnarok." There was a brief pause as the virus she'd installed months ago swept through the operating system.

"Access accepted."

* * *

With a flare of satisfaction, Elise watched Henry Voroninn's glum, beefy face appear on her vid screen. His eyes widened. "Captain! How did you..."

"A little computer magic, Henry," she told him. In fact, it had taken her an hour of delicate, nerve-racking work to contact him without setting off the safeguards Roarke's computer experts had planted in the *Raker*'s network. Elise grinned impishly. "I didn't get this job by nepotism alone, no matter what Price says."

The big man frowned in puzzlement. "I thought they'd disabled all our security systems."

She nodded. "Except for the virus I planted."

"Roarke turned his back on you that long?"

"Actually, I wrote it several months ago. It seemed a logical precaution to take, with the *Liberator* breathing down our collective necks."

"Hmph." He looked more grumpy than pleased. "Wish you'd said something about this earlier. I've been pulling my non-existent hair out trying to come up with an escape plan."

"Sorry, Henry." Elise shrugged. "I just wasn't certain it would work. For one thing, I had to find an opportunity to launch it, which was far from a sure thing. And once I did, the chances were good that Roarke's counter-virus systems would defeat it. We got lucky." She grimaced as she stretched, absently trying to pull the kinks out of her spine. "God knows it's about time."

"But can they detect our communications? If Roarke catches you at this..."

At the thought of her captor's reaction, Elise felt a chill skate along the nape of her neck. Faking confidence, she smiled comfortingly at her second in command. "Don't worry about it. I designed this program to allow me to communicate with the crew without being detected. We should be safe. As long as neither of us patches into the bridge, anyway."

Chapter Four

Roarke hunched in Elise's command chair, staring thoughtfully at the tips of his boots. Whether he liked it or not -- and he didn't -- he strongly suspected he was falling in love with Elise Morrell. Which presented him with a whole raft of problems, not the least of which was the lady herself, who was damned unlikely to indulge him. Then there was the problem of the Starforce High Command's reaction when he tried to keep her out of that prison camp.

If he wasn't so desperate, he'd be intimidated. Still, he'd never backed down from a fight in his life, and he certainly wasn't going to start now. It was just a matter of convincing Elise she wanted him as much as he wanted her, while simultaneously convincing the High Command they *didn't* want her. *Simple as getting sucked out an airlock.* And probably about that pleasant.

The bridge doors slid open to admit Yolanda Boniface, who paused to eye him on her way to her station. "How's the captive?"

He snarled.

She gave him a cheeky grin. "That's what I thought."

Before he could manage a suitably annihilating reply, one of the vidcreens flashed to life, split down the middle as if for a bridge conference. Surprised, Roarke pivoted to stare at it, wondering why one of his crew would call in through the ship's intercom instead of using the radio implant.

"Okay, Captain, so we can communicate," Henry Voronnin said as his face appeared on the screen. "What do we do now?"

Roarke jerked upright, knowing instantly that this conversation wasn't supposed to be happening. And he certainly wasn't supposed to be hearing it.

On the split screen beside Voronnin, Elise frowned. "That's a very good question."

"How did they do *that*?" Yolanda crossed quickly to the communications console.

"Bypassed the computer safeguards, probably. Do they know we're monitoring?" Roarke demanded, coming out of his chair to stalk closer.

Yolanda's narrow black brows drew down. "Doesn't look like it. We're patched in, but they're not picking us up."

"Good," he said, then shushed her so he could listen to Elise's plotting.

With a grin of pure homicidal cheer, Voronnin suggested, "Well, we could always release something lethal into the ventilation system."

"Suicide's counterproductive, Henry."

Her first officer gestured with a hand the size of a spacesuit gauntlet. "Who said anything about suicide? All our people are in their quarters. If we confine the gas to operations areas and the bridge, we won't put any of the crew in danger."

Yolanda leaned close to Roarke and whispered, "You're growling, Boss."

He stopped.

"Henry, the boarding party's wearing armor, and they have communication implants," Elise pointed out. "The gas might kill a couple of them, but the rest would go to oxygen packs. And then we'd have a bunch of pissed-off troopers looking for revenge. I, for one, do not want to go up against armor bare handed."

Roarke clenched his gauntleted fists. "Isn't that a damn shame?" He was growling again. He didn't much care.

* * *

Elise tapped a finger against her computer console, thinking furiously. "If only they didn't have those communication implants, we might..." Something flickered in her consciousness, and she stilled, trying to bring it into focus. The plan materialized with all the speed and detail of something that had been brewing in her subconscious for hours. She snapped her fingers. "Communication implants. That's it! Henry, we can broadcast a sonic stun pulse right into their implants. Boom. They go down and out, and we've got an hour to retake the ship."

He considered the idea, then shook his head slowly. "I don't think that would fly, Captain, not if they're taking standard precautions and scrambling their communications. Their implants will reject any signal that isn't in the right code, which means nothing of ours would get through."

"Henry, I'm telling you, this is the solution." Elise sat forward in her seat, unconsciously leaning toward him in her eagerness. "The *Raker*'s computer could analyze a sample of their communications and decode it. It'll take time, but it's not as though either of us has a more pressing engagement."

"That's the God's truth." Henry meditated a moment. "Could work."

"Of course it'll work." She lofted a teasing eyebrow at him. "My plans always do."

"Except when they don't," he said dryly.

Barely even registering the quip, Elise got down to business, her hands darting over her workstation console as she set up the program.

Watching her on the screen, Henry commented, "If this does go, it'll be our turn to take hostages. The *Liberator* won't fire on us if we've got Roarke."

"Mmmph."

"Then, once we're away, we take the whole lot of 'em to Elba. Let Roarke try playing his clever little games with CSSIntel."

"Elba?" Elise frowned uneasily, looking up at him.

He shrugged. "It's the only POW installation in the sector. We have to take them there. It's standard procedure."

"Right." She fidgeted, hating the idea. "Look, I don't know how much time I've got before he comes back. I'd better get on it. Morrell out."

* * *

For a long moment Roarke sat paralyzed, unable to believe Elise would even consider handing him over to those bastards in CSSIntel. Not after he'd held her in his arms this morning, relishing the tender sensation of her sweet, warm body against his.

Damn her. Turning on his heel, Roarke headed for the nearest hatch. Over his shoulder, he barked, "Yo, find that computer virus and kill it. And send somebody after that bastard, Voronnin."

Yolanda nodded and turned. From the corner of her eye, she spotted something white sitting beside the command station he'd left. "Hey, boss, you forgot your helmet…"

But the hatch had already closed behind him.

* * *

Elise stared at the vidscreen as the *Raker*'s computer worked to crack the boarding party's radio code, but she couldn't concentrate. She couldn't seem to shake the image of Roarke locked up in a prison camp.

CSSIntel had tortured him so badly he was still feeling the effects two years later. What would they do to him now, particularly considering he'd killed his original jailer to escape? Elise had an ugly feeling she already knew the answer to that one: they'd brutalize Roarke until he died, simply as an object lesson to the other prisoners. He wouldn't last a week, and his final hours would be unspeakable.

She wasn't going to do it. No matter what it cost her, she wasn't going to let those bastards have him. Even if it gave Admiral Scordillis the excuse he was looking for to break her, she was going to turn the boarding party loose on the first Rebellion planet she could find.

Elise scowled at the screen of her workstation as she considered the implications. It would mean the end of her career, the loss of her ship, everything she'd worked for so long. And yet, letting CSSIntel have Roarke would do something much, much worse.

That would strip away her soul.

She straightened in a burst of self-awareness. It wasn't just the principle of the thing, though she wouldn't have sentenced a dog to that hellpit. No, it felt a lot more personal than that. As if Roarke had assumed an irrational importance to her, despite the fact that he was the enemy commander who'd tried to kill her yesterday -- and who'd successfully seduced her last night.

Neurocuffs notwithstanding, it had been more than a seduction. There'd been tenderness in the touch of his hands, his mouth, in the way he'd looked at her as he'd entered her body. This morning he'd held her like a lover. Elise could have withstood the rest of his arsenal: the wicked skill, the ridiculously arousing sexual threats, even the intelligence, the sense of humor, the lupine good looks, that strong, amazing body. She could have withstood it all, except for the possibility that he actually cared about her, that he saw her as something more than a target in battle and in bed.

But did it matter? She was still a CSS captain, and he was still the enemy. They…

Behind her the room hatch sighed open. "You've been a very bad girl, Elise," Roarke rumbled.

She turned her head barely in time to see him coming for her, his handsome face like stone. Elise tried to duck, but in the armor he was far too fast for her. He caught her by the collar and hauled her out of her chair.

Before she could yelp a protest, Roarke stripped off her robe with one ruthless swipe. Elise swore, struggling, but a naked woman is no match for an armored man, and he was relentless. In seconds, he had her pinned to the bulkhead with the weight of his body while he banged a magnetic clamp against the wall over her head. Neurocuffing her wrists together, he caught them in the clamp's field.

"Roarke, what the hell do you think you're doing?" Elise spat, pulling uselessly at the neurocuffs, though she knew she wouldn't be able to break the clamp's magnetic grip; it was designed to hold several tons of equipment.

"We're going to have a little… talk." Roarke crouched to grab her ankles, fending off the kicks she directed at his head. He clicked neuroshackles around them and thumped a pair of clamps against the wall, then caught the shackles in the clamps.

"Do you chain all your bed partners, or is it just me?" Elise demanded between gritted teeth, subsiding in raw frustration.

"Just you," he said, his tone dripping honey. "Nobody else betrays me to CSSIntel before the sheets are even cool." She stared at him, sick dread rolling over her. "And yes, I did monitor your chat with

Voronnin." He straightened to his full height, looming over her like an armored wall.

Elise straightened her own spine, trying to ignore the way the shackles spread her thighs. "If our positions were reversed, you'd have done the same thing."

He braced a palm beside her head and leaned close. "In the first place, I wouldn't work for the bloody CSS. I'm picky about who I do my killing for."

Knowing a threat when she heard one, Elise stared up into his handsome face, so close to her own. "You won't kill me."

A combination of irritation and reluctant amusement flickered over his face. "You're right, I won't. But that still leaves me a lot of room to maneuver." Reaching into one of the pouches on his belt, Roarke pulled out a thick black cylinder with rounded ends.

Elise felt her face go cold as the blood drained from her head. "Price'll be thrilled," she muttered hoarsely. It was a neurowhip.

Cleansing anger flooded into her, flushing away the moment's fear. "Give me credit for some intelligence, Roarke. You and I both know you'd be the last one to use that thing on a prisoner."

"Now there" -- he flicked one of the setting rings on the barrel with his thumb --"is where you're wrong."

Before she could flinch, Roarke touched the neurowhip to her right nipple. Elise cried out as intense sensation rolled over her, so hot and fierce it took her a moment to realize what she was feeling was pleasure. Shocked, she stared up into her captor's hungry eyes.

"Oh, yeeaaah." He gave her the smile the Wolf

must have given Little Red Riding Hood. "Not only will I use this little toy on you, I'm going to enjoy it."

Still wearing that sensual carnivore's smile, Roarke lazily teased her nipple with the neurowhip. She gasped as phantom teeth nibbled gently on the pink bud.

"If you'll notice," he said in a mockingly pedantic tone as he ran the barrel gently over the curve of her breast, "the neurowhip has three setting rings, one for intensity, the other for the type of neuron being stimulated, a third for combination of stimuli you select. A readout tells you which settings you've chosen." His thumb flicked one of the rings, and she felt a delicate, arousing suction. "Though I didn't know about this particular group of settings until a certain female friend asked what I was doing with a sex toy in my quarters." His teeth flashed. "Evidently the neurowhip is a well-known piece of... equipment in some circles. Some enterprising CSSIntell agent must do a brisk smuggling business."

Again, he stroked the tube over her nipples, and another cascade of pleasure rolled over her. Adjusting the whip as he went, he raised the intensity until she clenched her eyes shut and groaned helplessly. It felt as though countless tongues were licking and sucking at her breasts, warmth and wetness and pressure flickering across her skin like flame.

"I've never used it this way. Hell, I've never used it at all." He watched her breasts tremble as she gasped. "This seems like a perfect time to experiment."

"Why?" she croaked, twisting in her bonds. Lush delight trailed the neurowhip as he ran it down her ribs. "I thought you were... AH!... angry..."

"Oh, I am." He drew an erotic circle around her belly button. "Not about the escape plot -- you're right,

I would have done the same thing -- but I'm pretty pissed about Elba."

"I wouldn't have... I wouldn't have sent you..." She shuddered helplessly.

He heaved an exaggerated sigh. "Now, that's the problem with torture. You can never tell if the victim means what she's saying, or if she just wants you to stop." Leaning close enough to breathe in her ear, Roarke whispered, "Do you want me to stop, Elise?"

The whip was tracing a curving arc low on her belly, just above her pelvic bone. Any minute now he'd go lower, find her most sensitive flesh. She didn't think she could stand it if he touched her there. "God, no," she whimpered. "Don't stop."

* * *

Aching, Roarke watched Elise writhe, her white, deliciously lush body twisting in the neurocuffs. Her eyes were closed, the long lashes fanning against the curve of her cheeks. Her soft lips parted as she gasped. Her nipples were tight little points on her full, swaying breasts, and her hips made tiny, involuntary thrusts.

He was rapidly discovering just how uncomfortable it was to get a lead pipe erection in boarding armor. But he didn't dare take the suit off. If he did, he'd take her.

And then neither of them would know the truth.

* * *

Elise opened dazed eyes and looked around for Roarke through a haze of pleasure. She found him kneeling at her feet, running the neurowhip up and down the inside of her thighs. Even though he wasn't actually touching the erect nubbin between her legs, the back spill from the device was providing a wicked stimulation every time he brought it close.

Roarke looked up, his black eyes meeting hers,

male and hungry, yet fiercely controlled. He was still wearing his armor. Elise realized she wanted him out of it. She wanted to see his glorious body naked, feel his hands, his mouth, his strong, warm strength. The neurowhip, intense as its stimulation was, couldn't give her any of that. But he was trailing the device up her leg, closer and closer to her core. The sensations it wrung from her made her back arch.

"No, wait, not like… uhhh… not like that," Elise gasped.

Blessedly, Roarke stopped. "Don't you want to come? I can tell how --" his corded throat worked as he swallowed "-- hot you are."

"But I want… you. Take off the armor. Please, Roarke."

His lids lowered. "Why? What difference does it make?"

He wanted coherent thought out of her *now*? "It's cold."

"I can make it warmer." He flicked one of the setting rings.

"No!" His obtuseness was beginning to drag her out of her luscious fog. "I mean it's empty. Not like… not like when you touch me."

"But it's all the same thing. Just skillful stimulation of nerve endings. Isn't that what you said this morning?"

"It was more than that." She swallowed, licking her dry lips.

"You think so? Let's see…" Roarke leaned closer and opened his mouth. Elise tensed, staring down at his dark head, so close to her pubic mound. This time the wet, hot tongue she felt stroke into her curls was real. And it was his. Elise shuddered, desperate for him. Roarke tilted his head back to look up into her face. "I wonder. If you close your eyes, can you tell the difference?" He lifted the neurowhip again.

"I don't want that thing. I want you." He was playing with her, damn it. She frowned, coming fully aware now, spurred by the restless blend of hunger and irritation he'd aroused so ruthlessly. "Is that what you wanted to hear?"

"Maybe."

"All right," she snapped. "Last night was more than sex, and we both know it. Take off that bloody armor, toss the toy out the airlock, and let's stop playing around."

Roarke's eyes flared with hot satisfaction as he tossed the neurowhip away. Reaching for the shackles, he freed her legs with a couple of violent jerks. She watched impatiently as he grabbed the 'cuffs and liberated her wrists as well. Elise stepped away from the wall and helped him attack his armor, tugging off the awkward gauntlets, popping the pneumatic seal on his chestplate. Together they hauled the torso shell away from his muscled chest, flung it aside, and went to work on the lower half of the suit the minute he opened its catches.

"This isn't just sex," Roarke told her fiercely, pulling his legs free.

"I know that. Hurry and get that thing off." As he stripped off the last, unwanted barrier of the skinsuit, Elise shot him a cautious look. "What do you think it is?"

"Hell, I don't know. Bed?"

"No, here." She turned and bent over the desk. "It always made me crazy when you'd threaten to come into me like this."

"Me too," he growled, and moved up behind her. His big hands caught her hips and tugged her back.

The smooth, rounded head of his erection brushed her bottom, lowered until it found her eager heat. He entered in a slick glide, filling her endlessly as she arched in pleasure.

"God, Roarke!"

"Yesssss!" He pulled her greedily against him, his hands going to her breasts to pluck and roll her hard nipples as he kissed her ear, the side of her neck, biting gently until she turned her face to his. Plunging his tongue into her mouth, he held his hips still. She didn't protest, wanting only to prolong having him within her.

They strained together like that, kissing slowly, awkwardly, their necks twisted, eyes closed. Elise felt Roarke shudder against her. "God," he moaned, "I want to drive into you, but it'd be over too soon. I'm too hot for you, I'd never make it last long enough."

Elise murmured an incoherent agreement even as she felt her own control eroding. Her hips rolled once, an involuntary thrust that buried his silken length a fraction deeper. She caught her breath. He felt so thick inside her, his body so strong around hers as he surrounded her with his arms and his chest and his powerful hips, cradling her in masculine power, in desire, in heat. No man had ever felt this way -- as though he completed her, enhanced her, yet made her more wholly herself than she was without him. She wanted more.

Teeth unconsciously biting her lip, Elise pulled away slightly, then drove back onto his width. He gasped. "Elise, don't. I can't..."

She thrust.

Roarke lost control. His powerful hands clamped into the curve of her bottom and dug in as he began to lunge, driving his long cock in and out of her. She quivered as ecstasy ignited in her cunt, searing brighter with each pistoning stroke. "God, Elise, I need you," he groaned, "I'm not going let you go again, I'm going... to keep you... AH! Whatever it takes..."

"Yes!" She threw back her head as he pounded her, his hips slapping against hers. The pleasure blasted her every inhibition, her every vestige of control. "Yes, keep you..."

He grated something else, but he was thrusting so hard she couldn't make it out, couldn't comprehend anything beyond the fiery length digging inside her, giving her no mercy, offering no quarter from the brutal delight.

Detonation. Elise convulsed in Roarke's possessive arms, screaming through her climax as her body tightened on his so ferociously, he made a startled sound. And came with a roar of pure male triumph.

* * *

When Elise next became aware, the edge of her workstation was digging into her belly, and Roarke was sprawled across her back, feeling heavy, sweaty, and utterly delicious.

"Mmmmm. That was..." She couldn't think of the words. Nothing seemed good enough.

"Yeah," he agreed blurrily. "Mmmm." After a long, languorous silence, he stirred. "I must be heavy." Gently he pulled away. She caught her breath as he left her. She realized she wanted to call him back, wanted his hot weight. Without him she felt curiously light, cool. And empty.

"I wouldn't have sent you to Elba," Elise said, suddenly desperate, though she didn't know why.

"Yeah," he said. "I just wasn't sure you knew it."

"What do you mean?" She pulled away from the desk, wincing a bit at the soreness in her muscles. It was an oddly satisfying ache.

"There's something happening between us, and it's not hate." He threw her a hooded black look. "I want more of you than what I can get by shackling you to the wall."

She grinned. "Though that has certain attractions I never would have guessed." Elise sobered. "But I'm not sure what either of us can do about it."

His expression turned wary. "What do you mean?"

Elise shrugged, making a helpless gesture. "We're on opposite sides, Roarke. If I don't manage to escape, I'm going to prison for the duration of the war. That doesn't sound like a particularly good way to start a relationship."

"I know that. I..." Roarke broke off, tilting his head as though listening to something. His dark eyes widened. "How did he get past the guard stationed in crew quarters?" he barked. Realizing he must be talking to someone through his implant, Elise grimaced.

"He didn't just walk through the bulkhead, Yo. I want to know what the hell..." Roarke broke off, eyes going narrow as he stared at Elise. "Forget it, I'm sure I know someone who can tell us. In the meantime, triple the guard and send out search parties. I want that bastard found, and I don't want any more *Raker* people getting loose!"

Elise stared at him, remembering she'd disabled Roarke's computer safeguards -- and the one man who knew she'd done it. "Henry."

"Yeah." He turned around and began hunting for his armor. "We'd better get dressed. And while we're at it, you can tell me how Voronnin got past the guards I had posted at the corridor junctions in crew quarters."

Frowning, she stood and made for a closet, stalling for time. She knew the answer, of course. Coalition ship designers were a cautious, paranoid bunch; there was an access tube that ran from the crew deck to the armory. A second tube was located just outside her quarters, also going to the armory. Nobody but senior ship's command staff knew about it. "Roarke, you know I can't tell you that. Regardless of whatever's going on between us, I have a responsibility to my crew."

He snorted. "Maybe, but not in Voronnin's case. For one thing, I don't think he feels much loyalty in return."

She frowned at him. "What are you talking about?"

"How do you think we monitored your transmission to him earlier?"

Finding a black one-piece ship suit, Elise pulled it out of the closet and put it on. "I assume you defeated my security program."

"Not quite, or he wouldn't have gotten loose." He grunted as he shrugged back into the torso armor.

One hand sealing the suit closed, Elise looked up. "What are you saying -- that he betrayed me?"

"Wouldn't be the first time."

"I've known Henry Voronnin since we were in the CSS Academy. He's not the type."

Roarke sighed. "Remember that anonymous tip that led me to you on that Tyus beach? Ever wonder where it came from?"

"What does that have to do with…"

"Who knew where you were headed, Elise?"

Elise felt her stomach sink. She'd called Henry before she'd gone for her swim that fateful night.

"Anybody that looked out a window."

"*He knew who you were.* Even gave your ship registry," Roarke told her. "The only person who could have blown your cover was Voronnin himself."

Henry, a traitor? It couldn't be. He was the most genuinely decent person she knew. It couldn't be.

Slowly, she moved to her desk chair and sat down. "But why?" The question sounded a lot more forlorn than she would have wished.

"Well, there's the fact that somebody with the CSS high command doesn't seem terribly fond of you. Not judging from the communique we got yesterday detailing your Superspace dropout coordinates. Hell, I met you expecting a trap -- which it was, but not for the *Liberator*."

Elise stared at him, wishing that for once she'd been wrong about the CSS's capacity for treachery. "That wasn't Henry. He'd have been killed if you'd destroyed the ship. No, I think Admiral Scordillis himself was responsible for that one."

His eyebrows lifted. "A nasty enemy to have. Which gives Henry a motive." Roarke moved to lean an armored hip on the desktop. "If Voronnin knew the admiral was willing to go to those lengths to get you..."

"Then setting me up on Tyus would make sense. It'd be the only way to save the ship. And since that failed, and since we survived your attack..." She dragged a hand through her hair as pain clawed at her. "He must have patched us into the bridge hoping to goad you into killing me. With me dead, Scordillis would leave the crew alone. God, Henry."

And now he was on the loose. Headed for the armory. He couldn't get at the beamers -- he'd need her voice command for that, CSS having a pathological fear of mutiny -- but he could get to the boarding armor. The armor wasn't locked down, because it had to be accessible to repel invaders even with the captain dead.

Which she might soon be, after Henry took the second access tube back to her quarters.

Elise lifted her head. "Roarke, you'd --"

The corridor door slid open, revealing two figures in black and gray CSS boarding armor. The visor of one of the suits slid back, revealing Henry Voronnin's familiar face, twisted in an alien expression of rage. "Damn you, Roarke, why won't you kill her? Are you that hot for her narrow little ass?"

"Henry," Elise growled, "you treacherous..."

Before she could open her mouth again, Roarke swept her out of her chair with one hand and tossed her into the corner. Her head struck the bulkhead with the force of his enhanced strength. Sparks exploded in a white-hot burst of pain.

* * *

Roarke dove after her, spinning to place himself between her and the mutineers. It was a risky move, literally backing himself into a corner, but he knew if he'd tried to defend her any other way, one of them would maneuver to his rear and take her. Triggering his implant, he barked, "Yo, get a crew down here! The goddamned escapees are in Elise's quarters!"

The smaller of the two promptly turned and rammed his fist into the bulkhead beside the door. Sparks showered. He turned and served the door to Elise's quarters the same.

"Your rescuers won't be getting in that way, Roarke," Henry told him over the sound of rending metal. "Not without a beamer torch and an hour's work, anyway." The big man edged toward him. "Let us have the captain, and we'll discuss this."

Roarke's lips pulled back in a snarl. "Go to hell."

"Be reasonable. There are two of us, and you don't even have your helmet. One good head shot, and your brains are all over the bulkhead. Either way, I'm going to kill her. Why die too?"

For a moment Roarke could see it: Elise, helpless in the merciless armored grip of these bastards. Rage scalded him. "Fuck you, Voronnin."

"I'll get her. One way or another." He was swinging his fist in a blurring roundhouse before his faceplate even had time to close.

Roarke blocked it away from his bare head and slammed out a counter punch. It struck Voronnin square in the chest, and he staggered, only to rear back and drive a kick right at Roarke's belly.

His first impulse was to dance aside, but Roarke caught himself at the last moment. He couldn't leave Elise unprotected. He swept down a block instead.

Too late. The booted foot hit him like a meteor. Even with the protection of his armor, the impact rammed into his belly with sickening force. Roarke gasped for breath, fighting to keep his feet and avoid being knocked into Elise, knowing he could easily crush her even as he tried to keep her alive.

Recovering his balance, he growled and shot two rapid-fire punches at Voronnin's faceplate. The assassin blocked the first, but the second staggered him.

Not daring to press his advantage for fear of leaving Elise vulnerable, Roarke stayed in his corner and waited for the next attack.

* * *

Woozily, Elise shook her head, blinking away the dancing gray spots that filled her vision. She must have blacked out for a moment. Something broad and hard was pressed against her, wedging her into a corner so tightly she could barely breathe. She heard Roarke curse viciously over a rhythmic series of crunches, the sound of something hard slamming and grinding into something that clanked and scraped with each blow. Still dazed, Elise pressed her forehead against what she suddenly realized was Roarke's armored back, and felt him shudder with impact. It was then that she recognized the sounds: hand-to-hand combat in armor.

Desperately she shook her head again, trying to make sense of the situation despite the hammer strokes of headache that made thought all but impossible. They were backed into a corner. It was the worst possible tactical position; Roarke couldn't maneuver at all. Why didn't he move, get room enough to defend himself?

The last of the mental fog burned away as she realized Roarke must be guarding her. Because if he didn't, Henry Voronnin would murder her like a child pulling the wings off a bug.

Looking up, she saw Roarke blocking punch after punch away from his head.

Damn. He couldn't keep that up. He was going to get himself killed trying to keep her alive. Stupid, quixotic…

What was she supposed to do without him?

Something hard closed around her ankle. Jerked, pulling her down and out. Elise yelled and grabbed for Roarke, but her hands slipped down the chill, smooth metal of his armor. She hit the deck hard, and her captor dragged out of her corner, right past Roarke's leg, scraping off a layer of skin on his knee joint as she passed.

Roarke glanced down, saw what was happening

and swore, grabbing for her, but a punch from Voronnin drove him back into the bulkhead.

A gauntleted hand closed brutally tight over her throat and jerked her to her feet. Elise gasped, fighting to breathe, clawing uselessly at the arm that held her. Gagging, she stared into the polarized plastic of her assailant's faceplate.

The visor slid back, revealing the smug, malicious features of Lt. Gloria Price. "Hello, Captain. Looks like I finally got you just where I want you."

Chapter Five

In frustrated rage, Roarke watched the second assassin drag Elise out of reach. He had to get her back before the bastard killed her.

Something blurred toward his face. He blocked it automatically, knocking aside yet another lethal Voronnin punch. Cursing under his breath, Roarke realized he'd have to take care of that treacherous son of a bitch first. Knowing he needed maneuvering room to do it, he lunged out of the corner, slamming a one-two combination into Voronnin's faceplate as he went by. The tough, armored plastisteel was designed to take a lot of abuse, but if you hammered at it long enough, it would give.

And that was just what Roarke meant to do.

He circled his hulking opponent, forcing himself to forget Elise's peril for the moment. It was difficult using martial arts techniques that called for agility in bulky boarding armor, but still he twisted his body into a powerful spinning kick targeted at Voronnin's skull.

With a roar of fury Roarke could hear even through the helmet, the big man grabbed his leg before the strike landed. Jerking straight up, Voronnin dumped him hard on his back, then stomped viciously down into his belly. Pain choked him, sickening and black. Voronnin drew back for another kick, but this time Roarke caught his boot. Clamping his other hand into his foe's knee, Roarke picked him up and hurled him away. Voronnin slammed into the bulkhead.

Rolling, Roarke sprang for him in a low, flat dive, managing to score another hard punch to the faceplate just as Voronnin landed a bruising kick between his ribs. But the helmet didn't give.

He just prayed Elise would still be alive by the time it did.

* * *

Black spots danced in front of Elise's vision as Price's ruthless grip cut off her oxygen. Even as she pounded the traitor's arms in an effort to break her hold, Elise realized she was deliberately spinning the assault out. In the suit, Price could have easily crushed her throat with one hard squeeze. Evidently she was enjoying herself too much to make it quick.

Elise's blows weakened as her strength drained rapidly. Even the pain was fading, drowned in a rising tide of darkness. With a sensation of mild surprise, she realized she was dying.

Abruptly the vicious grip relaxed. Wheezing, Elise choked down a gulp of air.

"Oh, Captain -- I just remembered," the blonde said, malice in her cold blue eyes. Elise didn't stir, hanging limp as she concentrated on breathing. Price gave her a quick, hard shake. "Wake up, Captain, you need to hear this. There's a message Admiral Scordillis told me to convey before you died. Are you still there?"

She managed a weak kick in the traitor's general direction.

"Good. Listen carefully now: your father is dead. The CSS had him assassinated a week ago. You're the last Morrell left alive. And soon… there won't be any of you."

* * *

Roarke managed to work his opponent into the same corner he'd just vacated, but he paid for it. Voronnin hammered a trio of blows into his torso so powerful the armor couldn't absorb that much force. Pain hammered him, and something grated ominously in his ribs. *Cracked,* Roarke thought grimly. Perhaps worse. He tried to back away, but sensing his weakness Voronnin followed, drawing back his fist for another pile driver punch to the ribs.

Roarke automatically blocked -- only to realize at the last instant the strike was a feint.

He looked up to see a huge fist coming right at his face.

Instinctively Roarke ducked, grabbing the arm as it passed overhead. Continuing the arc, he jerked down. Voronnin went airborne and slammed head first into the bulkhead behind Roarke. Plastisteel crunched. The assassin rebounded off the wall and slowly toppled.

Holding his abused ribs, Roarke cautiously moved close enough to see Voronnin's face. Through the shattered visor, his opponent's face was slack, eyes closed.

One down, Roarke thought grimly.

* * *

Elise stared at the blonde in stunned horror.

Obviously relishing her anguish, Price explained, "The Admiral suspected you might decide to step into your father's position with the Reform movement. That's why you've got to die." Smiling sweetly, she let go of Elise's throat so she could catch her by the shoulder instead. She drew back an armored fist that could shatter her captain's skull. "Any final words for the Admiral, Captain?"

Elise coughed. "Yes," she choked out. Her voice was barely a whisper, sandpaper rough. "Abort Omega Code Zero."

"What's that supposed to mean?" Price scowled, irritated. "If you're trying to stall...."

She broke off as her body snapped out to its full

height, jerked rigid as though by invisible strings. Her hands fell away from Elise and slapped down at her sides. Price's eyes widened. "What?" Her head snapped back and forth in her helmet, but other than that, she didn't move at all.

She couldn't. Despite the agony in her throat, Elise felt a feral grin slide across her lips.

"What's the hell is going on?" Price demanded, her voice spiraling into a screech. "What did you do?"

"I was..." Elise had to stop and swallow to get her abused vocal cords to work, but she still couldn't manage anything louder than a whisper. "...Expecting something like this from you. A month ago I programmed your onboard suit computer to lock the armor down at my command." Watching fear swamp Price's eyes as the blonde realized just how thoroughly she was trapped, Elise felt her grin broaden. "You know, I do have a message for Scordillis. Tell him I resign." Slowly, she drew back her fist.

"Captain..."

The punch landed squarely on Price's patrician nose. Blood spurted, accompanied by a satisfying howl.

"You have such a way with words." Roarke said into Elise's ear.

"I try." She redirected her triumphant grin over her shoulder at him.

Ignoring Price's nasal curses, he shook his head. "Here I was, desperately trying to finish that bastard Voronnin off in time to save you, unarmed and supposedly helpless as you are. I should have known better. You wouldn't be helpless stark naked in a tiger cage."

Refusing to subject her abused throat with any more attempts at speech, Elise smiled tightly.

Roarke frowned and put out a hand to lift her chin, tilting her head back so he could see her throat. "Let's see that... Elise, you've got her fingerprints branded into your throat. I'm amazed you can talk at all. Are you all right?"

"Fine," she rasped. As fine as she could be, anyway, under the circumstances.

He shot her a worried look, obviously doubting it. "Let me call my crew and see how they're doing with the door. We need to get you to a medic." Looking away from her, he said into his implant, "How are you coming with that laser torch, Yo?"

As Roarke talked to his people, Elise's attention fell on Henry, still sprawled unconscious on his back. His helmet faceplate was shattered into jagged chunks.

Taking a step toward him, she felt something roll under her foot. She looked down and saw she'd stepped on the neurowhip, lying where Roarke had apparently dropped it. Elise picked it up and idly twisted the setting rings with a thumb as she moved to stand over her former friend.

"What happened to you, Henry?" she murmured. "And why didn't I realize it?"

His eyes opened. "You always did underestimate me."

His hand flashed upward and dug into the waistband of her coveralls. The next moment she was on top of him and his huge hand was wrapped around her head. Slowly, he began to twist.

Elise gritted, "Planning to break my neck, Henry?"

"Yeah." His grip tightened. "Sorry, Captain."

She rammed the neurowhip through the hole in his faceplate and activated it. He howled, his massive body arching under her, his hand tightening convulsively on her head. Teeth clenched, she held the whip where it was.

The deck plate boomed in her ear as something heavy hit the ground beside them. Fingers closed over Henry's, fighting to pry them away. Out of the corner of one eye, she saw Roarke's white, desperate face as he fought to keep Henry from twisting her head any further. Pain lanced up and down Elise's neck, and she screamed as the pain spiraled, her voice blending with Henry's bellow. She felt bone grate just as Roarke finally managed to jerk Voronnin's hand away, scraping off a layer of skin in the process.

Henry's bellow cut off.

"I should have killed that son of a bitch when I had the chance," Roarke panted into the sudden silence. Reaching down, he tenderly pulled Elise away from her would-be killer.

"'S okay," Elise rasped, looking down at Henry. His eyes were fixed, staring. Dead. "I thought neurowhips weren't supposed to kill."

"They're not" Roarke frowned at the body. "Though I do think I heard something about not bringing them in contact with the victim's head..." Glancing at the readout of the whip she still held, he flinched. "Not at that setting, anyway."

Elise looked down. All three readings were redlined. Horror wound tight in her. "Evidently," she whispered.

* * *

Elise made a soft sound. Roarke looked quickly over at her, scanning her as she lay on the regrowth couch a few feet away. He'd ended up in Sickbay with her when the medic discovered the interesting fractures in his ribs.

The desolation on her face tore at him. "You had no choice, Elise, you know that. He was going to kill you."

She shot him a blank look, as though it was taking her a moment to remember who he was talking about. At last she shook her head, pale strands shifting around her shoulders under the gold light cast by the medifield. "It's not that." Elise hesitated. "Roarke, the CSS had my father assassinated."

He blinked. "You're *that* Morrell?"

"Didn't you know?"

"The dossier I had on you was fairly sketchy."

She nodded, then fell silent again.

He studied her. Her face was too pale, suffering etching the delicate features and pulling her lush mouth tight. Yet her eyes were dry. "You've seen news stories then?" she asked at last.

"Yes."

"How did they do it?"

Roarke hesitated, then admitted reluctantly, "A sniper from ambush. I understand he died instantly. They're claiming a rival member of the Reformists hired the assassin."

"They would."

"I'm sorry, Elise."

"I know." She paused. "When the medic releases us, there's something I want to show you."

He nodded and allowed the silence to claim her again.

* * *

An hour later, they stood in a gravitylock and waited for it to cycle. Slowly, Roarke felt his body becoming lighter as the gravity in the cubical decreased until his feet left the deck altogether. The opposite hatch opened, and Elise pushed off, drifting out of the lock to catch at a padded perch in the tank beyond. Roarke followed more slowly, scanning the area with his habitual caution.

It looked just like the ZG tank on the *Liberator*. Designed to allow crew to practice zero gravity fighting skills, it was outfitted with a number of hoop-shaped perches that protruded from the curving walls. Vid projectors allowed the occupants to program whatever background they chose for three-dimensional display on the tank walls; Elise had chosen a scene of the Earth from orbit. Roarke stared hungrily. He hadn't seen the home world since the war started, and he doubted he'd ever see it again. It was as heartbreakingly beautiful as always, a lovely blue globe splashed with green and ocher, swirled with blinding cloud cover.

"Before we started this mission, while the *Raker* was still in orbit around Earth, my father came up for a visit," Elise said softly. "I brought him in here and had the computer relay a sensor image to the projectors. This is a recording of that image." Her voice dropped. "He said Earth had never been more beautiful to him, because he was seeing it from the deck of my ship. Since then, I've been coming here whenever I felt the need for his guidance. It makes… made me feel close to him."

"I can't think of a better remembrance." His voice was a bit too husky, and he cleared his throat. He felt a sudden, vicious desire to hunt Frank Scordillis down and kill him for her.

"My father thought the Rebellion was wrong, you know." Elise brought her feet around so she could perch on the handhold. "He believed the only real route to change was from within. Otherwise you just exchange one dictator for another."

Roarke scowled. "The Rebellion is a democracy, not a dictatorship. We've already ratified a constitution."

"I know." She let go of her handhold and hung in the air for a moment, letting herself float. "As much as I loved him, I've come to realize my father was wrong, about that and other things. Some systems are so corrupt they can't be changed. They simply can't tolerate anything but evil. If you try to change them, they'll kill you. And if you just go along, they'll corrupt you." Softly she added, "That's what happened to Henry. And ultimately, it's what would have happened to me."

"I think you're selling yourself short. Enemy or not, you've never been anything but honorable." Roarke grimaced. "Even when I didn't want to admit it."

She shook her head, the small movement causing her body to drift in the air until she reached out and grabbed the handhold again. "Since I'd become captain, I'd begun to finally see what the CSS was doing. Often I was appalled, it was so totally opposite everything I knew to be just. I considered resigning a hundred times, but I always rationalized my way into staying."

She shrugged. "I reasoned that my father's enemies would use my leaving the service to make him look bad, I reasoned that I was protecting the lives of innocent Coalition civilians, I reasoned that soon he would be president and the corruption would end." Taking a deep breath, Elise added, bluntly, savagely, "But the fact was I'd worked fifteen years of my life to win this ship, and I didn't want to lose it."

"Sounds to me like you were guilty of being human."

"Unfortunately that's no excuse." She put her slim foot into the hoop and gently pushed. Slowly, her unbound hair forming a swirling halo around her head, Elise floated upward. "But now that doesn't matter. I've lost it all anyway. My crew, my ship, my home. My father."

He looked up at her as she hovered over him, her body long and lush in the white shipsuit he'd given her in lieu of the uniform she'd refused to wear any longer. "Elise...."

She was staring fixedly at the globe of Earth, its blue light washing her face in cool radiance. "Losing him... it's like when someone you love dies of a long, wasting illness. There's grief and pain, but there's also a kind of relief. Because it's over." Her eyes seemed to be growing larger, an effect caused by tears filling them, yet unable to fall. "I never realized how working for those bastards had eaten at me all these years. And without meaning to, he'd tied me to them." Impatiently, she dashed a hand over her face. The tears spun away, glittering in the earthlight. "But God, Roarke, it hurts."

Feeling helpless in the face of her grief, he pushed off from his handhold and floated to join her. "Elise..." Gently he caught her shoulders. She turned and flowed against him, wrapping her arms tightly around his ribs, the movement tumbling them both into a slow spin.

He felt her small, slender body shudder with pain. "They killed him. Roarke, the bastards killed him."

"I know, darlin'."

"There's no more of us left. Nobody but me. I'm alone."

"Shhh. You're not alone. I'm here." Gently, he kissed away one of the tears clinging to the feathered length of her lashes.

Suddenly her mouth was on his, desperate, fierce

with a hunger that caught him off guard. Roarke stiffened in surprise, then began to kiss her back. Her tongue swept into his mouth, so possessive and eager he felt his cock harden. Her slim body strained against his. Instinctively he tightened his grip, giving her the strength and closeness she seemed to need so badly.

"Help me, Roarke," she whispered against his mouth. "Help me forget. For just a little while."

"Anything," he moaned as the tank spun lazily around them.

"We need to anchor," Elise said, her voice hoarse with a razored combination of choking grief and sudden, furious need. "Anchor us."

Roarke reached out and snagged a passing handhold, then caught the one next to it with the other hand, bringing both of then to a sudden stop. Elise pulled back from him just enough to open the seal of her shipsuit, her mouth set in a line that trembled. He could only ache for her, even as his own hunger ignited as she wiggled out of the suit. She sent it sailing across the tank and reached for Roarke's seal. Ruthlessly, she dragged at it until it opened, clawed it back until it was off his shoulders and pulled down to his elbows.

Elise began to nibble on the thick swell of his biceps, then licked her way up his arm and across his shoulder, biting and tasting as she went. After wrapping her legs around his thighs to anchor herself, she stretched up his body to pull the suit down to his waist. Roarke moaned as his erection pressed into her flat belly.

Her long, cool hands trembled as they traced the plates of his pecs, then explored the weave of muscle that lay over his ribs. He felt her breath gusting warm over his skin, the brush of her fine pubic hair against his right leg, and shuddered himself in raw, erotic pleasure.

"If you keep this up," Roarke said, his voice husky and rough, "I won't be responsible for my actions."

Elise straightened, her hands bracing her away from his chest even while she held on with her legs. There was a hypnotic, witchy sensuality about her as her long hair flowed around her head, her gem-green eyes glittering at him through a sheen of tears, her breasts with their darkly flushed nipples taunting him. "Surely the captain of the *Liberator* can muster more self-control than that."

"I'll try," he muttered hoarsely.

"Good." And, wrapping both hands in the fabric of his coveralls, she jerked them down. His stone-hard erection sprang free into the cool air. "Because I'm getting to the best part."

* * *

Elise stripped the suit the rest of the way down his legs and tossed it across the tank. For a moment she let go and allowed herself to float, studying Roarke as she considered the possibilities. He was stretched out, his hands locked around the handholds, muscled arms bulging as he held his powerful body taut. It was a tempting picture -- and just what she needed. What she had to have.

Forgetfulness. If only for a while.

Making love in zero-g was tricky. Unless one partner anchored the other, it was easy to go into a wild, uncontrolled spin or even bounce off one another altogether. It took strength and self-control to provide your lover with the strong, steady brace needed, not to mention a willingness to stay completely rigid. Roarke hadn't even questioned why he should be the one to anchor them, though she knew he'd probably prefer to be in control. He seemed to recognize what she needed.

Looking down the length of his body, Elise saw the jut of his erect cock. She decided on the spot to reward him for his generosity.

Reaching out, Elise hooked an arm around his strong thigh and drew herself closer as she opened her mouth for the broad, purpled head. Roarke moaned in anticipation that would have made her smile at any other time. Now she just took him in without hesitation. The crown felt just slightly nubby as she swirled her tongue over it, then sucked it deeper inside. She grasped his hip, angled her body upward and sank, head first, down onto his erection.

Fellatio was the sole sex act that was actually easier in zero-g, since you could get into any position you needed to and suck as long as you wanted without worrying about muscle fatigue.

Roarke's back arched as he moaned in voluptuous pleasure. They drifted for a moment, then jerked to a stop as he remembered his task and grabbed hold of the hoops again. Slowly, Elise withdrew, paused to lick and bite gently at the crown, then took the thick shaft even deeper. And so she played, first pulling her body closer by her grip on his hips, then pushing away again, over and over until he twisted in helpless pleasure.

"If this is payback for using the neurowhip on your nipples," he groaned, "it's damned effective."

She didn't answer, too intent on the moment, on the feel and taste of him. Forcing away the pain.

"But for you, I'm willing to suffer." His black eyes closed. "As long as you don't stop."

Instead of taking his cock again, she pulled herself close to his groin and nuzzled his testicles. Sucking first one and then the other into her mouth, she tongued them, enjoying the shudder that ran through his powerful body. Returning her attention to his cock, she slowly licked up and down the thick length, then engulfed him for a few more long strokes down her throat.

"Elise." His voice had deepened into a rough growl. "If you keep that up, *I* won't be able to."

He was staring at her with that famished black wolf look in his eyes, and she realized his patience was eroding rapidly. But she wasn't ready for it to be over. Not yet.

Releasing his hard shaft, she worked her way over his torso, stroking the fascinating topography of his muscles, savoring the warmth of his skin. And his hooded gaze flicking over her body in that predatory way he had.

"Elise, let me suck your nipples," he purred.

"I don't know," she rasped, a jolt of pleasure at the idea stabbing through her desperation. "You've been a very bad boy."

"Just give me another chance." His eyes hooded. "I'll show you just how bad I can be."

"Well, all right." She let herself drift up his body, touching him here and there as she moved. Taking hold of his powerful biceps, she presented a nipple to his mouth. "As long as you're very, very bad."

Looking up into her eyes, he lifted his head and curled out his long tongue for a slow lick of the hard pink tip. Pleasure lanced through her at the contact.

Then it was Elise's turn to moan helplessly as Roarke began suck and bite and lick at the stiff nipple. Desire coiled in a tight, laced ball in her belly. She twisted her torso to present the other breast to his mouth, and he obligingly, hungrily, closed his white teeth over it. His tongue flicked at his trapped captive until she writhed against him, the strength and hardness of his body maddening her even more.

Roarke released her from his mouth, dark eyes burning into hers. "Now." And he arched his back, thrusting his hips upward in invitation.

"Yes," she moaned, and hurriedly pushed herself down his body. Ravenous, desperate, Elise wrapped her legs around his hips, caught hold of his hot shaft, and lifted herself until she could aim it at her slick pussy. Tightening her thighs, she grabbed his ribs and pulled until he sank into her, spreading her, filling her deliciously full. She shuddered.

"God, Elise…" Roarke twisted, pumping his hips to help her push his shaft deeper into her clamping flesh.

Driven wild by the force of her desire for him, Elise began to work, grinding her body against his, though she could scarcely bear the pleasure of the penetration. She could feel the muscle leaping under his damp skin as he struggled to both hold them still and provide a steady platform for her pleasure.

Gasping, she rode him, staring at his handsome, set face, watching the flex of tendon in his jaw as he fought to control his own passion. Forced to keep her strokes short, she circled her hips, letting his shaft gore her deliciously. Each thrust drove her pleasure that much higher, until her climax was just beyond the brush of her fingers, needing only one tiny nudge…

"Elise!" Roarke groaned. "I have to…"

His hands released the hoops and flew to her hips. Powerful fingers closed over her round buttocks, lifted her off his shaft, then drove her downward in one brutally deep thrust.

"Roarke!" she screamed, feeling it coming,

bursting along her nerves in a firestorm. "I love you!"

He bellowed in triumph and release. Deep inside her, she could feel his thick cock jetting.

Later as they clung together helplessly, he whispered in her ear, "I love you too, Elise."

* * *

Roarke floated in midair, relishing the feeling of Elise wrapped around him like a blanket, her body utterly limp, her skin damp and warm with pleasure. Her hair waved around them in the air currents, strands of fine silk shimmering in the blue recorded light of Earth. One of her long, slim hands stroked his chest, combing through the ruff of hair in sensual exploration. Her mouth was pressed against his breastbone, over his heart. He felt something wet against his skin he suspected might be another tear.

"What's going to happen now, do you think?" she asked, sounding sleepy.

"Well, you're not going to that damn prison camp, for one thing. Would you be willing to defect?"

"After what the CSS did? You'd better believe it." She bit gently at one of his nipples. He closed his eyes at the sharp pleasure. Resting her chin on his chest, she looked up at him. "I think I'm going to tell the crew what happened. All of it, including Scordillis' betrayal of us and Henry's assassination attempt. What they did to my..." She broke off. "My people deserve to know what the CSS really is."

"Will it make a difference?"

She shrugged. "Some of them will probably opt to stay in the service, either out of fear for their families or ambition, but I think those who can defect, will." Elise shot him a haunted look. "The real question is, will they be accepted?"

He nodded. "They'll have to undergo psyche

evaluations to make sure they're not spies, but once their sincerity is confirmed, there'll be no problem. Frankly, the Star Force needs all the qualified ship personnel we can get." He hesitated, then added, "That goes double for you. There's always a certain amount of political infighting involved in who receives captaincies, so it will be difficult to get you a ship given your background. But you're too talented to waste, and I will fight tooth and nail to get one for you. And I should be able to pull it off, too." Roarke smiled grimly. "The high command still owes me one for Nygaard."

She pulled away and stared. "You'd do that for me?"

"Yes. I'm not saying what I get you will be much of a ship, but..." He broke off and shrugged.

Frowning, Elise reached out and caught his wrist. Weaving her fingers through his, she stared at their joined hands for a long moment. He waited patiently for her to speak.

"I want to avenge my father," she told him finally. "But you and I have just discovered each other. I don't want to leave you. And frankly, I'm not sure I have any interest in political intrigue just now. Of any kind. Not even to get another ship." She looked up at him, her green eyes vulnerable. "I don't suppose there's an open berth on the *Liberator*."

"I'm sure something can be arranged," Roarke told her, his voice rough with the knowledge that she was willing to choose him over another ship of her own. Twisting his mouth into an evil grin, he added wickedly, "In fact, I can think of several interesting positions I'd like to put you in."

"That sounds... promising." But her eyes had drifted to the image of Earth, hanging blue and white against the stars. He could almost feel the grief beginning to ribbon its way through her again.

"But for now," Roarke said softly, "I think I'd rather just hold you."

"Yeah." She wrapped herself around him again, her body warm and sweat damp. "I like that idea."

He drew her closer. He'd finally caught Elise Morrell.

And he planned to hold onto her for the rest of his life.

Stranded
Angela Knight

Society-girl Alex has a smutty secret: she craves domination. One night, while fantasizing about the man who can claim and master her, Fate drops her in his arms. Literally.

Hawke's been alone in the "Goldfish Bowl" for far too long. When the Bastards drop a beautiful blonde into his life, he doesn't mind protecting her, but she's going to pay for it. By satisfying his every sexual need. But it won't be easy. Alex requires some very creative domination. And then there are the Monsters...

The sex is great, but will they survive being *Stranded*?

Chapter One

Alexandria Kenyon lay staring up at the ceiling fan circling lazily over her bed. Each moonlit rotation sent shadows spinning across the cherry colonial furniture, but she was far more interested in the erotic images flickering through her own mind. Her nipples rose hard and hungry under the lace of her camisole, and she ran her fingers over them, sighing in pleasure.

Closing her eyes, Alex pictured a man, broad shouldered and blond and feral, with hard hands and a long, hungry cock. And a mouth that rasped erotic orders.

He'd taken her prisoner. Now she lay on his immense bed looking up at him, bound and naked and breathless. He stood there with muscled legs braced wide, surveying her with a conqueror's smile, his cock jutting in cruel anticipation of his pleasure. "You're mine now, sweet. You challenged me and lost, and now I'll take you. Every way that pleases me."

Imagining the lust and triumph in her dream lover's gaze, she licked her lips and slid her other hand down the waistband of her little lace panties. *Bad Alex,* she thought as she stroked between the soft, slick lips. *Not politically correct, Counselor.*

She didn't care. Bob had moved out a year ago, and she hadn't wanted to get anywhere near a man after what he'd done to her. Now her libido was gnawing holes in her self-control. Yet cruising singles bars wasn't the kind of thing an Atlanta prosecutor could afford to do.

God, she needed a man. A bad man. A wicked dominant who'd grin in anticipation when he discovered the submissive streak she hid under the persona of ass-kicking prosecution lawyer. Brass-balled bitch by day, bound and gagged by night.

Oh, yeah. She slid a finger between her dewing lips. *Fuck me, Master.*

Yeah. Like she'd ever call any man master. She'd spent the first twenty years of her life trying to get out from under Daddy's suffocating protection. And he'd been trying to get her back under it ever since she'd moved out nine years ago.

Which was *not* a thought conducive to orgasm.

She added a second finger and slid it deep inside her pussy. Tugging her nipple with the other hand, Alex hummed at the lazy swirl of pleasure…

* * *

He slid one brawny knee onto the bed as she gazed up at him, quivering in a combination of arousal and fear. "I'm going to fuck you, sweet," he rumbled. "I'm going to suck those pretty pink nipples until you stop struggling and start begging. I'm going to get you hot and wet enough that when I drive my big cock into that tiny cunt, you'll hardly scream at all."

"No," she moaned, as his strong body mantled hers. "You can't do this to me. I don't want this."

"Don't lie to me." He lowered his head to one bare breast. "I'll have to punish you."

"If you release me, my father will pay you well!"

"It's not money I'm interested in." He gave the desperately hard nipple a slow lick. Pleasure sizzled through her. "It's you." Another slow, swirling lick. "Your pretty tits. Your tight, aristocratic pussy." He switched his attention to her other breast, considered the impudent point. Raked it gently with his teeth. "I'm going to tame you, Alexandria. I want to see you on your knees, that lush mouth sucking my cock like the slave you are."

"No! I'll never yield to you! I'm of royal blood!"

His gaze shot to her face and hardened. "No more.

I rule now. I conquered your lands as I'm going to conquer your body. You'll fall to me just as your castle did."

He slid a hand between her spread legs. She groaned in shame and pleasure as he found her wet and ready for him. Triumph shone in his eyes. "And something tells me my conquest won't take long at all."

* * *

As pleasure swirled around her masturbating fingers, Alex shuttered her lids and grinned at the fantasy she'd conjured. *I really should be ashamed of myself.* Two fingers stroked deep. *But I'm not.*

So she had a kinky streak. After twenty-nine years of playing by the rules, she was entitled to --

Blinding light exploded across the room, jarring her out of her sensual preoccupation. Alex jerked her head up and yelped in shock. The ceiling fan had disappeared, replaced by a glowing, six-foot hole. "What the…"

Something jerked her up off her bed and sucked her right into the blazing opening. She didn't even have time to scream.

* * *

"All right, damn it," John Hawke growled as he floated in the Caribbean-blue water. "I'm here. Give me whatever it is so I can go home."

Overhead, the tell-tale ring of clouds remained open. And stubbornly empty.

A bumblebee circled his head. He swatted it aside absently as he glared up at the clouds. Maybe they were finally going to send him that axe he'd been doggedly visualizing for the past month. If he thought about something long enough, sometimes the Bastards would send it to him.

Last time the gift had been a waterproof bag that turned out to contain five pounds of iodized salt. It had been more than welcome, since the mineral was otherwise unavailable on the artificial world of the Goldfish Bowl, with its freshwater sea and tropical temperatures. He'd have died of a fatal electrolyte imbalance without it.

Over the past year, he'd found the Bastards sent him whatever he couldn't catch, scrounge up, or make for himself, dropping it from the cloud ring they used as a sign. Of course, immediately afterward they'd send something that would try to kill him, so he never felt grateful.

He'd tried to ignore the ring this time, sick of playing their sadistic little game, but the Bastards had promptly triggered a migraine so severe, he'd had no choice but to swim out and wait. As usual, the headache had disappeared as soon as he'd obeyed.

There was a reason he called them the Bastards.

As he watched, the cloud ring began to sink toward him. Treading water, Hawke blinked at the sky. It had never done that before. Usually they just dropped the gift and let him dive after it.

The ring kept descending until it was about six meters over his head. Despite himself, he felt a sudden spurt of hope. Was it descending to scoop him up? Back in Afghanistan, the damn thing had just sucked him right off his feet, pack, body armor, and all. He'd almost drowned when he'd hit the water before he managed to cut his way loose from his own gear. So what were the Bastards up to now?

Something too big to be an axe plummeted out of the ring, falling right toward him. A piercing female shriek rang out.

Sweet Jesus, it was a woman!

SPLASH! Water flew skyward as she hit.

Hawke sucked in a deep breath and dove, afraid she'd drown. A trail of bubbles led him to her in the blessedly clear water. He could tell by the way she writhed that she was disoriented, not sure which way was up. Without his help, she didn't have a prayer.

He clamped a hand on her wrist and hauled her up until he could grab her shoulders from behind. Then, holding her pinned against his body despite her panicked struggles, he kicked toward the shimmering light above them with everything he had.

She broke the surface choking and fighting in animal panic, flailing arms and kicking legs battering at him. Luckily Hawke had anticipated that, which was why he'd grabbed her from behind. Now his greater strength kept her from drowning them both. "You're all right!" he shouted over her sputters as he began a one-armed stroke toward shore. "I've got you!"

Long, wet fingers clamped around his wrist in a death grip, but she had the sense to quit fighting. "What's going on?" She spat out another mouthful of water so violently she narrowly missed the bumblebee that lazily circled them. "Where the hell am I?"

"God alone knows, sweetheart," he told her grimly. "I sure don't."

It took only a couple dozen strokes to reach the artificial shallows, since what passed for ocean floor in the Goldfish Bowl resembled the bottom of a swimming pool more than anything else. When his bare feet hit the fine sand, Hawke waded up onto the beach, half-carrying his wet, trembling gift. The minute he let her go, she collapsed into a panting tangle of slender limbs and long hair.

"You okay?" He crouched beside her.

"I don't… I don't know." Blinking, she stared

wildly at the beach around them, visibly bewildered by her close brush with death. "I don't understand any of this."

Finally getting a good look at her, Hawke whistled silently. Even half-drowned, she looked like every wet dream he'd had since becoming a prisoner.

Hell, she looked like every wet dream he'd had since puberty.

She wore a pair of tiny panties that barely covered the shadow of her bush, and her soaked shirt was some kind of silk and lace thing that had gone perfectly transparent, revealing round, pert tits with hard little nipples. Hawke couldn't tell what color her wet hair was, but there was a lot of it, falling in tangled strands over that centerfold body.

When she looked around at him again, her gaze was sharp and considering. She recovered fast, he'd give her that. "You saved my life. I thought I was dead." Her eyes were a clear, crystalline blue, even more vivid than the Goldfish Bowl's ocean. Her nose was straight and narrow in her elegant, long-boned face, and her mouth -- damn, those were definitely dick lips. Full and soft and lush, the kind a man wanted to see wrapped around his cock. They made quite a contrast to that blue-blood diva face. She sat up, raking her hands through her hair, unconsciously trying to set herself to rights. "Thank you."

Hawke was rock hard behind his loin cloth. "Believe me, it's my pleasure."

But even as he imagined everything he was going to do to her, he wondered what the Bastards would do to make him pay.

* * *

She'd been rescued by Tarzan.

Alex blinked up at her savior, who wore only a

strip of brown hide around his narrow hips. Luckily, he had the kind of body that could pull off an outfit like that. Shoulders easily twice the width of hers, biceps the size of coconuts, and a six pack that made her want to purr, *It's Miller Time*! His legs were long and muscular, giving her the impression he'd easily catch anything dumb enough to run away.

Not that she had any intention whatsoever of going anywhere.

And his face -- well, he definitely didn't look anything like the parade of pretty boys Mama assembled for her approval every time she went back home. First, of course, there was the long, blond hair that lay in wet tangles across those quarterback shoulders. Daddy wouldn't have let him in the house with that hair. Yet he was intensely masculine, with a regally Roman nose and broad, high cheekbones. A broad jaw and square chin gave him the look of a heavyweight boxer, though a sensual, well-shaped mouth and smoky gray eyes saved his face from outright brutality. Judging by the hungry heat in his gaze, it was for damn sure he wasn't gay. That wasn't always a given with Mama's dinner guests, whether Virginia Kenyon realized it or not.

The question was, how the hell had she gotten from her bed to the feet of a sex god, with a dunk in the ocean in between? "Who *are* you?"

"John Hawke. And who are you?"

"Alex. Alex Kenyon."

"Nice to meet you, Alex Kenyon." Reaching out, he cupped her chin in long, strong fingers, tilted her head up, and leaned in close. "Very, very nice."

Even as her inner Southern Belle squealed in offended shock, his mouth closed over hers in a warm, wet slide.

Her heart, just beginning to slow its frantic beat after her brush with death, lunged back into a gallop. Automatically, she started to pull back in surprise, but his callused fingers tightened, holding her in place. His tongue stroked boldly between her lips as he kissed her with a rough, predatory hunger that made her nipples peak. She really should knock him on his backside for his gall, but God, it had been so long. And maybe he deserved a kiss for saving her life.

So Alex closed her eyes and kissed him back.

Then a wet hand boldly cupped her breast. The big opportunist was *groping* her! "What are you doing?" She jerked back, outraged. "A kiss is one thing, but saving my life doesn't entitle you to paw me."

Tarzan's luscious mouth curled into a dark smile. "Look around, Dorothy. You're not in Kansas anymore. This is the Goldfish Bowl, and I make my own rules."

He had a point about the Kansas thing. She'd already noticed it was broad daylight, which was pretty damn weird considering the moon had been shining just a minute ago.

And then there was the beach. Her Atlanta home was hundreds of miles from the ocean, so how had she got to the seashore?

Frowning, she turned to look out to sea. And stared. She sure wasn't in Georgia anymore. She wasn't even in Miami, despite the stretch of pristine white sand underfoot and the clusters of big palm trees inland.

For one thing, the horizon was far too close. It was almost as if they were an immense, round room -- if a room could be ten or fifteen miles across. And the sky… Alex tilted her head back and stared upward. It had an odd, milky quality, painted in swirls of iridescence -- not clouds, but patterns of moving light, something like the Aurora Borealis. She couldn't see the sun at all, yet the light was as bright as noon. "Where *are* we?"

Hawke rose to his considerable height. "Like I said, I call it the Goldfish Bowl."

"I can see why." It felt odd lying at his feet, so she scrambled up too, noting absently that he didn't offer her a hand. To her annoyance, her legs trembled. She stiffened them as he strode to a pile of equipment on the sand. "What are you doing?"

"I've got a bad feeling we're about to get a guest a lot less pleasant than you." He crouched and started picking through the gear.

"What kind of guest? And what makes you think that?"

"It's the pattern. They send me something, and then something worse shows up." Hoisting a pouched belt in desert camo, he buckled it around his narrow waist with the grim air of a man expecting eminent attack.

She propped her fists on her hips and frowned at him. "What do you mean, worse?"

"As in 'kill it before it kills you' worse." He strapped a short, sheathed knife to his ankle. Tarzan evidently had access to Velcro.

Finally he lifted something that looked like a stick attached to some kind of belt. As he swung it across one shoulder, she got a better look. "Is that a *sword*?"

"Yep." He belted the thick leather strap diagonally across his torso. The sheathed sword it supported was easily three and a half feet long, not counting the two-handed hilt.

He wasn't Tarzan, he was Conan the Barbarian.

Hawke turned toward her, settling the blade into

place with a shrug of those Olympian shoulders. "When I was first snatched, this weapon was an M-16. By the time I arrived here, it had morphed into this. Evidently the Bastards didn't want me having access to fire power."

"I have no idea what you're talking about. Could you please quit being mysterious and tell me what's going on? Who are the Bastards?" She was getting thoroughly fed up. "And how did I get here?"

He lifted his head and turned to stare off into the trees, his expression alert. "Same way I did, I'd imagine," he told her absently. "You were abducted by aliens. And I think you're about to find out why I call them the Bastards."

Aliens? Good God, she was stranded with a lunatic. "Is this some kind of joke? Because it's really not funny."

"Shut up."

Anger zapped her appreciation of his amazing butt as he turned his back on her. Nobody talked to a Kenyon that way. "Who do you think you are?"

He closed a hand around the hilt of his sword and levered the big blade out of its scabbard. "I said *shut up*. Something's coming."

Before she could tell him off, the bushes rattled. A roar split the air, loud enough to make her jump.

Something burst from the trees in an explosion of scales and teeth. Alex screamed like a fire siren as it lunged right at Hawke, snapping massive jaws.

"Get back!" he bellowed, running to meet the monster. Even as it tensed to spring, he swung his sword. Blade bit into scaly hide. The monster howled and reared, slashing at him with knifelike front claws. Hawke leaped back and circled. It turned with him, snapping.

Good God, it had six legs!

It scuttled on four of them while it tried to rake him with long, thin forearms, snapping and roaring like a nightmare cross between a Tyrannosaurus Rex and a scorpion. It was easily the size of a horse.

Alex wanted to run. She wanted to help him. But she couldn't do either, because she couldn't move. Her body was completely frozen with terror as he hacked at the monstrosity slashing and snapping at him like something out of *Alien*.

I've got to do something! It's going to kill him!

* * *

Hawke grunted in pain as the thing raked claws across his thigh.

Jolted out of her shock, Alex looked desperately around for a stick, a rock. Anything. She had to get her hands on a weapon.

At her feet lay what looked like a misshapen conch shell. She snatched it up in a sweaty hand and started toward them even as her every instinct howled at her to run away. She couldn't just stand around while a monster chowed down on the man who'd saved her life.

But before she could take another step, the thing screeched, took a step, and toppled into the sand. Alex had no idea what Hawke had done, and he didn't give her time to figure it out. The minute the monster was down, he pounced and started chopping. Purple blood flew. The thing roared and flailed, but he ignored its claws and kept hacking with grim intensity.

"Jesus," Alex whispered as the shell dropped from her lax fingers. *Note to self. Never piss off Hawke.*

Finally the thing's struggles subsided. Hawke's Ginsu imitation slowed. Finally, with one last chop for good measure, he rose from the twitching corpse. The only sounds were his harsh breathing and the lazy buzz of bumblebees.

Edging closer, Alex looked down at the thing. He'd cut off its head and one foreleg. The rest of it looked like it had been put through a Cuisinart.

It had six eyes.

This thing couldn't be real. Yet indisputably, it was. Just as indisputably, it hadn't evolved on Earth. Everything from the color of its blood to the weird structure of its muscles told her that. "Is this the alien that abducted us?" Alex whispered. She was shaking.

"This?" He wiped purple blood from his forehead and snorted. "Not likely. This thing is dumb as a post."

"It tried to eat us." She felt numb.

"We'd have given it a belly ache." Hawke turned to look down at her with a euphoric grin, visibly high on his dangerous victory. "I tried meat from one once. Gave me the runs like you would not believe."

Alex stared at him. "You *ate* one of these things?"

"A piece of it. Seemed only fair." He pulled a piece of leather from a belt pouch and started cleaning the blood off his sword. "It would have eaten me."

Suddenly she realized some of the blood running down his thigh was red. "You're hurt!"

He looked down at the gash cutting across one thigh and shrugged. "It's already healing."

"But it..." Alex broke off. As she watched, the wound narrowed, sealing over like a special effect in a werewolf movie. But that was impossible.

She stepped back, keenly aware of what he'd done to the alien lizard. No ordinary man could have done that much damage with nothing more than a glorified machete. "You're not human."

Hawke rolled his eyes. "Oh, give me a break."

"Your strength... the way you heal. You're not

from Earth any more than that… thing is!"

"I was born in Virginia." Glaring at her, he sheathed his sword with a slither of steel on leather. "It's just that ever since the Bastards took me, I've gotten stronger and harder to kill. Which is a damn good thing, or we'd both be monster chow by now."

She winced, suddenly feeling like a paranoid bitch. "You've got a point. Sorry. I guess this whole situation is just making me a little nuts."

"Tell me about it." Hawke slumped, suddenly looking weary as all the anger ran out of him. "Look, I'm going to wash this shit off. It stings. Wait here." Turning, he strode toward the ocean, stripping off his gear as he went.

"Wait!" Alex called, shooting a hunted look at the trees. "What if another one of these things come along?"

Hawke glanced back at her. "It won't. The Bastards never send more than one WTF at a time."

With one last uneasy glance at the cooling corpse, she hurried after him. "WTF? As in What the Fuck?"

He shrugged. "Seems to fit."

"Guess it does, at that." As Alex watched, he crouched and began to splash the blood off. Seawater turned pink as it ran in glistening trails down the ridges of his body. "Doesn't the salt sting?"

"There is no salt. This is more big-ass lake than anything else."

He was right, she realized, looking out to sea. There was almost no wave action at all, unlike every ocean she'd ever seen back home. "It's almost as though it's man-made."

"More like alien-made."

Alex wrapped both arms around her body. A cool breeze blew into her face, smelling of flowers and monster blood. She shivered, though her body had almost dried from its dunking. "I don't understand any of this."

"Join the club." He rose from the water, slicking his wet hair back from his head. "You know, I haven't had to shave once the entire time I've been here. My hair grows, but not my beard. I'm not sure why, but that bothers me almost more than anything else. Why do aliens care if I get stubble? Doesn't make sense."

"Why should it? Apparently nothing else does."

"Good point." Hawke waded back toward her. Cool gray eyes studied her with approval. "So, Alexandria Kenyon. What do you do back home?"

She forced herself to straighten up and stop huddling as he stepped out of the water. "I'm an attorney."

For a moment something flickered in his eyes. Then it was gone. "Yeah? I was a Marine. The aliens abducted me from the middle of a battle in Afghanistan. Must have been a year ago now. What day was it when they took you?"

Alex blinked, watching the water sluice down his magnificent body. It suddenly hit that she was completely alone with him on this planet, or space ship, or whatever the hell it was. God knew how far away Earth was. "July 7, 2004."

That stopped him in his tracks. "2004?" He frowned. "I've been here more than two years? That can't be right. It was March 2, 2002 when they took me, and only three hundred and sixty-seven days have passed since then. I've kept track."

So he was snatched during the war in Afghanistan, just a few months after September 11. "Could the days be longer here?"

"Not according to my watch." Hawke picked up

his belt and buckled it around his lean waist, then collected the rest of his weapons. "It's broken now, but the first couple of weeks, it worked fine. The Goldfish Bowl is on a twenty-four-hour cycle." Fastening the sword belt across his torso, he shook his head and dismissed the question. "Never mind, it doesn't matter. I'm not a Marine anymore."

Gray eyes lifted to meet hers. She felt her mouth go dry at the heat that flared in them. He started toward her in a long, sensuous pace, like a tiger stalking something slow and delicious. "And you're not a lawyer," he continued in a deep, velvet voice. "There is no law here."

That did not sound good, especially given what he was capable of. She looked him right in the eye anyway. "Wherever there are people, there are laws."

He lifted a blond brow as he stepped up to her, muscle sliding under tanned skin. A lot of tanned skin. "Sure of that, are you?"

"Absolutely."

"In that case, I guess that makes me the law." Hawke's gray eyes searched her face with predatory intensity. "At least as far as you're concerned."

Her mouth went dry, but Alex knew she didn't dare back down. She couldn't let him think he could bully her. "Just exactly what do you mean?"

"At least once every couple of days, sometimes more often, something's going to attack us. It may another WTF, like our scaly friend over there, or it may be a lot of small, ravenous things, or it may be something even I have never seen before. But whatever it is, I'm going to have to defend us both." His gray gaze intensified. "I'm going to bleed for you, Alex. I already have."

He had a damn good point, but she had no

intention of admitting it. "I'm not helpless."

"Aren't you?"

She tilted her chin at him. "Maybe I'll get superpowers too."

"Maybe. But maybe you won't." He straightened his brawny shoulders, silently drawing attention to his size. He was a good eight inches taller than she was. "And even if you do, somehow I get the feeling I'll still be stronger."

"So, what? That gives you the right to order me around?" She attempted a scornful laugh. A husky note spoiled the effect.

"Yes, actually. It does."

"I don't think so."

"You'd better. Our toothy friend is just a sample of what I've faced on this rock every single day for the past year. I've had to work my ass off to stay alive. Now I'm going to have to work twice as hard keeping you breathing too."

"I'll do my part."

"Yes. You will."

Damn, why did she have the feeling she'd just fallen into a trap? And why, she wondered, staring up into his brutal face, were her nipples getting hard?

"Sometimes the Bastards send a deer, and I have to hunt it." He took a step forward. Alex took another step back. "I kill it, skin it, and butcher it. I tan its hide to make leather for what clothes I have. I carve its hooves and horns into tools. When there's no meat, I harvest the local plants and berries."

"I can do that. I'm not afraid of work."

"I'm relieved to hear it." His gaze bored into hers. "And you'll do everything else I tell you to do, too."

"Or what?"

"Or I'll..." His sensuous mouth curled into a

smile. "... persuade you."

"I'll bet." Alex gave him her best regal glare. She'd learned the fine art of putting a man in his place from Virginia Kenyon, and she was willing to bet her mother's techniques would work just as well on Conan the Sex God. "What's your first order -- Master?"

The cold mockery in her voice would have made most men back off in a hurry, but Hawke didn't even blink. "Suck my cock."

She didn't even wonder what her mother would have done. She just bared her teeth. "Go to hell, Conan."

His gray eyes crinkled at the corners, amused rather than threatening. Was this some kind of test? "That's no way to talk to your lord and master."

"I won't be bullied into sex." But despite her anger, despite her offended dignity, something in her responded to his outrageous demand. Her nipples ached as they contracted even further into tight, ready peaks.

He glanced down, as if his attention had been drawn by the subtle movement of those hardening tips. "When I give you an order, I expect you to obey it," he said, still watching her breasts. "If you make me stand around arguing, we're both going to end up dead."

She fought the impulse to cover herself and silently cursed her randy libido. "Not when the argument involves sex."

"I just saved your ass. Twice, come to think of it."

"Thank you." Her heart was pounding. This shouldn't be turning her on, no matter how big, bad and gorgeous he was. "I'm willing to concede all that might deserve a gratitude hummer, but I won't be forced."

"So why am I getting the distinct impression you'd

like to be?"

Heat poured into her cheeks. On top of everything else, she was blushing. Fantastic. "Now you're just being insulting."

"Am I?" Hawke broke into a feral grin. In one smooth motion, he reached back and drew his sword. It hissed as it emerged from its scabbard in an endless length of gleaming steel. Biceps rippled as he placed the sharp edge just under her chin. "Get on your knees."

She swallowed, looking from the glittering blade to his hot, aroused gaze. "You do know the definition of rape, right?"

"Yeah. This isn't it. On your knees."

Had she misjudged him? Was she stuck on this island with an abusive superhuman creep?

Testing, Alex stared hard into Hawke's eyes. There was heat there, true, a hint of dark pleasure in what he was doing. But there was humor too. Like a kid playing a game.

A really big kid playing a really kinky game.

She relaxed slightly. Sword or not, she could sense he wouldn't hurt her. Dominate the hell out of her, yes. But he wouldn't hurt her.

Besides, wouldn't it feel good to just *play* for once? There was nobody here to judge her, nobody to find her a disappointment. Nobody to remind her of her responsibilities as a Kenyon. For once, she could be herself. She could act out her kinky dreams without fear. Hawke would be delighted to help.

"Alex." He said her name gently, with just a hint of artistic male menace. "I gave you an order."

Looking into his hard, deeply masculine face, she felt fine inner muscles clench and heat. Slowly, she dropped to her knees in the sand at his big feet.

Chapter Two

"That's better," Hawke purred, lowering the sword to reach for his loin cloth with one hand. He tugged the flap of leather out of his waistband and dropped it with a wet *plop*.

Alex sucked in a breath as his cock spilled out at her. It was beautiful -- a long, smooth column of hard flesh, flushed with lust, invitingly thick. Imagining how it would feel pushing its way into her aching core, she had to fight back a moan.

"Put it in your mouth."

She shot a look up at him. He was watching her, gray eyes narrow, sensual lips parted. She knew she should make some kind of effort to let him know he hadn't intimidated her. That she wasn't falling for the act.

Instead she caught his cock in one hand, leaned forward, and gave it one teasing lick of her tongue.

Hawke stiffened, sucking in a hard breath. Despite all his rough orders, she suspected she'd surprised him.

"How long has it been, Hawke?" Alex asked, caressing his thick length. She wanted to suck him, yes, but first she'd damn well let him know she wasn't a doormat. "At least a year, right? Probably longer, if you were at war before that."

"About... eighteen months." He stood rigid, as if he didn't trust himself to move. She wondered what he was afraid he'd do to her.

Cupping his heavy balls with her free hand, she gave him a gentle squeeze. "A long time without a woman."

"Yeah. I want your mouth, Alex. Now."

Smiling at the rough hunger in his voice, she

leaned forward until her mouth was a bare half-inch from the flushed head of his cock. But instead of engulfing him, she blew gently.

"You'd be wise not to tease me." There it was again -- that hot, male rumble that sent another stream of heat trickling into her core.

Gently, she closed her teeth over his cockhead and raked them across the flushed knob, drawing back until they clicked closed. "Or what?"

"Or I'll take you over my knee and beat that pretty ass until you squeal." His hand threaded through her drying hair to curve around the base of her skull. Not quite dragging her onto his cock, but close.

A glistening bead of pre-cum emerged from the flushed head. Alex licked the drop away with a flick of her tongue. The hard muscles of his belly laced. "Do I look like your slave?"

He laughed, the sound rough with need. "Half naked, on your knees in front of my cock? Yeah, as a matter of fact, you do."

She gave him another teasing nibble. God, she loved this. Loved the idea of taunting this powerful man until he was helpless with need. "Well, I'm not."

"Baby, I could change that by nightfall."

"I doubt that." The wildfire racing through her veins made her want to stroke herself.

Why not?

She released her hold on his cock and balls and caught her breasts in both hands. Cupping the full globes through the lace of her camisole, she squeezed her nipples and tilted her head up to meet his gaze. "But I'll bet I could enslave you."

Long fingers tightened around the base of her skull, reminding her he still held her. "Honey, you don't have the slightest interest in enslaving me." The corner of his mouth curled up. "Your eyes light up too much whenever I order you around."

She stiffened. That hit a little too close to home. "Bull."

He grinned darkly. "I'd bet a month's pay you're slick as melted butter between those pretty thighs."

"You'd lose."

"No, I wouldn't." He lifted the sword. Before she could jerk away, he rested the cool edge of the blade against the side of her neck. "Open wide, honey. I want to find out if you can do something with that mouth besides tease." The hand around her head pulled her closer to his jutting cock.

She resisted more for form's sake than anything else. Then, with a hungry moan, she opened her mouth and sucked the big head inside.

"Mmmm. More." He arched his back, gently forcing another inch of his shaft between her lips. She sucked him so hungrily, her cheeks hollowed. "Oh, yeah, that's right. Nice and obedient. I always wanted a slave girl."

Alex tightened her jaws, not quite biting down on his cock, but making sure he got the threat.

He chuckled, a dark rumble. "You're bucking for that spanking, sweetheart. Deeper."

She drew back to pull in a breath, then leaned forward and slid his cock so far into her throat, she gagged.

"Swallow it," he rasped. "You can take more when you swallow."

Obeying, Alex realized he was right. Pulling back to steal another breath, she tried again and worked him further down. He rewarded her by tightening his grip on her hair.

Then, slowly, carefully, he began fucking her

mouth.

* * *

Hawke threw back his head and groaned helplessly at the raw pleasure of Alex's lips around his cock. He'd had kinky dreams like this, but even back on Earth, he'd never expected to live any of them out. Hell, there'd been a time when a woman like her was a lot more likely to throw him in jail than suck him off.

Slowly, he stroked back into her mouth, fighting desperately not to come. He wanted to make this last as long as he could. He could feel her hot little tongue swirling around the crown of his shaft as she gave him sweet, rippling suction like a burning gift.

He looked down, watching hungrily. She'd wrapped one slender arm around his hip as she held his dick with the other hand. Those luscious lips pouted as they surrounded his cock. Shuddering, he carefully pushed back inside, then pulled out again, trying to moderate his strokes and give her plenty of time to breathe. Self-control wasn't easy with the ferocious climax building in his balls.

Particularly since a woman like Alex wouldn't have given him the time of day back on Earth.

But he could have her here. She wanted him. He knew that from the way her eyes glittered with arousal even as she bitched about his dominant bastard act. Why else would she blow him with a hot enthusiasm that was almost enough to make him come all by itself?

He was just enough his old man's son to take advantage of her hunger.

Hawke thrust into her mouth again, using the slightest bit more force than he needed, knowing it would make her hotter. Sure enough, she gave his cock a sucking pull so hard, it was all he could do not to spill on the spot.

Oh, yeah. She liked this game.

And he was more than happy to play it however she wanted. He'd pretend to be Master Bastard for her, and he'd fuck her any way she'd let him. But he'd make damn sure she never guessed where he came from.

Panting, he tipped his head back and listened to the delicious sounds of her mouth working his cock. A bee flew around his head, but he barely noticed, all his attention focused on the shimmering pleasure. With a strangled shout, he drove his cock hard into her mouth and let himself pump. "Drink it!" he growled. "Swallow my come. Now!"

She made an odd sound, a delicious little moan. And then she did exactly what he'd told her to do. The ripple of her throat sent his orgasm blazing up like pure oxygen on a forest fire. He roared.

Oh, yeah. He was going to take everything she let him have.

He just had to make sure she didn't get too much of him.

* * *

Hawke pulled his softening shaft out of Alex's mouth and sheathed his sword. "That was… nice." His voice was hoarse. He stopped and cleared his throat. "Come on, I'll show you the cave."

Still on her knees, a storm of heat rioting in her blood, she stared at him. "Nice? It was *nice*?"

"What, you want an Academy Award for best Blowjob of 2003?"

"2004. And no, what I want is for you to return the favor!" Alex gritted her teeth against the need to jump the arrogant bastard, kick his feet out from under him, and ride his cock all the way down.

He smirked. "We can't hang on the beach having

sex all day. Something'll eat us."

She rose to her feet and glowered at him as she dusted the sand off her shins. "I thought you said we'd hit our monster quota for the day."

Hawke shrugged brawny shoulders. "They could always change the pattern. I don't call 'em the Bastards for nothing."

"They're not the only bastards around here," Alex muttered.

Starting off toward the trees, he glanced back, a devilish glint in his eyes. "Now, is that any way to talk to your lord and master?"

"You want to know where you can sheath that sword, Conan?"

"You're just begging for a spanking."

"You and what army?"

"I'm a Marine. I'm an army all by myself."

"You do have enough ego for a platoon." She stalked into the trees after his broad back.

"I'm really going to enjoy turning that pretty little ass pink." Pushing a low hanging branch aside so she could pass, he grinned wickedly. "'Course, once I've got you bent over, who knows what I'll do next?"

Her unruly libido purred. Trying to ignore it, Alex glared at him as she ducked past. "Yeah, and once I find out where you sleep, who knows what *I'll* do next?"

"Fall asleep bound and gagged, with a pink, aching butt. Have I mentioned I like anal sex?"

She choked and stopped dead to stare. "You're not serious."

His grin was slow and lethal enough to make her heart pound -- and not with fear. "I just love forcing my cock into a tight little asshole and listening to the squeals."

Alex swallowed as he sauntered past her and reached for another low-hanging frond, holding it back for her. Determined to fight her perverse arousal, she managed a sneer. "You're assuming you can make me squeal."

His eyes narrowed. "Oh, I can make you do all kinds of things." He let it go, but she fended off the swat to her ass with one hand.

"We'll see." She strutted past him. God, she was beginning to enjoy irritating Hawke. It was like teasing the Big Bad Wolf. Sooner or later, she was going to get eaten.

She was hoping for sooner.

* * *

Hawke actually liked her, damn it.

He had not expected that. Oh, he'd known she'd be bright -- attorneys were rarely dumb -- but he hadn't anticipated her wicked sense of humor.

Then, of course, there was her sassy courage. After witnessing what he'd done to the WTF, most women would probably have hesitated to give him this much hell.

"You're assuming you can make me squeal." She really did need that spanking. And he was looking forward to giving it to her, too.

Hawke glanced over his shoulder as they approached his cave. She was watching his backside. "Enjoying the view?"

Alex jerked her gaze up to meet his. To his delight, she blushed bright red. "Well, the way it's just kind of hanging out there, bare and flexing, it's tough to miss. What, didn't you have a bigger piece of leather?"

"You saying I've got a broad ass?"

"No, actually it reminds me of a pair of cantaloupes." She winced. "God, did I just say that?"

Hawke couldn't help himself. He roared with laughter.

"Oh, shut up. Me and my mouth. My mother would be mortified."

"Actually, you have a very nice mouth. Given a little training..."

"A little *training*?" She stopped at the foot of the cliff to glare. "You rat, see if you ever get another BJ from me."

"If it's any comfort, you obviously have natural talent. Surprising, given your background." He leaned a shoulder against the cliff and settled back to enjoy her reaction.

Alex gave him a suspicious, narrow-eyed stare. "Now, what do you mean by that crack?"

He hadn't had this much fun in two years. "Blue-blood Southern Belles usually aren't hummer artists. And with that accent, I'd bet a month's pay you're FFV." *First Families of Virginia* was a very old term for the state's very old money -- people who could trace their ancestry back to the early colonial period.

She curled a lip, outraged. "Accent? I don't have an accent." There was a definite drawl in those A's.

"Forgive me, Scarlett. What *was* ah thinkin'?"

"Oh, kiss my ass." She huffed, then reluctantly admitted, "Okay, yeah, I'm one of *those* Kenyons. My father's Harold Kenyon."

He started, straightening away from the cliff. "Judge Kenyon?"

Delicate brows lifted. "Why, Hawke -- have you had professional dealings with Daddy?"

As a matter of fact, he had. Not that he had any intentions whatsoever of telling her that. "I was stationed in Norfolk for a couple of years. He made the papers about once a month." But Hawke had actually met the judge years earlier, at the Old Man's trial. Hangin' Harry was an intimidating bastard, particularly to a seventeen-year-old kid who was scared he was seeing a sneak preview of his own future. After watching the judge verbally flay his father at the sentencing, Hawke had decided the only way to avoid following in his father's bloody footsteps was to enlist in the Marines.

Good God. He'd just shot his wad in Judge Kenyon's daughter's mouth. Hangin' Harry would have a stroke.

Hawke was still contemplating that appalling thought when, like the Southern girl she was, Alex asked the question he dreaded. "So what'd your folks do?"

Well, Dad knocked over convenience stores until he killed a clerk, and Mom was a drunk who moonlighted as a stripper. Hawke was the first male in his family in three generations to avoid jail time. "This and that." He gestured at the rocks overhead. "The cave's up that way. 'Fraid you're going to have to climb."

The distraction worked. She looked up the cliff face, an expression of dismay growing on her pretty face. "Up there?" Then she processed what he said. "*Cave*?"

"WTFs don't like to climb either, sweetheart."

"Good point." Alex contemplated the cliff, visibly appalled. "So how do I get from here to there?"

"Grab a rock and start pulling yourself up. Don't worry, I'll be right behind you." Watching her pick out an outcropping to use as a handhold, Hawke smiled a little grimly. At least he'd distracted her from probing his background.

Because there was a fine old Southern phrase for his family too, and it sure as hell wasn't FFV.

White trash.

* * *

"Damn, Conan, you sure don't mind working." Alex stared around the cave in admiration.

He snorted. "Well, it's not like I can lie around all day watching TV and playing video games."

"Guess not." She'd expected cramped, damp, and dirty, but the cave was really quite spacious, with a high ceiling, curving rock walls, and a hard-packed sandy floor. Her attention riveted on the rear of the cavern, where a surprisingly big bed stood. The frame was made of thick bamboo lashed together with white nylon cords Hawke must have brought with him. To make a mattress, he'd sewn together a couple of blankets. The result looked fat and inviting. "What'd you stuff the mattress with?" she asked, moving over to get a closer look.

He shrugged. "Leaves, grass. Whatever was handy. I strung parachute cord across the bed frame to give it some support."

Alex nodded and kept exploring. A couple of clay oil lamps hung from the ceiling, supplying a flickering light. Several spears leaned together in the corner. The walls were lined with clay pots, hide bags, and baskets he'd woven out of vines. There were even a couple of military canteens wrapped in desert camouflage. She nodded at the containers. "What's in those?"

"Oil. Fruit. A few vegetables. Smoked meat. I fill the canteens with water twice a day."

Alex nodded. She'd seen the fire pit he used to smoke the food just outside, to one side of the cave. He'd also built bamboo drying racks that currently held several hides he was in the process of curing in the sun.

She squinted, her attention caught by what

appeared to be a bamboo platform leaning against the back wall. He'd tied the thick bamboo together with lengths of vine. Two wooden oars lay on the floor in front of it. "Is that a raft?"

"Yep." He started taking off his weapons to stow them neatly beside the bed. "Built it not long after I got here. Used it to paddle out to the barrier."

Interested, she turned toward him, absently waving aside a cruising bumblebee. "What barrier?"

"There's some kind of force field or something surrounding us. It's what holds in the water and atmosphere, just like a goldfish bowl." He pulled out a cloth and sat down on the edge of the bed as he drew his sword from its sheath.

Alex frowned. "What's beyond it?"

He shrugged, wiping down the weapon. "I couldn't tell. You can't see through it. It glows with a milky light during the day that's blinding close up. Apparently, it's the only source of light in here, since we don't have a sun."

She leaned against the cave wall. "Did you try getting through it?"

Hawke shook his head. "Pounded my fists against it so hard I capsized the raft. Didn't do a damn bit of good."

Alex frowned, considering the implications. "Weren't you afraid it would burn you, if it's glowing like that?"

"It wasn't radiating heat." He shot her a look. "Besides, it's not like I had a hell of a lot to lose."

She nibbled a thumbnail. "So if the walls aren't hot, and there's no sun, why is it warm in here?"

"I'm just a poor, dumb Marine, Alex. I don't know these things."

"Dumb, my ass. You seemed to have coped with

plunging back into the Stone Age pretty damn well."

"I haven't had a whole lot of choice." He sheathed the sword and put it on the floor beside the bed, within easy reach. "And I've had a great deal of time to figure out how to make what I needed." Rising from the bed, he gave her a wicked grin. "In between jerking off, that is." As her head snapped up in astonishment, he sauntered across the cave toward her. "Fortunately, now I've got you."

"You do know how to sweet talk a girl."

"Hearts and flowers have never been my thing."

She backed up a cautious pace. "I did pick up on that, now that you mention it."

"I knew you were a clever woman. Take off your clothes."

"I beg your pardon?"

There were an awful lot of white teeth in his smile. "I suddenly realized I haven't seen you naked."

She folded her arms and glared at him. "So therefore I should strip."

"It *would* help."

"Forget it, Conan."

"You've seen me naked."

"Only because you made me give you a blow job."

"Would have been tough to do otherwise. Besides, I thought you wanted me to return the favor." He tilted his head, long blond hair sliding over his brawny shoulders. "Licking those pretty little nipples won't be nearly as satisfying with them all covered up."

Alex's heart began pounding again. His blunt orders had a way of turning her on even as they rubbed her the wrong way. Besides, he looked so damn luscious. She'd never had a lover that damn big, and she yearned to touch him. Then, too, there was something about teasing Hawke that never failed to get her motor running.

"Weeeelll... Okay." She smoothed her palms down the front of her camisole. "If you insist."

He grinned wolfishly. "I do."

The fabric had dried from the heat of her body, and now the lace was just slightly stiff. Lifting the hem an inch, she watched Hawke's gaze sizzle.

Oh, this is going to be fun.

* * *

Hawke watched her lift the lace hem of that camisole with his heart pounding and his dick pressing into his loin cloth. Inch by taunting inch, she showed him her taut, tanned little belly, the curve of her waist, the rise of her rib cage -- and the sweet, full contours of her lower breasts.

As he caught his breath, willing her to lift the hem further, she purred, "Like what you see?"

Little tease. "Almost as much as I'm going to enjoy watching your ass turn pink," he growled.

"That's no way to talk." She dropped the camisole back over her centerfold body and gave him a smirk that was pure evil.

He almost snarled in frustration. "Take off that shirt."

"Make me."

"Don't tempt me."

"Judging by that hard-on, I'd say I already am."

Hawke gave her his best menacing smirk. "Your asshole is going to feel really good stretching around my cock."

She turned her back on him and huffed. "Bully."

"I've always wanted to ream a blue-blood belle. I hope you're a virgin."

Alex snatched the camisole off in one movement and threw it aside. "There. Satisfied?"

Hawke drank in the sight of her long, deliciously bare back. Her round little butt cheeks flexed each time she shifted her feet, bisected by the tiny lace thong that was more enticement than anything else. He reached for her. "No, but I'm going to be."

She yelped as he grabbed her by one forearm and hauled her toward the bed. "What the hell do you think you're doing?"

"I seem to recall promising you a spanking." Hawke dropped onto the bed and jerked her down across his thighs.

"What?" Alex tried to rear up, but he planted a hand across her back and kept her there. Her skin felt silken under his palm. Her pretty breasts felt so deliciously warm and soft pressing against his thighs, it was all he could do not to moan in pleasure.

"Stop that!"

"Not a chance." He let his free hand stroke boldly over the round, smooth cheeks of her bottom. She squirmed, but he held her still with no effort at all. She was completely at his mercy.

Hawke let the idea sink in for both of them as he caressed her tempting little ass.

"I'm warning you," Alex said breathlessly. "Don't even think it."

"Or what?" He traced a finger up the cleavage between her pretty haunches.

"Or..." She broke off as he reached the waistband of her thong. He wrapped his fingers around it. "Don't you dare!"

Hawke jerked. The string snapped. "You were saying?"

"Jackass!"

"That's no way to talk to your lord and master." He gave her butt a light swat. She bucked, screeching more in outrage than pain as she snapped her head around to glare at him. Despite the anger, there was even more arousal sizzling in her eyes. "I know where you sleep, you big jerk."

"Oh, come on, Alex." He reached down between her thighs to find the soft, furry lips of her labia. "A spanking can be sexy." Dipping a finger between them, he found her slick and snug enough to make his dick twitch in anticipation. He grinned. "And I'm not the only one who thinks so."

Chapter Three

Damn it, he was right. She'd had fantasies just like this -- being draped across some big sex god's thighs while he got ready to paddle her butt. And the reality was even hotter than her kinky daydreams.

Hawke slid that big finger inside her again in one long, seductive stroke that made her squirm. Alex gave him another testing buck, but he held her still without effort. She was completely at his mercy.

And God help her, she liked it.

"I think I need to repeat the new ground rules," he told her in that rumbling purr of his as he withdrew his finger from her body. "Rule one -- I am the master." That broad palm landed with a *SMACK*! Alex jumped and gasped, though the blow produced more noise than pain. "Rule two -- *you* are the sex slave."

"You are sooo full of --"

SMACK!

"Rule three -- you'll do exactly what I tell you to do." *SMACK*! That one was a little harder. She panted as her arousal grew. "Because otherwise, something's going to eat us." *SMACK*! He paused for another leisurely exploration of her pussy, which, shamelessly, had grown even wetter. "Why, Alex -- I do believe you're starting to enjoy this."

"Don't" -- she broke off to moan as he added a second finger --"don't flatter yourself."

He yanked his fingers out. *SMACK*! "Don't lie to the lord and master, Alex." *SMACK SMACK SMACK*!

Her yelp was genuine this time as her backside heated under the rain of burning slaps. "I'll 'lord and master' you, you big --"

SMACK! "I can keep this up all day, babe. How about you?"

Blood rushed into her stinging cheeks, and her tingling labia swelled. Every time he'd spanked her, he'd given her clit a little jolt. "Bully." The word emerged as a moan.

"Feeling abused, sweetheart?" Big fingers stroked over her blazing flesh. She squirmed. "Damn, that's a pretty pink. I do believe it's giving me an appetite." Before she quite knew what hit her, he tossed her lightly on the bed and knelt beside it. Alex lifted her head, dazed, as he hauled her thighs over his brawny shoulders. His smoke-gray eyes focused hungrily on her pussy. "And I know just the perfect appetizer."

That wicked mouth fastened directly over her sex, tongue stabbing right between her lips. His first lick pulled her back into a bow. "Jesus, Hawke!"

His only reply was a hungry hum as he went to work, flicking his tongue up and down over her opening, each pass catching her clit. Simultaneously, he reached up to capture her breasts. Long, strong fingers stroked her nipples, squeezing and plucking until she squirmed. "Oh, God!" she gasped, writhing. The extravagant pleasure made a deliciously arousing contrast to the sting of her paddled ass.

He licked. He suckled. He kneaded and twisted. Alex, her thighs draped over shoulders, arched her back and clawed at the grass-filled mattress. It was as if he'd pulled her favorite fantasy right out of her head and brought it to life. Groaning with maddened pleasure, she ground her pussy against his face. Obligingly, he closed his mouth over her clit and sucked hard. His tongue made a single searing pass over the little nubbin…

Alex screeched as her climax boiled up out of nowhere and drowned her in fire. Bucking mindlessly, she rode the molten wave home.

It hadn't even crested yet when he jerked his face away from her, grabbed her thighs, bent them up and back, and crammed the entire meaty length of his cock inside her. "Oh, yeah," he growled over her yelp, hauling her closer, working the thick shaft even deeper. "That's what I want!"

Stunned by the deliciously erotic violence of his entry, Alex could only blink at him. Hawke rose over her, his hard face brutal with hunger, his eyes glittering, both her knees cupped in his hands.

"Now," he said, giving her a feral grin. "Let's fuck."

He pulled out slowly. Heat skittered along her nerves at the sensation of his thick shaft withdrawing. The tip of him actually left her body. He leaned forward again. Her slick, tight flesh twisted as his length slid back inside. Fire curled into a hot ball low in her womb. "God, that feels good," Alex gasped.

"Mmmm," he agreed, and pulled out. Satin thickness caressed her sensitive inner core. Looking down between her thighs, she watched his abdominal muscles ripple as he pushed deep. "Oh, yeah. My own little sex slave," he rumbled, watching her face with hungry intensity. "So sweet and slick and hot. Mine to fuck however I want."

"Nooo," she groaned, not meaning the refusal.

"Yeeah." He drew out. "Oh yeah. I think I'll tie you up next. Maybe grease up that little ass and…" He slammed deep, making her yowl in a combination of pleasure and torment.

"Forget it," she gasped, writhing at the starburst sensations. "You're not putting that thing in my --"

Hawke laughed and began to pump in long, ruthless strokes. "Babe, once I've got you bound and gagged, you're not going to have much say in which little hole I bang."

Alex cried out, her climax cresting hot again. He was right. He was so damn strong he could do whatever he wanted with her.

At that thought, the orgasm he'd been building with every stroke of his cock launched up her spine like the Space Shuttle. She convulsed, helpless in his grip as his broad shaft worked in and out of her creamy sex. That was when she knew. Hawke was the man of her dreams.

Every last kinky one of them.

* * *

Grinding his teeth, Hawke ought for control. It wasn't easy, given the sweet pull of Alex's hot inner muscles milking his cock. It had been so damn long since he'd ridden a woman. Even then, it hadn't been anything like this.

He could still taste Alex on his tongue, salt and vinegar and musk. Her cunt clung and gripped him with every hard stroke as her lovely little breasts bounced. Her blue eyes glittered as her little pink tongue flicked out over her lips. Long hair the color of honey tumbled across the bed he'd never expected to see a woman in.

Sucking in a breath as pleasure clawed at him, Hawke thought about everything he'd ever imagined doing to a woman. Imagined tying her up. Imagined the tight, slick grip of her asshole as he gave it the fucking he'd been threatening her with.

She was his. Hangin' Harry's blue-blood daughter was his, and he could have her however he wanted. And the thought obviously turned her on just as much as it did him.

Hawke shuddered as the fire clamped hot claws around his balls. He felt a wave of it rolling up his cock. "I'm coming!" he gasped.

"Hawke!" She arched, eyes squeezing shut, pretty lips gasping. Her tiny inner muscles clamped and pulled at his cock in yet another climax. He roared, coming like a freight train in a blaze of heat.

His last thought before the fire took him was that he'd never had a woman like her.

And now that he had her, he was damned if he'd let her go.

* * *

With a sense of regret, Alex felt his softening cock slide from her body. Hawke collapsed beside her with a heartfelt groan. "You okay?" He was panting.

She whimpered, not quite up to speech.

He reared up on one elbow, concern in those smoke-gray eyes as he examined her face. "Alex? Did I hurt you?" A tight little line grew between his thick eyebrows.

He was really worried. The thought sent a bubble of pleased warmth rising in her. "I'm fine," she managed.

"Are you sure? I'm a lot stronger than I used to be, and I got a little carried away." He caught her by one hip and rolled her over to examine her backside. "I don't think there's any bruising."

"Hawke --"

"I really did pull those swats."

She grinned back over her shoulder at him. "Hawke, I'm fine. You didn't hurt me. As much as I hate admit it, I enjoyed every minute of it, including the spanking."

He searched her face. "You sure?"

"You know, you're completely ruining your image as a dominant asshole."

"*That* was a game." His sudden grin was wicked.

"Mostly."

Enjoying herself, she asked, "How mostly?"

Hawke sobered, his gray eyes going serious. "When something's getting ready to eat us and I give you an order, I don't want an argument. I realize you argue for a living, but whenever I'm fighting a WTF is not the time."

Alex snorted. "Give me credit for a little sense, Hawke. The only creature I want eating me around here is you."

He laughed. "I can't tell you how gratified I am to hear it."

"Gratified." Deciding it was time to start teasing him again, she stuck her tongue in one cheek. "That's a really big word for you, isn't it? I'm so proud."

"Smartass. You want *another* spanking?"

"Only if you promise to kiss it and make it well."

The humor drained from his eyes as he leaned down and tilted her chin in one big hand. "Love to."

Hawke's kiss was slow and sensual, his lips moving over hers in a silken possession that made her toes curl. His warm tongue slipped between her lips in a gentle mating stroke that made her sigh. When he finally lifted his head, she whispered, "You're really good at that."

"I'm really good at a lot of things… Ow! You bit me!"

"Oh, that was just a little nip, you big baby."

"I'll *give* you baby, wench!" Long, merciless fingers went for her ribs.

She shouted in laughter and kicked at him. "Get off me, you bully!"

"Watch where you put those bony little feet. Or…" He grabbed an ankle and wiggled the fingers of the other hand menacingly above her sole.

"Don't you *dare* tickle me!"

"Or what?"

"Or I'll…" She lunged for his ribs.

He convulsed with a booming laugh and let her go to fend off her hands. "Cut that out!"

"Ha! Conan is ticklish!"

"I'll give you ticklish!" The mattress rustled as they wrestled, laughing and panting.

* * *

Alex lay draped over Hawke's bare chest, listening to his heartbeat settle into the slow rhythm of sleep. Poor guy. Between fighting the WTF, banging her brains out, and having his secret ticklish spot discovered, he was worn out.

She yawned so hard her jaws creaked. Okay, so he wasn't the only one.

Alex settled her head more comfortably in the hollow between his shoulder and the swell of his right pectoral, smiling sleepily. She really should be more upset about this. She'd been abducted by aliens, for God's sake. She had court next week. Guilty pleas alone would take two days.

Grimacing, Alex pictured the long lines of drunks, petty drug dealers, and car-breakers who'd assemble in the courtroom Monday, waiting to plead guilty. Most of them would get probation, though a few would do time. Hours and hours listening to bullshit excuses. "I lost my job, Your Honor. That's why I had to steal my neighbor's stereo to buy crack." Yeah, right.

She released another huge yawn and hooked her arm around Hawke's broad ribcage. His skin still felt a little sweaty from their play.

A movement in the corner of her eye attracted her attention. She looked down to watch his thick cock slide into full erection. She blinked at it, remembering what it had felt like thrusting deep into her eager sex...

A loud, rattling sound brought her head up.

Hawke was snoring.

Alex buried her head against his chest and giggled softly. Maybe being abducted by aliens wasn't really so bad after all.

* * *

One Month Later

Concentration fierce in her eyes, Alex drew back the spear, her body silhouetted against the vivid blue of the Goldfish Bowl's ocean. The wind whipped the dark honey hair she wore tied up in a long ponytail. She wore only three strategically placed bits of leather and just enough cord to support them.

Hawke's cock thoroughly approved.

A drop of water rolled down one perfect breast. He gave serious thought to licking it off, but decided she wouldn't appreciate being interrupted. At least, not this minute. He'd learned over the past weeks that Alex was ferociously driven; once she'd attained her goal, she'd be more than happy to celebrate.

He watched her brows draw down as her eyes narrowed. Her little pink tongue stole out to the corner of her mouth, a measure of her concentration. Hawke felt his heart roll over in his chest.

She was just so damned adorable.

"Hah!" Alex drove the spear ferociously downward, her entire body surging with effort. The weapon bit into something below the water. She leaned into the shaft with her full weight, grinding down as whatever it was kicked up spray around her.

Finally the splashing stopped. Bumblebees buzzed lazily. He watched her rise on her toes to get a better look at her catch. "Yes!" Alex crowed, and levered the spear up. A bass flailed weakly on its flint point. "Look at that! By God, I did it!"

Hawke grinned, unable to resist her incandescent joy. "You certainly did."

She waded toward shore with her catch. "You get to clean this one."

"Sure do." He followed her, watching her delightful ass, clad only in a couple of bits of string he fully intended to snap. "A deal's a deal."

"I told you I could do it!"

"I never doubted you."

Alex lowered the struggling fish to the sand. "Uh, could you…"

Drawing his knife with a wry grin, he crouched to finish the fish off. She couldn't stand to see anything suffer. Hawke had only persuaded her to try spear fishing by offering to give her a pass from her usual fish-cleaning duties. He'd figured it was an important skill she needed to know. She had to be able to fend for herself if something happened to him.

Now, there was a thought to kill a good mood. The idea of Alex going up against a WTF or any of the Bastards' other nasty pets chilled him right to the marrow. Particularly since, unlike him, she'd never acquired superhuman strength.

Thing was, it did sound like something the Bastards would do -- take him out of the picture and leave her defenseless. Oh, Hawke knew she'd rise to the occasion -- there was some serious steel hidden under all that pretty fluff -- but he hated the thought of the fear and grief she'd feel if something happened to him. They'd gotten close over the past month.

Close, my ass, he thought dryly, watching her do an impromptu ass-wiggling victory dance around her catch. *I'm head over heels in love with her.*

That thought would have scared the shit out of him if they'd been back home. The more Alex talked about her blue-blood family -- her fiercely protective judge daddy and matchmaking mama -- the more obvious it was they'd hate him with a passion. Hawke might have enough medals for a platoon in his footlocker, he might have worked his way up from lowly private to lieutenant in the Marine Corps, but he'd still be trailer trash to them. Which was why he'd never let her worm the truth of his background out of him.

Oh, he'd learned enough over the past month to know Alex herself wouldn't care. She knew he'd worked his ass off to get where he was -- he'd told her that much -- and that was all she'd care about. To her, the fact that his daddy and brother were doing time would be irrelevant in the equation of what Hawke himself had accomplished. That ferocious sense of justice was one of the things he adored about her.

That, and those lovely tits. Among other things.

Oh, yeah. He had it bad. So bad, he was no longer all that sure he wanted to go home. Back home, the fact that he'd grown up in a seedy trailer park would matter. Back home, it wouldn't take Alex long to discover his mama drank most of the take-home pay he sent her.

Hawke knew he was probably enabling Ma's drinking problem, but he just couldn't stand the thoughts of his mother going hungry. And she did occasionally buy food, at least between pints of Mad Dog 20/20.

Okay, so he was a sucker.

But in the Goldfish Bowl, he could keep Alex in happy ignorance while screwing her brilliant brains out. Here he could slay all her monsters and bask in the adoration in her eyes. His mother would still be taken care of, since he'd be listed as Missing In Action and the Marines would continue to send her his pay.

Of course, the trick was, he had to keep killing the monsters. If one of them actually got him, Alex was fucked.

So he'd just damn well make sure none of them got him.

"I think I'm going to try to catch another one," Alex announced, wading back into the water.

"Good idea." Hawke trailed her happily. Walking a pace behind Alexandria Kenyon was no hardship; her ass was a thing of beauty. "We can smoke whatever we don't eat tonight."

"Oh, yeah. Or I could try to whip up a nice fish stew. A few potatoes, some carrots..." They tended his garden on a daily basis. Even weeding was more fun with Alex beside him.

No doubt about it. He had it bad.

Hawke watched her draw back the spear and go still in the water as she waited for her prey to swim by. From the corner of one eye, he spotted a ripple in the water. Something was definitely headed their way.

He frowned. Damn big ripple. Too big for a...

A head the height of his body rose from the water on a long, snaking neck. As they gaped at it, the thing roared, revealing a mouthful of shark teeth.

"Oh, shit," Hawke breathed, and grabbed her arm. "Run!"

* * *

"Faster!" Hawke roared, hauling her across the beach with running strides so long she could barely keep up. "A thing that size is not going to want to leave the water. If we can get inland, we're safe!"

But if we can't, we're toast, Alex realized grimly as

she poured everything she had in pelting over the sand at his heels. She didn't dare take time even to drop her spear.

SLAP! Something cold and wet wrapped around her left ankle. The beach flew up and slammed into her chest, ripping her hand out of his and knocking the spear from her grip. Instinctively, Alex tried to scramble back to her feet. She heard Hawke's bellow of horror at the same time she realized she was caught. Twisting around, she saw what had her and screamed.

A thick, meaty tentacle had wrapped around her bare ankle, suckers gripping her flesh. As she stared at it in frozen horror, it jerked, hauling her over the sand, back toward the edge of the water where the thing's head towered over the water. The arm had to be a good thirty feet long and thick as a python. "Fuck!" she screamed. "Haaawke!"

He lunged past her to pounce on the tentacle with a roar of fury. His sword caught the light as he lifted it and chopped down on the thick limb just beyond where it wrapped around her foot. Orange slime flew through the air, and the tentacle's grip convulsed. Alex shrieked as what felt like a dozen needles sank into her skin. "Hawke, its suckers have *spines*! Oh, *damn*, that hurts!"

He didn't look around, just held on and hacked as the tentacle dragged them toward its horrific owner. A second tentacle lifted out of the water and plunged toward them. "Look out!"

Hawke threw a quick look over his shoulder at the whipping arm, but instead of letting her go, he gave the tentacle another vicious chop, hacking right through the end that held Alex.

Despite the biting pain from the spines, she struggled to her feet as he jumped up. The second tentacle whipped down at him, but he ducked aside and slashed at it.

"There's another one!" she yelled, seeing a third arm rise from the water. "How many tentacles does that thing have?"

"Run!" Hawke bellowed, dancing around the flailing arm. "I'll distract it!"

"But…"

"Goddamnit, I said *go*!" He chopped. Orange blood flew.

Just as the third tentacle snapped around his waist. "Shit!" he bellowed, and twisted around to attack the arm with his sword. That sounded like a cry of pain; it must be digging into him with those spines. "Let go, you bastard!"

A weapon! She needed a weapon! Desperately, Alex whirled, looking around for her fallen spear. There! She spotted the long wooden shaft lying on the sand where she'd dropped it. She raced to pick it up.

But by the time she turned around with it, the thing had wrapped still another tentacle around Hawke's sword arm as it hauled him toward its fanged head. He wasn't making it easy; he'd managed to get his legs braced in front of him to resist its pull. His feet dug furrows in the sand, cords standing out on the side of his neck as he strained, face going bright red.

With a desperate scream, Alex lunged toward the tentacle holding Hawke's sword arm and drove the spear into it with every ounce of her strength. Both tentacles convulsed, coiling like snakes. Hawke cursed viciously as they dragged at him. Bright red blood snaked down his bunched biceps. The spines must be tearing the hell out of his skin.

She jerked the spear out and looked for another spot to jab.

"Look out!" Hawke roared. "There comes another one!"

Alex whirled, saw the meaty arm shooting right for her face, and ducked. She gave it a savage jab when it feinted at her, dancing out of its path. Shooting a look at Hawke, she tried to decide whether she could get in another shot at the ones holding him. He'd twisted his sword around and jammed the weapon into one of the tentacles, all the way up to the hilt.

"What the hell do you think you're doing?" he bellowed. "Get the fuck inland!"

"And leave you?" She danced and jabbed with her spear. "I don't think so."

The fourth tentacle suddenly whipped around to catch his left leg. It jerked him right off his feet. He cursed savagely.

She screamed as the monster lifted him off the ground and carried him toward its open jaws. "Alex, get clear!" he roared. His face was as white as parchment.

"Fuck that!" It was going to eat him!

The sheer blazing panic of that thought swamped every other consideration. Alex took off running straight for the thing's head. She had to get there before he did. Luckily, the thing wasn't lifting very fast, probably because Hawke was fighting for everything he was worth.

"Go back!" he bellowed.

The creature's massive head whipped around to stare at her with malevolent interest, but it had its tentacles full with Hawke. Membranes snapped back and forth across its huge yellow eyes. It plunged toward her, jaws gaping wide.

Moving faster than she'd ever moved in her life, Alex jumped aside. It missed.

"Hey, ugly!" Hawke yelled. "Over here, you slimy motherfucker!" He'd cut off the tentacle around his sword arm, and now he jabbed his blade savagely into the one that circled his waist. He bore down, twisting the sword.

The thing's head reared up with a shrill, ringing cry of pain. It whipped around and started hauling him toward its open mouth. Alex saw her own reflection in one huge, yellow eye... And stabbed her spear right into it with the entire weight of her body behind the blow.

The thing howled like a banshee. Its massive head whipped toward her as it lashed in agony. She tried to duck, but it clipped her shoulder. She went flying like a Mark McGwire home run. The sand came up at her face...

Chapter Four

Hawk shouted as Alex hit the ground and tumbled like a rag doll, but there wasn't one damn thing he could do about it. The remaining tentacles that held him lashed back and forth with the creature's death throes, threatening to tear him apart. Its spines ripped his skin in white-hot agony. He kicked, felt the one around his ankle tear away, but he was still trapped in the arm that held his waist. It flailed, flinging him upward. His stomach somersaulted as he shot skyward, flew twenty feet, then plunged down again.

The ocean shot up toward his face. *Fuck*! He sucked in a breath.

It was like slamming into a brick wall at thirty miles an hour. Cold and pressure rammed his face. And then he was underwater, being dragged relentlessly downward as the creature sank. Tendrils of red blood snaked past his eyes, mixed with streamers of orange. Huge bubbles rolled up.

The need to breathe clawed at his chest, but he fought it, sensing the tentacle was losing its grip. Black spots floated in front of his eyes, and he knew he was on the verge of losing consciousness. For a moment, it seemed easier…

And then a thought pierced his stunned brain.

Alex! Fuck, he had to get loose. She was up there hurt. He had to get free!

He shoved free of the tentacle and kicked, clawing and fighting toward the light he could see over his head. Too far off. He was never going to make it.

He had to. She'd risked her life to save his ass; he couldn't do less for her. Lips sealed and eyes burning, he kicked hard, driving for the surface.

His head exploded into air and blinding light. Hawke sucked in a desperate, furious breath. His body felt like solid lead, but he ignored his exhaustion and turned in the water, searching for the beach.

He spotted it. And there, lying on the sand, was a small, crumpled figure.

Alex. Goddamn her, she'd better not have gotten herself killed.

Hawke flung himself toward shore in what had to have been the ugliest swimming stroke he'd ever performed. Finally his feet hit sand, and he staggered up the beach to collapse beside her.

"Alex?" He turned her over awkwardly, ignoring the vicious stinging pain in his biceps from the thing's spines. "Alex, baby, be alive." His voice choked. "You'd better not be dead, you hear me?" He dropped his head on her chest and listened.

For a moment, he heard nothing but the buzzing of those damn bees, and his own heart stopped. Then…

Thump. Thump. Thump.

"Oh, Christ!" His eyes filled with tears. "Thank you, Jesus." He straightened and began carefully examining the woman he loved.

* * *

The first thing Alex heard was her lover's deep, sensual growl. "I am going to kick your ass unless you talk to me right now."

With considerable difficulty, she managed to pry her lids open. His face loomed over hers, dripping water onto her chest. There was a marked gray cast to his skin, and his eyes looked wild. She coughed. Everything hurt. "Is that any…" She had to stop to pant. "Any way to talk to the woman who saved your life?"

A broad, relieved grin broke over his face. "Saved it, hell. You damn near gave me a heart attack."

"Ingrate." She rolled over onto her side and groaned.

"You okay?" Tenderly, he ran a hand over her back.

"Everything hurts." Alex frowned, and cautiously rolled over onto her hands and knees. "But I think it all works. You?"

He sat back on his haunches and looked down at his flat, muscled belly. A set of horrific punctures marked his skin as if he'd be run over by a spiked tire, but the openings were already closing. "Motherfuckin' monster made hamburger out of everything it grabbed, but I'm already starting to heal."

With a sigh, she staggered upright. "I should be so lucky." Then, aiming a frown down at her ankle, she saw her puncture wounds were also beginning to close. "And apparently I am."

"Good." He clambered to his feet and stood there swaying as he glowered down at her. "I want you in perfect shape when I wallop that disobedient little ass."

"What?" She glared at him in outrage.

Gray eyes blazed. "I told you to leave, damn it! You disobeyed me and it almost *ate* you!"

"Well, if I had obeyed, it would have eaten *you*!"

"So?"

"So, I love you, you big dumbass! You're not becoming monster chow as long as I'm around to do something about it!"

For a moment, incredulous joy flooded his gaze. Then it vanished into a snarl as he poked a finger toward her chest. "Sorry, you're not distracting me that easily. The point is, when I give you an order, you do what I tell you to do!"

"Yeah?" Furious, fighting mad, she sneered at him. "Well, here's an order for you -- kiss my ass!" Snarling, she whirled around and stomped back toward the cave.

The next monster that came along could eat him with her blessings!

* * *

She loved him. The thought filled Hawke with giddy joy.

Which he had no intention whatsoever of letting her see. Alex had almost gotten herself killed, damn it. Trying to save him, true -- and he had to admit there was a good chance he'd be dead now if she hadn't. But when he'd looked around and seen her flying at that monster with that silly toothpick of a spear, he'd damn near had a heart attack right then. He'd thought the thing was going to eat her on the spot.

When Hawke remembered the monster's long, snakelike neck, all those teeth, how fast the fucker moved, it made him sick. He couldn't let her do that again. He'd rather die himself than watch something take a bite out of her. He had to make damn sure that the next time he gave her an order, she obeyed it.

Striding along behind her as she stalked toward the cave, Hawke eyed her round little ass, just barely clad in a tiny triangle of leather. A wave of violent lust rolled over him. He recognized it as the flip side of terror; he always got horny as hell right after a battle. He'd bet a month's pay Alex felt the same, no matter how pissed she was.

Suddenly he knew just what he was going to do to make sure she never took a chance like that again.

* * *

Damn it, all the little hairs were standing up on the

back of her neck. Hawke was projecting hot male menace at her so hard, he was damn near giving her radiation burns.

Perversely, Alex felt her nipples peak. He was probably going to spank her again before screwing her brains out. The thought turned her on even as it ticked her off. It was just not fair. Nothing she'd ever experienced made her as hot as John Hawke being a dominant asshole. He was so gorgeous, it wasn't as if he needed any other unfair advantages.

She stomped up the winding path toward the cave, acutely aware of the rustle of bushes behind her as Hawke stalked her. Rivulets of warm cream slid into her cunt with every step she took. Any minute now, he was going to grab her, rip her clothes off, and beat her butt. Then he'd slide that humongous cock into her aching pussy and fuck her until she saw stars.

She really should put up a fight. Just on general principles. She'd saved his life, damn it. Where did he get off being such a prick about it?

And to make matters worse, she'd blurted out that she loved him. Like he needed any other ammunition.

He hadn't told her he loved her back, either.

Alex brooded about that thought as she climbed the cliff up to the cave. She never found it an enjoyable trip anyway, and it was even worse now, with all the aches, bruises and puncture wounds she'd managed to collect during the fight. She was healing fast, but not that fast.

And horny on top of all that. It just wasn't fair.

After an interminable climb -- feeling Hawke's gaze burning her ass the whole way -- Alex scrambled into the cave. She'd really like to collapse, but that blazing glare was making her far too jumpy. Instead, she made for one of the canteens and slugged down half its contents.

When she was done, she wiped her chin and turned to look at him as he bent to dig through one of the leather bags. "Oh, hell," she said, grimacing as realization hit. "We forgot the fish."

Hawke shrugged. "Something else has probably eaten it by now."

"Guess it's veggies and fruit tonight."

He pulled a handful of cords out of the bag and turned toward her. "Actually, I had something else in mind."

Her heart gave an enthusiastic little jump. She backed up a pace anyway. "Like what?"

Hawke gave her a grin that was all teeth. "Like an in-depth discussion of why you're going to fucking *obey* me the next time I give you an order."

"Oh, come on, Hawke! It was going to kill you!"

"That's not the issue."

"Oh, hell yes, it is! If you think I'm just going to stand by and... Hey!" He grabbed her by one arm, kicked her feet out from under her, and pushed her down onto a fur pelt on the dirt floor.

The next thing she knew, he'd flipped her over on her belly, grabbed one wrist, and started whipping the cord around it. "You'll do what I tell you to do," he told her grimly.

"What the hell do you think you're doing?"

"Guess." He grabbed the other wrist and bound the first to it with a couple of ruthless loops.

"Hey!" Alex tried to flip over, but he dropped a knee in the small of her back and pinned her in place. Finished, he released her wrists. They dropped to the pelt over her head. "Cut it out!"

"Oh, no." Steel slithered as he drew his knife. She felt the cool brush of the blade against her waist as he cut the cord waistband of her leather thong.

"Let me guess," she snarled, frustrated and turned on as he sliced her clothes off her. "You're going to beat my ass again, right?"

"No," he drawled lazily, rising to his feet and tossing her bra and thong aside. "Actually, I've got something else in mind."

"What?" She twisted around on the pelt and glared as he went to the collection of clay jars against one wall of the cave. "What the hell are you doing?"

"Looking for the animal fat." Picking a jar up, he uncorked it, took a sniff, then capped it and put it down again. He chose another, opened it, and nodded in satisfaction. "There it is."

"What do you need animal fat for?" Alex watched as he headed back toward with the jar in one big hand.

Her heart began to pound. She knew damn well what he needed it for.

With a nasty grin, he bounced the jar in his palm and confirmed her fears. "Greasing your tight little asshole."

"Oh, no. Forget it." She tried to flip over, but he dropped to his knees and slapped a big hand in the center of her back to shove her flat. Before she could rear up again, he turned around and half sat on her facing her backside.

She heard the *clink* as he pulled the clay cork off the pot. "I'm afraid this is not a topic for debate."

"You'd force me?" Alex flinched as he used the other hand to part her butt cheeks.

"I don't need to use force, and you know it." Warm fingers stroked between her cheeks, seeking the little puckered opening. "I'll make sure you're nice and hot before I start your punishment."

She caught her breath as Hawke's long, thick

finger found her asshole and began to push. He entered slowly, the penetration both a bit painful and shockingly erotic. Despite herself, she felt a hot, scandalized arousal growing as he probed her. "You can't do this!"

"Sweetheart, I can do any damn thing I want to with you. You're the one who's tied up, remember?" The dark purr in his voice made her heart pound. "Oh, yeah. You're definitely a virgin there, aren't you? Nice and tight."

She swallowed as he drew his finger out of her and delved into the pot again. Her voice cracked. "I hope that's not what you use to cook with."

"Don't be disgusting. I whipped this up especially with you in mind."

"Well, that's a…" She squeaked. He was using two fingers this time, and the slow penetration stretched her brutally. "Damn it, that hurts!"

"Good. It'll hurt even more when it's my cock." He rotated those long fingers, and she caught her breath. "Oh, I'm gonna enjoy this. There's nothing quite as hot as working my dick into a pretty little sub's tight asshole."

Alex was feeling distinctly lightheaded as every bit of blood she had headed straight for her pussy. "I'm not a sub."

"Yeah?" He slid the forefinger of the other hand into her pussy. She caught her breath in agonized pleasure as he stretched both tight channels. "You're pretty damn creamy for somebody who's not a sub. Especially considering what I'm getting ready to do to your virgin ass."

She really ought to tell him off, but the sensation of his big fingers working her pussy and anus was just too overwhelming. Dropping her forehead to the pelt under her, Alex sobbed in a breath.

"I'm gonna fuck your little butt real slow," he purred in the menacing rumble that could make her cream even when he wasn't strumming her clit and fingering both holes. "Long, deeeeep thrusts. It's gonna hurt, but this is a punishment, so I don't have to be gentle."

"Bastard!" She shuddered, ferociously aroused.

"You bet. That's why you don't want to piss me off."

"I saved your life, you prick!"

"And I gave you an order you disobeyed." He jerked his fingers out of her, grabbed her hip, and flipped her over on her back. Then he moved around to kneel between her spread thighs. "Luckily for you, I think you need to be a little hotter before I start your punishment."

She watched breathlessly as he spread her lips, lowered his head, and extended his pointed pink tongue. Its first pass over her clit sent a sizzle through her that made her back arch. Then, as she writhed, he started eating her out. A moment later, two of those big fingers went back up her ass.

* * *

Hawke danced his tongue around Alex's hard little clit, enjoying the way she twisted against his mouth. Simultaneously, he fingerfucked her, in all the way to the knuckles. Her backside gripped him like a fist. Imagining what it would feel like to force his cock into that little hole, he growled in pleasure against her cunt.

Oh, yeah. He was going to give her a reaming she'd never forget.

And judging by her panting groans, she loved every minute of the preparations. He'd suspected Alex had a masochistic streak, but she was even more responsive than he'd hoped.

Which meant he could give her the assfuck he'd been dreaming of for weeks now. By the time he was done with her rectum, she'd never dream of disobeying another order.

Yeah, it was highhanded. Yeah, he should be ashamed of himself. But he really didn't give a damn. If being a prick was what it took to make sure she never again risked herself like she had today, he was more than happy to play sadistic bastard.

Particularly since he was so hard, he could drive nails with his cock.

She was grinding her wet little cunt against his face now, savaging her own backside with his fingers, on the verge of an explosion.

Hawke jerked his hand out of her butt and sat up, licking her hot juices off his lips. "Sorry, babe," he told her, watching the shocked fury roll over her face. "You don't get to come. This is a punishment, remember?"

Her eyes narrowed as her pretty mouth curled into a snarl. "You asshole!"

He grinned. "No. Yours."

Reaching for his loincloth, he jerked it away, freeing his aching cock.

* * *

Her heart pounding with a potent combination of arousal and fear, Alex watched Hawke grease his cock. He took his time, scooping out a dollop of the animal fat and stroking it up and down the jutting shaft, his gaze never leaving hers. His smoke-gray eyes seemed to smolder.

"You're going to want to fight it at first," he told her in a velvet rumble that made her nipples ache. "But your best bet is to push out with those little muscles while I force it in."

Licking her dry lips, she stared at his massive cock, hypnotized by the way it bobbed under his stroking hand. She was acutely aware of her wrists, bound behind her back as she knelt.

"Feeling helpless?" he purred. "You look it. Tied up and ready to take my cock up your virgin ass. All pretty tits and long legs and anxious eyes." Hawke grinned. "It's no wonder I'm hard as a rock."

"You do realize you're being a prick?" She sounded breathless, damn it.

"Oh, yeah." He caught her under one knee and flipped her onto her belly, then lifted her hips off the pelt. The movement spread her wide. With the other hand, he reached between her cheeks, parted her. His glittering eyes studied her, his angular face sharp with hunger. "What a pretty little rosebud asshole." He let go of her backside to grab his massive dick, simultaneously dragging her close with the other hand. "Don't worry, baby, I'm not really going to split it open." His teeth flashed. She felt something smooth and hot press against the delicate flesh. "It's just going to feel that way."

Alex's eyes widened as she felt the crown of his cock pressing against her anus in a savage demand for entry. The tiny opening reluctantly spread, admitting the knob a fraction. "Hawke!" she gasped. "That hurts!"

His eyes blazed up as he grinned. "I know." Another flaming inch slid inside. "This is what happens when you don't mind the big, nasty Marine." He licked his lips and grabbed her other hip, pulling her closer, slowly impaling her. His face tightened with voluptuous pleasure. "He ties you up and helps himself to your anal cherry."

Alex groaned, tossing her head as she tried to adjust to his relentless entry. His cock felt like a red-hot baseball bat.

"Push, babe," he growled. "Let me in."

Desperate to relieve the pressure, she obeyed. As the grip of her muscles eased, he sank deeper and deeper. Finally her butt was snug against his washboard belly. He released her hips and came down on top of her, big hands braced beside her shoulders. He gave her a conqueror's grin. "Mmmmm. Finally. Balls deep in your ass. I think I like it here."

"Oh, God." It felt like he'd shoved a burning torch up her butt. "Hurry up and get off already, you sadistic son of a bitch!"

"Not so fast. Here comes the good part." Slowly, he began to pull out.

She gasped. He wasn't kidding. The sensation was dark and exotic and really kinky, and it went on and on as he withdrew his big cock. Alex squirmed, catching her breath.

"Told you you'd like it." Hawke smiled smugly. "Now..." He thrust. Another wave of dark, hot pain. Then he pulled out again, very slowly, sending pleasure snaking along every nerve ending she had.

"I think you're beginning to get it," he rumbled. "Let's pick up the pace a little..."

Oh, God.

* * *

Pleasure wrapped around Hawke's balls like wet silk as he fucked Alex Kenyon up her deliciously tight ass. It wasn't the first time he'd tied up a pretty submissive for a thorough rectum reaming, but it had never been this hot.

She'd pissed him off, of course -- that was part of it -- and then there was the wicked kink of butt-banging

Judge Kenyon's virgin baby. But most of it was just the searing response she gave him every time he shoved his cock up that butter-slick channel and felt her squirm in painful pleasure.

Sweet Alex had a masochistic streak that brought his inner sadistic bastard roaring to the surface.

Not that it had ever been all that deeply buried to begin with.

Hawke drew out, listening to her conquered moan of delight. He pushed inside. She twisted, her tight, well-greased flesh gripping his cock. As he felt the little hole strain to take his invading width, she whimpered, a tiny, helpless sound that made his dick twitch in dark pleasure.

Oh, yeah. He was giving poor little Alex a very hard time. And damned if she didn't love it almost as much as he did.

Taking pity on her, he reached down and stroked his thumb over her clit as he forced his shaft in. She jerked and moaned.

"Like that?" he drew out, circling and strumming her clit.

Alex groaned, throwing back her head and arching her spine until her pretty nipples pointed at the ceiling. "Oh, God! Yes!"

"More?"

She panted. "Oh. Oh, yeah!"

Hawke gave her a dark smile. "Here it comes then."

Then he started fucking her -- long, hard strokes that tore a scream of tormented ecstasy from her mouth. He gave her no mercy at all beyond the thumb that stroked her clit as he rammed her ass.

"Hawke!" she gasped, writhing under his hard strokes. "Sweet God, I'm coming!" Tiny inner muscles clamped over his cock, pulsed as she convulsed in her bonds.

He'd never seen anything as hot in his life as the sight of Alex climaxing as he fucked her virginal ass.

Hot Roman candle bursts of pleasure began to shoot up his spine. With a roar of savage joy, he drove to the hilt and threw back his head, pumping Alex full of hot cum.

Chapter Five

Hawke collapsed against her, all hot, sweaty muscle and delicious male weight. She groaned in pleasure even as her violated ass ached in protest. He'd sodomized her without any compassion whatsoever, yet she'd never experienced anything so utterly arousing. Her climax had lit her entire nervous system up like an overloaded Christmas tree.

"Damn, Hawke," she wheezed. "That was rude, crude, and socially unacceptable."

"Yeah." He sounded distinctly smug. "Wanna do it again?"

"Give me a week to recover, and I'll think about it."

"Glad you approve." He reached for her bound wrists, grabbed the knife, and freed her with a single pass of the blade. She let her arms fall, but before she could get comfortable, he scooped her off the floor and carried her to the bed.

After laying her down on the thick mattress, Hawke went to rummage among the supplies against the wall. He returned with a wet cloth he put to use cleaning her well-fucked backside. She sank into a pleasant lassitude as he busied himself again before sliding into bed next to her.

As Hawke wrapped brawny arms around her, Alex nestled her head into the hollow of his shoulder and sighed in pleasure. "That was really hot."

"Oh, yeah."

"You're not a nice man."

"Nope."

"But if you think I'm going to just stand by the next time something tries to eat you, you're out of your ever-lovin' mind."

Hawke sighed.

* * *

Alex came awake slowly to the sound of a low buzzing. She opened her eyes and saw one of the ever-present bumblebees hovering over her head. She frowned. It seemed to be watching her.

She swatted at the thing. It ducked aside like a tiny helicopter, but it didn't buzz off. Instead it returned to hovering over her and Hawke. It still seemed to be watching her.

Come to think of it, those damn bees always seemed to be watching her.

And what the hell were they anyway? Narrow-eyed, she considered the insect. Now that she looked more closely, she saw that though it did sound like a bumblebee, it was matte black instead of striped. Its head was oddly shaped, much bigger than a normal insect's in promotion to its body. Rather than multifaceted eyes like an Earth bee, it had single-faceted ones set on the front of its "face," rather than on the sides of its head.

All of the bumble-things behaved strangely, too. Instead of buzzing around the local vegetation to feed on pollen -- or whatever -- they seemed more attracted to her and Hawke. Yet they never seemed to bite, meaning they weren't bloodsuckers like mosquitoes.

Suspicion tugged at her. "Hey, Hawke."

"Hmm?"

"What are those things?"

He opened one eye and followed her pointing finger. "It's a bumblebee, Alex."

"No, it's not. Look at it."

Hawke groaned. "Alex, baby, I don't give a damn."

"No, think about it. This is a man-made -- or alien-made -- environment. Everything in it was added for us to eat, use, or run from. So what are the bugs for?"

Hawke's eyes narrowed. One big hand flashed upward, and two fingers snapped closed around the bumble-thing.

"Damn, you're quick."

"I try." She scrambled onto her knees as he sat up. His eyes narrowed, and he squeezed so hard his fingertips turned white. His brows flew up and he opened his opened his fingers.

The bumble-thing took off, obviously unhurt by his attempt to crush it.

"You losing your touch, Hawke?"

He snorted as he eyed the circling bug. "Hardly. I don't know what that thing is, but it's no insect. I'd have crushed it otherwise."

"I'll be damned," Alex growled. "It may not be an insect…"

"But it's definitely a bug." He glared at it. "I'd bet a month's pay that thing is the alien equivalent of a camera."

"That's why they're always around, especially when we're fighting something." The bumble-things had been all over the place when she and Hawke had battled the wannabe Cthulhu with all the tentacles. She just hadn't registered them at the time.

"They seem to love it when we have sex, too." His jawline was tight with fury.

She snarled. "Peeping toms. Where's a fly swatter? I say we start eliminating a few winged spies."

A strange male voice spoke. "I suppose that's my cue."

With a muffled shriek, Alex jumped for the nearest pelt as Hawke lunged for the sword he'd left lying beside the bed. "Who the hell are you?" he roared at the tall, slim man who sauntered casually into their cave.

"I am Nathaniel Oritz Krikor," the man said, sweeping them a theatrical bow, arms spread wide. "Your humble host."

Whipping the pelt around her body, Alex glared at their visitor. He had an inch or two on Hawke himself, but if he weighed more than a hundred and fifty pounds, she'd be surprised. He wore a white linen suit that looked like it cost a grand or so, and his hair was a blond so pale, it matched the suit. So did the elegant leather loafers on his narrow feet. His irises were a strange, iridescent shade that shifted color every time he moved his head, from blue to purple to red to yellow, then back to blue again.

"What are you supposed to be?" Hawke snarled, eyeing the white suit. "John Travolta in *Saturday Night Fever*?"

Studying the invader's narrow, too-handsome face, Alex added, "Or an alien?"

Krikor threw back his head in a laugh that showed every perfect tooth in his head. It still sounded far too practiced for genuine humor. "An alien? Me? No, Ms. Kenyon, I'm afraid you and Lieutenant Hawke here have jumped to the wrong conclusions." He aimed a wide, bright smile at them, but there was something malicious in his eyes. "You weren't abducted by aliens. Believe me, aliens have no interest in our little Earth whatsoever. At least, not during your time."

Alex's jaw dropped. "But they do in *yours*?"

"Just what *is* your time, mister?" Hawke lifted his sword, rage in his eyes.

Krikor backed up a cautious step, smiling even more broadly. "Now, there's no need for violence here, Lieutenant."

"I strongly suggest you tell me what the *fuck* is going on, or you're going to experience more violence than you know what to do with." Each word dripped icy menace.

Now Krikor's artificial smile looked distinctly panicked. He shot a look at one of the hovering camera bees, then straightened his shoulders. "What you don't realize, Lieutenant, is that over the past year, you've become a hero to billions of humans. Many of them routinely check your data stream dozens of times a day to see how you're coping with the challenges of the Bubble."

"Billions of people?" Alex whispered. "Bubble?"

"*Data stream*?" She'd never seen Hawke so furious. He took a step toward Krikor. "What fucking *year* is it, asshole?"

The slender man blinked and licked his lips, his gaze flicking to Hawke's sword. "Using your calendar, it would be May 25, 2443."

* * *

Alex's legs went weak. She sank down on the bed, clutching her pelt. "Four hundred and thirty-nine years. We've come four hundred and thirty-nine years. Into the future."

"That's right." Evidently realizing he'd rendered them too stunned to attack him, Krikor straightened and fingered the elegant lapels of his suit. It must be some kind of costume; it was doubtful even menswear would remain that static for four centuries.

For that matter --"How come you speak English?"

Krikor shrugged. "I have a translator, of course. So does everyone else. Otherwise you wouldn't be so hugely popular." His iridescent eyes lit with greed. "And you are. Huge. We've made billions, just on merchandising alone."

It was impossible to take in. "You took us from our own time," she said blankly. "Aren't you afraid of, I don't know, changing history or something?"

Krikor laughed lightly. "My dear, one can't change history. It's already happened."

Alex looked at Hawke, feeling helpless and overwhelmed. "Do you understand any of this?"

Their host ignored the question. "At any rate, I'm here to tell you it's time for you to return to the twenty-first century. The Lieutenant's visa has expired and --"

"Visa?" Hawke demanded.

Krikor nodded. "Your time travel visa. Of course, that's not the actual term, but the concept is close enough. Now." He rubbed his thin hands together. "I'm pleased to inform you we have some very nice cash prizes waiting for you back home --"

"Prizes." Hawke's lips pulled back from his teeth. "This has all been some kind of fucking *reality show.* Only instead of eating bugs, I got to fight monsters!" Stiff legged, he began to stalk Krikor, whose expression shifted from smug to panicked with every step Hawke took. "What would you have done if one of those things had *eaten* me, you son of a bitch?"

The man cringed. "We'd have stopped it before you were really hurt."

"Yeah?" He jerked a thumb at Alex, who was crowding at his heels, steaming with fury. "What about her? Why'd you pull her into it?"

"Well, just watching you fight *C'kici* and *varitakor* had gotten a little dry. We decided you needed a love interest."

"But why kidnap *us*?" Alex exploded. "Aren't there people in your own time that would have played your stupid game?"

Krikor blinked at her. "Oh, we couldn't use

anyone from the present. Not anymore. *Everybody*'s heard of the Bubble. They all know the rules, so there's no fear. And if the contestants aren't afraid, there's no drama. Besides, you two are --"

Hawke's fist slammed into his face before he could finish the sentence. Krikor went down like a sack of cement as the big man threw his sword aside and lunged for his throat.

Alex flung herself on her lover as he grabbed the man's skinny neck and began to squeeze. "Hawke, no! Please! Let him go!"

He threw her a wild-eyed look over his shoulder. "He's not going to just get away with this!"

Softly, Alex said, "But Hawke, you can't do this. Let him go."

He looked down at Krikor's purpling face, his expression twisted with rage. Slowly, the fury faded. He released his hold and straightened off his gasping victim. "Yeah. I guess you're right. I can't just kill him."

"No." Alex calmly stepped around him, drew back her foot, and rammed her bare heel right into Krikor's balls. As the skinny little creep curled like a gagging shrimp, she gave Hawke an angelic smile. "Not until I got in my shot, anyway."

His answering grin was savage. "That's my girl. Let's --"

White light exploded over their heads from the glowing hole that had opened in the ceiling of the cave. Alex and Hawke stared up at it in horror. "Oh, sh --"

They were sucked off their feet before he could finish the curse.

* * *

" -- - it!" Hawke spat, just as his booted feet hit the ground in the pitch dark. Gunfire exploded around him. He hit the dirt more by instinct than anything else as the enemy fired wildly, probably reacting to the hole of light that had spit him out.

Hawke curled instinctively into a ball, his hands over his helmeted head.

Helmeted?

In the darkness, his hands explored his body, discovered familiar cloth where he'd been almost naked before. Holy crap, he was wearing his uniform again -- the same uniform that had long since been reduced to rags by alien fangs.

It's impossible. And yet, here he was. The show's bastard producers must have somehow duplicated all his gear. Including -- *Thank you, Jesus*! -- his M-16. He pulled the rifle off his shoulder and began firing it in the direction of the enemy. Somebody screamed.

Everything went quiet.

"Lieutenant!" Sergeant Ron Jacobs bellowed from somewhere nearby. "Lieutenant, what the hell was that light?"

Hawke took a deep breath and lied. "I haven't the faintest idea, Sergeant."

The Bastards had returned him to the exact moment he'd left -- two full years before they would abduct Alex from her bed. She didn't even know him yet, much less love him.

Why should she? He was just the Jarhead son of trailer trash. And she was Alexandria Kenyon, blue-blood Southern Belle.

Way out of his league.

* * *

Alex yelped as she fell out of the light, hit something soft, and bounced. "Oh, hell. Hawke?"

She blinked at the moonlight-washed furniture around her, then reached for the crystalline lamp gleaming in the dimness. A moment's fumbling turned it on.

Stunned, Alex stared at her surroundings. She was back in her own bed. And… She looked down at her chest. She was wearing the same camisole she'd had on when they'd snatched her a month ago.

It was as if none of it had ever happened.

A sense of hollow emptiness washed over her. Hawke. God, Hawke. If they'd sent her back to the moment she'd left, they'd sent him back too -- straight into the middle of the war in Afghanistan.

Two years ago.

Feeling sick, she rolled out of bed. He might be dead now. And even if he wasn't, how the hell was she going to find him?

But she had to. Somehow. She loved him, damn it. She wasn't about to lose him after everything she'd done to keep him alive. She'd fought a monster for him, for God's sake.

Think, Alex. What did she know? She knew his name. She knew he was a lieutenant in the Marine Corps. Her father had connections. Surely she could convince him to…

The doorbell rang.

Alex shot a glance at the clock. It was the middle of the night. Who would…

She was running downstairs before she even had time to complete the thought. Hope swelled in her chest as she skidded to a halt in the foyer, flipped the porch light on and snatched the door open. "Hawke?"

The tall man on the other side wore a Marine dress uniform and a chest full of ribbons. Her heart skipped in anguish. *He's come to tell me Hawke's dead…*

Then Alex registered the hard, handsome face under the shining black bill of his uniform cap. His blond hair was cut so painfully short, she hadn't even recognized him. "Hawke?" Her voice broke. "Hawke?"

Then she was in his arms.

They both started babbling at the same time. "I thought I'd lost you..."

"Jesus, I've been waiting so long..."

"What have you been?"

"I couldn't stay away any longer."

Alex grabbed his strong arms and dragged him inside, banging the door shut. "They just sent me back. How did you know?"

Hawke studied her face, his gaze fierce and hungry. "You'd told me it was 2004 when they took you. I served out the rest of my tour while I waited until the Corps transferred me back to the States. A month ago, I managed to track you down, but I didn't dare approach you, because I knew you wouldn't know who I was yet."

She closed her eyes, imagining it. "Oh, Hawke."

"Then today I went to the ATM, and there was ten million dollars in my bank account that just appeared out of nowhere. I knew it was the prize money. I figured that must mean you were on your way. So I pulled up outside your house and waited until I saw the flash."

Alex blinked. "Ten million? Hell of a prize. How are you going to explain it?"

"According to the bank and a lawyer or two, I've developed a rich relative." A faint smile curled his mouth. "Think Judge Kenyon would mind a wealthy son-in-law -- even if he did come from trailer trash?"

"What?"

Right there in her foyer, he swept his hat off, dropped to one blue-clad knee on the marble floor, and took her hand. "Alexandria Kenyon, will you marry me?"

She sucked in a gasp as joyous tears prickled her eyes. "Oh, God, Hawke, do you really have to ask? Yes. Oh, yes."

"John." His gaze searched hers. "My given name is John."

The tears swelled hotter. "I love you, John."

He grinned. "Even though I'm a dominant asshole?"

Alex pounced on him, knocking him onto his back. His medals pricked her breasts as she dove in for the kiss. "Since I'm incredibly kinky -- oh, yeah."

His mouth tasted of mint as his lips moved hungrily against hers. She slid both hands up into his short-cropped hair as his own went to her ass and pulled her astride him. His fingers felt deliciously warm on her spine.

By the time they both came up for air, Hawke's eyes were smoky with passion and growing heat. Alex pushed herself up to straddle him and contemplate the best way to get his uniform off.

Cupping one of her breasts through her camisole, he grinned. "Oh, I remember this. I considered ripping it off you."

Starting work on his intricate gold buttons, she narrowed her eyes. "Lieutenant John Hawke, don't you dare."

A big, warm hand slid under the lace hem and went looking for bare flesh. "I'm going to have to teach you to read Marine command insignia. I'm a captain now. God, I've missed these breasts."

She closed her eyes as his clever fingers did wonderful things to a nipple. "And they've missed you."

"Oh, come on. We'd just made love when the

asshole showed up."

"You mean you'd just banged me up the backside playing Master Bastard."

He winced. "Sorry about that."

"No, you're not. And neither am I." She managed to drag another button from its buttonhole, exposing a tempting sliver of abdominal muscles. "You Marines sure wear a lot of clothes, Captain."

Hawke laughed and reached for one of the hooks holding his tunic neck closed. "Let me help you with that."

"Thank you." She rose off him to stand astride his hips, pulling her camisole over her head. "By the way, I am not making love to you on this cold floor when there's a perfectly good mattress upstairs. Which doesn't crackle, rustle, or sag, unlike the last one we played on."

"Have I mentioned you have the most gorgeous tits I've ever seen?"

"Yeah? Maybe I'll let you kiss them." Alex turned with a teasing roll of her ass. "If you can catch me." She sprinted for the stairs.

Hawke caught her before she got four more steps. She rode up the stairs across his brawny shoulder.

Five minutes later they were naked in her bed, and Hawke was demonstrating exactly how much he'd missed her nipples. Each long, wet stroke of his tongue made her squirm, while the big hand exploring between her thighs sent sweet pleasure sizzling through her body.

For her part, Alex caressed the hard ripples of muscle sheathed in satin skin. Being back in civilization hadn't made him go soft -- in any sense of the word, judging by the warm, thick cock nestled against her hip.

She wrapped her fingers around it and smiled lazily as he gasped.

"You're distracting me," he protested over her nipple, his free hand gently cupping her other breast.

"Good." Alex stroked the length of the bobbing shaft. "I'd hate to think I was losing my touch."

"Noo." His voice sounded distinctly strangled as she brushed her thumb over a bead of pre-cum. "You're definitely in no danger of that."

"Good." She grinned impishly. "'Cause, you know, I was getting worried. I mean, you've been here thirty whole minutes, and you haven't tied me up yet."

Hawke lifted his head. Smoky gray eyes sizzled over his feral smile. "Are you disappointed?"

"Who, me?"

"Alex, love, are we getting bored with foreplay?"

She wriggled under him. "Well, I *am* really, really wet..."

With a low, menacing growl, he reared back onto his haunches between her thighs, grabbed her knees, and spread her wide. She yelped as his thick cock speared into her in one hard thrust.

Hawke grinned down into her startled eyes. "In that case, it has been an awfully long" -- he drove in all the way to the balls --"long" -- pulled out and jammed in again --"*long* time."

Her entire nervous system jolting with each thrust, Alex wrapped her calves around his back. "Tell me about it."

As his massive shaft worked in and out of her creamy sex, she grinned happily. *One thing's for sure -- Mrs. Alexandria Hawke will never, ever be bored.*

Epilogue

They were married a year later, after twelve months of living in glorious, engaged sin. Hangin' Harry gave his daughter away with a proud smile in a church ceremony that was the biggest social event of the year. He hadn't even flinched when Hawke had told him about his father. To the old man's credit, his new son-in-law's status as a war hero seemed to weigh more than the millions he'd inherited from his mythical relative.

He and Virginia were already hinting broadly about their yen for grandchildren.

Hawke and Alex had every intention of obliging them -- and enjoying the process thoroughly.

Chain of Kisses
Angela Knight

For years, Prince Admiral Arles of Tor has been obsessed with Gisel Vanda, who jilted him at the altar. When Arles discovers the lovely runaway is now a mercenary space captain, he captures her, determined to get Gisel out of his system. He soon discovers she's even more intelligent and beautiful than he remembered. Too bad she's also a political liability he can't afford…

Gisel bitterly regrets jilting Arles, and her love for him still burns bright. Even as he tests her with acts of erotic dominance, she sees the opportunity to redeem herself. But with a murderous enemy closing in, can love survive the demands of royalty?

Chapter One

When we walked into the Bolthole, I took one look around… and every instinct I had began to howl. My hand dropped instantly to my beamer. Galon had taught me a smart mercenary listens to her hindbrain if she wants to live long enough to retire. He'd never steered me wrong.

At my side, my security chief frowned, tufted ears flattening as he joined me in scanning the bar. Pinj was a Javat -- two meters of muscle, fangs and claws. His long, lush fur was the color of the pink ryrstone cliffs of his home world, its deep rose a stark contrast to the blue of his enormous eyes. "Where in the Great Dark is everybody? This place is usually crowded ass to elbows."

He was right. The Bolthole was always packed with mercenaries, pirates, and spacers of every species, drinking, arguing, gambling and getting into fights. Yet absolutely no one sat at the softly glowing tables or the winding bar that radiated light over the room. Even the strippers were nowhere to be seen.

"Bolthole," I asked the bar's computer, "what's going on?" I didn't draw my beamer, despite the itch in my gun hand. Quite. Most stations didn't allow you to walk around strapped, but only an idiot went unarmed on Infinity Station.

"Adin Valin leased the bar for the next hour, Captain Bera," Bolthole said in its liquid purr. "He wishes to speak privately with you without risk of eavesdroppers."

Pinj and I exchanged a long look. "How much did he pay for that?" I demanded.

"I'm not authorized to release that information."

Pinj's tail thumped against my booted ankle as he

lashed it restlessly. "Well, at least we know this *keritz* has money to throw around. May he be equally generous with us."

"Maybe." I frowned, carefully cultivated mercenary paranoia lifting the hair on the back of my neck. If I'd brought anyone but Pinj along on this meet, I'd give serious thought to hitting my thrusters.

Luckily, the Javat was a match for anything in this part of the galaxy, up to and including a Fafnarian warrior. I'd once seen him take out a pirate in full boarding armor barehanded.

Not that I was exactly helpless. Galon had made sure of that over the decade he'd spent turning me into the warrior I'd become. I'd needed every minute of that training as I'd captained the *Valkyrie's Quest* for the past two years. That had included some ugly ship-to-ship combat and boarding actions.

And then there was the Fafnarian I'd killed to avenge Galon's death… A too-familiar stab of pain sliced me at the thought, and I shoved the dark memory away.

I'm not a pampered princess anymore. There was some solace in that anyway, though it was little comfort when I slept alone in the bed I'd shared with my captain for the five years we'd been lovers.

After he'd saved me from my own poor decisions twelve years ago, Galon became my protector and my teacher. Finally his feelings for me became anything but fatherly, though my own emotions for him had never run as deep. I'd always regretted that, but my heart belonged to another man, and I couldn't seem to get it back.

I dragged myself out of what threatened to become my habitual spiral into guilt and regret. I needed to concentrate on getting this job. We were running low on funds, and operating a mercenary company wasn't cheap. Neither was keeping the *Valkyrie's Quest* and her crew supplied with fuel, oxygen, and food. Our last contract had paid well, but it had ended six months ago, and our cushion was getting thin.

So despite my doubts, I led Pinj to a table with a good view of the door and sat down with my back to the wall. Instead of taking the seat beside me, my security chief moved to stand just behind my left shoulder, where he proceeded to loom. I didn't protest. Between the seven-centimeter claws and the mouthful of very sharp teeth, Javats made intimidating bodyguards.

"Would you care for your usual?" Bolthole asked.

"No." I wanted to keep my head clear. "I will take a cup of ch..." Before I could get the rest out of my mouth, my communication implant blared in my skull so loudly I almost jumped.

"Captain, we've got a problem." Executive officer Gayne Chrys sounded as cool and controlled as always, but there was a note of tension in her voice that made my gut clench. *"Three Torrean warships have just dropped out of Superlight surrounding us. They've powered weapons up."*

Pinj swore a stream of impressive Javat curses, his blue eyes wide, his pupils pinpricks. I froze, my eyes flying wide. Torreans? *Odin's Blind Eye*! *"What registry?"*

*"*Baldur's Vengeance, Yggdrassil *and* Mjölnir.*"*

My heart began to pound in long, furious lunges as an explosion of crazy joy took me by surprise. Mjölnir was Arles's ship! *He's come for me*!

Yes, and whatever he's after, it's nothing good, I told my inner idiot princess. *"We're on our way,"* I said to my XO, rising from the table.

"What shall I tell Adin Valin?" Bolthole asked as we strode toward the door.

"Nothing," I snarled back. "It was a Loki-cursed trap."

"We've got to get to the shuttle and pray Arles doesn't blast us to hell before we reach the ship," I told Pinj.

The Javat's ears pricked as he stared at me. "Who the Great Dark is Arles?"

"Captain of the *Mjölnir*." Among many, many other things.

His nostrils flared, scenting me as we rounded the Bolthole's entry door. "What did you do to *him*?"

"To start with," growled a low, deadly voice, "she jilted me at the altar and made me a laughing stock to the Empire."

I jerked to a stop a heartbeat before I could slam nose-first into an armored chest. Torrean ceremonial armor, intricately engraved with the coat of arms of the Royal House of Tor. Nobody wore that armor but the prince himself.

Arles.

My gaze flew upward, but his helmet visor was polarized, and I couldn't see his face.

A clawed hand clamped around my upper arm, but before Pinj could snatch me away, the five armored men around the prince had their weapons pointed at the Javat's head. I heard their beamers whine, powering up.

"Don't shoot!" I yelled, throwing my hands up.

"Captain, let's get the fuck out of --"

"You're not going anywhere," Arles told me coldly. "Except with me. Because otherwise, that ship of yours is going to be a ball of ionized gas. I *will* order it fired upon."

I licked my dry lips. "That's not necessary."

"That depends on you. Don't test me, Gisel."

"Gisel?" Pinj said, staring from my face to Arles's menacing faceplate. "You've got the wrong woman. Her name is Zel Bera."

"No, it's not," Arles said. "Join the legion she's lied to, Javat."

"Let him go," I told the prince in a low voice. "Let *Valkyrie* go. I'll come with you."

"Do you honestly think you're in any position to negotiate?"

"They don't deserve to die, Arles. Your quarrel is with me."

"It certainly is."

"Captain..." Pinj gathered himself, rage flaring in those blue eyes. I knew he was ready to fight for me, despite the fact that he had no chance at all against seven Torean warriors in combat armor. He knew it too, but he'd die trying. He was just that loyal.

"Stay out of this, Pinj," I snapped.

"But --"

"I'm going home. It's time." I jerked away from my security chief and gave Arles a look that silently pleaded with him not to kill those I cared about.

He gave me a very slight, very cold nod.

Working fast, I commed the ship's computer to give it my instructions, then reached out to my XO. *"Gayne, I'll be returning to my home world with Captain Arles of Tor. He's promised not to fire on the* Valkyrie, *so you should be safe. I've transferred the captaincy over to you, along with the balance of our funds. You'll need to find a contract as soon as possible. The Adin Valin contract... fell through."*

"Wait, what? Captain, what in the Great Dark are you

doing?"

"Something I should have done a long time ago," I said. *"Good luck, Captain."*

"But Zel --"

"I'm sorry. You've been a good friend." Blinking my stinging eyes, I cut communications, unable to bear it any longer. Avoiding Pinj's bewildered stare, I turned to Arles, who gestured me ahead of him with a mocking little wave. I strode past him, head high.

At least he had the sensitivity to wait to put me in chains until we were out of Pinj's sight.

* * *

I gave the manacle on my right arm a restless tug, and it responded with a metallic chime. I couldn't see a damn thing. A blindfold bit into my temples, wrapping me in sensual, intimate darkness.

The lack of vision only made me more aware of him -- his scent, that faint tang of spice and masculinity, the heat of his big body standing just to the left of the bunk he'd chained me to, the slight rasp of his breathing. I had always been acutely aware of Prince Arles of Tor, once my intended, now my captor.

The reason I could never love Galon.

The bed dipped under his weight as he sat down beside me. I quivered like an animal, imagining his nudity. The way he'd looked that night a dozen years before was branded on my memory.

Arles's broad back had flexed as he'd used the light whip, the perfect, tanned hemispheres of his bare ass working in concert with the leap of thigh muscles and the snap of brawny arms.

The girl had squirmed and sighed every time he hit her. Even as young as I'd been, I'd known she loved it. The smell of sex hung in the air like some kind of musky, exotic spice.

Arles touched my nipple, brushing calloused fingertips over the hard nubbin. Just once, but I still caught my breath at the liquid heat that rushed through me.

"Sensitive little breasts." His voice rumbled in the intimate darkness of my blindfold. "I wonder how you'll taste. Shall I find out?"

Saliva flooded my mouth, and I swallowed. I didn't answer.

"I asked you a question." His fingers closed over my flesh in a pinch carefully calibrated to give more pleasure than pain. Yet the potential sting floated just beneath the delight like a dark promise. "I want an answer. Shall I taste you?"

"You'll do as you please. You always do."

"True." He twisted, released, flicked the nipple back and forth, sending warm delight lapping along my nerves. "But a show of submission on your part might appease me."

"I rather doubt it."

"But can you afford to take the chance?" Another hot pinch, this one with a hint of sting. Perversely, I felt heat flood my belly. "My reputation is not exaggerated."

"I never thought it was."

"Perhaps a silk flogger." He brushed his hand over the sensitive flesh of my left breast, gave me a caressing squeeze. "Right across these pretty tits. I would enjoy watching you dance."

"I've heard that of you." I tried for a tone of mild contempt, but my voice sounded too high, too breathless. I silently cursed myself. I could usually act more skillfully for my enemies.

Unfortunately, I'd never seen Arles as a foe. Even now, bound and naked, I remembered the thoughtful boy who'd first taught me strategy over endless games of Conquest.

The prince was even more skilled now, a conqueror of two worlds who'd driven the Fafnar from Torrean space with his ruthless, brilliant tactics. When he'd captured me, I'd known I was in trouble.

I wasn't really surprised, though. I'd known the prince would eventually demand a reckoning; my actions had done too much damage to his reputation. Anybody who watched the news vids knew that.

Now Arles traced one finger down my torso, dipped suggestively into my navel, and paused at the neatly trimmed edge of my bush. I managed not to squirm. "I have a suspicion you're wet," he said, his voice dark and low. "Are you? Do I arouse you, Gisel?" He laughed. "Odin knows you've made me hard and hot."

His fingers dipped between my spread thighs. Both of us groaned at the slick, tight flesh he found.

"Ripe," Arles murmured. "Ripe as a peachango. Ready for my cock. Is that what you want, Gisel?"

"Do you care what I want?"

"Not really." I could almost feel his purring laughter, soft as fur draped over cold steel. "I care what *I* want. And what I want is to taste you, beat your sweet little ass, and grind my cock deep in that tight little cunt. Which is exactly what I'm going to do."

His mouth covered my nipple in a breath-stealing rush. Sensation exploded across my nerves -- the gorgeous rake of his teeth over the hard tip, the wet heat of his tongue sweeping circles over jutting flesh, his lips tightening in a hard, drawing suction. I gasped. My chains rattled, gold links ringing as I writhed in helpless lust.

Arles growled back, his voice rough and male as

he settled over me like a mantle of hard muscle and warm skin. His scent flooded my head, dark with alien spice and masculine musk. Instinctively, I tried to curl my arms around his strong back, but my chains pulled tight. I was still helplessly spread-eagled beneath him.

"Mine," he rumbled, lifting his head from my breast. "At last."

And he levered up to kiss me.

It was a burning kiss, a devouring kiss, all tongue and thrust and bite. I moaned, losing myself in his taste as I arched into his tensile brawn. But even as I savored his ferocious sexuality, some part of me squirmed in shame. My mother had taught us that craving a man's dominance was weak. We were princesses, born to rule, not submit.

But as the prince kissed me like a conqueror, I realized I did not care. The queen's teachings had cost me my world, my honor, and the man I loved. I was tired of running from Arles of Tor. There was no point. He had me.

He'd always had me.

By the time he broke the kiss, both of us were panting. I could feel his cock against my belly like a length of pipe, velvet over iron. "I believe I owe you a spanking," he murmured in my ear, his breath tickling my skin.

"Somehow I don't remember that particular debt."

Arles gave my earlobe a retaliatory nip, then levered off my spread-eagled nudity. Something clicked, and my chains fell lax with a soft rattle. Despite my blindfold, I tried to bolt from the bed.

The prince snaked an arm around my waist, spun me around, and pushed me back down. My stomach hit hard thighs, and I felt a cool draft across my bare ass. I twisted, driving an elbow at his face. Arles jerked aside, avoiding the blow.

Before I could launch another attack, he grabbed my flying fist in one hand, captured the other wrist, and dragged them both behind my back. The manacles' magnetic fields engaged, locking them in place. The chains draped down over my hip, the links cool against my hot skin -- leaving me helpless across Prince Arles's knees, just as I'd been in my most searing fantasies.

I tried to rear onto my feet, but he arrested my surges with a hand between my shoulder blades, pinning me like a toddler.

It was said the royalty of Tor had been gene-sculpted for combat, creating warriors who were faster, stronger, and smarter than any commoner. As I struggled against his iron hold, I began to believe the rumors. He could crush me if he chose.

"Now," Arles said, not even winded. The bastard. "Let's see what shade of pink this pretty ass turns." He brought his palm down on my butt with a loud *smack*. I swallowed my yelp.

Another smack as his hard hand met my soft backside, then another and another. The flesh heated with each swat. "Arles, you son of a bitch!" I kicked at him, trying to lever off his lap.

"That's no way to talk about my mother," he said mildly, controlling my struggles with no effort at all. The smacks came faster, igniting my ass into a bonfire blaze as I kicked and cursed.

Despite my curses, heat burned deep in my juicy pussy. Odin's Blind Eye, I wanted him. Each stinging swat only increased the craving.

"Do you have any idea of the scandal you brought down on both our Houses, you spoiled little brat?" Arles growled between blows. I realized rage steamed beneath his taunting dominance. "You spat on all the Torrean warriors who fought and died to protect your wretched little world from the Fafnar." *Swat! Swat*! "My people battled the lizards for years to drive them from Swanhilde space, and how did you reward us?" *Swat, swat swat*! "You jilted me at the altar and made a mockery of the treaty between our worlds." *Swat! Swat! Swat*! "My brother had to marry that little whore sister of yours to salvage the treaty, and she's led him a merry dance since. And all this time, I didn't know if you were alive or dead!"

That last was followed by a smack so hard, it was all I could do not to scream. My eyes stung, and I blinked furiously, determined that the captain of the *Valkyrie's Quest* would not cry.

Worse still, every accusation carried a shameful cargo of truth. I *had* betrayed him and my own people. I *had* run away. And for what? Cowardice. And not even fear of him, but fear of my own desire for him. What a stupid waste. "*I am sorry*!" I blurted, meaning every syllable. "Odin's eye, I'm sorry!"

"We'll see, won't we?" He freed my wrists and dumped me on his bunk, then stripped the blindfold from my eyes. As he straightened over me, I blinked my vision clear -- and gaped up at him in helpless lust. *Gods, he's grown more beautiful.*

He looked like one of those ancient Earth statues given life as he stood there with his big, bare feet braced. Muscle worked over his body in rolling curves, veins snaking along massive biceps as corded tendons flexed. His shoulders looked as wide as a wall compared to his tight waist and long, strong, warrior's legs.

But it was his face that riveted my gaze.

Arles's eyes were the burning green of jungle

leaves backlit by the sun, made even more striking by the brilliant gold sunburst around his pupils. He stared at me, his nostrils flared like a hunting beast's, as though he drank my scent from the air. His cheekbones rose in chiseled juts, framing his roman nose and sweeping down to the hard angle of his broad jaw. His mouth was drawn tight with temper, but I remembered the lush sensuality of those lips. I'd stared at them for hours as a girl, dreaming of virgin kisses.

Blue hair fell around his shoulders, iridescent with flashes of green and purple, its inhuman brilliance the mark of his gene-sculpted royal blood. Its silken length led the eye to the matching cloud of iridescent azure curls that spread across his broad chest, narrowing to a thin trail snaking south over his tight abdomen.

Right to his cock.

The thick staff angled upward with the force of his lust, flushed hot red, balls drawn tight, fat plum head gemmed with a crystalline bead of pre-cum.

"Beautiful," Arles rumbled, his gaze flicking from my face to my nipples, down to my sex, my legs. "Damn you, you're even more beautiful." His eyes narrowed, green as a leopard's glowing in the dark. "You're going to pay for it all, Gisel. Everything you've done to the House of Tor you'll come to rue under my hand."

I stared up at him, feeling suspended in a moment of raw lust as thick and hot and bright as sun-warmed honey. "Yes," I croaked, my lips dry. "Let me pay my debt."

His upper lip pulled back, flashing teeth in a soundless growl, and he fell on me. Big hands jerked my legs wide. He paused just long enough to position his cock between my pussy's slick lips. Then he impaled me in a single, furious thrust, forcing my tight, wet flesh to stretch wide around his ruthless shaft. Stuffed halfway to the throat, I yowled out my pain and delight.

Arles froze. "Did I hurt you?"

"No," I gasped. "No, I want more!"

His grin twisted, eyes going hot and narrow. "*Take* more, then." Bracing one hand on the mattress, Arles wrapped the other around my ass, lifting me into his thrusts. He filled me as Galon never had, a searing invasion that ignited every nerve in my cunt. As he rolled that muscular ass, I tossed back my head and howled. Every entry rode the edge of pain, but it was followed by slick, gliding pleasure.

So I wrapped my legs around his waist and bucked into his thrusts, loving the furious ride, needing it, craving it. Craving *him*. "Arles! Odin's eye, I will pay as you please. Just forgive me."

"Not in this life," he growled, ramming his cock so deep I shouted in genuine pain.

The prince rumbled something that sounded like an aborted apology and moderated his strokes. I convulsed, coming in waves, ecstasy replacing the pain to blaze up my spine like a shooting star.

"Odin's balls!" Tendons worked in Arles's powerful throat as he threw back his head and rammed deep. His cock jolted inside me, shooting streams of thick heat into my pussy.

I screamed, drowning in another wave of sumptuous, pulsing orgasm. But even as I writhed, I wondered if Arles meant what he'd said -- that he'd never forgive me.

I craved that forgiveness anyway.

* * *

Twenty members of Arles's crew sat around the octagonal serving tables in the *Mjölnir*'s mess. As we walked in, their voices filled the room with a cheerful babble of jokes, tech talk, and the usual playful taunts, reminding me of happier days aboard the *Valkyrie's Quest*.

But as they spotted Arles leading me toward the officer's table, all conversation died away. Men and women alike turned to stare.

No wonder. A length of gold chain led from my jeweled collar to the prince's big hand, and manacles bound my wrists. My bonds were as finely crafted and gem-studded as any jewelry I'd ever worn, but no one would mistake them for anything but symbols of my sexual captivity.

I lifted my chin and met the curious gazes, freezing my expression into one of cool disdain. I might wear chains, I might have lost everything I'd built over a dozen years, but I was still a royal princess of Swanhilde.

Still, the walk to the captain's table stung. Women smirked and men leered at the nipples visible through my filmy thrall tunic. One spacer made a comment that triggered barks of crude laughter.

My hands curled into fists. I wanted to rage at them, but I muzzled my fury and reminded myself of my bargain with Arles. I owed him this. And he had let my crew live.

Even as I drew my shoulders back and stiffened my spine, eyes widened all across the room. Everyone promptly found something else to look at. The snap of heads turning to gaze elsewhere looked almost synchronized. *What the Great Dark...*?

Which was when I noticed the tension in Arles's broad shoulders and his white-knuckled grip on my leash. I couldn't see his expression -- I walked at his heels -- yet I could almost feel the radiating heat of his anger directed, for once, at someone other than me.

I stared at his stiff spine in speculation. Perhaps he was simply a jealous man, yet some naive part of me hoped he'd felt my shame and silently defended me with a glare.

Ridiculous thought. Why would he care? Especially given that shaming me was obviously the intention behind the sex-thrall tunic and chains.

But as I trailed him across the gleaming faux marble floor to the table reserved for senior officers, I remembered the boy I'd loved. Arles had been an idealist then, devoted to his father's vision of imperial honor and responsibility.

I'd been eight years old the summer my mother had hand-fasted me to Prince Arles. Even then, the tall, handsome fifteen-year-old had fascinated me. He'd been kind, showing me the model starcraft he'd built, even teaching me to fly the little toy around the palace.

I'd proceeded to break one of my mother's priceless Elderkind vases with a particularly ill-aimed dive. To my astonishment, Arles told our parents he was to blame. Though he suffered his mortified father's thundering wrath, he didn't reveal I was the true culprit.

I'd been deeply grateful. Queen Zerelda expected her daughters to be worthy representatives of our royal House. Had Arles not claimed responsibility, Mother would have ordered the captain of the Royal Guard to flog me with his sword belt. It would not have been the first time, nor the last.

From then on, I'd worshipped my prince. And that was how I thought of him -- *My Prince,* as though he were a hero from some ancient tale.

We spent hours together in the years that followed, arguing ancient battles and plotting wild strategies to defeat the Fafnar. I came to adore Arles with all the passion in my young heart. No wonder Galon hadn't been able to dislodge him.

But Arles was no longer that boy, as I was no longer the foolish girl trembling before her mother's anger. It was past time I took responsibility for my sins.

I had indeed shamed the royal House of Vanda and voided the treaty that had been in place since our parents had hand-fasted us when I was a child. It was a good thing Emperor Ragnar had not abandoned Swanhilde to its fate, or the Fafnar would have enslaved my people and wiped out my royal House. They'd done as much on the other worlds they'd preyed upon.

We'd have had no hope of defending ourselves. Swanhilde's people were artisans and poets, farmers and philosophers. The Torreans, on the other hand, were the finest warriors in human space, which was why my mother had sought the treaty with Emperor Ragnar to begin with.

My stomach clenched as I considered the fate I'd almost brought down on my world. *I deserve anything Arles wants to do to me.*

The prince sat down at the server and waved me to the high-backed seat next to his. I settled into the chair, feeling its warm, dark blue padding shift and move around me until it cuddled my body like a living thing. I glanced over the room, lifting my brows. Every seat in the mess was of the same expensive type. "You pamper your crew, Captain."

He shrugged. "Small comforts are the brick and mortar of crew loyalty. My people are well paid, and I treat them with respect. In return, they never hesitate to follow me wherever I lead." Arles grimaced.

"Including more than one brawl with the lizards."

"That couldn't have been much fun." Fafnarian warriors are built like biped tanks, more than two and a half meters tall, with armored black hides and claws like daggers. "I've had a scuffle or two with them myself. I killed one, but I damned near bled to death doing it."

Arles's brows raised. I doubted he believed me. "What possessed you to even make the attempt?"

I shrugged. "He'd killed my… captain, Galon. I was…" So blind with rage and grief I went after the reptilian fucker with a quark-splitter axe. "It was a wonder I lived through the fight at all. The captain has been dead two years now, but I still miss him."

Green eyes narrowed in a flicker of jealousy before the expression vanished from his face. His gaze went cool as he eyed me, analyzing, studying me as if he saw far more than I wanted him to. With his sensor implants, he probably did. Finally, he nodded shortly and turned his attention to the tabletop menu display.

I watched his clever fingers tap meal choices for both of us. I was not surprised he didn't ask my preferences. I was his thrall, not a guest, and he wanted to make sure I knew it.

While we waited for the server to produce our plates, the prince propped his elbows on the table and studied me. I decided it was time to own up to my mistakes.

"I was a stupid girl twelve years ago, Arles." I had to force my gaze not to drop. "I know you may not believe me, but I've rued my flight every day since. It was cowardly, and I was not raised to be a coward. I have spent the last dozen years trying to become a woman who could meet her own eyes in the mirror."

Arles bared even white teeth, not sympathetic in

the least. "While my House endured the shit-storm of rumor you left behind -- rumors my enemies used against me to erode my reputation and stain my honor."

I swallowed. "Yes, I've seen the news vids." The galactic gossip coverage had been brutal. Reporters brought up my jilting him in every story about his victories.

"And we won't even mention your sister's antics once she became my brother's wife." The prince grimaced. "Had I not redeemed myself in the Fafnar war, the Torean nobility would have refused to acknowledge me as my father's heir. You damned near wrecked my career before it even began."

"I know." I blew out a breath. "And I regret that."

"Meals are served," the table announced before I could say any more. Panels in its gleaming surface opened, and the server lifted our plates into place.

I picked up my fork, only to put it down again, unable to eat for the tension knotting my belly. "I wish there was a way to atone for my actions."

"There is." Arles studied me with a gambler's cool calculation. "My tour of duty here is done. I'm returning to Tor. If you truly mean to make up for your transgressions, serve as my thrall until I find a wife."

I gaped at him. It was one thing to parade around his ship on a leash, playing sex games. To do so on Tor, where the news services would beam every juicy detail to Swanhilde… "But my mother…"

"Yes, I imagine it will be quite the scandal. A Swanhilde princess in bondage to her former betrothed." Another woman might have mistaken the nasty curve of his mouth for a smile. "Fortunately, you've seen to it that I'm inured to scandal. You, however, will experience the same depths of shame I knew when you jilted me before the whole of my father's empire."

Outrage shot through me, and I almost told him exactly what I thought of his offer. But even as I opened my mouth, I saw the cynical glint in his eyes.

So I shut my teeth, sat back in my seat, and wrestled my anger until I could make my own calculations. Galon had taught me to read an opponent's intentions, and I knew when I was being played. "And if I refuse?"

"Then I fuck you for a week, punish you as it suits me, and set you free. You'll go back to your ship and hide from your mother and your people while you tell yourself you're not a coward." Arles shrugged his broad shoulders. "Your choice, Gisel. Just how sorry are you?"

He expects me to refuse.

And if I did, my life would proceed just as he predicted. I had built a comfortable identity as Captain Zel Bera, fighting other people's wars, courting death for money, just as my mentor had. Very good money, true, but still, only money. And one day I would lose -- and die, just as Galon had.

It was not as if I defended my world and people, as Arles did. I'd studied his spectacular battles with the Fafnar, and I knew he'd fought with brilliance and guts.

If I went to Tor with him, I could finally face my mother and confront my wretched sister. I'd long since realized Isa had manipulated me into running, probably intending to wed Arles herself so that she could one day be Empress of Tor. Arles, being no fool, had wanted nothing to do with her, and she'd ended up with his brother. Jarrat was a handsome, witty man, but he was not the heir. Isa must have been beside herself with rage at the way her plans had backfired.

While I set all that to rights, I could atone to the boy Arles had once been. My young paladin.

"I accept."

Arles's eyes widened in astonishment, only to narrow as his lips parted in a snarl.

Here it comes, I thought.

Chapter Two

The field shackles held me a foot off the ground, arms and legs spread helplessly wide in mid air. Hanging by my wrists and ankles should have been murderously painful, but the shackles' null-grav field reduced my weight until the strain was no more than mildly uncomfortable.

"So how do you like our recreational facilities?" Arles drawled, all lazy, wicked humor. His mood had improved since he'd strung me up.

"You Torreans have an interesting concept of recreation." I eyed the surrounding chamber with a combination of dread and arousal.

A varied selection of whips, clamps, and dildos occupied niches in the bulkheads, along with assorted toys I couldn't identify despite my extensive spacer's education in kink. Larger devices stood around the room, constructed of leather straps and gleaming rods that curved in suggestive shapes, obviously engineered for bondage.

As if to complete the dungeon effect, the walls and floor appeared to be built of irregular black stone blocks. Torches clamped to the walls provided the only illumination, the flames casting sinister shadows.

I realized much of the scene must be a three-dimensional projection over the real chamber. "Isn't this supposed to be a military vessel?" I curled my lip to disguise my nervous excitement behind a show of contempt. "How the hell does bondage play encourage order and discipline?"

"Torreans enjoy erotic games." Arles paced around me, studying my nudity with hooded interest. "And as I said, I like to oblige my crew with the... simpler things."

"Especially since you get to reap the benefits."

"Of course." He stepped in close to cup one of my bare breasts. His long fingers felt deliciously warm as he stroked and weighed my flesh, eyeing the full curves like a connoisseur. "And what lovely benefits they are."

"Thank you -- I think."

"Oh, don't thank me." Arles leaned in, and I caught my breath. His mouth closed over my nipple, sucking hard, licking and nibbling and tugging until the glittering pleasure made me want to writhe in my bonds. I controlled the impulse, but it took every ounce of discipline I had.

At last he released his erotic hold to smirk into my eyes. "You're going to wish you were a hag by the time I'm done with you."

Arles gave my nipple a teasing flick with his tongue, then leaned back to observe its stiff, rosy jut. His hand lifted, holding a small golden object studded with emeralds. Before I could ask what it was, he attached it to my nipple, and the thing promptly clamped down so hard, I swore in startled pain.

Meeting my gaze, Arles grinned like a wolf. "Does it hurt, darling?"

"Yes, you bastard!" The clamp seemed to be chewing now, its gemstone jaws opening and closing on the aching pink peak. Every bite sent fire radiating through my chest until I could only speak through gritted teeth. "When I get down from here, we'll see how *you* like wearing them... on your balls."

"Now that's no way for a thrall to talk." He produced another clamp and let its jaws snap closed on the other stiff, ruddy nipple. Smiling like a devil, he stepped back to watch his little toys gnaw.

Odin's Blind Eye, they stung! Fire blazed a trail

along my nerves, and I ground my teeth against a shout. Just before my control shattered, the pain vanished, replaced by a dark, radiating delight. I arched in surprise as each nipple pulsed in time to my racing heartbeat. "Gods! What the Dark is that?"

"The clamps produce a field that stimulates the pleasure receptors." Arles flashed his teeth at me. "And a few others. I'm sure you can guess which ones."

The left clamp began to sting again, just as the right produced a sweet throbbing. They started alternating, first torturing my tits, then pleasuring them like a man's wicked mouth. The waves of sensation intensified until I twisted in the air, panting and tugging at my bonds. Arles watched my helpless reaction, his powerful arms crossed as he rocked back on one booted heel.

I've got to regain control, I thought desperately. *I can't make this too easy for him. I have to hold his interest, or he'll grow bored.* Arles had a reputation of going through mistresses like canapés.

I stared at him, struggling to mask my expression. He'd stripped off his blue uniform jacket, which left him in black trousers and gleaming armored boots that rose above the knee. Judging from the smirk he gave me when he noticed my besotted gaze, he knew I loved every ripple of his chest, every gleaming blue strand of his shoulder-length hair.

He turned his back and sauntered to a selection of whips hanging from the wall. The play of muscle rolling from his shoulders to his tight waist so enthralled me, I didn't realize what he was doing until he turned with a light, long-tailed whip in his hand.

I drew in an alarmed breath. He grinned at me and gave the whip an echoing *snap*. I'd been fantasizing about this moment for a decade. Heat clenched in my belly, followed by a stab of cold fear. "Bastard," I breathed.

"Bitch." He strolled toward me, letting the whip trail on the floor at his heels. I watched in helpless fascination as he lifted it to strike.

Arles paused, staring into eyes I suspected had gone wide and wild. "Are you sure you want to be my thrall, Gisel? Wouldn't you rather go back to the *Valkyrie's Quest*? My agents tell me you've become a respected mercenary. Why would you give that up to be my slave?"

I swallowed. "I'm tired of hiding. I am a princess of Swanhilde, and I've shamed my blood long enough. I want my honor back." *I want* you *back.*

And there was the truth of it, naked and stark in my brain. I still loved Arles. I wanted him. I would suffer any punishment he chose if it meant his forgiveness.

Lifting my chin, I stared into his jungle cat eyes. I didn't flinch as he swung the whip.

The lash hit me right across my breasts, adding a hot sting to the throb of the clamps. I sucked in a breath, but I didn't scream. The whip was lighter than it looked, black silk rather than leather. Which didn't mean it wouldn't hurt, especially if he put that gene-sculpted strength into it.

Arles gave me a demon's smile, his green eyes taking on a hot glitter as he watched the pink stripe rise across my breasts. "Niiiiice," he purred, and began to prowl around me, studying my body as I hung helpless in the air.

Heat pooled low in my belly as my sex tightened and grew wet. Gods, I wanted his cock. I wanted him to fuck me, ached to feel him pound his hips into the cradle of mine.

The click of his boots stopped right behind me. A quiver of helpless anticipation rolled over me, and I closed my eyes, fighting not to pant. Arles stepped in so close I could feel his breath on my ear. "I love your ass." He cupped one cheek in his long, warm fingers, squeezed, stroked. "It's so round and tight and perfect. I want to fuck it."

The tip of his tongue flicked out to caress the curve of my ear, and I jerked in surprise. He chuckled and caught my earlobe in his teeth for a gentle bite. Goose bumps rose on my arms.

He drew away, only an inch or so. "Ever taken it up the ass, Gisel?"

"*No…*" I bit my lip. A bit too much moan in that. *Control. Control it, damn it. Don't give him too much too fast. Fight him, or he'll get bored.*

"I'll wager you're tight as a miser's fist." Arles reached under my ass, seeking the mouth of my pussy. He pushed a finger in deep and growled in arousal, the sound rumbling in my ear. "Thor's balls, you're wet. You do like this, don't you?"

I said nothing. The clamps still worked their evil sorcery on my aching tits. Arles pumped the finger in my sex, sliding between slick, swollen lips, each stroke sending another jolt of pleasure up my spine. His thumb circled my clit, adding to the heat that boiled in my veins. I was surprised I didn't steam.

"I asked you a question, thrall." His voice had gone icy. "Answer me. *Do you like this*?"

My teeth sank harder in my lower lip, and I braced in the shackles. His boots clicked on the stone floor as he stepped back, getting room to swing.

The lash cut a furrow of bright pain across my shoulder blades. I clenched my teeth and managed not to scream.

"Answer me!" he snapped, and struck again, this time cutting across my ass.

"Fuck you!"

"Yes, you will, but not yet." Another blazing blow. Despite the burn, I knew he'd pulled his stroke. "You want this, don't you?" Another blow, then another, and another, as the clamps shot pleasure through the pain in sweet little darts. "*Do you want this*?"

"Yes!" I yowled. The words burst from me before I could clamp my teeth shut. "I saw you with Rilla the night before our wedding. I saw you beat her, watched her dance under your whip. You were supposed to marry *me* the next day! I should have hated you. Instead I've dreamed of that night for years. *I want this*!"

The stinging blows halted. "Who the Dark is Rilla?" He sounded honestly confused.

I hung there limp, panting. I knew better, but I told him the truth anyway. I'd lied enough, especially to him. Especially to myself. "One of Isa's retinue. A blonde. Big tits."

"Are you talking about the little slut who drugged me?"

"She drugged you?" I frowned. I hadn't known that.

"She served me wine laced with some Swanhilde aphrodisiac. I realized what was happening, lost my temper and beat her ass for it. But I didn't take her. I wanted *you*." Arles stalked around me to study my face. "You *saw* that?"

"There was a spy chamber next door to your bedroom," I told him. "Isa and I watched you flog her and fuck her with the butt of the whip."

His eyes widened with astonished realization. "No

wonder you took to your heels. Rilla was an experienced submissive, Gisel, and I knew it. I would never have treated a seventeen-year-old girl that way. Particularly not *you*."

"But Isa said…" Even as the words came out of my mouth, I winced at my own stupidity.

"Isa's a manipulative bitch," Arles said, impatient. "You have to sift everything she says like rose flour to pick out the lies." His green eyes narrowed thoughtfully. "But you were barely more than a child. Of course you believed her." He turned away, angrily snapping the whip against the floor. The crack echoed from bulkhead to bulkhead like a lightning strike. "All of this, everything that happened, all the scandal. All because of that spoiled little bitch. And I fell for it."

Hope bloomed in me for the first time in years, unfurling giddy petals in my mind. It made me stupid. "I love you, Arles. I've loved you from the time I was eight years old."

Arles froze, his shoulders tensing until they were as rigid as marble. He pivoted to face me. His eyes blazed with incandescent green rage in his white face. "*I don't care*."

"But you said…"

"*Why* you ran is irrelevant. You're political poison now, Gisel. For the past decade, you've been the subject of countless rumors and foul jokes -- with me the punch line of every one. Do you really think I'd be stupid enough to marry you now? Every enemy I have would dredge up every old rumor to paint me a fool. They'd seize my father's throne, put a puppet in my place, and siphon the Empire's wealth into their own pockets. I will *not* be replaced by thieves and liars."

I stared at him, stricken, sick. "I'd never have run had I known you'd pay such a cost."

"I believe you, but it doesn't matter." Arles stalked closer until he could glare into my face. I controlled the impulse to shrink away. "I am to rule an empire, and you made me look like a witless, love-struck dupe. Every bloody battle I fought to reconstruct my reputation would be wasted if I married you now. The warriors who fell in my service would have died for *nothing*. The only way I can spike my foes' guns is to parade you before all of Tor on a leash." He bared his teeth in a savage, tortured grimace. "You can never be anything to me but a sex-thrall."

* * *

I stared at Arles. To my horror, my eyes began to sting. I ground my teeth and fought for control, but a tear slid down one cheek, painting a cold, wet trail on my hot skin. "*I am sorry*!"

Arles leaned close enough to kiss. "Not as sorry as you'll be when we reach Tor."

Hot-eyed with rage, the prince freed me from the field restraints and hauled me across the chamber to one of the bondage devices. He ordered me to kneel on the padded bench and started buckling me in, thighs spread wide, ass thrust out, arms extended out front and locked in restraint bands.

Sweating, I listened to his boot heels click on the deck as he stalked away. Over my shoulder, I caught sight of him selecting a small jar from one of the wall niches. I quickly jerked my gaze away as he headed toward me again, dipping his fingers in the jar as he came. My sex clenched and heated in nervous arousal. I knew what was coming next, and it was going to hurt.

I was right.

"Now," Arles rumbled, his green eyes hot. "Let's see how tight this tempting little ass really is."

I felt his oiled fingers between my helplessly spread thighs, seeking the tight pucker of my asshole. He pushed, sinking the finger deep. I stiffened at the alien sensation of his entry, then caught my breath at the dark pleasure as he withdrew.

He laughed in a low, masculine growl of excitement. "If I didn't know better, I'd swear you're a virgin."

"I am," I confessed on a gasp. He was using two fingers now, probing ruthlessly deep. My channel fought the entry, and I tried to release the clamping muscles. Resisting would only make it worse. Besides, I had no real desire to fight him. Shamed excitement flooded me as his ruthless fingers greased my ass.

"You mean Galon never got around to using this little hole?" His voice held an edge like a quark-splitter's blade. "I'd have thought you two would have been more adventurous than that."

I froze, silently cursing myself for letting him catch me off guard. Of course Arles knew about Galon. The spies of Tor were legendary for their ability to penetrate any security, learn any secret. Once they'd learned my new identity, they'd have ferreted out every detail of my life. Including my relationship with Galon.

His thumb joined the fingers in my ass, stretching me ruthlessly. "I asked you a question. Did Galon ever use you like this?"

"No," I gasped, shivering at the ribbon of exotic pleasure threaded through the pain. "He feared hurting me."

Arles laughed in a short, humorless bark, and pulled his hand away. "I have no such fear."

I looked back over my shoulder to see him open his uniform fly and free his rigid cock. He started stroking the thick lube over his shaft, staring at my ass with predatory heat. I licked my dry lips. He looked up, caught my gaze, and grinned like a wolf as he sauntered closer. The smooth, thick head of his cock brushed my anus. He leaned in and began to push.

The entry was slow and searing as his big shaft drilled relentlessly deep, forcing the tight, tender flesh to spread for his pleasure. "Oh, yes," Arles growled through set teeth, "I think you just may have the tightest ass I've ever fucked."

"Bastard," I gasped.

"Darling, you have no idea." He worked in another stinging, ferocious centimeter. "But you will. Before I'm done with you, you'll know exactly what I'm capable of."

Clenching my fists, I fought him, clamping down hard. I knew better, but my body had other ideas. It didn't care for his invasion.

"Ooooh, yes," Arles growled. "That's it. Tighten up. You can't keep me out, but it feels so sweet when you try."

Finally he stopped, buried so deep I could feel his balls pressed against me. I tossed my head at the vicious ache, trying to relax my protesting inner muscles. He paused a moment before he began to slowly pull that endless dick out of my tortured channel.

Which is when ribbons of delight started twining around his retreating cock. My eyes went wide, and my bound hands curled into astonished claws.

Again the prince thrust, triggering a wave of thorny pain that made me grit my teeth. But when he started pulling out again, that wicked, erotic sweetness rose again, growing even greater when he reached beneath me and found my clit. I shuddered in delight and suffering as he fucked me, long and slow and deep.

"Yes. Oh, yes," Arles whispered roughly. "I knew you'd love it -- eventually."

The prince fucked me with seductive sadism, shoving into me as he teased my clit, before withdrawing slowly, letting me feel every hot centimeter of that thick shaft. I squirmed in my bonds, battered by waves of pleasure and pain so intense I was no longer sure which was which.

"Did you love him?" Arles snarled, circling his hips until his cock seemed to screw its way into me.

I knew he meant Galon. "No," I gasped. "I tried, but I couldn't. You wouldn't let me, you bastard."

The prince stopped in mid-stroke. I looked over my shoulder to find him staring at me with a puzzled frown. "You're telling the truth." His sensor implants no doubt told him as much. "You spent years with him. You were his lover…"

"But I loved *you*." I threw back my head and groaned at the searing sensation of his cock impaling me like a stake. "He deserved more from me, but I could never give it to him. I tried, but my heart just wasn't mine to give. You had it."

Arles's lips drew back from his teeth. "Good." He began another slow, silken withdrawal. I shuddered as the exotic pulses rolled through me. "I could never forget you either. And I tried. Odin's Blind Eye, I tried."

He started to grind, fucking me hard, fast, sending blasts of raw sensation along my shuddering nerves. His hips hit my ass in fast, meaty slaps. The orgasm took me by surprise, bursting in my skull like a thunderclap, followed by rolling throbs as savagely delicious as his cock. I screamed, drowning in fire. My muscles jerked and quivered.

Arles shoved to the hilt, his head snapping back as if from the impact of an invisible fist. His cock jerked deep in my ass. He roared, a raw, masculine bellow of pleasure and conquest.

We writhed, coming, flying, locked together in convulsive pleasure until the climax died, leaving me limp and sweating. Panting, I listened to him breathe in rasps, the sound harsh in the chamber's stillness. I ached to hold him, ached to be held, but I was still bent helplessly, locked tight in leather and steel.

Loneliness chilled me. I'd never felt so far from him, even when I'd been half a galaxy away. Arles might use me, pleasure me -- he might even love me in some hidden corner of his soul -- but I would never be anything more to him than his thrall.

One day the man I loved would be emperor, and he would never let either of us forget it.

* * *

It took two weeks to make our way back to Tor, and Arles spent every off-duty moment taking me in ways I'd never even heard of. We worked our way through every device and toy in the ship's erotic dungeon as he demanded my utter submission. He fucked me until I was sore and limp as a rag, even as I discovered a euphoric high under his ruthless hands.

Afterward, we'd retire to his quarters, where the prince would hold me with a lover's tenderness. Sometimes he'd make love to me on that narrow bunk, his kisses gentle, each touch of those big hands as sweet and stirring as a virgin's dream. When Arles finally slept, I'd lay staring at the bulkhead in the dark, trying to ignore the tears rolling hot down my cheeks.

It was at such times that Galon's ghost whispered his disappointment. Playing at erotic submission was one thing, but I'd let Arles enslave my spirit. Otherwise, I would never have allowed him to treat me with such contempt. If I really wanted him, I had to fight for his respect.

It was time I start acting like the captain of the *Valkyrie's Quest*.

But I'd wrecked Arles's political life once. Did I have the right to do it again? And what price would our respective kingdoms pay? I was no longer an ignorant girl, to act blindly without thought for the consequences.

So as I lay in the prince's arms each night, I sought a way to cut the Gordian Knot that bound us. But every plan I considered was riddled with too many potential pitfalls. I could see no solution, except to play the thrall and wait for an opportunity.

There had to be a way.

* * *

In far too little time, *Mjölnir* reached Tor. I still felt bitterly torn when I boarded the prince's sleek little captain's launch for the flight down to Asgard, the capital city. With Arles piloting the craft, I sat alone in the rear passenger section, watching out one of the long viewports as the planet swelled around us in shades of green, blue and ocher.

We landed on the palace's small flight pad in the center of the vast green maze that was the royal gardens. I looked up, heart beating hard with anxiety, as Arles came into the back of the craft to collect my leash. "Come, Gisel." His grin looked twisted. "Our public awaits."

"Lovely." I rose to follow him toward the airlock. He glanced back at me just before he opened it, and I thought I saw a flash of guilt in his green eyes. Then he straightened his shoulders, turned around, and strode down the gangplank, my leash wrapped around his fist.

I followed, three paces behind on the end of the thin chain, out into the glare of the Torrean sun and the gaze of the media.

The Palace of Valhalla spread before us, familiar to me from countless childhood visits -- a massive structure built of silicaslate blocks that glittered in the afternoon sunlight. The walls appeared white at first glance, but with every step you took, a rainbow of iridescent color rolled across them. Between the silicaslate and the palace's astrogothic architecture -- all tall, arched windows and soaring spires -- Valhalla looked as mythic as its namesake.

Emperor Ragnar strode down the garden's winding silicaslate path, a tall, broad-shouldered man dressed in silver-trimmed black velvet, his shoulder-length blue hair braided with gemstones that clicked as he walked.

"Father!" Arles walked into his arms, and the two men thumped each other's backs as they hugged in joyous welcome. Unlike my mother, Ragnar had never seen the need for emotionless royal reserve.

I winced as I saw a cloud of tiny devices fly past the royals, headed right for me. Though no bigger than a pea, each cambot was equipped with powerful visual and auditory sensors, as well as the artificial intelligence to use them. The cameras transmitted the vid they shot to their respective news agencies, which would edit the footage, package it with appropriate arch commentary, and beam it out to the ten worlds of the Torrean empire.

The cambots darted around me like a swarm of bees, each projecting the three-dimensional logo of its home newsie, each shooting vid of me in my jeweled chains. I resisted the urge to swat.

A princess of Swanhilde turned sex-thrall. My mother would have my head on a pike.

At least Arles had allowed me to wear something a bit more modest: a white gown that bared my arms before skimming the length of my body to flow around my sandaled feet. I'd piled my long red hair atop my head and bound it there with fine gold chains and emerald gemstones to match my manacles. Maybe the newsies would mistake my bonds for a fashion statement.

Probably not.

I tried to ignore the flitting cameras as I waited a discreet distance from Ragnar and Arles, now deep in low-voiced discussion.

Just beyond them stood the usual gorgeous herd of courtiers dressed in rainbow shades of shimmersilk and velvet. They stared at me with their heads together, gossiping for all they were worth. I ignored them too, until a familiar figure emerged from the midst of the crowd.

I hid a wince.

My sister wore a haut couture gown in metallic gold that drew the eye to her small, lushly curved body. Isa looked so much like our mother, with her flaming red hair and delicate, elfin features that I had to look twice to make sure it wasn't Queen Zerelda slinking toward me like a cat.

But no, Mother didn't slink.

"Well met, Gisel." Isa stopped before me, hands on hips, voice just loud enough to ensure that the cambots began to orbit her as well. "It has been too many years since you ran away."

I lifted a brow, keeping my expression cool, almost bored. "You mean since you *manipulated* me into running. What exactly was the point of that, Isa?"

She raised her chin and looked down her nose at me -- quite a trick, considering I was a head taller. "I have no idea what you're talking about."

I smiled faintly. "Of course you don't."

Isa glowered, a soft petulance in the line of her mouth I'd never noticed when I was her adoring little sister. Then a sudden glint of sadistic anticipation flashed in her eyes. I braced, recognizing the signs of a foe about to go for the jugular.

"I hope you have something more suitable for tonight's ball than the rag you're wearing," she drawled. "Our mother is on her way from Swanhilde to attend. She means to celebrate your homecoming."

I felt my face go as still as a mask, a royal's programmed response to any devastating news. "Indeed?" I sounded barely interested. I wanted to throw up.

"She's so pleased the prince has brought you home." Isa's gaze flicked deliberately to my thrall collar. "Just think how... delighted she'll be to see you've found your *proper* place."

"And how does she feel about yours?" I asked, as I would never have dared a decade before. Isa would one day be queen, and I'd always treated her accordingly. "Judging by the newsies, you've made our mother's heir a camera whore."

Incredulous rage flooded her eyes. "How dare you, cow!" Isa's small fist flew toward my face.

Her hand slapped into Arles's palm, though I hadn't even seen him turn. He glared down at her, his father at his shoulder, glowering. "Isa..."

"I could have ducked," I told him. "She's slow."

"I'll show you slow!" my sister hissed. "I'll beat you like the slave you are!"

Lifting a brow at her, I raised my manacled wrists and smiled sweetly. "Hitting a chained woman -- tut. Did you forget the cambots, dear?"

"You fucking bitch!" my sister spat, and shot a spiked heel at my shin. I stepped aside, and the kick missed. Suddenly Arles had his hands full as she lunged for me, screeching. He looked taken aback as he contained her frenzied struggles.

"I'll take her." Jarrat appeared from the midst of the crowd to grab his wife's wrists and drag her away. Spinning her around, the big man pulled Isa across his shoulder and straightened.

"Put me down, you lickspittle!" She pounded his back with her fists, feet kicking a meter from the ground in hysterical fury. "I order you!"

He rolled his eyes, shook his head, and turned away. Long blue braid swinging, Arles's brother strode off, carrying his wife, who howled at me, "I hope he flogs you bloody, thrall bitch! I am your *queen*!"

"Best not let our mother hear you say that, Isa!" I called back. The courtiers snickered.

Ragnar sighed, his expression resigned. He looked at Arles and angled his head toward the palace. "Attend me."

His son nodded, caught my leash, which he'd released in the struggle with Isa, and drew me after him as the two men strode into the palace. Their respective teams of bodyguards closed in around us, eight very big men in the red and blue of the palace guard. Swords swung at their hips, the only weapons permitted in the Imperial presence since the assassination of Arles's mother by one of her own guards.

Personally, I'd always thought that particular policy was just begging for trouble.

Chapter Three

The emperor's private inner chamber was just as I remembered it, with its tall, arched windows, intricately patterned carpet, and bronze statues of the gods in heroic poses. Arles, Ragnar, and I sat on thick cushions around a low, inlaid table covered with trays of food and glasses of wine. I nibbled a canapé and kept my mouth shut, aware that, as a thrall, I was being treated as the guest I most definitely was not.

I damned near choked when Ragnar met his son's gaze and said, "What in the name of Odin's Blind Eye do you think you're doing?"

Arles didn't even flinch at the emperor's obvious anger. "Having drinks with my father. Unless you have something else in mind?"

"Don't play dumb with me, boy. It doesn't suit you." He stabbed a ringed finger in my direction. "I'm talking about parading a princess of Swanhilde on a leash! Have you lost your mind?"

"Gisel turned her back on her rank when she fled twelve years ago." Arles's voice was so even he might have been talking about one of the canapés. "Now she's just a mercenary I captured in battle. She chose to become my thrall in exchange for the freedom of her crew. I am hardly the first Torrean captain to take an enemy prisoner."

"She's the daughter of my ally, Arles! You are humiliating Zerelda in the imperial media!"

"Zerelda's daughter has been humiliating this family in the media for years," Arles observed coolly. "Turnabout is fair play."

"Gisel is not Isa. She isn't responsible for her sister's actions," Ragnar snapped.

"No, but she *is* responsible for her own." Arles

took a deliberate sip of his wine. "She jilted me, remember? I've been cleaning up the resulting mess ever since."

"Gisel was barely more than a child, frightened by the sight of her bridegroom flogging another woman," Ragnar growled. "And yes, I do know exactly what happened that night."

Horrified heat flooded my face. *Oh, Odin's blood*!

Even Arles's cheeks darkened. "I was drugged."

"So I've been told. And I don't blame you for whipping the chit; I'd have done the same. But you were a grown man, and Gisel was seventeen. We failed her in not tracking her down before she flew off with that Galon Teve character. Though I suppose it was lucky he found her, or she'd be dead now."

Arles sighed. "I'm aware of that, Father."

Ragnar turned toward me and studied my face, his gaze probing and intent. "My spies tell me the child I knew has become a warrior. When I think of you going up against one of the lizards with nothing more than an axe..." He shook his head. "How the hell did you survive?"

"Your Excellency, I didn't *survive*," I told him. "I hacked off the bastard's head and cremated Galon with its skull." I'd shot them both into the nearest star. My captain's body had flared bright, blazing like a Viking's pyre an instant before it vanished.

Both men sat back on their cushions, brows shooting upward in surprised respect. Ragnar glanced at his son, his expression calculating, before he transferred that narrow gaze to me. "You do realize I can order Arles to set you free."

I hesitated, surprised at the instant "*No*!" that rang in my mind. I forced myself to consider the idea. It was certainly tempting, especially considering my mother's probable reaction at tonight's ball. And yet... "Arles believes parading me as a thrall will spike the guns of his political foes. I think I owe him that much."

He snorted. "You don't owe any of us anything, girl. We're the ones who failed you by not keeping you safe."

I gestured, sweeping that away. "Arles is your heir, Your Excellency. I don't want the Torrean Empire to suffer for my actions by giving your foes ammunition."

"Fuck our foes," Ragnar snapped. "Gossips and schemers, the lot of them. Arles can silence them if he stays on Tor and does a little work to build alliances among the nobility. He has no need to make a pawn of you. Hell, if he has any sense, he'll make you his wife."

"No." Arles rapped out the word in cold, unadorned refusal.

"Forget your pride and look at her, boy." The anger had drained from Ragnar's voice, leaving only weariness. "She has intelligence and courage, and the combat experience to use them. I wanted her for you even when she was a girl, but she'd be a far better empress now."

"Oh, our enemies would love that," Arles growled. "Given the dance Isa has led Jarrat, just imagine what they'd say of Gisel."

"And Gisel will prove them wrong." Ragnar leaned an elbow on his knee. "You forget, you'll have time to win them over. I have no plans to die anytime soon."

"Neither did Mother." She'd had been killed by an assassin when Arles was only five years old.

"And I still grieve, but not even an emperor can gainsay death." He grabbed his son's hand in an urgent grip. "Don't sacrifice a love like your mother and I shared for nothing more than your own damned pride. And you do love Gisel, don't you?"

I expected another stark "*No*."

Instead Arles sounded as tired as his father. "Yes, I love her. I can't think of a time when I didn't. But I won't plunge the Empire into chaos to have her."

"Damn you, Arles." Ragnar threw up his hands, gems clinking softly in the long, braided blue hair as he fell back in his seat to glower. "You'll do as you will, no matter what it costs us all."

"No, Father," Arles corrected grimly. "I'll do as I must."

* * *

That night I watched my mother stride across the ballroom at the head of an entourage of diplomats, courtiers, and royal bodyguards. It took all my discipline and training to keep the sick dread off my face. I felt a hand close comfortingly over my arm, and I looked around to see Arles give me a nod of encouragement. I smiled at him, surprised and oddly warmed, though he still held that damned leash in his hand.

Zeralda came to a stop before me and flicked her fingers. Instantly the courtiers melted away and the bodyguards fell back to a discreet distance, where they eyed the crowd with the intensity of career paranoids. Behind us, the four men of Arles's Imperial Guard did the same.

"Hello, Mother," I said, studying her cautiously. Zerelda appeared not one day older than she'd been when I'd run away. A tiny woman who barely came up to my shoulder, her features were as fine and delicate as a Faery queen's under a cascade of red curls bound in a complex arrangement of braids and gemstone clips. The ethereal effect was enhanced by her gown, which fluttered around her body in sheer, pale blue petals, shimmering softly in the golden ballroom light.

I felt like a bear next to her, faintly ridiculous in the peacock-blue gown that swirled to mid-thigh and bared my long arms even as it displayed my abundant cleavage. Between my height, my breasts, and the muscle I'd built for hand-to-hand combat, nobody would ever mistake me for a Faery anything.

"Gisel... oh, my love..." To my astonishment, Zerelda pulled me into her arms, hugging me close despite our awkward difference in height. Her voice broke with genuine emotion. "I feared I'd never see you again. I thought you dead."

Astonished, I put my arms around her and tentatively returned her hug. "Ah... I'm sorry I worried you." *I didn't know you'd care.*

She pulled back to meet my gaze. There was vulnerability in those striking, blue-violet eyes, astonishing in a woman who'd always been so utterly self-controlled. "I sent agents out when you vanished. They searched for years, but they could find no sign of you."

"I was aboard the *Valkyrie Quest* under an assumed name," I told her. "I became a mercenary."

"So Ragnar tells me." She added dryly, "Apparently I need to hire away a few of his spies." She squeezed my shoulders. "I am glad you're home, Gisel. I have missed you so."

"And I've missed you," I told her, a sense of unreality stealing over me. Where was the hard-eyed queen who'd palmed me off on a series of nannies -- when she wasn't chewing me out for dishonoring my House?

Zerelda sighed. "If you missed me, I doubt it was

very much. I made so many mistakes with you, my dear. I was so angry when you ran away… at first. Then when it began to seem that I'd lost you forever, I started to think about everything I'd done wrong. I can't blame you for fleeing." She shot Arles a hard look. "Especially after what you saw the night before you were to marry *him*."

Arles stared back at her, impassive. Behind him, his bodyguards watched hers, hands light on the hilt of their swords.

"No, I am the one who was wrong," I told her. "Running was the act of a coward. My thoughtlessness could have destroyed Swanhilde. We're fortunate that the emperor elected to hold to the treaty and defend us from the Fafnar." I took her small hands in mine. They felt fragile and cold. "I am so very sorry, Mother."

"What else were you to do? I drove you away with my demands. And you could have so easily died…"

I squeezed her hands, seeking to warm them. "Mother, you did not drive me away."

Zerelda shrugged. "I gave you no reason to stay, either." She looked down at our linked hands. Her thumb touched the jeweled manacle around one wrist, turned it back and forth so that the thin chains clinked softly. "Do you want me to free you from him?" Though she did not look up, the queen spoke in a low, deadly voice that told me she meant every word. "I vow to do whatever it takes. Even if it means war."

My jaw dropped as I stared down at her bent head. My gaze flew to Arles, who stood so tense and still he might have been cast in bronze. His face was expressionless, but anger flashed hot in his eyes.

"No, Mother," I told her hoarsely. "I have made an agreement with the prince, and I mean to keep it."

He relaxed fractionally.

She looked up, examined me as if she'd never seen me before. Perhaps she hadn't. "You love him."

I swallowed. "Yes."

A muscle flexed in her jaw, and she turned that look on Arles for a long, long moment. The anger drained from her eyes, and she sighed. "Then do as your heart demands. I want only your happiness." My mother squared her shoulders and gave me a smile that looked a trace tense. "Seek me out tomorrow. We will speak more of this in private."

With that, Queen Zerelda walked away, royal pride in every stride.

As I watched her entourage close in around her, I noticed a crowd of Torrean nobles hovering nearby, accompanied by the usual cambot swarm. Isa stood among them, her face white, her fists clenched at her sides. She shot me a killing look and stalked off.

"Come," Arles said in my ear, handed me my leash, and offered his arm. "I want to speak to you somewhere a bit more private."

I hesitated, wondering what he was up to, then coiled the chain in my free hand before hooking the other into the crook of his elbow. He guided me across the gleaming ballroom floor, his bodyguards surrounding us like wary wolves.

The orchestra played the first notes of the "Stellar Waltz," and dancers began to circle the floor in a colorful, shimmer-silk blur, whirling in stately circles.

We escaped down a corridor, his guards' boots ringing on the faux marble. Arles stopped to touch a spot on one wall, and a door slid soundlessly open. I hadn't even known it was there, for it was camouflaged by a vidfield that made it look just like the wall around it. We all slipped inside, and the captain of Arles's bodyguard closed it behind us, frustrating a dozen cambots who weren't quite fast enough to make it through.

"That's better," Arles said in satisfaction, turning to usher me down the narrow corridor. "The thing I hate most about being home is those damned cambots. I can't go to the head without a swarm of them checking to see if I wipe my ass."

I laughed, remembering that frustration well. "Gods, yes. It's maddening."

Trailed by his guards, we rounded one corner, then another, before Arles opened a door into darkness. He led the way out into a moonlit corner of the palace garden. The only sound was the soft patter of water and the plaintive *churrr-churr* of night birds calling for mates. I glanced up, past the leafy trees that screened this section of the garden. Stars spread across the sky in a bright bloom of light, and Tor's two moons rode the sky, a fat, full moon in the east, a smaller one in the west.

"Beautiful night," I murmured, and gave Arles a smile. "Very romantic."

He didn't smile back. "Yes."

I frowned at him as he turned toward the captain of his guard. "Dolph, give us a little privacy, please."

Nodding, the big guard -- he was fully as tall as Arles -- pivoted to his three fellow agents and gestured. They faded into the surrounding leafy shadows with such skill, I wouldn't have known they were there had I not seen them go.

Arles drew me over to a bench and tugged me down to sit. I eyed him warily, not sure I liked the grim line of his mouth. "What's wrong?"

"This is not working."

My heart seemed to crash through the pit of my stomach. "What isn't?"

"Making a thrall of you." He looked away from me, staring across the moonlit garden. "I release you from our bargain. You may return to Swanhilde with your mother or go back to the *Valkyrie's Quest*, as it suits you."

I stared at him, stunned. "But... why? You told Ragnar --"

"That was before I watched the cambots orbit you and your mother during your reunion." He frowned, flexing one big hand on his knee.

"So? When she wants privacy, she activates a jamming field. Any vid the 'bots shot wouldn't be useable."

"As we all do. But watching those 'bots brought home to me that my father is right. I have no business using you to resolve my political problems. I can handle my foes myself. I don't need to drag you through the muck to do it. Not that politics was ever my real reason for any of this."

I shook my head, bewildered. He'd been so adamant about keeping me only a few hours before, despite Ragnar's obvious disapproval. "I don't understand."

Arles took my hands in his and met my gaze, his green eyes almost painfully naked in their vulnerability. "I took you captive because I wanted you. Actually, that's not strong enough -- I *craved* you. I wanted to make love to you, talk to you, *be* with you. But my pride would not let me simply seek you out. What kind of man would go crawling to the woman who jilted him? So I seized on Torrean politics as an excuse for your capture."

Now my heart was in my throat, catapulted there by hope. "What are you saying?"

He hunched over my hands, his expression

troubled. "I thought only of myself -- *my* needs, *my* foes, *my* throne. I never really considered how you would suffer." Shaking his head, he added, "No, your mother was right. None of this was your fault. I can no longer pretend it is."

The words were out of my mouth before I knew what I was saying. "Arles, I don't care why you took me. I only want to be with you. I meant what I said -- I love you."

"As I love you." He said the words without hesitating.

For an instant, joy blazed incandescent in my brain.

Then he spoke again. "But what I told Ragnar is still true. I won't plunge the Empire into chaos for our happiness. Too many innocents would suffer -- including you. You'd become a target for my enemies if it comes to civil war, and --"

"I do *not* need your protection!" I shot to my feet, fisting my hands as rage flooded in to replace my aching devastation. I started pacing, fingers worrying my leash as I tried to regain control of my temper. "I'm a mercenary, Arles. I killed a Fafnar warrior with an *axe*, for Odin's sake. I may have played submissive for you, but that does not mean I will allow myself to be victimized. Any foe of yours will regret fucking with me."

He rocked back and studied me in wary surprise. "Yes, you've got a formidable reputation, but Torrean politics..."

"...are considerably more civilized than the wars I've fought." I raked my fear hand through my hair, my chains clinking. "Arles, I've killed enemies with my bare hands. I held Galon in my arms as he died and comforted him despite my grief. And then I got up, hunted down his killer, and avenged him, though that damned reptile almost gutted me. I've spent years doing whatever it took to keep my people alive and win wars for those who hired us." I shot him a savage look. "I would be an asset to you, you bloody fool."

The prince stared at me as if stunned by my fury. "I have no doubt of that, but --"

"Oh, give it up, Arles." My sister strolled from the shadows. "You're going to make her your princess, and everyone knows it."

He frowned at her. "This is a private conversation, Isa. Go back to the ballroom."

"You're not emperor yet, Arles. You can't order me to do a damned thing." She sauntered closer to eye me, her expression frigid with contempt. "So you're going to be Empress of Tor."

I stepped back warily, instincts howling at the feverish glitter in her moonlit eyes. "And you'll be queen of Swanhilde."

"Of course. I'm the oldest, raised to rule. I spent hours at our mother's side, learning all the boring bullshit she cared to teach me. While you..." She curled a lip. "You played combat games with the handsome prince. The girl everyone loved. *Empress* Gisel. *He should have been mine*!"

The stiletto dropped from her elegant sleeve to fill her hand in a length of gleaming steel. She lunged, driving it at my chest.

* * *

I had no idea she was so fast.

But Galon had spent years teaching me to fight. I swept up my manacled wrists to wrap the chain around the knife, dragging it out of her hand and into mine as I pivoted aside. I slammed my elbow into her chin, sending her staggering backward. My elbow jangled viciously.

Isa shook off the impact. "You bitch," she snarled, and barreled toward me.

For a moment I was tempted to use the knife I'd just taken away from her. But I couldn't bring myself to hurt my sister, so I hooked one foot between hers and tripped her. She fell right into the bench, her head hitting the silacaslate seat with a *thunk*. I winced. My sister tumbled limply backward, out cold.

"Gisel…" Arles broke off. He was on his feet, but he stopped in mid-step, an expression of disbelief on his face. He looked down at the bloody blade point protruding from his chest. "Odin…" He dropped to his knees.

Behind Arles, the captain of his bodyguard jerked the sword from the prince's back and flicked the gore from its length. He smiled in demonic satisfaction and raised his weapon over Arles's head.

I flung myself into a roundhouse kick that cracked into the assassin's chin. Something snapped, sharp as a breaking stick. His body spun from the force of the blow to collapse in a boneless pile, his head twisted on his broken neck.

I knelt beside the prince. Blood soaked his dress uniform from the wound that pierced the left side of his chest. "Arles!"

"Missed his stroke… the traitorous fuck," my lover panted, rolling over onto his belly as he clawed his attacker's fallen sword into his hand. "Hit the lung, missed the heart." Arles pushed himself onto hands and knees, still holding the weapon. Sweat gleamed on his white face. He coughed, his breath bubbling wetly.

Oh, not good.

"Where the hell… are the rest of my guards?"

"Here, my Prince." Two more agents streaked out

of the dark, swords lifted. I leaped to meet the first, ignoring my manacles, the knife held in a fighter's easy grip.

The traitor parried my blade and swung his own at my head. I threw out both arms, snapping the chain tight between them, deflecting the blade. We spun apart and began to circle.

"Damn it, Gisel, get out of here!" Arles reeled to his feet, one hand clamped to his wounded chest, the other gripping the sword. He bared his teeth and charged the remaining guard before he could skewer me from behind. The man spun away to meet him.

Even badly wounded, Arles had the strength of the gene-sculpted warrior he was. You'd never know he was hurt as we engaged the traitors, blades ringing in the relentless rhythm of attack and parry. Sweat rolled down my arms and thighs as I labored to keep my opponent from gutting me with his longer blade.

Arles growled like a leopard, ignoring the blood rolling down his side. His foe charged him, and he spun aside, striking even as he whirled. His blade chopped into the traitor's chest as if he were slicing soft cream. Choking on a scream, the assassin collapsed.

My opponent's gaze flicked toward them, and I saw my opening. I lunged inside his guard and slashed my blade across his throat. Blood sprayed hot across my face. He reeled back from my attack, clutching his throat as he stared at me in shock. His knees gave under him, and he toppled, eyes going empty and fixed.

"Where's the fourth guard?" I spun to stand back-to-back with Arles.

"That's a very good question." Together, we scanned the darkness.

Voices rose in shouts, and we tensed, staring

toward the rustling bushes and listening to the click of running boots on the silicaslate path.

"Arles!" Ragnar shouted, emerging from the bushes with a crowd of agents. One of them was the missing bodyguard, who'd evidently gone for help.

"We seem to have traitors in our midst," Arles spat, not lowering his weapon as he glared at the agents. "Evidently Isa has bought at least some of them off."

"Again?" Ragnar swore so viciously, I knew he was thinking of his dead wife. "I thought our security practices were supposed to catch traitors!"

"Yes, well, apparently they didn't work." Arles swayed, going ghost-pale. "Oh."

I hooked one arm around his waist, bracing him against my side. "Your Excellency, the prince is hurt. One of the guards ran him through."

The emperor's eyes widened before he rapped out an order. "Doctor Cavo, get your ass up here!"

The guards parted to allow a man in court garb to step through, towing a trauma unit. "I'm here, Sire."

Arles lowered his weapon and sat down on the bench to let the doctor treat his wound, though he kept a wary eye on the agents. They appeared not to notice as two of them slapped forcecuffs on Isa, who still lay unconscious in the grass. The others fanned out to search the gardens.

Ragnar and I watched as the doctor coaxed Arles to lie down on the bench so the trauma unit could treat him. The device moved to hover a centimeter from his wounded ribs, humming and chirping as it coaxed the bleeding to stop so he could be transported to surgery.

I was vaguely aware of cambots circling us like gnats, but they were the least of my worries. I was too terrified I was about to lose Arles.

The prince ignored both the doctor and the cameras in favor of briefing his father on the attack. "Gisel… saved my life," he told the emperor in a ragged voice. "They'd have finished me if… if she hadn't helped fight them off." Arles's vivid gaze flicked to me. "Wearing manacles, armed with nothing more… more than a knife. Killed the one who… who stabbed me."

Ragnar glanced at me, brows lifted. "My spies were right. You *can* fight, can't you?"

"That's not all she can do," Arles said, reaching past the doctor to grab one of my manacles. He pressed his thumb to a gemstone, and the collar and chains fell away with a musical rattle. I stared at him, startled. "To hell with the politics, my enemies, and my pride. Marry me, Gisel."

"What?" I gaped at him helplessly. "But…"

"When Isa went for you with that knife, I felt my heart stop." He ran his thumb over the thin flesh of my wrist, tracing the fine blue vein there. I felt the hair rise on the back of my neck. "You are everything I have ever wanted, everything I love. Life without you wouldn't be living at all." Staring into my eyes, he breathed, "Please, Gisel, please. Marry me."

And I said the only thing I could say. "Yes."

Chapter Four

The wedding took six months to plan, largely because Arles insisted on an affair grand enough to make clear how much he valued me. In the meantime, Ragnar and my mother waged a ferocious media campaign to transform me from the butt of sexual jokes into the royal heroine who'd saved the prince from assassins.

For once, the media cooperated, interviewing damn near every member of the *Valkyrie's Quest* crew, along with the grateful residents of various planets we'd helped protect from would-be invaders. Never mind that we'd been well paid to do so.

By the time my friends and allies were finished singing my praises, I barely recognized the heroic woman warrior they'd turned me into. Arles and I found ourselves the stars of an interplanetary romance that had become a mass obsession in the Empire.

No less than four different BioVids were produced, none of which had a cursed thing to do with reality.

Still, the end result was exactly what Ragnar intended. None of his political foes dared say a word against either of us for fear of suffering the wrath of the entire Empire.

I doubted the golden haze of political stardom would last, but I planned to make the best of it while it did.

Isa was charged with conspiring to assassinate an imperial heir. She could have faced the death penalty, had a panel of doctors not ruled her mentally ill. Luckily, the therapy seemed to work. During my weekly visits to the Imperial Center for Mental Health, she seemed much calmer, no longer the shrill psychotic who'd tried to kill me.

Her doctors believed the pressure of life as the royal heir was responsible for her illness and suggested removing her from the line of succession. My mother readily agreed and declared me the heir to the throne. She and Ragnar then started work on a treaty to bring Swanhilde into the Torrean Empire.

Arles's brother, Jarrat, finally obtained the divorce from Isa he'd wanted for years. He promptly started enjoying his new sexual freedom with a parade of exotic beauties from around the Empire.

Meanwhile, Arles and I did a great deal of smiling and a great many interviews. By the time the day for the wedding arrived, I was ready to kidnap him, drag him aboard the *Valkyrie's Quest*, and flee to the most remote world we could find.

But since I knew the cambots would probably track us down, I resisted the impulse.

* * *

Our wedding day arrived in a sensory assault of color, music and glittering candlelight. The palace throne room was barely recognizable under drifts of rare red roses, shipped all the way from Earth and arranged in exquisite Elderkind urns older than Earth's pyramids. Every breath I took was scented with perfume from exotic petals.

Thousands of guests from Odin knew how many planets watched as Emperor Ragnar presided over the ceremony in his iridescent robes of state. I barely heard his Imperial blessing of our union, too busy gazing helplessly at my impossibly handsome groom.

A rainbow of military honors glinted on Arles's broad chest, dazzling against the somber, dark blue fabric of his dress uniform jacket. He'd worn his azure hair loose around those powerful shoulders, emeralds glinting from braided locks on either side of his strong warrior's face.

But none of that gemstone glitter could match the happiness blazing from his eyes.

Arles and I repeated oaths of love and fealty to one another before he gave me a kiss so passionate I knew it would lead every vid cast in the Empire for a week.

We then had to endure a reception ball and the attentions of a swarm of cambots. I smiled until my cheeks went numb, and Arles visibly fidgeted with the need to get me to himself. I was chatting up the ambassador from Earth when the prince's control broke.

"Excuse me, sir. I need to borrow my bride for a few days," Arles said, and swept me into his arms, along with several meters of white nanosilk skirt. He carried me out as I called hasty goodbyes to the laughing guests, my lace veil swirling in our wake. How he avoided tripping on my train, I will never know.

* * *

"I thought we'd never escape that lot," the prince sighed, kicking the door to his chambers closed as he swept me inside. He wasn't even breathing hard, despite carrying the combined weight of me and my wedding gown down half a kilometer of palace hallways.

He put me down on my jeweled high heels, and I got busy trying to untangle myself from the gown's extravagant, pearl-encrusted skirt. "Yes, well, I don't think I'm ever going to escape this dress."

Arles gave me a wolfish grin. "Why don't I help you with that?"

I lifted a brow at him as I wrestled layers of stubborn fabric. The thin, diamond bangles he'd given me rang together with every tug. "According to the Newsies, you *do* have a talent for getting women out of their clothes."

"A skill I'll be restricting to you from now on."

"You'd better." I gave him a cheeky grin. "I'm a dangerous woman."

"Yes," he rumbled, his smile wicked, "I know."

Moving around behind me, Arles kicked my nanosilk train aside and went to work on the gown's countless tiny fasteners. It took him ten minutes and some quiet swearing, but he got them all open. I squirmed out of the tight bodice and began hauling the dress over my head.

Arles stepped around me and sprawled in a chair to watch, shamelessly enjoying my struggles.

I finally tunneled free of the gown and its layers of petticoats, then pulled off my veil before dragging the whole pile over to my new walk-in closet. I stuffed the lot into the auto-fold hamper, which devoured them with a series of chirps. A moment later the unit huffed a blast of jasmine-scented air and spat them all out onto one of the closet shelves, neatly cleaned, packaged and vacuum-sealed.

"Mmm." The sound was very male -- and very hungry.

I turned to find Arles eyeing me with predatory interest. A heavy, full-length mirror in a gildwood frame stood just behind his chair, and I realized why he was staring. I now wore only a corset beaded with pearls, a pair of tiny lace panties, and jeweled high heels that made my legs look endless in white lace stockings. A long pearl necklace draped over my corset-mounded cleavage to swing at my waist. Even I had to admit the view wasn't bad.

"I knew you'd look luscious in that corset." It had

been yet another gift from him, having arrived just in time for the wedding gown's final fitting. The designer had not been happy with either of us for the addition.

Sprawled in the armchair in his dress uniform, Arles gave me a buccaneering smile. "Come here." An erection looking damn near as thick as my wrist bulged beneath his snug black uniform trousers.

"Well now," I murmured. "Whatever do you have in mind?"

"I haven't tied you up and fucked you hard in three whole days." There hadn't been time. "I find I'm feeling… neglected."

"Can't have that." I sauntered toward him, strutting just a bit on those ridiculous heels.

Arles rose to his feet, lithe as a panther, and pulled the seal of his dress tunic. I watched him shrug out of the jacket, powerful muscle bunching and releasing under a silken thatch of iridescent hair. Bracing his booted feet apart, he tossed the tunic aside and waited for me.

My tiny panties were already wet through. Not that it mattered. They didn't have a prayer once he got those big hands on them.

Smiling up into his hungry eyes, I stepped into his arms. Just as I expected, he slid his palms over my hips, found the fragile waistband, and tugged. The lace snapped, and he dropped the remains on the floor.

His mouth crashed down on mine, hot, wet and famished, in a ruthless kiss of possession and need. I kissed him back, opening for the teasing thrust of his tongue, the nibbling capture of my lip as his hands slid up to cup my corseted breasts.

When we finally reeled apart to breathe, Arles smiled down at me, the animal heat in his gaze tempered by tenderness. "Wife," he whispered.

I smiled dreamily up at him. "Husband." Neither word had ever sounded so sweet.

* * *

Arles turned me to face the mirror and wrapped his strong arms around my waist. With a sigh, I leaned my head back against his chest, admiring the contrast between us. I've got a mercenary's body, lean with fighting muscle, but dressed in that corset I looked as lush as any courtesan.

"Take hold of the mirror," Arles ordered, breath hot on my ear.

Lifting a brow, I met his gaze in our reflection and reached upward, meaning to take hold of the carved posts at the top of the mirror's heavy gilt frame. Before I could touch it, my arms jerked forward until my diamond bracelets clicked against the posts. I gave my wrists a tug, but the bracelets appeared stuck fast to the mirror.

"They're force cuffs!" I stared at him over one shoulder. "You gave me diamond force cuffs as a wedding gift?"

He grinned like a wolf at a lamb. "It does seem so."

"Well, that's a relief."

Now it was his turn to blink. "Oh?"

"I was afraid we were going to start having boring married sex."

Green eyes narrowed. "I'll show you *boring*."

I smirked. "Oh, dear. Am I in trouble?"

"Yes." His hand landed on my ass in a swat that made me bounce on my jeweled heels.

I glared. "That hurt!"

"It was supposed to." He eyed my butt. "Now you have a pink handprint on one lovely cheek. I do believe it needs company."

"Don't you..."

Six hard swats landed on my butt until I danced and yowled, squirming from side to side in a vain attempt to avoid the stinging blows.

"Now that," he announced at last in a tone of relish, "is a really pretty shade of pink."

I glowered at him, butt flaming. "I married a brute."

"Poor thing." Arles slid an arm around my waist and reached down to finger my sex. I caught my breath at the luscious penetration. I hadn't known I was that wet. "You do suffer so." His teeth flashed. "Or at least, you're going to."

"Oh, good." He added another finger to the one probing my sex, and my eyes closed in delight. "I hear suffering is good for the soul."

"Now that you've brought it up..." He cupped both breasts, still covered by the corset. To my surprise, the pearl-encrusted fabric slid down of its own accord, baring my nipples even as it lifted the soft mounds.

I blinked. Of course, a nanosilk garment could assume different styles depending on its programming, but somehow I hadn't expected this. "You rigged my corset?"

"I certainly did." He caught my long pearl necklace in both hands and started dragging the strand back and forth across my stiff pink nipples. "Backfired on me, though. All through the reception, I kept thinking about what I could do to you with it. That's why I stayed behind you all night -- I had a hard-on like a blast cannon I was hiding behind your skirts."

"Pervert." I sighed, enjoying the sensation of those cool, smooth pearls rolling over my breasts.

"Oh, darling, you have no idea -- yet." He

murmured some command I didn't quite catch. Pleasure bloomed in my chest like the brush of feathers over sensitive skin. I gasped in helpless delight.

Arles grinned behind me. "The corset is laced with neural implants, just like those nipple clamps I used on you. Which reminds me..."

He brushed his fingers over the pearls covering my bodice. The fabric began to squeeze my breasts like strong, cupping hands. As the corset fondled me, Arles caught my nipples between thumb and forefinger, first pinching, then flicking, then raking his blunt nails over the tight, pink tips. A hot sting zinged through one breast as the corset's implants added a little pain to the pleasure, like a dash of spice in a sweet dessert.

Soon I whimpered in helpless delight as alternating pulses of pleasure and pain jolted through my body. I could do nothing except watch my reflection writhe in Arles's arms, my wrists still bound to the mirror as he tormented my breasts and finger-fucked my pussy. He looked so big standing behind me, all hard muscle and demanding eyes, casting a sorcerer's spell on me with every stroke and pinch.

"Fuck me!" I moaned at last, trembling on the edge of a climax that burned just beyond the next caress. "Arles, for Thor's sake, fuck me!"

"Yes!" Arles said in a hot growl. He grabbed me by the thighs, lifted me right off my feet, and spread me wide before driving the whole hot length of his cock into my cunt. His open fly ground against my ass as he began to thrust, plastering me against the mirror. The cool glass pressing against my bare breasts only added to the sensory assault.

I threw back my head and screamed as I fought to roll back onto Arles's meaty cock. I had no leverage, held off the ground as I was, so I hooked my high-heeled feet behind his knees and ground backward, taking that big shaft as deep as I could get it while he pistoned his muscled ass, relentless as a machine, sweat rolling down his brawny torso and slicking his chest hair flat.

His cock bored in and out of my gripping flesh with just the perfect friction, raking pulses of pleasure through me with every pass. The first deep pulse rippled through my belly. I came, my body jerking helplessly against the cool surface of the mirror in time to each blazing pulse.

Arles roared, his head thrown back, fingers digging into my thighs as he rammed me against the glass, burying his cock so deep his balls teased the lips of my pussy, filling me full.

We tumbled into the aftermath locked together, breathing hard, sweat-slick, his big hands still gripping my legs, my feet still wrapped around his calves. The muscles of my thighs jumped and quivered as he finally lowered me to my feet.

"Thor's Balls," I managed. "If I weren't bound to this damned mirror, I'd be a puddle on the floor."

"Then I'd better turn you loose and put you to bed, because I'm no better off." He reached for my wrists and touched something. My arms sprang free, and I lowered them to my sides, wincing at the ache in abused muscles.

Arles swept me into his arms again, this time with an audible grunt. Apparently I'd finally managed to tire even his gene-sculpted body.

He carried me to the huge, circular bed that ruled the room. A veiling canopy of transparent curtains draped from a single gilded ring set in the ceiling. Urns of white roses surrounded it.

Opposite that stood a gilt-wood armoire near a

massive dresser that was damned near bigger than my entire cabin on the *Valkyrie Quest*. A carpet the length of my captain's launch covered the floor in vivid, swirling patterns of blue and green.

The bed's sheets felt impossibly smooth and soft against my sweating body as I sprawled on the mattress, stunned limp by pleasure.

Arles did something to my corset, which popped open like a clamshell. He peeled it off me, dropped it on the floor, and started shedding his boots and pants. I ogled him shamelessly, enjoying the revelation of powerful thighs and hard calves. Even spent as he was, there was wicked promise in the swing of his cock. I licked my lips and considered the possibilities. Arles had a short recovery time.

But before I could reach for his tempting length, he slid into bed next to me. Arles spoke the next words in a quiet voice, but the stark truth of them reverberated all the way to my soul. "I love you, wife."

I discovered I couldn't breathe, as if I'd taken a hard blow to the chest. Several minutes passed before I could speak again. "And I love you, my husband. I always have. I always will."

Arles smiled at me, and for a moment I saw the boy he'd been all those years ago. He drew me against the warm strength of his big body and sighed in pure contentment, as if all was right with his world.

Arles of Tor loves me. My paladin. My prince. My heart filled with such blazing joy I was amazed it didn't glow through the walls of my chest. Blinking away tears, I snuggled into Arles's arms and drifted off to sleep.

Armored Hearts
Angela Knight

When interstellar mercenary Captain Nick Rand rescues a beautiful enemy from his own men, he thinks she's the answer to his vampire prayers. On the verge of starvation thanks to the destruction of his hemosynther, he's in desperate need of a female blood donor.

Lieutenant Zara Tahir needs him as badly as he needs her. Without Nick's blood, Zara's overactive immune system will kill her.

But Zara has no intention of embracing captivity. She's willing to exchange blood for blood, maybe even play a kinky game or two with the handsome vampire dominant. Still, he's the enemy, and she can't allow herself to see him as anything more.

Then Rand's enemies make things a lot more complicated...

Chapter One

Hunger chewed Captain Nick Rand until he felt like a bone in a wolf's jaws. It wasn't just a hunger of the body, though his gut felt hollow and his hands had a tendency to shake. Didn't matter how much food he ate, how much water, coffee, or whiskey he drank. None of it touched the craving that gnawed at his brain, making it hard to think about anything but what he needed. Even now, when the enemy might be drawing a bead on his skull, all he wanted was blood. Hot, red and seductive as a siren -- a taste that reminded him of sex and the cool touch of a woman's hands.

Rand fought to ignore that bottomless need. He didn't have time for it now, no matter how hungry he was. Enemy temp shelters surrounded him, dome shapes dappled with camouflage until they were indistinguishable from the forest floor.

They made his shoulder blades itch.

Invisible, a silencer field muting the sound of his footfalls, he padded between the shelters, beam rifle raised as he swept its muzzle from side to side, scanning for potential attackers. His stomach growled so loudly he wondered if the noise could be heard outside his silencer field. He ignored his hunger, fighting to concentrate past the savage need. As he'd been fighting for every endless hour of the previous nine days.

Instead, Rand focused on the familiar process of searching the enemy camp. He could hear the rasp of his breathing in his helmet as he ducked into one empty tent after another, though the silencer muted the sound past four or five centimeters.

In his helmet com, he heard the murmur of his

men reporting in as they filtered through the camp, searching for the enemy. They had no more luck than he'd had. The Falaran Coalition battalion had melted into the surrounding forest, leaving behind smashed equipment, hastily abandoned meals, and wrecked temporary shelters. Apparently, they'd been alerted to the approach of the G.A.E. force at the last minute, dropped everything, and run like hell. Wise of them, considering they were outgunned and outmanned. The colony was small, without the economic resources Godsson's more established planetary population could command. Their armor was certainly no match for the G.A.E.'s.

Still, they could have left someone behind. Maybe in camouflage armor like his own, surrounded by a field of energy that bent light, rendering the sniper invisible.

But you could bend all the light you wanted to, and it wouldn't stop Rand from picking up your scent. Vampires had great noses. And great speed, great endurance, and enough raw strength to take on a mech unit with no backup at all. Which was why he had been hired in the first place, despite the G.A.E.'s disdain for mercenaries in general and vampires in particular. The generals who led the Glorious Army of the Enlightened didn't know a damned thing about war. Nick Rand, on the other hand, had spent the past two decades fighting in a dozen wars on a dozen planets. His combat reflexes weren't just muscle memory -- they were burned in all the way down to his DNA.

Which was why the G.A.E.'s brass had decided they could ignore his food preferences.

He moved in a liquid glide into the next tent. Sweeping his rifle over the whole space in a smooth arc, he ordered a sensor scan. The answer came back a heartbeat later.

Sensor scan completed. No enemy located, said the computer implanted at the base of his brain. He breathed deep, scenting the air just to be sure. And froze.

The tent belonged to a woman. Actually, more than one. Perfume lingered in the air: lilacs and star roses and the natural scent of female bodies. Rand inhaled, drinking in the lush aroma. His eyes closed for just a heartbeat as he imagined the taste of blood and pussy.

Months. It had been months since he'd had a woman. Godsson taught females were corrupting influences who'd blunt his soldiers' warrior instincts. He insisted women belonged at home, teaching their children piety and submission to the will of their Most Exalted -- i.e., Godsson himself.

Yeah, right. Why the female cultists tolerated this airlock blow, Rand had no idea. It was no wonder the million or so Falarans had refused to join Godsson's six million plus worshipers, badly outnumbered or not.

I should never have taken this fucking job. Never mind that he'd needed work. Peace had broken out all over with its usual rotten timing. Absolutely no one had been hiring. Had it not been for Godsson's decision to invade the neighboring planet Falara, Rand would have been forced to find a security job, and he hated bodyguard work with a passion.

But after a year with the G.A.E., the idea of keeping some arrogant prick alive was starting to sound pretty damned good. For one thing, he wouldn't be slowly starving to death among zealots who considered him a pervert.

He wished G.A.E. HQ would quit fucking around

and send him a new hemosynther. The last time he'd commed them, Supplies and Requisitions claimed the 'synther was on order, scheduled to arrive from Earth next week in a shipment of medical equipment. Rand had told the requisitionist it had better, or he was coming to HQ to sink his teeth into something with a pulse.

The man had blanched. As if Rand would touch his sweaty neck with a nine-meter radiation probe. His blood would probably taste like burned coffee and stale doughstries anyway.

Growling under his breath, Rand left the tent -- and heard the scream coming from the other end of camp. A woman's voice, crying out in rage and pain.

He was running before the echo died.

* * *

If she hadn't been so sick, she could have made the G.A.E. bastards pay a higher price when they found her in the middle of the camp. Unfortunately, it had been more than a month since her vampire had died, and Lieutenant Zara Tahir was deep in blood sickness.

They surrounded her, a yelling, laughing mob of massive shapes in helmets and black armor emblazoned with Godsson's halo and planet logo. Those suits gave them enough raw power to take on a blast tank and win.

Even so, Zara hadn't made it easy for them. Even in her lighter V.S.S. armor, she had the advantage in speed and agility. She'd fought so ferociously she'd triggered a spontaneous nosebleed. Feeling the hot wetness rolling down her upper lip as she spun and kicked, Zara snarled. It had been far too long since she'd tasted vampire blood. Wouldn't be long before her own immune system killed her.

Not that these fuckers would give it the chance.

They were pissed, and they planned to kill her. And worse.

It took all ten of them to get her down, spread eagled, and stripped. Their strength enhanced by their mechsuits, they shredded her light V.S.S. armor like wrapping paper. Hands clamped down on her arms and legs, pinning her to the camp's packed dirt so painfully, she knew she'd have bruises.

Assuming she lived that long.

"Hold her still!" A man in lieutenant's armor straightened, reached down to his belt, and clicked something. The groin cup of his armor slid aside, revealing a jutting erection.

Zara bucked again with a desperate wrenching twist that caught her captors by surprise. Snatching a fist free, she plowed it at the officer's balls. He jerked back and she missed, though so narrowly she felt the brush of his pubic hair against her knuckles. "Shit!" he swore, spinning away. "That's it, bitch!" To the men around him, he snarled, "Don't you fuckin' let her move. I'm going to teach that cunt her place. You can have whatever's left."

When he returned a moment later, looming behind the men who held her down, the lieutenant held a pulse rifle in both hands. He aimed the rifle butt at her face.

Knowing the blow would quite likely kill her, Zara sneered. "Go ahead, you cowardly son of a whore."

The butt flashed as it began its descent…

"What the fuck is going on here?"

At the furious male roar, her attacker stopped dead in mid-swing, his eyes widening behind his faceplate. The whole mob jerked to face the roar's owner, their body language shouting guilty alarm.

Good, Zara thought. *A senior officer.* Maybe he'd

save her.

Then again, maybe he wanted to be first in line.

She'd heard Godsson had recently decreed that raping enemy female combatants was not a sin. They were, after all, unnatural creatures in daring to resist Godsson's "holy" plans for the colony. He said it was his warriors' responsibility to teach them proper submission.

That kind of callous bullshit was exactly why Zara had joined the Falaran Coalition Army. She had no desire to live under any cult leader's thumb -- especially an asshole who called himself God's Son.

"We, ah... found an enemy combatant," the mob's leader stammered.

"Yes, Lt. Godshammer, I know," the officer said, his voice steely with sarcasm. "I heard her screaming from the other end of the camp. What, you boys thought you'd commit a war crime or two? Not on my watch. Get the hell away from her."

"But His Most Holy said --"

"You are not raping that woman, Godshammer." His tone dropped into a menacing hiss. "*Get. Off.*"

They let her go and scrambled away with a speed that was almost comical. Without even being told, all ten fell into formation, lining up at attention as if hoping it would save them from their commander's rage. The lieutenant paused to close his groin cup, fumbling in his haste.

Zara lay in the dirt where she'd been left, too bloodsick to do anything else now that the immediate threat was over.

Boots padded toward her. "Are you all ri..." The officer broke off.

Oh, hell, what now? She looked wearily up at him as he stared down at her.

Zara froze.

He was the biggest damn vampire she'd ever seen in her life. It looked as if they'd turned somebody who'd been genetically engineered to begin with. She'd heard rumors that the G.A.E. had hired vampire mercenaries in response to the Falaran Coalition Army's Vampire Defense Program. Godsson had ranted against vampires being perverts too many times for the G.A.E. to produce them outright, so hiring mercs was the best their army could do.

In any case, the G.A.E. had obviously gotten its money's worth. The vamp -- a captain by his shoulder stripes -- was at least two meters tall, and his shoulders looked about a meter wide in his black combat armor. His open faceplate revealed a sharply sculpted face that was all chiseled masculine angles and eyes the metallic gold of ancient coins. What she could see of his black hair appeared to be cropped short, emphasizing his brutal masculinity. Even as his staggering male beauty hit her, she realized something much more frightening.

Judging from his pallor and the raw hunger in his eyes as he stared down at her, it had been a week or more since he'd fed.

"Shit," she said wearily. "Your hemosynther's on the blink."

"You blew it up nine days ago," he told her hoarsely.

* * *

Sweet Jesus, the grunts had captured a bloodsub. Rand glanced around for downed G.A.E. bodies -- unconscious or dead -- and was surprised there weren't any. They'd been lucky she hadn't managed to take a few of them out before they got her down. Bloodsubs had more than enough strength, speed, and skill to take on armored troopers and kick their collective asses. That was, after all, what 'subs had been designed to do... along with keeping their vampires alive and sane.

And where the hell *was* her vampire? If he'd had a woman like this, he sure wouldn't let Godsson's thugs lay a glove on her. Not as long as he was still breathing, anyway.

Which meant her vamp had to be dead.

The bloodsub lay panting in the shreds of her red Vampire Support armor, looking like a gift from the gods, beautiful even with dirt smeared all over that luscious body. Her legs looked delightfully long and curving, her breasts round and white, with candy-pink nipples that seemed to beg for his teeth. Her waist was tiny, her hips just wide enough to cradle a hungry vampire. And her swan's throat was white and long, carotid beating a rhythm of temptation Rand could hear where he stood.

Her face was fully a match for that exquisite body, from Slavic cheekbones to full pink lips, green eyes wide as she looked up at him, lashes long and feathery. A gorgeous blonde mane of hair foamed around her face. He wanted to wrap it around his fist while he fucked and fed on her. Now.

Rand fought down the lust enough to manage speech. "Are you all right?" he asked hoarsely. "Did they..."

She shook her head and climbed wearily to her feet. "You got here in time."

Rand tried not to stare as her lovely breasts juddered with each panting breath. Dragging his famished gaze away, he turned at the approach of the small squad of men he trusted at his back. The five jogged up in their black mechsuits, staring at the naked

Falaran. He picked out a familiar round face with guileless blue eyes. "Corporal Rainsley, check the shelters. Find this woman something to wear."

"Yessir." Rainsley turned and loped away like the earnest young idealist he was.

Rand turned back to the captive -- only to find her staring at him with a bloodsub's erotic hunger. Rand had to fight the impulse to fall on her like the ravening animal he was one deep breath from being.

Nine days. Nine hellish days without blood, surrounded by Godssonist zealots he didn't dare feed from. It would probably set off a mutiny, Godsson's theology on the subject of vampires being what it was. Rand had worked too hard for too many years to win a reputation as a capable, coolly disciplined merc to blow it all just because he was a little hungry.

Scan that woman, he ordered his computer implant. *What's wrong with her*?

Her body temperature is abnormally high, and it appears her immune system is attacking her cells. High probability of blood sickness. I estimate it has been weeks since she's drunk vampire blood.

Well, shit, Rand thought. He had never actually seen a sub with a case of blood sickness, but he knew how it worked. Her immune system was killing her as it tried to destroy the vampire virus that infected every cell of her body. She needed a blood exchange in order to reinforce the virus, subdue the autoimmune disease, and return her body to health and strength.

Rand had exactly what she needed. As if in an effort to seduce him, her body was pumping pheromones that called to his with such power he had to fight the instinct to jerk her into his arms.

Rainsley returned to hand her a bundle of clothing. She took it, thanked him stiffly, and started to dress, her gaze wary, her movements slow with exhaustion. Her hands shook.

Rand growled, gesturing at the bruises that speckled her smooth skin like blue and purple camouflage. "This is utterly unacceptable. The next man I find abusing a captive will..." He let a little pause develop and bared his aching fangs, letting their imaginations fill in the threat. "... Definitely regret it."

Lieutenant Godshammer spoke up again, sullen rebellion in his eyes. "Begging the Captain's pardon, but His Holy Exalted did say we have an obligation to, ah... discipline female soldiers for their lack of femininity. I realize you don't walk the True Path..." Which was the bastard's "subtle" way of reminding his fellow soldiers that Rand Was Not One of Them. "... But we have the right to --"

"Commit war crimes?" Rand demanded, losing his temper. "Violate the interplanetary treaty Godsson himself signed? Because that's exactly what the attempted rape of an enemy combatant is, lieutenant."

"But --"

"But nothing. I took an oath to uphold the Treaty of Vermillion when I became a mercenary, and I will not permit those under my command to violate it because somebody has a fucking boner. Is that clear?"

Godshammer flinched away from the rage on his face, though the man obviously tried to suppress his reaction.

When he said nothing, Rand looked from the lieutenant to his accomplices. "I will review your combat comps' recordings of this incident, from the moment you first detected her until I pulled you off. You'll be informed of my decision." He swept another acid glare over them. "Dismissed. Finish securing this base. And if you find any other enemy combatants, notify me."

At that, all the men saluted, lowered their faceplates, and scattered, armored boots thumping as they hurried off.

Rand turned toward his new captive and took her elbow, steering her gently toward a nearby shelter. "In here. I'd like to have a word." He had to get her somewhere private. It wouldn't do to lambaste his men for trying to rape her, only to let them see him taking her blood. Never mind that he could smell her desperation, which was every bit as great as his own. They knew nothing about the relationship between bloodsub and vampire dominant, wouldn't understand the difference between a blood exchange and rape. Still, he needed her. Had to have her.

If she lets me.

* * *

Zara found herself impressed by the enemy vampire's iron will. If anything, he had to be in worse shape than she was. That was saying something, because every cell in her body was howling its need for release, for the lushly erotic sensation of fangs sinking into her throat, drawing off the brutal pressure that had been building behind her eyes for weeks.

Never mind that he was her enemy, never mind that she didn't even know his name. Their bodies recognized each other on a level that went beyond politics or war or anything but raw, sexual craving. Each could fulfill the other's hungers. That was all their bodies knew. All they needed to know.

She followed him into the temp shelter he'd seemed to pick at random. It was wrecked and empty, clothes, e-flimsies, and furniture scattered wildly, a mark of her fellow soldiers' desperation as they'd fled. They'd been too badly outnumbered, in too poor a position, to do anything else. Falaran High Command had given the order to retreat, and they'd obeyed.

Zara had volunteered to do her bit to delay the enemy, knowing what she was letting herself in for. It wasn't as if she could have kept up with the desperate retreat anyway. Lieutenant Colonel Kassir had initially refused to allow her self-sacrifice, until Zara reminded the woman she was dead regardless. The last of the Falaran vampires had died in the Battle of the Sar Caverns five weeks before. Without a vamp to help her subdue her rampaging immune system, she'd be dead within the week. If her life was lost anyway, she wanted it to mean something.

The ploy had evidently worked; most of the others seemed to have escaped while she'd distracted the Godssonists. She hoped.

"I am in need," the vampire captain told her, his voice a dark, seductive rumble. Startled, Zara met his golden eyes. They seemed to blaze in the dim light. "May I take you?" he asked.

She laughed, the sound a little wild as she hunched her chilled shoulders. The fever had to be getting pretty high. "You remind me of a courtly wolf, asking the lamb's permission to eat her."

"Sometimes even a wolf needs the veneer of civility." He moved closer until his broad, armored body loomed over her like a wall.

Zara studied him carefully, suddenly aware of just how alone they were -- and how much stronger he was. Yet nothing had forced him to come to her rescue. Hell, he could have easily gone to the head of the rapist line. "It's more than a veneer, I think," she said. *And maybe if I give him what he needs, he'll give me what I need. Better not ask him yet, though. What if he says no? I'll wait until he's done -- and hopefully in a better mood.* Decision made, she smiled slightly. "Yes, Captain. Yes, you may have what you need." *Have* it, not *take* it.

He studied her, his gaze intent, intimate. "What if I need more than your blood?"

Zara licked her lips, suddenly aware again of how very male he was. How handsome, how tempting. She shouldn't, she knew she shouldn't.

For both vampires and their V.S.S., drinking blood was a deeply intimate act. In fact, interstellar vamps like the captain often had dominant/submissive relationships with those who fed them.

Things were a little different on Falara because she and other volunteers had allowed themselves to be infected in order to better defend their people from invaders.

She still needed him. "You can have that, too," Zara said hoarsely.

The vampire smiled and took off his helmet, putting it down on the bunk. As she watched in growing tension, he removed his armored gauntlets, dropping them beside the helmet with a soft, heavy thump.

Zara controlled her instinctive flinch when his hands lifted to cup her jaw, his skin cool against her feverish flesh. "Thank you," he said, his voice deep, sensual. "Thank you for your blood." Leaning down, he breathed against her mouth. "Your trust." His lips soft, he kissed her, suckling her mouth, tasting her lips. "Your body."

He deepened the kiss, suckling, nibbling gently before his tongue swept in to possess her mouth, swirling and licking. Zara's knees weakened, and she sank into him, his armor hard and chill against her body. She wished suddenly, violently, that she could touch him.

When he finally drew away again, he gazed so deeply into her eyes, it seemed he saw clear to her soul. He stepped back and took her shoulders, then turned her gently until her back was to him. She realized his air of desperate restraint was gone. Now he seemed to be spinning out the moment before taking her, savoring the erotic anticipation.

She felt her nipples pebble against the material of the one-piece unisuit one of his men had found for her.

Smoothly, his hands moved up her arms to the closure of the uni, unsealed it, and pulled it off her shoulders to hang from the crook of her arms, leaving her breasts naked under his eyes. "You will not regret your generosity, lieutenant."

His long, strong fingers flicked delicately at the hard tips of her nipples, then gently pinched and pulled, sending a jolt of pleasure up her over sensitized nerves. "My name," he said in her ear, "is Captain Nick Rand." Big hands cupped her breasts, pulling her back against him.

He lowered his head until she could feel his breath blowing along her pulse. "And I promise you, captor or not, I will not take anything you don't choose to give. Ever."

A sudden, hot pain made her spine arch as he sank his teeth into her throat. He growled in pleasure and gathered her closer, pinching her nipples with sweet, wicked skill.

Zara gasped as he released one aching breast and brushed his free hand down the front of the uni to find her bare cunt in the unsealed opening. Long fingers stroked between her lips. She'd begun creaming the moment she saw him, and now she was richly wet. A thick, tapered forefinger slid easily into her core as he pinched and squeezed the hard tip of one breast with the other hand. His mouth moved over her flesh, feasting from her throat. He rolled his armored hips against her ass. She wished she could feel the length of his cock against her back, knew it would feel hard and demanding.

Closing her eyes, she sagged against him, surrendering herself utterly to the vampire's appetite. *This is only the beginning*. Her body leaped at the thought, hot with need and lust. *Once he's had my blood, he'll want to fuck me next. Godsson's zealots being the jealous assholes they are, he probably hasn't had access to a woman in months.*

She shouldn't do this. He was the enemy, and she shouldn't sleep with him, no matter how much she wanted to. It was wrong.

But oh, sweet God, how she wanted to. The thought of sex with him despite every dictate of common sense maddened her with its sheer kinky recklessness.

Gasping, Zara rolled her butt back against him hard, imagining the bulk of his cock driving inside her.

Pleasure unspooled through her like hot satin ribbons. His fingers pinched her nipple even harder, as a second finger joined the one plundering her juicy cunt. He drew hard on her throat, drinking her blood as his fingers pumped, his thumb flicking over her clit. Each skillful strum over her nubbin intensified the pleasure until she writhed against his armored chest, pumping her hips, gasping, whimpering.

With a scream that blended pain, delight, and erotic surrender, Zara came in the arms of her vampire enemy, barely aware of his rumble of predatory delight as he fed.

The last juicy throb faded, and she went limp in his arms, sagging, weak-kneed. "Oooh, my God," she moaned. "That was so good."

He rumbled back at her, a hum that sounded more than a little satisfied. And very male.

When he was through, he drew his fangs carefully from her throat. Pressed a surprisingly tender kiss to the point of her jaw. "I feel a little strange asking this, under the circumstances, but what's your name?"

She grinned, enjoying the delicious post-orgasm glow. "Lieutenant Zara Tahir. Vampire Support Specialist."

"Thank you, Lieutenant Tahir." He pulled away slightly. Turning her head, Zara watched as he lifted his wrist and raked his fangs over the skin until blood dripped. Then, to her blank astonishment, he put the sliced wrist in front of her mouth. "Drink, Zara."

She half turned in his arms, staring up at him with wide eyes. He was actually going to give her his blood?

"I know you need it," he said softly. "I can feel the heat of fever rolling off your skin. You're bloodsick. That's why you didn't kick the collective asses of those fucking rapists."

"Not rapists," she said hoarsely. "They didn't rape me."

"Because I stopped them."

She licked her lips, smelling the intoxicating scent of his blood. "Yes. You did."

"Drink, Lieutenant." His tone made it a dominant's order.

She bent her head to his bleeding wrist. Sealed her lips over it. The taste flooded her mouth, rich and coppery, but with a hot pepper edge that was more than human. She swallowed, once, twice. Started to lift her head.

"More," he said softly. "You need it."

And so she swallowed again and yet again.

Swallowed at his murmured urging until heat rushed through her with a dizzying intoxication. When she finished, she felt stronger, as if his blood was already bringing her immune system under control, restoring her body to her previous power, speed, and agility.

Her previous life.

"Thank you," she said softly. "You didn't have to do that."

The vampire met her gaze frankly. "We need each other."

"Yes," she said steadily, "We do. But you could have taken me by force."

His gaze cooled. "No, actually, I couldn't. And I won't."

That sounded like a vow. Zara wondered if he'd keep it.

Chapter Two

With her blood rushing through him, Rand felt normal for the first time in days. Unfortunately, he didn't have time to savor the sensual pleasure of being at full strength -- or enjoy the bloodsub as he so badly wanted to do. "I'm taking you back to our base, so you need to pack," he told her, "and you need to do it fast. We don't have much time before we're scheduled to blow this camp."

The lieutenant swore softly, but she didn't argue. Instead, she led the way out of the shelter, Rand at her heels, trying not to watch her distracting ass roll under the uni with every long stride.

They moved through the camp, Zara obviously taking the shortest route she could, as if she was worried the G.A.E. was about to start dropping bombs on her head. Meanwhile the men bustled around them, searching the base for abandoned equipment and weapons. Many of those they passed carried armloads of gear as they headed back to the transports.

Zara ducked into one of the shelters at last, Rand at her heels. It was a hell of a lot neater than the tents he'd searched earlier, with none of that sense of desperate soldiers trying to grab what they could.

"Who were you trying to buy time for?"

"No one." She bent to open the storage locker at the foot of her bunk.

Rand brought up his pulse rifle. "Step away from there, please." It would be too damned easy for her to grab a pistol from the locker.

She glanced up and froze, eyes widening at the weapon he held. Lifting her hands slowly, the lieutenant took a long step back. "You said to pack. That's what I was doing."

He gave her a deliberately easy smile. "Just making sure we don't have any misunderstandings." *Like you shooting me in the head*. "Unlock it, please."

Her gaze didn't leave his face, but the locker clicked open, as if obeying an order from her computer implant. "Your men took my rifle when they stripped me."

Rand reached down and flipped open the locker. He didn't see any obvious weapons, just neat stacks of uniforms, underwear, a spare pair of boots, and packages of emergency rations. He removed each pile and put everything on the bunk, his computer implant scanning for explosives and hidden weapons.

It would be a shame to end up dead because he underestimated her. And that would be so easy to do, particularly given those deliciously distracting tits, her big, earnest green eyes, and the taste of that sweet blood.

Yeah, distracting.

But neither Rand nor his computer found a damn thing. Satisfied, he stepped back, and pointed the barrel of his rifle in a deliberately aggressive gesture designed to remind her that screwing with a vampire wasn't a good idea. "Go ahead."

Expressionless, Zara picked up her pack and started slipping the neatly folded clothes into it, working quickly, but without any sense of panic.

"So," he asked again, hoping for a more honest answer, "who were you trying to buy time for?"

The lieutenant slanted him a look. Her long, graceful hands didn't pause in their work. "As I said, nobody. I just figured I wouldn't be able to keep up, and I didn't want to delay the retreat. I was pretty bloodsick."

"You didn't have transportation?" A camp like

this should have had a dozen troop transports.

"We'd lost some of our vehicles during the Battle of Sar. We couldn't fly everyone out at once." She shrugged. "As sick as I was, I didn't think I had that much more time anyway. If I was going to die, I wanted it to do some good."

Rand eyed her lovely profile under its tumble of shining blonde hair. "Either way, you did make a pretty good distraction. You had to know the bastards would line up for a shot at you." Silkily he added, "Have you always wanted to be a martyr?"

She shot him a look that glittered with dislike. "I didn't plan to be taken alive."

"Obviously you miscalculated."

Zara shrugged, her mouth tight.

He spotted a cube-shaped image projector sitting atop a rickety bedside table. The device was evidently voice activated, because it was cycling, projecting three-dimensional images of Zara's family and friends into the air. There were several of a teenaged Zara with an older couple standing in front of a waterfall, probably during some long-ago vacation. She had her father's stubborn jaw and her mother's expressive eyes.

Zara went right on packing, pointedly ignoring him and his rifle. The projector started on more recent images: Zara with a handsome blond man, both in the light skintight Falaran armor of the type worn by vampire teams. In one shot, the blond stared at her, smiling, his expression besotted. She looked back at him, wearing the kind of warm smile you gave a good friend.

"That your vampire partner?"

She glanced up, saw what he was looking at. Grief drew hard on her features before her expression froze and she returned her attention to her packing. "Yes. He was killed saving my life. Deliberately stepped between me and a pulse blast that would have blown off the back of my skull."

And she feels damned guilty about it. Guilty enough to martyr herself by distracting a G.A.E. team bent on rape. The thought sent a wave of protective rage through him all over again. "You were lovers?"

Zara shrugged, not looking at him. "He was my partner. My vampire." Grief darted through the green depths of those lovely eyes. "My friend."

Given the man's besotted smile, Rand would bet his captain's bars the vamp had wanted to be more than her "friend." Which probably also factored into the suicidal guilt.

Still, there must have been a sexual dimension to the relationship. They'd been a vampire team, after all. Sex came with the territory.

Yet the couple evidently hadn't had the kind of intense chemistry that led to passion. Rand was willing to bet he knew what was missing.

She slung the pack onto her shoulder and turned to look at him. Which was his cue to test his theory.

Rand reached into one of the pouches on his belt and pulled out a set of neurocuffs. "Hands on top of your head, please."

And there was the proof he was looking for -- that startled blink, the flood of sensual awareness in her eyes. She swallowed and obeyed, a betraying tremor in her hands before she rested them on her head.

Rand stepped around behind her and clipped one bracelet on her right wrist, then pulled her arm down. She lowered the other arm for him without being told so he could cuff that one too.

He smiled darkly. *Oh, you are a submissive, aren't you? And I'll bet your vampire wasn't a dominant.* Which wasn't surprising. The Falaran Coalition's vampire program hadn't featured the elements of submission and dominance typical in galactic circles.

But Rand definitely *was* a dominant. And he was beginning to suspect he'd finally found the bloodsub of his cold and lonely dreams.

* * *

Zara froze as the vampire cuffed her. Both arms went numb as the field the restraints generated blocked signals from her nerves, paralyzing them at the shoulder. Unlike old-fashioned handcuffs, there was no chain connecting the slender metal bracelets. None was needed. Once you were cuffed, you couldn't do a damned thing, though your captors could arrange your arms like a doll's. Even a mechsuited trooper couldn't break such cuffs, assuming you could get a pair on him to begin with.

She was helpless.

Rand began patting her down, his big hands sliding over her body, looking for weapons. He didn't grope, yet there was something acutely arousing about the brush of his palms over the curve of her breasts, down her torso, then passing between her legs before sliding along the length of each thigh and calf. He took his time about it, his hands thorough, searching her for any sign of blades, beamers, or projectile weapons. If she'd had any, he'd have found them.

But she had nothing. Nothing except an acute awareness of the enemy captain behind her, wide as a wall, all muscular male power and ruthless vampire hunger.

The key word there is enemy, Zara told herself. *Doesn't matter how sexy he is, he's G.A.E. Working for a fucking con man who invaded the planet trying to force us all to worship him.* She shouldn't find anything at all sexy about Captain Nick Rand. Even if he was the embodiment of every forbidden fantasy she'd ever had.

"Let's go, Lieutenant," the vampire said. He gestured toward the tent opening with the muzzle of his rifle. She could feel his gaze on her nape, burning male need focused like a laser sight. Squaring her shoulders, she drew herself to her full height and stalked out of the shelter and into the blazing afternoon sunlight.

* * *

The troop's transports set down in the camp's central landing pad one by one, sleek aerodynamic bullets masked by camo fields, floating downward on their repellers like fall leaves drifting to earth. The vampire directed Zara to the line of soldiers waiting to board one of them. A big hand cupped her elbow, ready to lend support or restraint as needed.

Or it may have been more gesture of possession, warning off the G.A.E. grunts who eyed her with a molten blend of lust and contempt. "Bloodwhore," somebody muttered behind her.

"Vamp sure made her yell, didn't he?" another answered.

Humiliation detonated in her skull, heating her cheeks like a torch. Zara knew she must be blushing redder than the trim on the vampire's armor.

Rand turned his head to look back at them. "You got something to say?" His tone could have frozen liquid nitrogen solid.

There was no answer.

"I didn't think so." He faced front again, standing behind her like a blast wall.

The men were justifiably cowed. No matter how strong a mech might be, vampires were faster. By the time a mech reached for a vamp, he'd have driven a combat blade into the base of the mech's skull.

No wonder Rand had his own troops thoroughly intimidated, for which Zara was damned grateful as they seated themselves among men who now busily ignored her.

Bloodwhore. The word dug its claws into her shrinking soul despite her best efforts to fight it off. She must have squalled like a cat in heat when Rand sank his fangs into her.

An enemy vamp, for God's sake. Was she utterly without pride?

Zara grimaced, imagining Andre's hurt at her lust for the enemy. He'd haunt her for the rest of her life. *Not that he's not haunting me now…*

She'd never felt the desire for her partner that she felt for this enemy vamp. She'd wanted to, God knew, but her partner just hadn't… affected her that way.

Thing was, she'd fantasized about vampdoms and bloodsubs since she'd gotten her hands on a forbidden sex vid at the age of sixteen. The vampire hero had been so very male, so dominant and irresistible. Zara had masturbated to the scene of the heroine surrendering her throat to him so many times, she'd had every word of dialogue memorized. Every gesture and growl and helpless sigh.

So when the G.A.E. invaded and a desperate Falaran Coalition had launched the Vampire Defense Program, Zara volunteered to become a Vampire Support Specialist. The vampire virus had transformed her body, making her bones denser, her muscles more powerful, her cells more responsive to healing.

"Reality never lives up to dreams, Zara," her mother had warned, but she hadn't listened.

Her mom had been right. Reality had turned out

to be a lot less erotic than her kinky little fantasies. Andre Miron had been a decent, big-hearted guy with a wide grin and unflinching courage that led him to leap to the defense of anyone who needed it. And yet he'd never lit up her body the way this enemy vampire had.

She'd wanted to give Andre the love he deserved, but she'd never been able to do it. Never.

And then it had been too late.

Some nights she dreamed of the instant the pulse shot burned a molten, blazing hole in Andre's face as he shoved her out of the way. Those were the nights she woke with tears on her face and a molten, blazing hole in her heart.

Why hadn't she been able to love him?

That a G.A.E. vampire made her cream when Andre hadn't felt like emotional treason. She couldn't let it happen again. She *wouldn't* let it happen again.

No matter what Rand might do to her.

* * *

Rand knew some people who needed killing. The fact that they were supposedly on his side meant exactly nothing.

He sat next to his captive, getting more and more pissed off as Zara's luscious female scent took on acrid notes of pain and humiliation.

Meanwhile, the men who'd attacked her surrounded them in the transport's seats, trading indignant glances and shooting glares at Rand for spoiling their war crime fun.

Then there was that little prick, Lieutenant Godshammer, who was fucking well going on report whether his father-in-law liked it or not. And what kind of army would assemble a chain of command like that? Even if Colonel Lordsvengeance hadn't been engaging in blatant nepotism, the grunts would believe he was.

And they had good reason to think so. Godshammer had been reaping the rewards of his father-in-law's favor for months, including first pick of the spoils from the Falaran camp.

That thought added to Rand's irritation. While he and his team had been searching the base for snipers, the rest of the men had fucking looted it. They'd used their sensors to find the most valuable gear, ammo and supplies, along with whatever loose screens and creds the Falarans might have been left behind, and taken it all.

Rand might be a mercenary who fought for creds instead of loyalty, but he'd never stolen the loser's shit, either. He wasn't a fucking thief.

Now Godshammer and the rest of the thieves sat on the transport counting their creds and playing with their looted toys -- other people's screens and trid cubes -- heads together over forbidden games, goggling at Falaran porn. Saying self-righteous crap about the Falarans' moral decay while nursing hard ons under their armor. Rand could smell their arousal.

Good thing Zara couldn't. She looked spooked enough as it was, her eyes fixed on the transport window she sat beside. Something bright flared just beyond the glass, and he followed her gaze.

The transport banked over the ground, and Rand saw a wing of G.A.E. fighters blowing hell out of the Falaran base. Just past Zara's shoulder, a God's Judgment 5000 swept over the camp, strafing it with quantum missiles that sent fireballs leaping into the blue sky.

Watching Zara watch the camp burn, Rand winced.

* * *

The G.A.E. base called Heavensgate spread below the transport: clusters of hemispherical tents dappled with the same blue and violet of the fern-trees that surrounded them. Fall had come to the foothills, and rolling lilac waves lay under the cloudless pink Falaran sky.

The transport rocked on its repeller fields as it touched down among the clusters of G.A.E. craft. The men lined up to disembark, ignoring Rand and Zara in favor of whatever screens and games they'd managed to steal.

It occurred to Zara that Godsson might be in for an unpleasant surprise. Since taking over the Heaven colony thirty years ago, he'd maintained an iron control over the media his people had access to, especially the comp screens he'd declared tools of the Evil One.

Now thousands of his soldiers were getting exposure to ideas his theocracy hadn't vetted -- particularly when it came to the common knowledge that Godsson had an extensive list of interstellar convictions for running cons on a dozen planets.

Zara grinned darkly, enjoying the thought that Godsson's greed could be the thing that brought him down. Too bad it might not be in time to save her people.

Or Zara herself, for that matter.

When the vampire stood and took her elbow, she allowed herself to be shepherded off the transport, the pack slung over her uni-clad shoulder. Given Rand's rank, the pair of them were the first to disembark from the transport. Zara's shoulder blades itched from all the glares aimed her way.

"Ignore them," the captain murmured as they

walked up the aisle to the hatch. "Don't give them the satisfaction of giving a shit what they think."

Easy for you to say, she thought resentfully. *You're not the one they're calling a bloodwhore.*

Though in the eyes of these fanatics, being a vampire was probably worse. Not that Rand acted like a man with anything to be ashamed of.

Maybe he did know what he was talking about, at that.

So she let him guide her down the transport's ramp, trying to look as if she hadn't done anything wrong and didn't give a damn if anyone else thought she had.

Her attention fell on a tall, angular man who stood at the foot of the ramp. His hair was nothing more than a thin fringe, his mouth almost lipless under a beaky nose, his eyes as blue and frigid as an ice-melt lake. He wore a colonel's comets on the high collar of his red and black uniform. She recognized him from recon reports as the commanding officer of this base. *Colonel Lordsvengeance.*

And he looked thoroughly pissed off. The glare he aimed at Rand could have burned a hole in three meters of ultranium bulkhead.

He turned that glittering attention on Zara next, and her stomach instantly coiled into a sick knot. There was something almost erotic in that frigid stare, a kind of lust, but not for Zara's body. *What this bastard wants is pain.*

Given half a chance, he'd torture her for the sheer pleasure of listening to her scream. By comparison, Godshammer looked almost wholesome.

"I won't let him have you," Rand promised, his voice so soft a human couldn't have heard him.

Zara threw him a grateful look. "Thank you," she

whispered.

"For the record, Captain," the colonel announced in a subzero voice, "You are not to pursue... *war crimes* charges" -- he grimaced in distaste at the phrase -- "against any of my men. Particularly not Lieutenant Godshammer."

Rand stiffened. "It *was* a war crime. They attempted to rape this woman, Colonel."

"Don't be absurd." Lordsvengeance curled a thin lip at her. "This little bloodwhore asked for it, and in any case, His Most Exalted has ordered the faithful to discipline Falaran females who dare take up arms against His divine will."

Furious, Zara opened her mouth, only to feel Rand wrap a big hand around hers, the motion hidden by his body.

"Godsson signed the Treaty of Vermillion," the vampire pointed out. "He agreed those under his command would not sexually assault enemy combatants."

"An agreement with infidels is not binding on His Most Transcendent."

"That's not surprising," Zara snapped, "Considering he's a fucking con ar --"

"Enough!" Rand snarled, his armored fingers clamping down on hers, almost tight enough to break bones.

She shut her mouth so fast, she tasted blood.

The colonel looked her over the way he would a poodle who'd puddled on his boots. "I wonder," Lordsvengeance mused in a silken voice, "if this creature knows where her Falaran battalion has holed up. Perhaps I should... ask her." There was something eager and repellent in those cold, cold eyes that made Zara's guts freeze.

"Come now, Colonel," Rand said blandly. "Do you seriously think the Falarans would have told a *female* anything worth knowing?"

The officer made a sound somewhere between frustration and agreement. "Good point, I suppose." His lips curled in a chilly smile. "Besides, at the moment you need this little whore with her blood still pumping. After the hemosynther arrives, I'll take her off your hands and discipline her as she so richly deserves."

Rand inclined his head. "As you say, Colonel."

For the first time, the man deigned to address her. "It would be to your advantage to make yourself useful, bitch." He curled his thin upper lip. "Otherwise you could find your life much shorter than you'd like -- and very, very painful." He started to turn away, then paused. "Do remember what I said about those war crimes charges." His chilly gaze flicked toward Zara. "Especially given that taking a female for sexual use makes you just as guilty as those you'd accuse."

Expressionless, Rand said, "I won't be filing a report."

"See that you don't." The colonel strutted away.

Once he was gone, Rand turned to Zara and said in a low, deadly voice, "What the hell was that?"

"He --"

"That man is a psychopath, Lieutenant," he said through his teeth. "You do *not* want to be at his mercy."

"No," she admitted in a small voice. "I really don't."

Rand sighed, sounding weary. "When I said I wouldn't let him have you, I meant it. But I'd just as soon not have to go to war with him -- not until I'm ready for it, anyway." His gaze heated. "But I'll tell you what I am ready for." His teeth flashed in a predatory smile. "You. And this time, I want more than a taste."

Zara swallowed as her nipples drew into hard points.

* * *

She was intensely aware of Rand's hold on her elbow as he steered her through the clusters of dome-shaped shelters that made up the base. His armored fingers felt cool and powerful.

Excitement buzzed through her, frothing in her blood, even as she told herself she had no business letting this man get to her. No business responding to him like this.

Yet even as she lectured herself, her heart pounded, and she had a humiliating suspicion that she was going wet between her thighs.

This was far too much like the fantasies she'd had -- those rough erotic dreams of her college years which had inspired her to join the Vampire Defense Program to begin with.

Zara edged a guilty glance up at the features visible through his helmet visor: that handsome, intensely masculine face.

What would his body look like? How would his cock feel, stroking hard and deep into her pussy? Her mouth went dry with need at the thought of the raw pleasure she'd find in that driving penetration, the feel of his mouth on her skin, the sharp, sweet penetration of his fangs.

This enemy captain was the embodiment of every fantasy she'd ever had, as Andre never had been. Andre, her friend and partner, whom she'd hurt with expectations he could never meet. Couldn't even understand.

The fact that she might actually *want* to be spanked made no sense to Andre. His bewilderment made her feel like she really was a bloodwhore. She'd carried so much guilt about her fantasies for years -- guilt that had only intensified when Andre died saving her life.

How could she feel this intense desire for the enemy? Yes, she had to let him feed on her. Without Rand's protection, she'd face an ugly death at the hands of that psychotic colonel, not to mention all the other fanatics on this base. She couldn't afford to piss the vampire off.

So yes, she had to submit to Rand. She might even have to sleep with him. He was a vampire mercenary, and that's what he would expect. But sleeping with him, letting him feed from her, did not mean *wanting* him like this.

She had to get control of this craving.

No, what I really need to do is escape. Get out of this place, and away from these vicious fanatics. Away from the vampire's seductive temptation, before she lost herself. Before he seduced her into giving up more than blood and body.

Before he turned her into a traitor.

Zara straightened under his hand, pulled her shoulders into a military posture, and prepared to do battle against her own need.

Rand steered her into his tent. It was ruthlessly Spartan; its only furniture was a bunk barely big enough to accommodate his brawny height, a locker, and a small folding table and chair. She was relieved to see his bunk was the only one there.

"You don't have a tentmate?"

He shrugged. "Nobody wanted to share a shelter with a vampire." Dryly, he added, "Evidently they think being damned is contagious."

"That or they're afraid you'd be overcome with bloodlust and attack them in their sleep."

He snorted. "I've *never* gotten that hungry."

As Zara moved further into the tent, she noticed images cycling over the table's surface. It was evidently the kind that did double duty as a computer. She eyed it as it displayed shots of Rand in a variety of uniforms, surrounded by grinning uniformed people with fangs. Fellow vamp mercenaries?

Another shot appeared, this one of a lovely older woman with dark hair and Rand's clever green eyes. Zara frowned at the nagging feeling she knew the lady from somewhere. She had no idea why.

Rand stepped around Zara and headed for the bed. She stared, instantly forgetting about the image sequence.

He touched the seam at his throat and the top half of his mechsuit split open, collapsing so he could strip it off like a coat. The lid of Rand's locker slid aside, probably in response to some signal from his cybernetic implant. He folded the suit coat and stowed it neatly away.

Leaving his chest deliciously bare.

Feeling as if she were sinking into honeyed need, Zara stared, her eyes drifting over the thick muscle, the ridges and hollows of hard male strength.

Rand's hands went to his mechsuit's crotch. The armored cup slid open at his touch, freeing his erect cock. It was just as thick and hard and elegant as her fantasies. Zara licked her lips at the delicious erotic possibilities inherent in that impressive shaft.

Her gaze flicked from that tempting cock to the width of his shoulders, the washboard ripple of his muscled belly. She licked dry lips. The man was everything she'd ever fantasized about in her lonely bunk.

Especially the hot, predatory glitter of his eyes, the white flash of the tips of his fangs in his smile.

His eyes locked on hers, Rand stripped off his mechsuit pants. His waist and hips were so narrow, they emphasized the width of his torso. He sat on the bed and bent to open the seal of his boots. Zara stared, hypnotized, at the strong curve of his back. Muscle rolled under skin still sheened with sweat from wearing armor.

He stepped out of his boots, then stowed everything in the locker. After settling the helmet and gloves in with the rest, he put the boots together beside the locker.

At last, he straightened and turned toward her, catching her staring. His mouth curved slowly as he walked toward her, his shoulders rolling with every confident male stride. "See anything you like?"

Zara jerked her eyes away from his aggressive predator's stare. She felt her face go hot, and cursed her fair complexion. "I… I… Don't…"

He reached out, fingertips brushing coolly over her jaw. "Such a pretty blush."

Before she could figure out how to react, Rand pivoted on a bare heel and walked away, giving her a luscious view of his bare ass. He dropped on the bunk, leaving her standing there shaking, her nipples pebbled tight inside her borrowed uniform. Embarrassed and hot at the same time.

"Do you want this?" He lay back, elbows on the mattress. "It doesn't have to be sex between us. Though I'll admit, I'll be painfully disappointed if it's not." His gaze hardened, amusement draining from his green eyes. "I'm not that bastard Godshammer. I do take no for an answer, and I will protect you."

He meant it. The thought brought her a sense of relief, along with a twinge of guilt. What would happen to him when she ran? And she would run. She didn't dare hang around waiting for Lordsvengeance to decide to torture her. Her gaze slid from his. "Thank you."

His eyes narrowed and chilled as if he read her mind. "That said, I won't let you escape. If you try, I will come after you and I *will* catch you."

"Understood." Something tightened low in her belly.

"And you like that idea, don't you?"

Lie. The thought flashed through her skull. *Don't let him know how much power he really has*. "Don't be absurd."

His smile went hot, intimate. "You know better than to think you can lie to me. Vampires can smell a lie." His dark smile broadened. "And that's not all we can smell."

She knew exactly what he meant, and felt her cheeks heat. The fact he could scent her need was almost as galling as it was intriguing.

Wrong. This is so wrong. And yet some part of her really didn't give a damn if it was wrong or not. Zara wanted him, craved the hot burn of his fangs in her throat, the feel of his hands gliding over her skin. Wanted him and really didn't give a shit about wrong or right, or anything else but satisfying the hot need he inspired.

She realized she was staring at him, at the hard elegance of his body. At the strength in those big hands. At the cock curving over his ridged belly and pointing at his chin, ready and arousing.

"You don't want to tell me no, do you?" His hand

drifted down the length of his beautiful chest, coming to rest just over the thick jut of his cock. She wanted to touch him even more than she wanted to feel that big hand on her skin.

"You're a submissive."

Zara started, her eyes flying to meet his, her lips parted instinctively on a lying denial.

"Don't bother. I sensed your reaction when I handcuffed you." Golden eyes watched her with hooded interest. "I heard your heart leap when the cuffs closed around your wrists. It beat even faster when you felt me behind you at the perfect distance to bite or kiss -- you didn't care which."

"I… I… You…" She stammered, couldn't think of a lie -- and realized she didn't want to tell one anyway.

She felt what she felt. Needed what she needed. And it didn't matter what she was supposed to feel, supposed to want. She wanted what she wanted, and she was going to take it.

Take *him*.

* * *

"I need a bloodslave." Rand said the words boldly, watching her eyes flicker as she reacted. Yeah, she was a submissive. It was obvious in the tremble of that soft mouth, and the jut of the nipples beneath her borrowed uniform. "And you need a dominant. That's what you fantasize about, isn't it? A man willing to do all the things to you that you've ever dreamed of. You crave that every bit as much as you need my blood."

She looked away, a beautiful blush spreading over the lovely contours of her face. "Yes."

"Yes, what?" Damned if he'd let her off the hook. He did not want any confusion or doubt or simple misunderstanding about what either of them wanted. It would be too easy otherwise to make a mistake, especially given how much he needed her. Wanted her.

"Yes, I want a dominant." He felt his cock lengthen another inch at the erotic possibilities in those exquisite eyes. "I've always had fantasies about..." She swallowed. "You. Vampires."

"That's why you became a bloodsub."

"V.S.S.," she corrected. "Vampire support specialist."

He laughed, though not at her. When she shot him an offended glare, he elaborated. "It always amuses me, how the military has to invent acronyms, prettying everything up."

Her expressive mouth flattened. "You mean the way your colonel talked about making me talk without ever using the word 'torture?'"

"First, he's not *my* colonel. But yeah, he is a son of a bitch. And like I told you, I'm not going to let him touch you."

"How are you going to stop him? He outranks you."

"You let me worry about that. All you need to know is that I take my responsibility to my submissives seriously. That means I don't do anything they don't like. So what *do* you like?"

"I don't know." Her gaze slid away from his again. "I've never done... *this* before."

"Well, what do you fantasize about?" And God, he'd love to hear all about any kinky thing she wanted to tell him.

She smiled, her expression open. Honest. "I fantasize about a lot. But there can be a lot of ground between fantasy and what someone likes in reality."

"Then I'll give you a safe word -- a code to use if I do something you don't like. Or if something hurts more than you want."

"How about the words, 'stop, damn it'?"

"Smartass. The code is 'abort.' Use it. And I'm not just talking about when something hurts physically. I mean if you start having a panic attack or it just gets too damn intense for you." He met her gaze, his own level, ignoring his nudity. "The point of this relationship is not abuse. It's sensual pleasure, even if that pleasure comes from having your ass caned."

Her eyes widened just slightly and her lips parted. *Direct hit,* Rand thought. There was a little masochist in the soldier after all.

Not that he was surprised. Most soldiers had a little masochist in them, whether in a sexual form or not.

He sent a pulse through his computer implant, and the magnetic restraints released, dropping from her wrists to thump down on the shelter's plastron flooring. "Take that uni off."

Zara licked her lips nervously and brought her arms around, one hand rubbing at the opposite wrist. Her gaze never left him, flicking from his face to his erect cock, down his legs to the bare feet crossed at the ankle.

She licked her lips again and reached up to follow the seal of the baggy uni. It split open on a V of creamy skin, revealing the sweet cleavage between her unbound breasts. Pointing the way to the dip of her belly button, then further down to the rise of her pubic bone.

She shrugged in an elegant little gesture, and the uni slid to her elbows, baring those delicious breasts, round and firm and insanely tempting. Her nipples were sweetly erect, rosy and distended with blood.

His fangs twinged.

She straightened her arms, letting the uniform

drop down the length of them -- it really was ridiculously big on her -- to catch on her hips before tumbling to her ankles.

For a moment she stood there, slim and delicious, all her lush curves on display, breasts and hips full and tempting, the narrow nip of her waist between them. Feminine as she was, there was muscle beneath her silky skin that revealed she'd worked to build her strength in the endless wait between battles.

If we'd met on the battlefield, I would've had to kill her. Rand thrust that dark thought away. It hadn't happened… At least, not so far.

He swore in that moment that he would never raise a hand to this deliciously vulnerable woman. Even if she tried to escape, he'd find a way to keep her safe.

Though there was something intriguingly erotic about the thought of chasing her… Then again, he found something erotic about damn near everything where Zara was concerned.

While he'd been distracted by another wave of lust, she toed off her boots and stripped away the last shreds of her V.S.S. armor. Once a suit lost its structural integrity, it was little better than tissue paper.

"Pick up the restraints and come here."

Zara dropped into a graceful crouch and obeyed, then rose to bring the cuffs to him. Her eyes were cast downward in unconscious submission, and her hands shook ever so slightly as she held out the neurocuffs, whether in fear or excitement. Something was definitely making her heart pound.

He inhaled, testing her scent. Yeah, that was arousal.

She could have feared him. Maybe *should* have

feared him. And yet it seemed she believed him when he said he wouldn't hurt her.

Reassured, Rand sat up on the side of the bed. "Come here." He gave her a deliberately menacing smile. "I want to... *discuss* your endangering yourself by smarting off to the colonel earlier."

Her expression was more intrigued than anything. "What exactly do you have in mind?"

He grinned wolfishly as he lifted the cuffs. "What do you think?"

She opened her mouth to answer, but he grabbed her wrist and jerked, tumbling her down across his lap. He pinned her there while she was still yelping. "Give me your other wrist."

She kicked, but it came nowhere near him. "Fuck. Off!"

His palm landed on the delicate curve of her ass in a loud, meaty *swat*!

"Ooowww!" She kicked again, and he took a moment to admire the working muscle of her gorgeous little ass.

Rand inhaled, testing, and confirmed she was still thoroughly turned on. Sniffed again.

Oh yeah. He'd somehow stumbled on the little submissive of his dreams. The one he'd been looking for all his years of being a vampire.

Capturing and cuffing her wrists one by one, he paused to contemplate her pretty backside with wolfish anticipation.

Then he proceeded to turn that delicious little butt a bright rosy pink, dotted with handprints.

Chapter Three

Zara had fantasized about being spanked so many times. Imagined the sting of a hard palm landing on her ass, the rough growl of a male voice rumbling orders.

There was something that just got to her about being helpless like this. About the sound of his hand igniting a fire in her ass with those ruthless swats. Yeah, it hurt more than she expected -- enough to have her cursing and yowling by turns. But it was also more arousing than her hottest fantasy.

And the way he looked at her, all blazing lust. Yet something in his eyes made her feel… beautiful. And, oddly, safe. As if she could trust him to protect her, could surrender, knowing he wouldn't go too far. As if his focus were more on what she wanted, needed, than on his own desires.

Though he definitely enjoyed beating her ass. She felt intensely aware of the long velvet-skinned arch of his cock against her ribs as he held her in place across his lap.

He paused his furious swats. She lay over his hard thighs, panting in a mixture of pain and desire. Wondering what he planned to do to her now.

He brushed his fingers delicately across the curve of her ass. "Very pretty. Very… pink." Laughter infused his voice. "How'd you like that, captive?"

Wanting only to incite him into doing something else equally delicious, she spat the first thing that came into her head. "Fuck off!"

The next impact of palm on butt was so hard, she damned near swallowed her tongue. "Now, is that any way to talk to your captor? I asked you a question, prisoner." *Swat*! "How." *Swat*! "Did." *Swat*! "You."

Swat! "Like." *Swat*! "That?"

Given the pain radiating from the site of that last blow, Zara swallowed the impulse to spit another obscenity. Silence ticked.

"Maybe I'll just check for myself." A finger brushed the swollen lips of her pussy. Slid between them to dip into her core.

Both of them groaned at the thick, slick cream he found there.

"Mmm. Seems you enjoyed your spanking almost as much as I did." This time two fingers dipped into her. Pushed deep even as his thumb strummed over her clit. Once. Twice. Playing her pussy, strumming notes of heat and delight with every inward dip and thumb swirl. "This is a really nice pussy you've got here. So very wet and tight. I can't wait to drive my cock into it."

Judging by the broad heat of his erection butting against her ribs, she could believe it. Imagining how delicious it would feel, she wanted to beg. "Don't!"

He stilled. "Do you want to abort?"

The cold wording slapped her back to sanity. He was asking if she wanted to use the safe word he'd given her. For a moment she was tempted, just to find out whether he really would stop. Especially given the goad of that iron hard on.

"No! No, I don't want to stop!" Which was why he'd given her a code to begin with -- so he could tell whether she really meant stop, or had just lost herself in playing the role of reluctant captive.

"You sure about that?" He jerked his fingers from her pussy and hit her ass again in another juicy slap.

"Oowww! Yes, damn it! I'm sure! Do not abort!"

"In that case..." He opened his knees wide, dumping her on the floor, though he held her waist to make sure she didn't hurt herself. Rising to his feet, he pulled her onto her knees.

Face to head with his cock. A teardrop of pre-cum beaded on its slit, a glistening testament to his arousal. She swallowed, her mouth dust-dry.

"Put that pretty mouth to good use." He wrapped a big fist in her hair and pulled her in, his free hand guiding the big shaft between the lips she opened for him.

He tasted of salt and man as he filled her mouth, hot and thick and maddening. Imagining how he'd feel stuffing her wet and empty pussy, she groaned in need.

And began to suck. Hard. Eagerly. Swirling her tongue over the underside of the shaft, licking the sensitive vein that ran along its length.

"That's right," Rand said, low and rough. "Suck me hard. Take me deep." He thrust, stopping just shy of gagging her, then began rolling his hips with ruthless control.

God, it was so delicious, so erotic feeling him mouth fucking her. Hands cuffed behind her, paddled ass burning, unable to resist even if she'd wanted to. And God, she didn't.

What she wanted was to be fucked. To feel him everywhere. To savor all the promise of pleasure his hard body offered. His shaft slid back and forth between her lips, making her imagine how he'd feel in her pussy, driving ruthlessly deep. Velvet over iron, solid and primitive.

Primal male to her hungry female.

"That's enough." He arced his hips, pulling his cock free from her mouth.

"No..." Zara groaned, breathless and frustrated. She leaned forward, trying to recapture his cock, but he stepped clear.

Laughing, he caught her jaw in his fingers and pulled her head up to meet his gaze. "When I say no, that's what I mean."

Scooping her off the floor, he dropped her on the bunk hard enough to bounce. "I have something in mind."

Then he pounced, pushing her backward onto her bound wrists as he lowered his head to capture a nipple in his hot, skilled mouth.

His tongue swirled over the pebbled point between gentle bites that let her feel the points of his fangs. Not penetrating -- quite. The wet sensations were overwhelming, sending her arousal spiking until she pumped her hips in helpless lust.

Rand braced his weight on his elbows as he rested his body diagonally across hers. Zara moaned as his thumb flicked one nipple as he suckled and teased the other.

And there was nothing she could do about it, even if she'd wanted to. The restraints around her wrists held her arms paralyzed beneath her.

Rand started working his way down her body, pausing here and there to kiss, lick, and bite. Each time she thought he was going to break the skin, but he held back. His restraint only stoked the anticipation.

He stopped to swirl his tongue over her bellybutton, making her squirm at the ticklish sensation. Then lower, nibbling gently.

By the time he rose to slide between her legs, draping her knees over his shoulders, need coiled into a tight, fierce knot between her thighs.

She raised her head, watching down the length of her body as he parted her. Licked. His gaze lifted to meet hers as he grinned wickedly. "There's nothing like the taste of wet pussy." His tongue thrust deep into her cunt.

"Rand! Oh, God!" Rolling her head back, Zara gasped. Waves of pleasure surged through her in time to his thrusting tongue. Settling down, he reached one hand up her body and went after one tight nipple, squeezing, pinching, twisting, while he licked in and out of her slick cunt.

She moaned as he lapped up and down each side of her vaginal lips, then swirled the tip of his tongue over and around her clit.

Her arousal intensified, until she writhed with it, suspended in the web of pleasure he wove. "God, Rand, you feel so good!" she gasped. "Fuck me, please, fuck me…"

The burning fuse of her pleasure suddenly detonated in a deep, rolling orgasm. She screamed, head thrown back, hips grinding.

"And that sounds like my cue." He pulled away, snatched her off the bunk as if she were weightless, and flipped her over. Spreading her with one hand, he aimed his cock with the other and thrust into her from behind.

She shrieked into the mattress, high, shrill and abandoned.

"Felt that, didn't you?" he asked, a note of dark laughter in his voice.

"Yes, you bastard!"

"That's no way to talk to your dom." He drew the length of his cock out of her body, then thrust deep. "I'm afraid I'm going to have to punish you for that."

Then he started driving, fucking her hard, his shaft so thick, so long, the muscle of his thighs pressing against hers, his long fingers gripping her hips as he ground in and out.

Those ferocious sensations built the pulses of her climax, driving them higher, faster. She convulsed helplessly, yowling under his pounding hips. "Rand! Oh, God, more!"

* * *

Rand watched Zara writhe, her slim back twisting, silken ass hunching against his groin, pussy gripping him, slick and snug. The pleasure was so intense he had to fight not to come. "God," he groaned, "You feel so damned..."

He held on somehow, listening to her gasping whimpers of delight, his fangs aching, until finally he could stand no more. Shifting his hold from hips to shoulders, he pulled her upright, then wrapped a hand into her hair. Dragged her head to one side.

And bit.

The taste of her blood filled his mouth, pumping sweet and hot. His cock jerked as his lust skidded out of control. He drank as her pussy rippled around his length and his balls emptied in burning pulses. She screamed again, stiffening in his grip. "Raaaaand!"

He growled possessively back at her.

The pleasure faded slowly, leaving her limp and sated in his arms. Rand withdrew his fangs carefully and started licking the small wounds; his vampire saliva would make them heal much faster.

She only moaned. "God, that feels good."

"Yes," he agreed in her ear. "It certainly did." He paused to caress her softening nipples as he pulled his cock from her sex. "Thank you for the gift of your submission."

"Believe me," Zara breathed, "the pleasure was mine."

Rand smiled and eased back, ordering his computer implant to open the neurocuffs. The restraints released, and he stripped them off her wrists before bending to scoop her up. Zara draped her arms around his neck as he carried her around the bunk to put her down on the mattress.

"That was delicious," she sighed.

Rand licked a drop of blood from his lips. "I thought so."

He moved through a flap into the hygiene closet that held the shelter's toilet.

He picked up a cloth and flicked it, activating the release of moisture from its fibers. Rand cleaned himself off with the wet cloth, then refolded it and dropped it back on the stack to disinfect itself. He grabbed another cleaning cloth and carried it out to Zara.

"Spread your legs," he ordered. She obeyed, looking half asleep and he reached between her thighs to her lovely pussy.

He put the cloth away, then returned to slide into the bed, spooning the warm curve of her body with his and wrapped his arms around her. "Sleep, Zara," he murmured.

She sighed, her breathing deepening, her slim body going lax.

He inhaled the scent of her hair, enjoying the warmth of her soft skin, savoring the memory of her body rolling against his as he drank from her. As she came in his arms.

He'd claimed her. She was his now. His submissive. His woman.

His captive.

Rand frowned a little, uncomfortable with the thought. It was one thing to play at holding a woman prisoner, to pretend to force her submission as part of a sexual game. It was another thing entirely to take a prisoner to bed. Yes, he felt reasonably sure she'd meant it when she gave her consent, especially given the scent of her arousal.

But could a prisoner truly give consent?

Unfortunately, there was no way to free her. If he even tried, Lordsvengeance would do everything in his power to kill both of them. And the bastard would make sure they died in the worst way he could manage, probably after torturing Zara for any intelligence she might possess.

Rand's jaw clenched as he stroked her slender shoulder. He'd sworn to protect her, and he'd do it.

Lordsvengeance would have to go through him to get to his submissive. And if the fucker tried, he'd find out exactly why you shouldn't piss off a vampire.

It wouldn't be a lesson the colonel would enjoy.

* * *

Zara woke some hours later to the smell of meat and spices. She sat up on her elbows on the bunk to see Rand, fully dressed in light G.A.E. armor, arranging a pair of steaming trays, utensils, and drinks on the small table.

"Something smells good."

"I made a run to the mess tent," he explained, as she took another appreciative sniff. "I figured being stared at by a tent full of horny, resentful assholes wouldn't be particularly good for your digestion."

"You figured right." She rolled out of the bed, picked up her uni, and got dressed before taking a seat at the table. She removed the tray's lid, releasing a wave of steam fragrant with the scent of roasted meat and spices. "Mmm." Zara picked up a fork and dug in, quickly discovering that it was every bit as delicious as it smelled.

For a moment there was silence as they made short

work of the food. Rand ate every bit as heartily as she did. Godssonists superstition notwithstanding, vamps ate food and had no more problem with sunlight than ordinary humans.

Once her stomach was comfortably full, Zara headed for the curtained alcove and used one of the cleansing sheets to bathe the dried sweat of combat and passion from her skin.

Emerging, she bent over the duffle she'd packed with her clothes and gear. She could feel Rand watching her lazily from where he sprawled on the bunk, his armored ankles crossed.

As she dressed in a clean uniform -- one that actually fit -- Zara asked, "What are your plans for the day? I mean what do you want me to do?" Looking over at him, lounging there looking big and handsome in his black armor suddenly brought home to her what an uncomfortable position she was in.

He might be her lover, but he was also an enemy officer.

What the hell am I doing?

As a lieutenant in the Falaran army, it was her duty to escape -- even to kill him.

And yet even if she did such a thing, what the hell would she do next? She was in the middle of a G.A.E. camp. Even if she succeeded in killing Rand, she was unlikely to make it to freedom.

But Rand, who'd protected her from his own murderous men, would still be dead -- a victim of his own generosity.

Assuming she succeeded. A V.S.S. might be strong, but Rand still had at least double her strength. Probably more. She didn't have a prayer against him.

None of which changed the fact that he was the enemy, and Zara still had a duty to escape.

* * *

His table chimed. Zara looked around in time to see a familiar face form above the tabletop. "Good morning, darling."

Zara had heard the voice in hundreds of newstreams: Adela Rand. She gaped. *Darling? Adela Rand is calling… Oh.*

"Hi, Mom," Rand said cheerfully. "Made any gossip streams lately?"

One of the galaxy's richest women gave him an urchin grin. "Oh, you how it is. I can't scratch my ass without winding up on the 'stream." She looked him over with what Zara thought was a trace of maternal anxiety. "I see you're still in one piece."

"So far." He rolled off the bunk, walked to the table and dropped into a chair so he could study his mother's image.

Zara fidgeted, more than a little uncomfortable. "Do you want me to step outside, give you two a little privacy?"

"God, no. Somebody'd probably shoot you -- while 'trying to escape.'" He gestured quotes in the air, then snorted sardonically. "Might even be true."

Adela studied her so closely, Zara wondered if she had spinach clinging to her teeth. "Who's this? And why is she wearing a Falaran Coalition uniform?"

"Mother, meet Lieutenant Zara Tahir. She's my… guest. Zara, this is my mother, Adela Rand."

Zara had to swallow before she could manage, "It's a pleasure to meet you, ma'am."

"I'm delighted to say the same. That's a V.S.S. insignia on your uni, isn't it, dear?" The woman's eyes narrowed as she studied the stylized golden V pinned on Zara's high collar.

"Yes, ma'am."

"Well, that's one way to solve the hemosynther problem."

Rand blinked. "How'd you find out about that?"

"I make it a point to be well informed about my only son. Especially since you won't tell me a damned thing. I would have sent you the 'synther, Rand."

"It's not your job to provide me with supplies. It's my employer's." Frowning, he changed the subject. "So. Are you on Falara yet?"

"Oh, yes. I'm meeting with Godsson in an hour, in fact. We're supposed to be discussing those ideas I have for his new Falaran territories. So far he seems to be very enthusiastic."

A muscle worked in Rand's jaw. "I trust your bodyguards are staying on their toes."

"I can handle myself, Nick. I used to be a merc too, if you remember."

"Which won't keep you from getting blood all over that pretty suit."

"It's in Godsson's best interest to make sure I stay safe, given his eagerness to cut a deal."

Zara had held her temper about as long as she could. "You might want to keep in mind that Godsson doesn't have this planet yet. He's not in a position to make deals."

Adela studied her in the fraught pause that followed. "It's only a matter of time, I'm afraid. The Falaran Army is outnumbered and outgunned. The newsies say the capital is expected to fall in a week -- perhaps two at the outside. I'm afraid you find yourself in a rather uncomfortable position."

The woman was so calm about discussing the virtual enslavement of a million people. As if Falara were some corporation she was buying. Zara opened her mouth for a hot retort.

But before she could spit out something ill advised, Rand covered her hand where it lay fisted on the table. "Enough, Zara."

"But..."

"Zara." Something about the look in his golden eyes made her close her mouth. It wasn't anger, or even a dominant's arrogant demand that his sub shut up. It was more like a plea for understanding, and a promise that he would explain. Just not now.

Adela's lips pursed as she eyed him, then flicked a glance at Zara. "The lieutenant's not just a solution to the hemosynther problem, is she?" She sat back in her chair with a satisfied smile. "It's about time."

"Oh, for God's sake, Mom, she's a prisoner of war."

"You don't fool me, Nick. You always know exactly what you want, and you get it. And then you don't let go."

Zara found her tongue at last. "Ma'am, we just met last night." She grimaced. "Under circumstances that were far from ideal."

"He rescued you somehow, didn't he?"

"Ma."

"That's what I thought." She nodded, satisfied. "She'll do, Nick. You always were a smart lad."

"That's not what you said when I was seventeen."

"You were *seventeen*. Too much testosterone, not enough brain development." Seeing Zara's confusion, Adela explained, "On the night he's talking about, we fought over his wrecking his brand new sports zipper. Damn near killed himself plowing into a traffic buoy."

"There was barely a scratch on me."

"Because you were incredibly fuckin' lucky. There wasn't enough left of that flyer to flatten into a sheet of aluminum foil. I almost passed out when I saw the remains." To Zara she added, "I said something unwise about his need to be more responsible and told him he was grounded. The next thing I knew, he'd ditched his bodyguards and *poofed*. I was still losing my mind when he finally called three days later and told me he'd become a vampire -- *and* joined Valentine's Vamps."

Zara studied him, bemused. "Why in the hell did you do that?"

He shrugged. "I figured otherwise I'd grow up to be another pampered asshole corporate prince. I knew a lot of guys like that, and I didn't want to become one."

His mother grimaced. "Yes, but you didn't have to become a merc instead, damn it."

"You told me enlisting in Randal's Raiders was the making of you."

"Well, yeah," she admitted. "But that was *me*. You were my baby boy, and I didn't want anybody shooting at you."

"Getting shot at did me good. Knocked all the asshole out."

"I wouldn't go that far," Zara murmured.

Adela laughed. "Oh, I do like her. She'll keep you humble."

"Would you stop?"

"But I'm having such fun..." To Zara she added, "He must have done something right -- he grew up to be a hell of a man."

Rand grinned, obviously pleased at the compliment. "Thank you, ma'am."

"I could use you in the company, you know." Adela grimaced. "I just had to sack my Chief Operations Officer for being a pampered asshole corporate prince."

Rand flicked a look at Zara. "I'll think about it."

"Really?" Adela looked startled. "The last time we talked about this, you refused to even consider quitting."

"Getting shot at is losing its appeal."

"It has appeal?"

He laughed. "I love you, Mom. Tell those bodyguards they better not let you get hurt, or corporate prince or not, they'll find out just how big an asshole I can be."

"I'll be sure to pass the message along." Her gaze grew serious. Weighted. "Take care of yourself, son."

"You do the same." His expression went equally grim. "I hear Godsson's a tough negotiator."

Her jaw flexed. "So am I. I love you, Nick."

"I love you too, Mom."

Adela's image disappeared.

Rand stared at the empty air left behind by his mother's vanished image. Anxiety lashed him like a dominant's neurostim whip until he wanted to steal one of the camp's pulse fighters, fly to Godsson's base, and blow hell out of anyone who threatened Adela Rand.

Unfortunately, that wouldn't be a good idea.

Oh, he could steal one of the flyers without much trouble, but he'd have to endanger Zara to do it. Without armor she'd be vulnerable as hell, and the Godssonists wouldn't hesitate to blow her pretty blonde head off.

Too, once he was in the air, his vampire advantages disappeared. He was a good pilot, but only that. The mercenary pulse pilots defending Godsson's headquarters were the best money could buy. They were literally jacked into their machines, and their reaction time was even faster than his. To make matters worse, Godsson had been able to hire a lot of them because all the other mercs were as desperate for work as Rand had been when he'd taken this Godawful job.

Luckily, Mom had a small army of skilled and nasty bodyguards to keep her safe.

Zara was another story. She was now in far more danger than his mother, and her only protection was Rand. So he needed to get his head out of his ass and take care of her, because the shit was about to hit the turbos.

It was time to put his contingency plan into operation.

* * *

Rand, Zara thought, looked incredibly pissed off. Worried as hell, too. It was obvious he loved his mother a great deal, and was convinced she was in some kind of danger.

Well, Adela did plan to meet Godsson, the target of more than one Falaran assassination plot. What kind of business deal was worth that sort of risk?

But why did he seem so convinced she was in imminent danger, as if someone was actively gunning for her?

Maybe he was just intensely protective. Zara felt that way about her parents too, which is one reason she'd gone to war to begin with. The Godssonists were a threat to the whole planet, including her family. She'd felt driven to do something about it, even if that meant becoming a Vampire Support Specialist in order to maximize her effectiveness in combat.

At least she hadn't blindsided her mother with that decision the way Rand evidently had. Then again, she hadn't been a teenager, either. Not that her parents had been any happier about the idea than Adela, but

Zara had been twenty-one. At the end of the ferocious argument that had followed, both her parents had basically flung up their hands in disgust.

"Go. Do what you want to do," her mother said. *"You will anyway."*

"Just be careful," her father added. *"We do love you, even if you drive us crazy."*

They'd understood the sense of duty that drove her. They should. They'd instilled it. They…

Rand rose from his seat in a muscular rush of vampire speed that sent Zara jolting back to the present. She looked up at him in alarm.

"Get your boots on," he said over his shoulder, moving to kneel beside his foot locker. "We need to get the hell out of here."

"Why? Where are we going?" Did he intend to race off after his mother? Surely not. An officer couldn't just up and leave his post. Not without getting court martialed, anyway.

He gave her a hard smile. "We're going on a picnic."

Zara blinked. The expression on his face was entirely too grim to go with those words. Whatever he intended, it was a hell of a lot more than a picnic.

She hesitated a moment, watching him flip up the lid of the locker and pull out a small pack. "Exactly what do you have in mind?"

He looked up to give her a wicked smile. It didn't even look forced. "Eating. You do that on a picnic."

"I have heard something about that, yes," Zara said dryly, watching him take items out of the locker and start tucking them into the pack.

"Good to know you're not completely uncivilized out here on the ass of nowhere. Boots, lieutenant."

Frowning, Zara stepped into the boots and bent to

close the seals. Rand, meanwhile, pulled his beamer rifle out of the locker. "You carry that on the base?"

"I do when I'm escorting a prisoner."

"Take many prisoners on picnics?"

"I do when I plan to eat them." He put down the weapon and pulled a pair of neurocuffs out of the locker. "Stand up and assume the position."

Zara felt a hot spark of desire at the rough command. Swallowing, she turned to cross her wrists at the small of her back. "Which position is that?"

"Bent over and sucking my dick." He stepped up behind her and clipped the restraints on.

As the neurocuffs closed around her wrists, her arms instantly went numb and limp. Kinky or not, she hated walking with her arms cuffed behind her. "You do know the colonel's not going to like this."

"Actually, I just commed him to ask him to sign off on this little outing, and he has no problem with it."

She blinked, taking that in. "He doesn't?"

"No." Rand bent to collect his rifle and pack. "I told him I was taking you out to question you about the location of the enemy bases. Somewhere without inconvenient witnesses."

"And he bought that?" Zara hadn't known Rand for very long, but even she could tell that sounded out of character for him. Especially given his views on war crimes.

"Yeah. Fortunately the colonel expects everyone else to be as vicious as he is. Plus, he's not the brightest laser probe in the kit."

"So how'd he get to be a colonel?"

Rand shrugged. "Probably did the right favor. The Glorious Army of the Enlightened is built largely on cronyism. Most of the guys who hold high rank helped Godsson set up his giant Ponzi scheme when he hit

Heaven thirty years ago." Heaven, naturally, was the name of the Godssonists' planet, located the next star system over.

"You do realize whatever you have in mind is not going to be that easy?"

"Don't worry, darling." He dipped his head to speak in her ear as he took her elbow and guided her out of the tent. "I've made plans."

Chapter Four

They approached the guard standing watch over the camp's landing zone, with its pulse fighters, transports, and two-seat zippers. The private saluted Rand, the gesture crisp.

Rand returned it. "Leaving camp with the colonel's permission."

The private's eyes went distant. Evidently he was using his helmet com to talk to the base computer. It must have confirmed Rand's statement, because the man came to attention and snapped another brisk salute. "Have a good… lunch, sir." His gaze flicked to Zara, making it clear just what he thought Rand would be eating.

"I intend to," Rand said, though Zara saw a muscle flex in his jaw, as if he didn't like the look on the private's face. Taking Zara's elbow again, he urged her toward one of the two-seater zippers.

Since her wrists were bound, Rand belted her in, then slid behind the zipper's flight stick. They lifted off a moment later, repeller fields boosting the streamlined little craft skyward.

It was a crisp fall day, the sun bright, the sky vividly pink. Falara's towering fern-trees had lost their bright gold shades as the planet's version of chlorophyll drained, leaving behind their natural purples and blues. The contrast between the leafy, rolling landscape and the brilliant sky was breathtaking as Rand banked the zipper over the camp.

Easing the flight stick forward, he sent the zipper shooting off into the rose sky just as the sun's glowing gold corona broke over the horizon.

Rand went silent as he flew, his expression gone so grim again, Zara wondered if she really was about to be tortured. Maybe he thought he needed whatever information she had to ensure his mother's safety.

Zara didn't want to believe it, especially after the way he'd held her so tenderly the night before. He didn't seem like another G.A.E. thug, but he *was* a mercenary. He wasn't fighting for his planet or his religion. He was getting paid.

Then again so was she. Probably not as much as an interstellar merc, but still.

Had she been suckered? Was this whole thing some kind of sick game he was playing?

She was feeling distinctly paranoid by the time they approached a low mountain range Zara recognized as the Granites. Rand took the zipper down, balancing the craft on its repeller fields. He piloted it right up to the cliff until the stone was so close, Zara started getting nervous. A hard gust of wind could smash the craft against the unforgiving granite.

Abruptly the black stone in front of the zipper's nose wavered and vanished, revealing the opening of an enormous cave. The zipper slid into the opening, its landing lights flashing on to illuminate the cave.

"This is Theta Base," Zara said, surprised. The Falaran army had moved into the network of natural caves, using it as a base for months. Then the G.A.E. had attacked, wiping out the base and killing all three thousand Falaran soldiers.

"Yeah," Rand said absently, as he brought the little craft in for a landing.

"My vampire partner and I visited this base once," she said. "It was a pretty good facility. The Falaran army spent a lot of time and money extending the existing cave structure."

"Yeah." Rand grimaced. "We had a hell of a time

digging them out. Lost a lot of men doing it, too. Which is why we ended up not using the base, because the Godssonists are superstitious as hell."

Zara stared at him as he unbelted and freed her from her own safety straps. "What, they think the place is bad luck?"

"They think it's haunted."

She blinked at him as she rose to her feet. "You're kidding me. Haunted? But there's no such --"

"Baby, I'm telling you, those people are gullible."

"I noticed," she said dryly.

"Which is why we're reasonably safe, at least for the time being. None of the Godssonists are likely to show up here without good reason." He gave her a wolfish smile. "So we don't have to worry about being interrupted while we... play."

"Ah." She eyed that smile, not sure she liked the looks of it.

Rand laughed. "Your eyes are the size of ration disks. What's the matter, darling, don't you trust me?"

"No."

"Smart girl." Taking her by the elbow, he guided her out of the hatch and down the short flight of steps to the stone floor.

Zara looked around warily. The cave was the base's secondary landing zone, so it wasn't quite as big as the main cavern. It could accommodate a couple of smaller transports and a zipper or two. The stone walls and floor were artificially smooth, thanks to the Falaran Army's laser borers.

The cavern entrance had disappeared behind the camouflage field again. Looking closer, Zara noticed several round holo projectors attached to the stone walls.

Rand put on his helmet and flicked on its light,

then slung the rifle and pack over his shoulder before taking her elbow. "This way."

Zara let him urge her through a smaller opening in the smooth granite walls into the complex of tunnels and caves beyond. Without his helmet light, she wouldn't have been able to see at all in the cool darkness.

"Where the hell are we going, Rand?"

"I told you, we're having a picnic."

"In the dark?" She shot him a narrow glance. "I don't know how you interstellar types do it, but Falarans have picnics outside, in the bright sunshine, where they can listen to the featherlites sing and eat actual food. None of which describes choking down dry emergency rations in a fucking cave."

"This 'fucking cave' has something the great outdoors doesn't -- a complete lack of armed assholes."

She lifted a brow at his rifle. "Present company excepted."

Rand gave her that wolfish grin he did so well. "You've quite the mouth for a woman walking in a fucking cave with a vampire."

"Yeah, I'm a risk taker."

He moved so suddenly she had no time to react. One minute she was walking along beside him. The next, he'd pounced on her, swept her up in his arms, and dumped her across the shoulder opposite the one with his rifle and pack. She yelped, startled, the sound becoming a screech when his gauntleted hand smacked her raised butt. "Hey!"

"That's the thing about being a risk taker. Sometimes it bites you on the ass." He raised his faceplate and nipped her hip.

She kicked furiously. "Put me down, bloodsucker!"

"You really are pushing it, entrée." He popped her on the ass again. "Better be careful, or I may decide to tenderize my food."

He was so damned outrageous, she found herself laughing. "You do realize your food may bite back?"

"God, I hope so."

Lying across his shoulder as he bore her through the cave system, she grew aware of how incredibly dark it was.

And how totally alone together they were. Which wasn't a bad thing, considering the alternative was being surrounded by the enemy.

He is *the enemy,* she reminded herself. Odd how hard it was to remember that with his big hand riding her ass. "Put me down."

He didn't even break step. "No."

Her heart pounded with a delicious blend of excitement, anticipation and a little dread. *He can do anything he wants with me out here,* she thought. And the thought didn't scare her a bit.

Zara thought of Andre, her first vampire lover. He must have been just as strong, but he'd never tried to carry her. Probably because this kind of display was a dominant's trick, designed to make a submissive aware of his sheer physical power.

And it was working. She felt aroused and anxious and eager, all at the same time. What was he planning? Another spanking? Maybe he'd make her suck him off while he…

Rand stroked a big hand over her thigh, the armored glove cool and hard. "You're going to be delicious." His voice was a purr of rough velvet, deep and intimate.

Zara swallowed, remembering the feel of his cock thrusting deep as he penetrated her from behind. She thought of his way hands and mouth and the sweet, stinging bite of his fangs. The copper taste of his blood as he'd fed her, saved her. The man was the embodiment of every vampire fantasy she'd ever had.

She could just relax and enjoy whatever pleasure he decided to give her. This time there'd be nobody to overhear her screams of ecstasy. Or to think she deserved to be punished for the sexual desire they believed women had no business feeling.

Rand was nothing like that kind of narrow-minded bastard. He valued her passion as much as his own. In fact, he went to considerable lengths to intensify her enjoyment in every way he possibly could.

She could relax while he took control. She was free. Whatever happened afterward, she'd worry about *afterward*.

So Zara relaxed, enjoying the sweep of big hands along her thighs and calves, stroking up to the curve of her ass. Distinctly possessive.

Rand turned into another tunnel. The opening they'd just walked through vanished behind them, assuming the appearance of smooth stone. Another camouflage field.

"How many field generators did you plant, anyway?"

"As many as I need." He turned right, walked through the cavern beyond and ducked into another tunnel opening, which also disappeared behind a camouflage field.

"Why *did* you put all this in place?" She'd love to think it was because of her, but he hadn't even known she existed until last night.

"Contingency plans. In war, you have to have plans, and then plans for what you'll do when the first plan fails. And then a third plan in case the second plan goes out the airlock too. Otherwise you have a tendency to get dead."

"So the Godssonists won't find us until you're good and damned ready to be found."

He nodded his helmeted head. "Exactly. Which means you can relax and concentrate on all the kinky sex I've got planned."

"Do you have contingencies for that too?"

"Actually, I'm playing that by dick." He laughed, the sound wicked. "Luckily I'm a very creative guy."

"I noticed." Arousal rolled through her like heated syrup. What was he going to do with her? What were these kinky plans of his?

He turned again, and put her down on a soft, yielding surface. A mattress, she realized, placed directly on the floor. Glancing around cautiously in the spill of light from his helmet, she found they were in a stone chamber only a little bigger than his tent. Stacks of boxes stood around them, but she couldn't read their labels in the dim lighting. "You really are serious about those contingency plans, aren't you?"

"You have to be when you work with psychotic assholes." Noticing that she was tensing, preparing to roll off the mattress, he dropped his voice to a dominant's growl. "Don't you move."

She froze, staring up at him as he towered over her. The light on his helmet blinded her so she saw him only as a tall silhouette with powerful armored shoulders.

Rand turned, sliding the strap of his rifle off his shoulder and putting the weapon down. He took the pack off and fished around inside it as he knelt beside the mattress. A moment later he reached for her again, taking her cuffed wrists and spreading her arms wide.

Sitting back on his heels, he studied her, the light on his helmet sweeping the length of her body. "Mmmm, you do look tasty," he said in a deep, low voice. "And you're completely at my mercy. I can do anything I want to you. You can yowl and scream and moan all you want and no one will hear you. My own delicious little picnic."

Her nipples tightened against the fabric of her uni as she stared up at him, hypnotized.

"The problem is, my dinner is overdressed." Bending, he ran a finger down the seal of her uni from its high collar, over the rise of her ribcage and down to the dip of her navel, then lower still, between her legs. The uni parted, the light on his helmet following his fingers, making her intensely aware of his gaze.

His hand slid between her thighs, cool on the vulnerable flesh of her labia. He spread the fabric further apart so he could stroke between her lips. "You're pretty wet for a woman at the mercy of a vampire," he observed in that dark voice, a purr of amusement and distilled sex. "You like this, do you?"

One of those armored fingers thrust upward, sliding easily inside her pussy. She gasped as he filled her, penetrating her all the way to his knuckles. The chill of his armored hand was shocking and raw and erotic. She caught her breath.

"Spread your legs," he ordered, cool, demanding.

Zara obeyed before she even had time to think about it, her thighs instinctively parting. His armored fingers pumped, setting up a lush, erotic rhythm. He was right. She really was wet.

She worked her hips, humping his hand in shameless pursuit of ecstasy. His thumb found her clit, circled. Delight rolled over her, waves of it, sweet and seductive. A second armored finger slid in, driving into her slickness, the sensation intense.

Groaning, Zara panted, humping his hand, straining for more of that luscious sensation. He reached up her body with his free hand, pushing aside the edges of her suit. Found an aching, eager nipple to squeeze.

"You have such pretty breasts," Rand murmured, low and seductive. "So pale, like mounds of cream. Especially compared to your rosy little pussy." The light on his helmet danced from her breasts down to her sex and back again, tracking the movement of his eyes.

"God, that feels so good," she moaned, closing her eyes and rolling her head against the mattress.

"And it's about to get even better." To her intense disappointment he released her pussy and nipples, leaving them aching. She raised her head, arms still flung helplessly wide, as he rose from the bed and took one of her booted feet in his hand. He found the boot's seal and traced his fingers down its length. It split wide open over her shin, and he pulled it off, setting it neatly aside. He did same thing to the other boot and set it down with its mate before picking something up off the floor.

Whatever it was gleamed as he fastened it around her ankle. She identified it when her leg instantly went as numb as her manacled wrists. Neurocuffs. "What are you…"

"You're a fighter. I don't want you to fight." The light on his helmet flicked up to her face. "Later, you can fight."

What the hell does he mean by that? Before she could ask, he put the other shackle on her ankle. "Now," he rumbled, "you're really helpless."

He pulled her into a sitting position so he could

start stripping the uni off her shoulders and down to her waist, then dragged the sleeves down her arms, then raised her hips to pull the suit off. At last he lay her down and arranged her spread-eagle. The cuffs paralyzed her arms and legs. There wasn't a damn thing she could do to flight him. He could arrange her body in whatever way suited him.

Which left her naked, shackled, and wildly aroused.

Rand rose from the mattress and stood beside it, his helmet's light taking a slow tour of her nudity, lingering on face, breast, and pussy. Half blinded, she waited to see what he would do next.

"There we go." Reaching up, he took off his helmet and set it down beside the mattress. The helmet light swung up toward the ceiling of the cave and brightened until it illuminated the space in a soft glow.

Licking her lips, Zara watched him remove his armor, listening to the soft metallic clicks, and the sigh of the armor's seals. He dropped the gauntlets beside the helmet, then removed his boots and placed them together opposite her clothes. He set aside the top and bottom of the suit next, revealing his powerful body. Finally -- God, *finally* -- he was completely naked.

He took a small jar out of his pack. Straightening, he unscrewed the lid, his big cock bouncing with the movement.

"You're going to like this." Rand smiled wickedly down at her, anticipation in his gaze as he reached into the jar and scooped up a generous portion of gel.

"What are you going to do to me?" The question was half joking, half flirtatious, but it came out sounding all hoarse.

"Whatever I want." One corner of his mouth tilted up. "And I want to do a good bit."

Kneeling beside her, he started smoothing the substance over her chest. It was cold, and she sucked in a gasp, then gasped again as the gel seemed to heat on her skin.

Zara raised her head to look down the length of her body as he spread the substance into an even thinner layer, paying particular attention to her breasts and nipples. Once her torso was completely slick and glistening, he started massaging it into her arms and legs, his big hands warm against her skin. Some of the cold numbness retreated from her paralyzed limbs.

Her skin shimmered under the gel with a rainbow sheen in the light of the helmet. With every moment that passed, it seemed she grew more sensitive, particularly her nipples. Zara's breathing roughened, her heart beating faster and faster.

Rand scooped out more of the gel, reached between her thighs, and began slicking it over her labia and jutting clit. She sucked in a hard breath, feeling that sensitivity increase until it seemed her pussy throbbed in time to her heartbeat. Aching, she waited for whatever he might want to do to her.

At last, he sat back on his heels, studying her with satisfaction. "There. All done."

She laughed. "God, I hope not."

"Feeling neglected, darling?"

"More like dying of anticipation."

"Well, we can't have that." Rand put the jar aside and picked up his pack again. Taking out several metallic objects, he slid them one at a time onto his fingers. At first she thought they were rings, but he pushed them down no further than his fingertips.

What the hell did he have in mind? Zara had read a great deal about vampire sexual techniques, and she wasn't familiar with any that called for rings. "What are you doing?"

"This." And he reached down and hovered his hand just a few centimeters over her skin. A brilliant crimson spark leaped from his fingertips to dance over her glistening skin. Pleasure exploded in her senses, so intense she gasped.

He grinned at her. "Like that?"

"What the hell?"

"They call this neuroplay. It's the newest thing in vampire circles. The gel conducts and intensifies the sensations I create with these neuro stimulators." He spread his hands, displaying his rings. "The light show is just a pretty plus. Speaking of which…"

The helmet light went out, leaving them in complete darkness thick enough to stir with a spoon. He reached out and began to run his hands just above her skin, tiny bolts leaping and dancing from his fingertips. The sparks changed from red to yellow to green to purple, a rainbow chasing his hand through the darkness. Every one of them sent waves of sensation across her skin, sometimes pleasure, sometimes stinging bites of pain.

Zara cried out, gasping as he played her body, conducting a symphony of sensation and color.

Taste flooded her mouth -- orange bursting on her tongue as if she'd bitten into a piece of the fruit. Next came cherries and mango and chocolate and mocha. "What… What's that I'm tasting?"

"Well, I did promise you a picnic." He stroked sparking fingers over her nipples, triggering a tiny electrical storm above her skin. Color chased color with every gesture he made, swamping her with the sensation of phantom teeth nibbling as phantom tongues licked and danced. She panted, groaned, loving the vivid sensations.

Sound was next: snatches of flute music, drums and harps, sweet notes that hung in the air, accompanying the vivid light show he created. He cupped her breast in one hand and bent to take its nipple in his mouth, suckling, his tongue swirling over the exquisitely sensitized flesh. Simultaneously, he floated his free hand over her skin, triggering the sensation of a feather stroking and tickling. That was followed by the feel of tiny mouths sucking, precisely echoing what he was doing with his own.

Rand licked and nibbled his way from one breast to the other as she panted over a snatch of classical guitar and the taste of crisp, sweet apples.

All the while, he watched her face in the light of the sparks, his gaze fascinated and possessive as he studied her reaction to what he was doing. Sensation piled on sensation, heat rolling over the skin to the piercing notes of birdsong and Vivaldi.

Her neurocuffed arms and legs spread helplessly wide, Zara watched the rainbow light show Rand's hands wove in the darkness. She'd never felt like this before. Never known this kind of hallucinogenic storm of eroticism -- taste and music and color, overwhelming her dazzled brain until she seemed to float in it, suspended in delight.

Rand rose and moved between her thighs, spreading them wider. She could only twitch helplessly. The light winked out as he gripped her sweating flesh, giving the sparks no room to dance. When he released her, they danced again, a tiny lightning storm.

She tasted wine, something fruity and sweet, as he spread the lips of her pussy. Rand touched slick, juicy flesh, and chocolate rolled over her tongue, laced with caramel. The notes of Wagner's "Tristan and Isolde" floated in the air like a sweet, distant echo.

He contemplated her sex in the rainbow light spilling from his fingers. Spreading her legs wider, he draped her thighs over his shoulders, giving him maximum access to her pussy.

The light winked out as he held her, leaving her panting in the dark again, feeling the slick sensation of his tongue licking her labia, circling her clit, lapping and stroking.

Zara rolled her hips, groaning in a battered lust. He went on licking, each stroke of his tongue inflicting delicious pleasure. The gel he used made her skin so hypersensitive, the flickering laps felt even more overwhelming.

As he feasted between her thighs, he reached one hand up her body and hovered it just over her breasts. Again, colors rolled in a rainbow of energy dancing from finger to finger. She tasted cream, oranges, and peaches.

Zara had no idea how he was working his erotic magic. *I need to ask him,* she thought, only to have the thought disappear in another wave of feathered delight. Half maddened by pleasure, she rolled her hips against his working mouth, feeling the press of his teeth and the flick of his tongue.

His fingers found the opening of her pussy, slid in and began to thrust, teasing little strokes that piled on top of all the other sensations. "Rand! Oh God, Rand, fuck me! Please, oh please…" What she wanted was his cock. Needed it, craved his solid width stroking inside her juicy pussy, driving to the balls and filling her completely.

His right hand drifted from one breast to the other, trailed by sparks and tiny flickers of colored lightning. "Rand, please, I need your cock, please!"

He moved in an abrupt, desperate rush, as if he couldn't stand waiting any longer. Rearing between her thighs, he took his glorious erection in hand and aimed it for the opening of her pussy. Her hungry flesh opened under the pressure of the big shaft, the smooth tip sliding inside, followed by slow, delicious centimeters that forced her walls to spread, filling her until he could get no closer and his hips were pressed tight against hers.

He drew out, taking his time. "You're mine now," Rand gritted out. "I'm not going to let you go." He drew out, thrust inside again. Hard.

Zara rolled her head against the mattress. His cock was so thick, so long and perfect. "The colonel may have other ideas."

"I don't give a fuck about the colonel." He drew out and thrust in again, the sensation raw and breathtaking. "You're mine now, and nobody is going to be able to get through me to get to you."

At those words, the orgasm detonated behind her eyes in a liquid rush that stormed from her pussy, right up her spine to her overwhelmed brain. Zara threw back her head and screamed.

Rand struck for her throat, sinking his fangs deep into her flesh. One hand fisting in her hair, he drank, holding her head still as he fucked her, thick cock grinding in and out.

And every last sensation was utterly real, not a thing of technology and chemistry. Nothing but his body and hers in an ancient, sweet dance. Male and female and desire.

Her orgasm strengthened with every swallow he took of her blood, every thrust of his cock into her wet and eager flesh.

The pleasure rolled on and on, so intense it made

bright flashes light the darkness of her closed eyelids. The pleasure of it lifted her up even as he held her safe in the cradle of his arms.

Rand drove all the way to the balls, and she heard his climactic growl against her throat as he drank her blood.

By the time he was finished, she had neither the strength nor the ambition to lift her head. Removing the cuffs, he rolled over with her and simply held her there in the dark. Limp, sated, she concentrated on breathing and listened to his ragged panting as he licked the bites on her throat, his vampire saliva helping the tiny wounds to close.

* * *

Half dozing, Zara lay in Rand's arms, enjoying the sweet peace she found in listening to his heartbeat. Finally she sighed and stirred. "This is nice..."

"Just nice?" He sounded more amused than offended.

She laughed. "Okay, it was a hell of a lot more than nice, and you damned well know it. I was just thinking that we need to get back to the base before the colonel loses what passes for his mind."

"Not just yet."

Something in his tone sent adrenaline flooding her bloodstream. Zara raised her head and looked into his eyes. "Why not? Is something going on you're not telling me?"

"Oh yeah, I'm just not going to tell you what it is."

She'd have laughed, but the cool, grim tone of his voice told her he was serious. She also knew there was no use trying to badger him for more information. First, because dominants didn't badger. Second, he was her captor and didn't owe her a damn thing.

Especially not information she might somehow

use to escape.

The thought had the effect of throwing ice water over her lazy mood. *What the hell am I doing? He's the enemy. He's working for the Godssonists. No matter how handsome he is, no matter how kind he is, he's still working for the motherfuckers who are trying to take over my planet.*

She tried to ease away from him, no longer interested in the illusion of safety he offered. The arm around her shoulders tightened, holding her in place. "You're not going anywhere."

"I can't sleep like this."

"Try." There was so much cool command in his voice, she knew she wouldn't get away without an out-and-out fight. Which she wouldn't win. She was stronger thanks to the blood he'd given her, but her body still hadn't recovered completely from the long starvation. Besides, he was a vampire.

Resentfully, Zara settled back into Rand's arms. A moment later he stirred, caught her upper arms, and lifted her off his chest. She glowered at him, irritated. "I thought you said we weren't going anywhere."

"We aren't." He rolled over, lifted the pack, and started fishing around inside it.

He pulled out a knife.

Zara tensed as fear shot into her bloodstream, far different from the delicious anxiety she'd felt earlier. "What are you going to do with that?" She had to work to keep her voice from shaking.

"We're on a picnic, remember? I still owe you dessert." He ran the blade diagonally over his chest. It wasn't a deep cut, or particularly long, but blood welled, dark red in the dim light. Rand lay back down beside her and gathered her into her his arms. "Drink."

She hesitated, wondering what game he was playing now.

"Do it, Zara." His voice sounded softer now, intimate and deep. "You need it."

He was right. Even after drinking from him last night, she could still use another infusion because she'd been so bloodsick.

Cupping the back of her head, he drew her mouth to the wound. "Drink."

With a sigh of erotic delight, Zara began to swallow, the taste of copper rolling over her tongue. *He doesn't act like a man who's just playing me.* A player would want to keep her weak, giving her just enough blood to keep her immune system from killing her, but not enough that she'd have the strength for an escape attempt. But if he was as kind and compassionate as his actions suggested, why would he work for the Godssonists?

His blood sang to her senses. Yet cold rationality told her he was an enemy even as her warm heart insisted he would never hurt her.

She had no idea which instinct to believe.

* * *

A chime woke Zara and she opened her eyes as the dim light suddenly brightened from the helmet still resting beside the bed. Rand reached out a long arm, grabbed the blanket that lay in a messy pile and flipped it over both of them. "Answer," he ordered his helmet. His voice vibrated with tension, and she realized he was afraid. Zara tensed. He'd never sounded afraid, even when he'd been facing down Lordsvengeance.

Adela Rand's image appeared, floating in the air over the helmet projector, the three-dimensional image so vivid it was as if the real woman stood there. "He's dead," she announced. "And I'm not. Where are you?"

Zara felt Rand relax, his breath whooshing out as

if he'd been holding it. "We're in my bolthole."

Adela smiled. "That's a relief. The last time we talked about this, you said you had no intention of hiding out. Though I'll say again, only an idiot wouldn't take cover when he faced three hundred to one odds."

Zara blinked. "What the hell is going on?"

"My plan worked," Adela said, before turning to her son. "So why did you resist the temptation to play King Leonidas?"

"Things changed."

"I see that." Adele's eyes flicked to Zara, who felt heat rising to her face. The blanket might have saved their modesty, but it was painfully obvious what they'd been doing. The older woman frowned. "You do realize they're going to come after you if this works? They'll want to take you hostage, use you for a bargaining chip so the rest of the rats can escape the sinking ship."

"They're not going to take me."

"Don't do anything melodramatic, Nick. You have something to live for now."

"Yeah, I do. And no, I don't intend to go down in a rain of plasma."

"Good." She looked as intensely relieved as he had when her face appeared in the projection. "So you're putting the plan into action?"

"Yeah."

"Excellent. Everything's in motion from my end. My team will be hitting the base in about ten minutes, so you'd better be prepared. Some of the Godssonists may get away and come gunning for you."

"They won't be able to find me."

"What are you going to do if they do?"

"Don't worry, Mom." He smiled slightly. "I have a

contingency plan."

They agreed to check in with each other at one-hour intervals and said their goodbyes.

No sooner had Adela's image vanished than Zara demanded, "What the fuck is going on?"

"We're taking care of your little Godssonist problem." He sat up, grabbed the top of his armor, and started pulling it on, preparing for battle.

"So I gathered. And I hope that message was encrypted, or we're fucked."

"Don't worry, darling, we always use galactic grade encryption. The idiots who work for Godsson won't be able to crack it. Anyway, they're a little too busy fighting for their lives right now to worry about intercepting messages from me." He rolled to his feet, picked up her uniform and tossed it to her. "Get dressed. I hope we're not going to get company, but I'd just as soon they don't catch us naked if we do."

Zara snatched her uniform out of the air and put it on, then rose and slid her feet into her boots. As she started closing seals, she said, "If you knew it was possible we'd be attacked, why the hell did we have sex?"

"Because I also knew it was going to take Mother and her mercs time to reach Godsson and kill him. I figured we'd have a good three hours, four at the outside, before the shit hit the airlock."

"I don't understand. And God, I wish I had my combat armor."

"Yeah, I wish you had your armor too. Otherwise, you can rest assured we wouldn't be hiding in a cave. We'd be helping my mom's mercs take the base right now."

"But I don't understand how you and your mother got involved in trying to stop the Godssonists. You're a mercenary. They *hired* you. Why did you switch sides?"

"Because I never should have gone to work for them to begin with." Rand shook his head. "I've fought in six wars and four corporate conflicts, and I know the kind of nastiness combat brings out in people. But the G.A.E. has a viciousness born of fanaticism."

"Yeah, we were unpleasantly surprised too," Zara said dryly. "I mean, they're just one star system over, and we've always traded with them. We kind of pitied them for being so damned gullible as to fall for Godsson's con. Then the next thing we know, they're invading and massacring people."

"Godsson's a greedy bastard," Rand told her. "He saw an opportunity to rob your people and add to his power base. He figured you'd cave once you realized how badly he had you outnumbered."

Zara snorted. "Not very fucking likely."

"He should have seen that coming, but he's stupid on top of being greedy." His lips twisted. "I should have known better than to have anything to do with the G.A.E., but at the time they came knocking I was broke and needed the work. When I first started to realize how ugly this war really was, I told myself I was a professional, and I'd taken the damned job. Then a few months ago, Lordsvengeance and his little band of psychos slaughtered an entire village of noncombatants right in front of me." He stared off into the distance as if at some brutal vision. "Kids and old people, because everybody else was off fighting. And they killed every mother-fucking one of them. Massacres happen sometimes, when you've got an asshole in charge -- that doesn't mean the whole army is evil. Then I discovered killing noncombatants had become policy. Godsson had decided that was the best way to break the Falaran Coalition's will to fight."

"And it backfired on them, because it just made us fight harder. We didn't want to be ruled by the kind of asshole who thinks like that."

"According to the Treaty of Vermillion, that kind of shit is a war crime punishable by death. I took an oath to uphold that treaty, and I don't break my oaths."

"I can understand that." Zara had no trouble believing that, considering his outrage when he found his men attempting to rape her. She frowned. "But why did your mother get involved?"

"Because I told her what was going on. Mom may have moments of ruthless practicality, but she agrees with me: you just don't massacre whole villages of children and old people."

"Why didn't she just go to the Interstellar Union, get them involved enforcing the treaty?"

He snorted and turned to flip the lid off one of the crates piled up around the chamber. "Involving the Union would have taken months, maybe years of political bullshit, with Godsson claiming innocence while he went on looting Falara. Meanwhile God alone knows how many people would have died. That's why I got my mother involved instead of using some of my other contacts in the government."

Zara blinked. "She must be spending millions on this."

"Yeah, but when you own your own planet, you've got it to throw around. Luckily there are an awful lot of unemployed mercenaries right now, not to mention her own small army of security. They're still outnumbered, but their equipment and training are far superior, and their officers can actually find their dicks with both hands. Which is more than I can say for

Godsson and his thugs."

"And Godsson really believed she wanted to do a business deal in the middle of a war?"

"That was the trickiest bit of the whole thing," Rand admitted. "We were worried he wouldn't fall for it. Luckily, he's a greedy bastard. All she had to do was wave money in his face and talk about a partnership. He couldn't resist the idea of being associated with Adela Rand. He probably thought he could leverage the publicity into more worshippers."

"Moron." She gave him a searching look. "So that gave your mother and her men the chance to kill him?"

"Yeah." His expression went grim. "She set up a high level meeting with Godsson and his senior cronies. She planned to take in a cadre of fighters and take on them all. That was the part I was most nervous about, because it would mean a pitched battle between her mercs and his bodyguards, and she could end up dead. But she insisted, and I couldn't come up with a better plan. Luckily, she pulled it off -- thank God."

Hope bloomed in her chest for the first time in months. "The whole invasion will collapse now that your mother's cut the head off the snake."

"Probably. Godsson's surviving cronies will start fighting it out to see who gets to be god now, while the rest of the G.A.E. just struggles to get the hell off Falara."

"And good riddance to them. But what's this about an attack on Heavensgate Base?"

Rand shrugged. "Mom's insurance policy. She figured Lordsvengeance would try to take me hostage in order to force her to let him and his thugs go. Then he'd most likely kill me, given that he's basically a vicious psycho."

"Assuming you didn't tear his head off his

shoulders first," Zara said. "You *are* a vampire."

"A vampire facing three-hundred-to-one odds. I'm good, but I'm not good enough to defeat an entire battalion of Heavensgate mechs."

He waved a gesture at the surrounding cave. "I set up this bolthole as a contingency in case I needed somewhere to retreat. I'd originally intended to go after Lordsvengeance at the same time Mom attacked Godsson. Then you came along."

"Wait a minute -- *I'm* the reason we're out here instead of back at the base, kicking Lordsvengeance in the balls?"

He shrugged. "I didn't want to risk you."

"Rand, I'm V.S.S." Zara glowered at him, offended. "Defending my planet is why I enlisted in the program. I've been at war for two years, and I can assure you I haven't been sitting on my ass. I'm not some helpless little civilian."

He glared right back. "Zara, you don't have a mechsuit. They blew it up."

"Only because we left it behind. We should have packed it!"

"And make Lordsvengeance instantly suspicious? POWs do not need mech armor."

Zara deflated. "Yeah, okay." She studied him. "You're serious? We came here to protect *me*? Why?"

"I said I would not let them have you and I meant it. Look, if Lordsvengeance took you, he could force me to surrender."

She winced. "And if they forced you to surrender, they could force your mother to give up and let the G.A.E. escape."

"Exactly. Which is why we've got to be prepared for anything the bastards do next."

Chapter Five

Zara studied Rand's handsome profile, gilded by the setting sun. There was a fine muscle ticking in his jaw as he gazed out through the opening of the landing cavern. He was fully armored, his helmet sitting on the stone floor by his hip as they sat together, his pulse rifle across his lap.

Sitting cross-legged beside him, Zara held one of the spare pulse rifles and a pack full of ammo clips on the floor beside her. It had been more than an hour now, and she was starting to hope they wouldn't have to fight.

She joined Rand in scanning the horizon for oncoming craft. She'd have enjoyed the view if the situation hadn't been so tense. The sun painted the blue, rolling hills with gilded light and turned the sky to a blazing crimson decorated with gilded clouds.

Judging from Rand's grim expression, he wasn't thinking about the view. "Wish you were helping your mother's mercs take the base?"

"Yeah." He rolled his broad shoulders. "I feel like a coward sitting back here safe while everyone else -- including my mother -- fights the battle I started."

"We can always go back to the base."

"I won't put you at risk." He looked at her, his expression hard, determined.

"Why not? I'm just a prisoner. Yeah, we've had some pretty good sex but..."

"You're not a prisoner. Not anymore." Rand gestured in the direction of Heavensgate. "The people who took you prisoner are currently getting their asses kicked."

"And I should be doing the kicking. Or at least help you do it."

"Not if it means getting killed."

"Why do you care? I can see if we'd been lovers for months, but we only met last night."

"Sometimes realizing someone's special doesn't take very long."

She studied him, and felt something unfurl in her chest. Something that felt like hope or joy. Something she had no business feeling for a man she'd met only the night before.

Rand glanced off over the hills again, like a man who felt painfully vulnerable. "I've looked for someone like you all my life. I would've wanted you even before I became a vampire. Your intelligence, your wit, that suicidal bravery of yours..." Now he turned back to her, his expression intense. His voice lowered, going deep and rough. "And your generosity. You were willing to feed me even though you were a captive."

"I didn't see that I had a hell of a lot of choice."

Now his golden eyes flashed in irritation. "You could've said no. I wouldn't have pushed it. But even as bloody and wounded as you were, I could see you responded to me because you knew I was hurting. My men had just attempted to rape you, and yet you were willing to let me take your blood because I was hungry."

"You weren't just hungry. If you've simply skipped a meal or two, I would've said no. I'm not that big a martyr." She shrugged. "I thought maybe I'd get lucky and you'd let me have some of your blood before I fucking died of blood sickness."

"Yeah, I'm sure that was a factor. But you were also surprised when I offered you my wrist. You didn't really expect me to feed you. And yet you were willing to give me your blood anyway." His gaze searched hers. "You were willing to trust me with your *life*. When I fed from you, I felt a sense of connection between us I have never felt for any other woman in my life. The dominance and submission, the sex -- that's a nice plus. But this..." He gestured back and forth between them. "The thing between us, it's not just nice. Yeah, maybe it is just starting. Maybe this is only a newborn love, but I want to see what it grows up to be."

Zara blinked, stunned and startled. Wondering what the fuck to say. Wondering if she dared admit that she, too, felt more than she'd feel for some vampire one-night stand, no matter how handsome.

Rand sighed, and his expression turned brooding. "I want something out of this damn war besides blood and terror and an inability to look at myself in the mirror." His jaw flexed in a restless roll of determination. "I'm done with being a mercenary. I'm done with killing. Fifteen years of this shit is more than enough."

"Frankly, I'm surprised you lasted that long."

"It hasn't been this damned bad before," Rand explained. "I spent most of my career fighting with the same mercenary unit. There was a wonderful sense of comradery in fighting together. In knowing someone else always had your back."

Zara nodded, remembering her brief, sad time with Andre. "I can understand that."

"Unfortunately, my unit broke up when our commander decided to retire. Then there was the lack of warfare going on across the Interstellar Union, so most of the other vampires started looking around for something else to do with their lives. I was sitting in a bar getting loaded when this G.A.E. recruiter came in looking for mercs. I didn't know a damn thing about the Godssonists, and I didn't take the time to do my research." He curled a lip in disgust. "And it bit me on the ass. Hell, it didn't just bite my ass, it took a huge chunk out of it. Two years I've spent fighting this war and training the people who've been brutally raping Falara." He turned to her and reached for her hand. She gave it to him, her chest aching. "I know how you feel about your people. Do you think you can forgive me for what I've done?"

Zara smiled. "Rand, you and your mother have *saved* my people. Or at least given us the first real chance we've had in two years. And you took a hell of a risk to do it. Your mother could have died killing Godsson, and Lordsvengeance will kill you if given the chance." She brushed her fingertips against his cheek. "The way I see it, you saw evil and had the guts to do something about it. If more people had that kind of courage, the human race would be a hell of a lot better off."

Rand grinned in obvious relief. "I did what I had to, baby. Otherwise my mirror and I would have come to a parting of the ways." He paused, his gaze searching her face. "Mom and I have been talking. She's planning to create a new philanthropic organization on Falara to help your people recover from the war. And she's asked me to run it. I've got more experience killing people than helping them, so I'm going to need a lot of on-the-job training. Mom says she's got some experts lined up to help, so I shouldn't fuck it up too badly."

Zara smiled slightly. "Knowing your compulsive perfectionism, you'll be the best thing that ever happened to Falara. Besides, I've heard a lot about your mother's charities. She does good work."

Rand leaned toward her, his gaze intense. "Would

you stay with me, help me? You'd make a great liaison between the charity and the Falarans. They might be more inclined to cooperate if you're involved."

She grinned, warmth expanding in her chest at the request. *He wants me to stay with him*! "It would be my honor."

"And you'll do a damned good job -- assuming we actually win this thing. A hell of a lot can go wrong. I..." He broke off, and his head snapped around toward the landing zone's opening. "Oh, fuck."

She followed his gaze and swore, seeing a pair of bright, slim shapes in the distance.

"Team transports," he told her grimly, rising to his feet in a powerful rush of mech servos and vampire muscle. "They're coming this way."

Her mouth went dry as she scrambled up to stand next to him, peering at the horizon. "Maybe they'll pass by. Could be headed to the spaceport."

"They're going in the wrong direction. The spaceport is east. Fortunately they're not flying very fast -- probably worried about taking fire."

"How the hell did they know we're here? We could have gone anywhere after we left the base."

"It's like they've got some kind of..." Rand turned to her, his gaze flicking up and down her body. He froze, staring hard at her belly as if he could see right through her flesh. Which, given his sensors, he probably could. He started to swear in an impressive roll of profanity.

"What?" she demanded, alarmed.

"There's a nanotracker stuck to your stomach wall. It's broadcasting on a frequency we don't normally use, so I never noticed it."

Horrified, Zara looked down at herself. "When the hell did they do that? I never had any kind of surgery..."

"They probably slipped it into your food."

She looked up at him, staring. "Why didn't they tell you? Did the colonel suspect..."

"If he had, I assure you we'd both be in cells right now. Lordsvengeance is a career paranoid who plays his cards close to the vest. Probably because all the upper echelon Godssonists are constantly trying to stab each other in the back."

"I'm crying for them," Zara growled. "Now what the fuck are we going to do?"

He lifted the rifle, checked the charge. "We're going to give them a very warm welcome."

* * *

Zara lay on her belly, tension running through her nerves, her cheek pressed to the pulse rifle's stock. The weapon's muzzle was barely a centimeter from the camouflage field that disguised the entrance to the tunnel she lay in.

Rand had run back to their sleeping chamber, returning with a signal blocker she'd tucked into a pocket of her uni. The blocker would prevent the enemy from picking up the signal from the tracker.

Now he waited in the landing cavern's larger tunnel, the one once used for transporting supplies into the base. They'd attack once the two transports touched down in the landing zone.

Zara spared a futile wish for an anti-craft battery, but the G.A.E. had stripped those weapons from the Falaran base after capturing it. Presumably about the same time they'd removed the bodies and sent cleansing bots in to remove all the blood.

"I was able to divert a lot of supplies for my bolthole, but a pulse cannon would have been a little much," Rand had told her. *"Even the Godssonists keep a better eye on*

that kind of thing than that."

The hum of repeller fields became a deep bass thrum as the two ten-man transports came in for a landing, touching down next to the two-seat zipper they'd arrived in.

Assuming there really were ten men on each craft, she and Rand faced ten-to-one odds. Maybe more. Zara swallowed and licked her dry lips.

As one transport came to a featherlight rest, the other skidded and bounced on its landing gear before it finally stopped. Apparently, whoever was running the show had been able to find only one good pilot when they'd fled the mercenary attack on the base.

As Rand had predicted, the two craft had parked with their noses toward the tunnels. There wasn't room for both of them in any other position.

The doors slid wide on each of the crafts. Armored men raced out, rifles at the ready, evidently expecting to encounter fire.

They weren't disappointed. Zara drew a bead on the first man out the door of the nearest transport. Her shot took him perfectly through the faceplate, one of the few spots of vulnerability on mechsuits. He tumbled off the ramp as she shot the mech immediately after him, though the next two survived because they tucked and rolled. They came up firing, but both missed the camouflaged tunnel.

Zara went right on laying down fire with all the skill and speed she'd worked so hard to learn since becoming V.S.S. She put a number of the Godssonists down, but others managed to take cover at the rear of their transport.

She was distantly aware of shouts and screams of pain as Rand tore into the men emerging from the transport he'd targeted.

Just as they'd planned, he shot the first three, who'd fallen as he charged out to engage the rest at hand to hand. It was risky, but it also took the enemy thoroughly by surprise. Besides, Rand's vampire strength was a lethal advantage.

Hanging back and shooting was problematic anyway, since the Godssonists' armor would deflect everything but a faceplate shot. And a faceplate was a relatively small target, especially when the enemy was moving fast.

Rand's armored fists and feet, on the other hand, could shatter mechsuit plates, driving shards of armor into the wearer's body.

Then there was his speed, and the vampire grace that kept drawing Zara's attention despite the circumstances. His agility and power were breathtaking as he spun, leaping off his feet and slamming fists, elbows, and feet into his opponents, dropping most and forcing others to retreat as Zara tried to pick them off.

Then she had no more time to keep an eye on him. She had her own hands full, as the men in the transport she'd targeted raced to the rear of the craft, where they fired back at her. Most of the shots slammed into the walls on either side of the tunnel where she lay; the mechs were unable to see exactly where she was because of the camouflage.

If she didn't keep them ducking, they'd be able to target her by shooting toward her fire. She had to keep rolling from side to side to prevent them from homing in on her.

The firing trailed off a moment, and Zara scanned for targets. She tensed, spotting a man darting toward Rand. Her bolt sliced across the front of his mask, and he screamed, hitting the floor in a tumbling roll.

Zara frowned, wondering if her blast had really done any damage. Then a shot hissed over her head, missing her by centimeters, and she forgot about her last target in favor of returning fire. By the time she looked for the man again, he was gone.

Zara rolled again. Just in time; another shot hissed through the spot where she'd just been. *They're zeroing in on me,* she thought.

It wouldn't be long before she would have to fall back and take cover in another tunnel where she'd be less vulnerable.

She swung her rifle back toward the other craft, where Rand still fought its defenders, alternating pistol fire between ferocious blows. Blood sprayed from one man's helmet, and he went down hard. *That one won't be getting up,* she thought in grim pleasure as she fired at one of the men trying to get to safety behind the transport.

At least she was keeping the attackers from the second transport from giving Rand any trouble. It seemed none of them quite had the guts to try to cross the open floor with Zara waiting to shoot them.

Spotting a man trying for Rand, she fired, taking him high on the chest. Unfortunately, the bolt was deflected by his armor, and he kept moving.

Rand leaped up, flashing into one of those incredibly graceful moves vamps did so well. The roundhouse kick took down two Godssonists who'd had the bad judgment to try to come after him side by side. Pieces of both helmets flew as the attackers dropped.

Zara was drawing a bead on another of the fighters when she saw a flurry of movement in the corner of one eye. She jerked her head around just in time to see a boot coming right at her face.

Light exploded behind her eyes and she screamed as blood flew from her nose. She flipped over onto her back, trying to roll away from the shot the man was probably about to fire into her skull.

Instead she felt hard hands grab her by the arms and jerk her right up off the ground. The rifle flew from her hands. He dragged her out of the tunnel, despite her efforts to jerk away. He was just too damned strong in his mechsuit.

"Now, bloodwhore, let's go have a talk with your fanged boyfriend."

Zara's blood ran cold in her veins. She'd recognize that voice anywhere: *Lordsvengeance*.

Somehow she got one eye open despite the radiating pain from her broken nose. His faceplate had a furrow burned across it, and she realized he was the man she'd hit with the glancing shot. "I almost got you, you bastard!"

"Almost isn't good enough, you little slut. And you will pay for it, believe me." Something cold pressed against the underside of her jaw: the muzzle of a plasma pistol.

He hauled her across the floor toward Rand. Her skull throbbed viciously with every step, and she wondered why his booted foot hadn't taken her head right off. Evidently he must've pulled the blow.

"Get out of the way!" Lordsvengeance bellowed at the Godssonists between him and Rand. Startled, they scuttled aside. The colonel shoved the pistol hard against her jaw. "Surrender, you bloodsucking bastard, or I'll blow your slut's head off!"

Rand froze, staring at them, horror on his face.

"Good job, sir!" one of the men yelled. It sounded like Zara's would-be rapist, Godshammer. "You got the bitch!"

"I'm not joking, fucker," Lordsvengeance snarled, ignoring his son-in-law. "Throw down that pistol."

Looking at Rand's anguished face, Zara could almost read the thoughts flickering through his mind. The whole counteroffensive would collapse if he were captured.

"Now!" Lordsvengeance's voice spiraled into a shriek as he dug the pistol harder into Zara's jaw. "You've got about three seconds before I do something your slut will not recover from!"

Rand's gaze met hers, and she realized he was going to give up. For her. "No!" she screamed. "He'll just kill me anyway!"

And Rand and Adela, too, once his mother surrendered -- as she would. The mercenaries she'd hired were unlikely to go on fighting once Adela was dead. Even worse, Lordsvengeance might be able to step right into Godsson's shoes and continue the invasion. This whole thing would be for nothing.

But if Lordsvengeance killed her now, Rand would survive. And he'd make damn sure her killer would not.

"I'm not kidding, fucker!" the colonel screamed, jamming the pistol into her face so hard, she couldn't suppress a scream. He was so focused on Rand, he seemed to have forgotten that he held anything more than a victim. "If you don't, your bloodwhore --"

Zara twisted, torquing in his grip to slam the blade of her hand against the muzzle of his pistol, knocking it aside with her V.S.S. strength. A blast fired into the ceiling, so close she felt it burn past her face. She wrenched out of the colonel's hold as his grip went slack in surprise. Wheeling, she rammed her fist into his faceplate, which spiderwebbed as he shouted in shock and outrage. Stunned by the impact, he staggered backward, trying to bring the pistol up. Zara wrenched it from his hand, reversed the weapon, and fired into his faceplate. The blast took him through one startled eye and blew out the back of his helmet.

Lordsvengeance fell, armor clattering on the cavern's stone floor.

Zara curled a lip. "I'm not a bloodwhore, you sociopathic motherfucker."

"Lordsvengence!" Godshammer shouted, taking a jolting step toward his dead father-in-law.

Rand spun, grabbed the back of Godshammer's neck, and slammed the lieutenant's head down into his lifted knee. Faceplate and skull crunched.

Tossing him aside, the vampire leaped into a whirling, enraged flurry of kicks and punches that took down five men in rapid succession. He whirled toward the rest, big body tensed, fists lifted. Zara dove for her rifle and drew a bead on the nearest soldier's head.

Rifles hit the ground as the remaining Godssonists threw their hands up. "We surrender! Don't kill us!"

Rand snatched up the nearest weapon and covered them. "Get the neurocuffs," he growled at Zara.

Grinning widely, she looped her rifle's strap over her shoulder and obeyed her vampire dominant.

* * *

Zara and Rand forced the survivors to strip off their armor at gunpoint, leaving them only their thin skin-suits. She held a rifle on them while Rand cuffed the eight survivors, including the four wounded, none of whom were in any condition to resist. Her head ached savagely, but she planned to make use of Rand's medkit as soon as their last prisoner was restrained.

Headache notwithstanding, she and Rand had survived. No wonder Zara was having so much trouble maintaining a stern expression. She was giddy with sheer relief.

As she watched the prisoners, Rand placed a set of portable force field projection disks around them. The cage the projectors created would keep the Godssonists out of trouble until Adela's mercenaries could send a transport to pick them up.

The moment the field popped into being, Rand turned and took three long steps toward her. She went into his arms with a moan of delight. He kissed her, his lips hot, demanding, his tongue sweeping into her mouth, stroking and sweet.

By the time they drew back, they were both panting. "Bet the prisoners enjoyed that show," Zara joked, though in fact, she didn't particularly give a damn. Thanks to Rand, the Godssonists no longer mattered.

"Give me some credit," he rumbled. "I've got the field keyed so they can't see through it. Though we can damn well see them."

"Good," she said, and rose on her toes to take his mouth again.

When they finally had to separate long enough to breathe, Zara managed, "I have a confession to make."

He grinned down at her wickedly. "I hope it's about some particularly kinky sexual activity you'd like to do with me."

"Close." Feeling vulnerable and a little shy, she smiled. "The reason I took the chance of jumping Lordsvengeance wasn't because I knew he was going to kill me otherwise, or even because I wanted to save Falara." She stroked her fingers over his cheeks. "Not that those things weren't a factor. It was because I wanted to save you more than anything else. I think..." She bit her lip. "I think I'm falling in love with you.

The thought of you dying hurts too damn much for it to be anything else."

Joy flared in his golden eyes, so brilliant as to be almost incandescent. "Thank you," he breathed. "I will take care of your heart, Zara Tahir."

She smiled. "And I'll take care of yours."

* * *

Six Months Later

Rand studied Zara with wicked appreciation. His new wife was gorgeously naked, dressed only in a pair of float restraints around her wrists, ankles, and forehead.

He'd used them to arrange her deliciously naked body in midair, bent and spread wide to give him maximum access to the sweet ass he intended to torment and enjoy. He'd attached a pair of stimulant clips to her nipples. She moaned softly as they created the sensations she was being licked and suckled, alternating, with varying degrees of pressure from pleasant to stinging.

But it was the ecstasy cat he was most looking forward to using. Unlike those of a real cat o' nine tails, the whip's nine lashes were thin neurostim fields that allowed the user to create sensations of pain or pleasure at his whim. Snaking holograms showed the location of each lash, which could also be combined or stiffened for various erotic effects.

Rand liked to keep the focus on pleasure -- depending, of course, on Zara's needs. Still, an ecstasy cat was a tricky toy to play with, requiring constant adjustments and careful monitoring of the bloodsub's reactions.

Rand was a master with it.

And they had all the time to play they needed.

They were, after all, on their honeymoon.

Besides, they'd earned it. They'd had to work hard the last six months, helping his mother get the Rand Falaran Foundation up and running. Then there'd been the challenge of rebuilding a planet devastated by two years of looting and war. So when Rand and Zara had spotted the opportunity to get married and escape for a week, they'd been more than ready.

Now it was playtime.

Rand shook the whip out and watched the holographic lashes curl across the floor. The cat produced a convincing slithering sound. It was designed to simulate the noise real leather would make.

"Ready, love?" he purred.

Her beautiful ass cheeks flexed deliciously at the sound of his voice. Her bent pose spread her labia and displayed her pink, tightly puckered anus. He eyed them lecherously.

"Does it matter?" she asked, her tone arch.

Rand grinned wickedly. "Not really." He brought his arm around and down to lay the lash across that deliciously fuckable ass.

Zara jumped as the wave of hot delight rolled across her skin everywhere the lashes touched. Her gasp made his cock twitch hard behind his fly. Thumbing the butt of the whip, he added a slight sting to the mix and aimed his next shot directly at her waiting asshole.

Imagining that little anus stretching reluctantly wide around his aching cock, Rand grinned in anticipation.

He was going to give it a reaming his luscious little wife would never forget.

Then, while he pumped her full of cum, he was

going to sink his fangs into that swan throat. And make her climax so hard she'd see stars.

* * *

Zara moaned in delight as her new husband flicked the cat's lashes upward, directly into her spread labia. One of them hit her clit, sending such a hot jolt of pleasure up her spine, she couldn't bite back her scream.

"Like that?" Rand asked wickedly, in that velvet-and- hot-whiskey voice of his.

"God, yes." She shuddered, unable to do more in the restraints that held her suspended in midair. She was utterly at her dominant's mercy, his to do with as he wanted.

And she'd never been more wildly aroused in her life. Her fantasies of a scenario just like this were the reason she'd become a bloodsub in the first place.

But not even her fantasies had been this good.

Now the vampire sauntered around in front of her. He wore only a pair of black skinsuit pants and knee-high leather boots. His magnificent chest was bare. Muscles flexed as he crouched in front of her and reached one big hand under her body to remove the clamps from her nipples. Zara moaned in disappointment as the phantom mouths released her.

Rand's answering grin was so dark, she felt a hot spurt deep in her hot cunt. "Don't worry," he said, a rogue's grin stretching his handsome mouth. "I'm not going to neglect those pretty tits." Long, strong fingers cupped her in warmth before he stood and stepped back.

And sent the neurostim lashes flicking right at one stiff little peak.

They landed with a fierce sting that tore a gasp from her mouth. Before she could cringe, he snapped his wrist again. This time ghost tongues licked across both breasts, wet and hot. She closed her eyes and gasped.

"Hold that pose," her husband ordered.

Zara opened her eyes just in time to see him open his fly, freeing his long, delicious cock.

"And yes, every centimeter is going up your ass," Rand told her, wicked laughter in his voice. "But first..." He caught the broad shaft in one hand and stepped closer, presenting it to her mouth. "Open wide, darling. It's time to suck your husband's cock."

With a helpless groan of arousal, she obeyed. He angled his hips and slid his length inside in one careful thrust that stopped just short of the back of her throat. Eagerly, she closed her mouth around him and began to feast on the silken shaft, using tongue and teeth and lips with all the skill Rand had taught her.

"Very good," he said, his voice rasping. "You do know how to use that pretty mouth. Let's make it a challenge." She saw him draw back the whip. "Don't bite."

Zara heard the soft *whoosh* sound effect as the lashes flew through the air and down across her ass. She stiffened, but this time the blow was a pleasure so pure she moaned around Rand's thick cock.

Then, as she sucked him eagerly, the vampire set about teasing her with the cat, sending its lashes dancing over her skin in waves of delight, driving her closer and closer to orgasm.

* * *

Her mouth felt wet and hot and skillful on his shaft. Rand thrust lazily, spinning out the pleasure of her oral worship, watching her long, slim body writhe as he laid on the whip. He aimed each blow carefully for the little dip in her heart shaped ass, knowing the lashes would curl around and down over her anus and labia and right across her clit in impacts of fiery pleasure.

With his vampire senses, he could feel Zara trembling on the verge of orgasm as she reveled in the kinky fantasy of being "forced" to suck his cock.

Knowing it would enhance her sense of submission, he fisted his free hand in her thick blonde curls and deepened his stroke, rising on his toes and angling his hips so he could drive more and more of his dick down her throat.

"Mmmm," he purred. "There's something about fucking a pretty sub's mouth..." He deepened his voice into menace. "But it's still not as hot as fucking her ass. How about it, Zara? Ready to get that tight little asshole reamed?" He gave her one last deep thrust, deliberately making her gag before quickly pulling free.

She looked up at him, dazed. He could feel how close she was to coming, how desperately turned on she was at the thought of what he planned to do to her.

Rand gave her his best demonic smile as he turned and picked up the tube of lubricant he'd left on the bed for just this moment. Tossing down the whip, he flipped open the cap and squirted a line of the lubricant all the way down the length of his cock. Slowly, he began spreading it over his shaft.

"God, I love getting a sub chained and spread, ready to take it up the ass. It's so good, Zara. Feeling a woman's tiny, puckered anus stretch wide as I force my dick in, centimeter by centimeter. Listening to her whimpers. Especially when she begs me to stop, when she moans my cock is too big." She was staring at his ferocious erection like a bird hypnotized by a snake. "Know what I do then?"

Zara licked her lips. "Ream her harder?"

He grinned. "That's right, bloodsub. You going to give me an excuse?"

She shivered. "I don't think you need one."

"Not with you." He gave his grin a darkly menacing cast as he sauntered around behind her. "After all, you're an enemy captive." Eyeing her helplessly bent body, he added, "With a gorgeously tempting butt and a tight little asshole just begging for a good, hard fuck."

This time he actually heard her swallow.

Rand reached for the softly furred lips of her cunt, spread wide by her position. As he expected, he found her so snug and deliciously creamy, he was almost seduced from sodomizing her.

He suspected, however, she'd be disappointed if he didn't carry out his threat. This first night as husband and wife, she deserved to enjoy her favorite kink.

She needed to be claimed. Wickedly. Utterly.

Besides, he was harder than a length of neutron cannon, and he could think of no better place for his aching prick than her tight little asshole.

Taking his thick, well-greased cock in hand, Nick stepped up to Zara's pretty curving cheeks and aimed for her rosette pucker. Looking down at the rosy tip resting against her tiny opening, he grinned in anticipation. And began, slowly, to lean into her as he sought to force his way inside.

But Zara was just as tight as he'd known she'd be, and the muscled ring resisted him.

He set his feet wider apart, caught her by one silken hip, and arched his back, using his buttocks to drive his cockhead past her instinctive resistance. Slowly, so slowly, the glans began to disappear inside, vanishing into her deliciously snug ass.

* * *

Zara gasped in arousal and pain as her husband's massive cock stretched her anus millimeter by evil millimeter. She squirmed in her restraints, but the float cuffs held her helplessly still. "It hurts!"

He leaned down until he could breathe into her ear. "Good." And slid another painful fraction of shaft up her convulsing rectum.

She closed her eyes, feeling cream flooding her empty cunt. "God, you're a bastard."

"Umm hmmm." He reached down and around her thigh to stroke her clit. The sizzle of pleasure blended with the hot fire of the cock steadily working its way deeper. "And you're a luscious bloodsub with the tightest asshole I've ever had the pleasure to fuck. Now be a good girl and relax those little muscles for my wedding celebration."

With a helpless whimper, she sought to obey, concentrating on opening herself to her lover's use.

Finally he stopped, his hips snug against cheeks. "In," he said, dark laughter in his voice, "up to the balls. How does it feel being skewered on your husband's dick, baby?"

"Painful," she groaned.

"Get used to it, darling. From this end, it feels hot, snug and sweet, and I'm not going to stop any time soon." His fingers flicked and circled her clit as he began to pull out.

The withdrawal was as overwhelming and delicious as his entry had been overwhelming and painful. And those long fingers knew just what to do to intensify the delight, caressing her clit in time to each ruthlessly deep stroke.

Cuffed, helpless, impaled on her vampire

husband's ass reaming cock, Zara closed her eyes and moaned in pleasure.

* * *

Listening to Zara's delicious little moans, Rand grinned. Not only did she have the most delicious butt it had ever been his pleasure to ream, but she loved being dominated. Her arousal grew hotter every time he taunted and threatened, teased and pleasured. She definitely loved being fucked like this as much as he loved doing it.

He could smell how creamy she was, could almost taste it on his tongue as her juices drenched his clit teasing fingers.

Oh, yeah. Zara Rand was ready for a good, hard buggering. And he was more than ready to give it to her. He wanted to make her come while he shot her asshole full of hot vamp sperm -- and sank his fangs into that pretty white throat.

"Hold on, darlin'," he growled, "I just ran out of mercy."

He began reaming her. There was no other word for it. He leaned into her, gripping her hips with both strong hands, pumping hard, sawing his thick cock in and out until she writhed helplessly in her restraints. "Stop!" she gasped, maddened at the torturous blend of pain and pleasure. "I can't stand it!"

He paused. "Are you using your safe word?"

She panted, gasped, and managed, "No!"

"Then I don't care," he growled in her ear. "You're mine, and I'm going to fuck your ass till I empty my balls. God, you're tight!"

Still riding her hard, he wrapped one muscular arm around her chest and started teasing her nipples, rolling the little peaks with one hand.

Reaching the other hand under her, he slid it

between her pussy lips to find her clit again. Zara screamed in pleasure.

With an animal roar, Rand shoved his cock all the way in, impaling her with one last brutal thrust. Releasing her breast, he grabbed her chin and dragged back her head. Before she could do more than gasp, he bit deep into her throbbing carotid.

Zara screamed again, writhing as he fed. Between her cheeks, his cock jerked in her anal grip, pumping his cum deep.

Long moments passed before Nick felt sated enough to free himself from his wife's ass and throat.

He looked down at her in satisfaction as she hung limp in her restraints. She probably felt too wrung out to move, after the multiple orgasms she'd enjoyed.

Her little anus gaped, swollen and red and smeared in cum from the pounding he'd given it. Given her bloodsub metabolism, it would soon be healed and tight again.

"You do realize," Rand purred, "you're mine now. And I'll never let you go."

Zara turned her head to look at him, her blue eyes languorous under her tangled blonde mane. She smiled slowly. "Good. Neither will I."

He swept her out of the air and into his arms, then carried her to bed. Settling her down on the wide mattress, he slid in beside her and pulled her close. Dropping out of character as wicked dominant master, he murmured in her ear. "I love you, Zara Rand."

"And I love you too, Nick Rand," she breathed, snuggling against him.

They went to sleep entwined together.

One.

Blood and Steel
Angela Knight

Elyn Castel spent fifty years as the slave of a vampire sociopath. Now, thanks to cyborg bodyguard Jarl "Blade" Bladin, Kruz is dead. Now Blade is after Elyn, and she knows she's finished if he gets his hands on her. But escaping the cyborg is easier said than done...

Chapter One

Fleeing in terror wasn't something Elyn Castel did. People ran from her, not the other way around. Besides, when you've spent fifty years as the slave of a sadistic sociopath, there's not much anyone can do to inspire terror. It's all been done.

But Elyn ran now, and she ran hard.

She darted down the concourse in long bounds that made the humans gape, leaping over tables filled with diners, spinning around astonished space station security guards, ducking the angry clawed swipe of a huge A'vi warrior.

Her sensors told her Jarl "Blade" Bladin matched her stride for impossible stride. But when the ill-tempered A'vi tried for him, one swing of an armored fist sent the massive alien down with a crunch and a started, agonized "*Chik!*" The pursuing security guards had to stop to help the injured T'ir.

You should never piss off a guy named Blade. Particularly not Jarl. Elyn's master could have told you that, had the vicious fuck still been alive. Blade had done a very thorough job on Kruz. She'd thank him for that, if only he hadn't targeted her next.

Elyn's cyplant whispered, and she shot in the direction it indicated, a service corridor that snaked out to one of the station's ten huge cargo holds. She could lose Blade there if she got lucky, kill him if she had to. Or die if she failed.

Odd. A few months ago, Elyn would have viewed the prospect of dying as a relief. But Kruz had still lived then, vicious blight that he was. She had no interest in dying now. She was curious about what life would be like as something other than a slave.

Elyn might not deserve to live, but she wanted to

give it a try.

As she ran for the service corridor, she was acutely aware of the distance between her and her objective. Cold star-flecked blackness lay beyond the towering transparent walls of the concourse, along with the elegant white shapes of the great passenger liners and cargo ships that orbited alongside Kring Station. Beyond them lay the vast blue arc of Cameron, with its landmasses in a hundred shades of green and brown. A thoroughly beautiful view, had she not been running for her life.

Being what she was, Elyn was fast. She reached the service corridor and plunged into it like a bucktor diving into its burrow. Blade was much bigger, being engineered for heavy combat, which made him slower and a fraction less agile. Still, no human and damned few aliens would have had a prayer against him. Elyn, however, was not human, and she could run him into the ground.

Unfortunately, there was nowhere to run *to*. Her ship didn't board for hours yet, and she'd have to shuttle over to it. Blade would be on her long before then.

She had to either lose him or fight. She didn't want to fight; he'd kill her. If Blade could slay Kruz, with his vampire strength and towering size -- not to mention his centuries of murder -- Elyn had no chance whatsoever.

So she listened to the ring of boots on the corridor behind her with dread in her heart. The nanotekker made no other noise, said nothing, barely seemed to breathe hard, while Elyn sucked air in desperate gulps. It was more like being pursued by a hunting cat than a man, given his silent predator's focus and lethal determination.

You couldn't reason with a man like that. You could only get the hell away from him. Assuming you could.

The corridor's gray walls blurred past, and her armored boots banged furiously on the floor with each gazelle spring. Her heartbeat filled her ears with pounding desperation.

At last the great double doors of the cargo warehouse loomed, locked against anyone who did not have the entry code. Elyn, of course, had hacked the code, and the doors slipped soundlessly open when her cyplant transmitted it. She charged inside, immediately ducked left and leaped to the top of a stack of cargo crates ten meters high. Without hesitating, she began to bound from stack to stack, each leap carrying her further into the hold's poorly-lit gloom.

By all rights, the hold's doors should have stopped Blade. Elyn wasn't surprised they remained open for him. Being Tekker, his nanoplant system was even better than hers when it came to hacking.

As the doors finally rumbled closed, she spotted the hiding place she was looking for and leaped down to duck into a narrow gap between two crates. It was barely wide enough for her shoulders, so she turned sideways and froze with her back against one stack.

Stealth field, she ordered her cyplant.

Processing, the cybernetic implant responded, before adding, *Stealth field in place.*

Implants throughout her body had begun generating a jamming field that would hopefully confuse Blade's sensors. The field was designed to make her body's assorted readings blend into the background readings. Even the sounds she made would be dampened. There was a lot of equipment in here, along with organics from a hundred worlds, including living creatures in stasis. With luck, Blade would be unable to pick her out against the noise.

She worked with ruthless discipline to control her breathing. Had she run far enough into the hold?

Elyn scanned for him. For a moment, her sensors picked him out plainly as he moved slowly through the hold, searching. Then he was simply gone. He'd raised his own jamming field.

As she'd known he would. Now it was time for a brisk game of cat and mouse while she tried to get out of the hold before he could track her down. Luckily, her cyplant had already located a servoid passage. Used by the small maintenance servoids that kept the hold clean, Elyn knew the passages were barely wide enough for her. Blade would never be able to fit his powerful shoulders into one.

The trick, of course, was reaching the passage before he found her. *Get that door open*, she told her cyplant, and leaped down from her hiding place.

She landed in a four-point crouch, knees bent, rolling on her toes, fingertips spread on the floor. The stealth field damped the soft thump to a bare whisper. Pausing, she listened, but heard nothing except the hum and buzz of stasis units and other electronics. Silent as a ghost, Elyn headed for the servoid passage as her comp worked to hack it. Sweat trickled down her spine as she slipped shadow-quiet between the towers of crates.

She spotted the passage door through a gap in the stacks, a circular indentation in the curve of the bulkhead. Ghosted toward it. Twenty meters. Ten. Five. Two. Sweat beaded her upper lip. *Have you unlocked the passage*? she asked her cyplant.

Yes.

Logically Blade would know one of the passages was her objective; otherwise she'd trapped herself in here, and he'd know she wasn't that stupid. But there were six of the passages scattered around the enormous hold, and he had no way of knowing which one she'd pick. He'd have to guess, then somehow determine her approach to it. Not being an idiot, she'd chosen a circuitous route.

Open it, Elyn thought, and sprinted, a bucktor running for its life with a greatfang right behind.

Stars exploded in her skull, and she went down in a hard skid, so stunned she barely even felt the pain. A massive weight landed on her back, smashing her into the deck. "Got some bad news," a deep voice rumbled in her ear. "Your stealth field is not as good as you think it is."

Fucking Tekker sensors.

Elyn twisted, slammed an elbow back, connected with something hard, heard a grunt. Tried to eel free, but he'd hooked a thigh over her right hip and an arm under her left shoulder. *Going for a headlock,* she realized, and slammed her head back. Another grunt as she connected with his jaw. Which was apparently solid tritanium, because the blow didn't even rock his head.

"Damn it, I'm not going to kill you!" he snarled.

She didn't dignify that with an answer, too busy writhing in his hold, bucking hard against his strength. Anybody but a nanotekker would have had a hell of a time holding on to a desperate, pissed-off vampire, but Blade controlled her furious struggles with ease.

"Elyn, if you'd just --"

Rage popped her fangs, and she turned her head and sank them into the palm of his hand.

"Kakshit! Bitch!" His right arm released its python

grip on her shoulder. She barely had time to realize that was a very bad sign when blackness exploded in her skull.

* * *

The little vamp went limp. Blade shook his stinging hand and ordered a scan. *Unconscious but not severely injured,* his nanoplant told him.

He'd pulled the punch just enough. *How long will she be out*?

Estimated three-point-two minutes.

He jerked field restraints out of a belt pouch and went to work twisting them around her wrists. A nanoplant-transmitted order activated the flexible coils, and they snapped rigid, tightening just enough to dimple the skin. He dug out a thigh set and wrapped them around her upper legs just above the knees, then followed that up with an ankle pair. *Sedation field,* he ordered them.

Sedation field activated, they chorused.

There. That would keep her out until he told the restraints to allow her to regain consciousness.

His captive safely trussed, he got to his feet and considered her, rubbing his jaw. Between the head-butt and that elbow strike, he'd have a set of impressive bruises. A human would be dead.

Vampy could hit.

She also had a very nice ass. Actually, the whole package was gorgeous, which was what had gotten his team killed. Elyn Castel looked at most twenty-four, with an oval face and not much in the way of cheekbones, dewy, unlined skin, and a delicately long nose above a full mouth. Her eyes were huge and green when they'd been open, lashes long and feathery as a doll's, with a tumble of bright golden curls to match. She had the body of a triddie star, breasts high and full, waist smaller than the spread of his big hands, legs that reached into next week.

A pretty neat trick for a woman pushing seventy. She'd been just nineteen when that bastard Kruz had assassinated her mother and enslaved her. Fifty years ago. Fifty years as a slave to one of the nastiest assassins in human space, a fate Blade himself had escaped only because she'd warned him.

He owed her for that. But by playing sexual bait for him, she'd also gotten both his team and his protectee killed, and he owed her for that too.

He'd killed Kruz, who had murdered Blade's people so bloodily and spread his protectee's guts all over the man's own house. Those six deaths were only the latest of Kruz's total. The bastard had been killing for three centuries, many of them murders for hire. Others had apparently been for the sheer joy of it; the vampire had particularly enjoyed butchering women.

Which was why Blade had taken more than an hour to finish him -- and Kruz had deserved every instant of blood and agony.

Now he meant to deal with the others responsible, starting with Elyn Castel. Next he'd hunt down No'bin Urthar and Stig Daven, Kruz's vampire henchmen, who had directly participated in the murders. Regardless of what he did with Elyn, Daven and Urthar were dead. And he fully intended to take his time killing them.

Blade bent and picked her up, then draped her across one shoulder. She was surprisingly heavy. Despite her delicate build, she was more muscular than she appeared, and her vampire nature gave her bones and muscles an extra solidity.

He started for the nearest door, one hand resting on her delicious ass. A very talented ass too, as she'd demonstrated during his seduction that night six months ago. Elyn knew how to use that lush little body of hers in inventive, skillfully erotic ways.

Nanotekker that he was, Blade knew his way around a female body, but she'd still shown him a thing or two. He was looking forward to finding out if she had any other tricks up her pretty sleeves.

She owed him, and he fully intended to collect.

* * *

Elyn woke into nightmare.

She was naked and bound in force restraints, spread-eagle across a bunk in a ship's cabin she didn't recognize. *But he's dead,* her disoriented brain shrieked. *Kruz is dead! This isn't supposed to happen again*!

He'd fooled her. Somehow he'd made her think Blade had killed him, but he was still alive, still capable of plunging her into horror. There'd be knives next, digging into her ass, her back. And Urthar, smirking like a demon as he plied his lash under his master's command, tearing screams from her raw throat.

The vampires would lap up her blood and pain like cats sharing a bowl of cream, repulsive tongues tracing over her skin until she wanted to vomit. Kruz's dick would rip into her dry cunt in merciless thrusts until she screamed her throat raw.

Kruz loved listening to her scream. He'd told her so often enough.

The door chimed and whispered opened, and she jerked her head around, expecting to see Kruz stroll in, moving with that insouciant grace, so astonishing in such a mountainous brute. No'Bin Urthar and Stig Daven would be right on his heels, eager to share in her suffering.

Instead, Blade filled the door, dressed in black skinpants and gleaming black boots, an equally black shirt open to bare his elegantly muscled chest. He gave her a lazy smile that faded as he took in her expression.

"You've got to go," she told him frantically. "He's coming, he's here, somehow he survived…"

Dark eyes flickered. "Who's here?"

"Kruz! He's still alive!"

His expression hardened with suspicion. "Are you trying to play me?"

Panic clawed at her with icy talons, making it hard to think. "You're Kith, you fool! If he gets his hands on you, he's going to enslave you! It'll all be for nothing." Kruz had punished her viciously for warning Blade and allowing him to escape.

Blade's eyes widened. "You're serious. Oh, Stellar Gods." He crossed the cabin in three long strides, bent over her, and started stripping off the restraints from her ankles and wrists.

"You've got to run," she whispered, terrified and obsessed. "Leave me. He'll be here any minute. You can't take me with you -- he'll find us. He'll know where I am. I can never escape. He always finds me. Always…"

"Elyn, he's dead!" Blade sat down and dragged her into his arms. He felt so strong and hard, almost as if he could protect her. But he couldn't. No one could. "I killed him three months ago. He can't hurt you."

"No, he's still alive, he tied me up like he always --"

"That was me, damn it." His powerful arms tightened around her, and he stroked her hair. "I was just being a smartass. Trying to play a bondage game." He growled a curse, the sound raw with self-disgust. "Apparently not one of my better ideas."

Elyn froze, afraid to hope. Some bone-deep part of her soul had always known Kruz was still out there, just waiting for her to relax her guard. She'd had countless nightmares that began just like this: herself, naked and bound, Kruz walking in with Urthar right behind him.

"Are you sure? Are you *sure* he's dead? He's so fucking cunning, and he loves tricks, loves to make you think there's a chance when there's not. This is just the kind of thing he'd do."

"Oh, he's dead, all right," Blade told her with grim certainty. "I'd show you a memage, except I don't think you need to see that much gore right now."

Well, that would be proof -- a memory image taken directly from Blade's recollection of the incident. Faint hope rose through her fear. "No, please -- show me. If he's dead, I need to see it."

"All right." He sighed. "Here, look."

The next instant, a three-dimensional image filled the air beside the bunk. The corpse was covered in blood, its decapitated head lying a meter away. Crimson splashed Kruz's broad, brutal face and hatchet nose. His icy eyes were wide with astonished fury, while his narrow lips lay open over his fangs.

Elyn was no stranger to violence, so despite the blood, she could make out the deep wounds across the corpse's chest, arms, and legs that looked as if they'd been hacked with a nanoknife. The quantity of blood was consistent with his wounds; it splashed the bulkhead and puddled on the deck around him in wide red pools.

"It's him," she whispered, astonished. "You really did it. You killed Kruz."

"And I find myself very glad I took my time." He stroked a hand through her hair again. "You don't have to be afraid anymore."

"The newsies all said he was dead." Elyn sank

against Blade's side as she stared at the image. "And I didn't feel him in my mind. He'd always been there, ever since he'd turned me. I hoped he was dead, but deep down I was afraid it might be some kind of trick. He knew you were hunting him, so maybe he --"

"He didn't. He's definitely dead." Blade studied the image with grim satisfaction. "Really, really dead."

Elyn closed her eyes. "Thank you." Pressing her lips against his cheek, she kissed him. "Thank you."

* * *

As her lips brushed his cheek, Blade felt the tears beading her long lashes. He winced, silently cursing himself. The mental damage she'd suffered at Kruz's hands was obviously far greater than he'd realized. In his defense, she'd showed no sign of rape trauma during that night six months ago. Just the opposite. She'd made love to him with a hungry passion that suggested she wanted him just as much as he wanted her.

So he'd tied her up tonight intending a display of dominance to drive home the idea that she'd better cooperate. But the minute Blade had walked into his quarters, he'd realized his mistake. She'd been pale as frost, her green eyes huge and helpless, her body racked by rolling shivers of animal panic.

Blade had been shocked by the contrast between that terrified woman and the tough, competent warrior who had eluded him for three months. Her irrational conviction that Kruz was still alive told him everything he needed to know about her treatment at the vampire's hands.

For weeks now, he'd been wrestling with what to do about her role in the death of his team. He'd thought that since she'd been able to warn him of Kruz's intention to enslave him, she could have also warned him his people were in danger too. He was beginning to realize how astonishing it was that she'd been able to warn him about anything at all.

Suddenly a slender hand cupped his head, curled into a fist in his hair, and dragged his head down to meet Elyn's hungry mouth. Blade stiffened in surprise as she suckled his lips, licking and biting with delicate greed.

He drew in a started breath that reemerged as a moan. He'd never had anyone kiss him like a drowning woman gulping air. Her tongue thrust between his lips in hot demand, and she slid across his lap, straddling him. He was instantly aware that she was gloriously naked, her bare breasts full and warm against his chest. All that lay between his cock and her cunt was the thin fabric of his skinpants.

Her free hand moved to cradle his face, her fingers warm and tender as her tongue swirled around his. She rolled her hips, pressing her weight deliciously against his hardening shaft, brushing her hard nipples back and forth across his chest. The friction was exquisite, perfectly calculated to drive him out of his mind.

Arousal hit him like a storm, despite his bewildered confusion. What had happened to the panic-stricken woman who'd greeted him when he'd walked in?

"Wait, I'm getting whiplash," Blade panted when she broke away from his mouth to begin nibbling her way to his ear. "Weren't you scared out of your mind a minute ago?"

"He's dead," Elyn growled against his mouth, her hands moving to fist in his shirt. She ripped it off his shoulders with one hard, twisting jerk. "I'd have been his slave for decades more, but you killed him. You *freed* me. I don't have to murder anymore. I don't have to crawl to him. I don't have to suffer. *And I want to fuck.*"

He blinked at the rough demand and swallowed hard, his mouth suddenly full of saliva. She slid off his lap, grabbed the heel of his boot, and hauled. Fasteners popped and the boot slid off his calf.

Elyn went to work on its gleaming mate, her eyes fierce as a hawk's. When the second boot thumped to the floor, she grabbed the waistband of his skinpants. They tore away in her grip, leaving him resting on his elbows with his cock lying hard and heavy against his belly. He blinked up at her.

Elyn stared at his shaft and slid onto the mattress until she crouched over him like a feline predator. Her blonde hair tumbled across his thighs in a cascade of cool silken curls as she lowered her head. Her long fingers felt warm as she wrapped them around him.

And her mouth -- Oh, Stellar Gods, her mouth was hot and wet, lips sealing hard, tongue sliding back and forth around his shaft. Every time she sucked, pleasure spiked in his blood, a hot thrum that followed every flick of her tongue and stroke of her fingers.

His eyes tracked the swing of her breasts, and he sat up to cup them. They filled his hands, the skin impossibly smooth and warm, nipples flushed a delicate rose. He teased one with thumb and forefinger, pinching and stroking. She purred around his cock, a soft feline rumble of hunger and pleasure.

He reached with his other hand to stroke down her back, enjoying the contours of delicate shoulder blades, the dip of her waist, the curve of her ass, at once strong and feminine. He didn't think he'd ever felt anything as smooth as her skin, so ripe and soft beneath his fingertips.

He explored her lovely backside, dipping between her thighs until he found the tight, wet opening of her sex. He caught his breath in anticipation as he slid two fingers inside her.

She growled in delight even as she sucked him so hard, his feet twitched in helpless pleasure. "If you keep that up," he managed despite his dry mouth, "I'm going to come way too soon."

Elyn pulled off him so abruptly he blinked and bit back a moan of disappointment. Which died as she planted one hand in the center of his chest and pushed him onto his back with a hard shove. She was astride him before he had time to register her intentions, one hand aiming his cock upward as she rose above it. Her green eyes glinted at him, cat hungry, and then she sank, impaling herself in a breathless swoop that ripped his breath from his lungs.

"Stellar gods…" he wheezed.

She growled at him, showing fangs. He blinked. They looked very sharp, and white enough to glow.

Elyn began to ride him. Slowly at first, as if to savor the sweet sensation of his cock buried so deep. Blade's head spun at the feeling of wet silk heat rubbing the length of his shaft, then down and down and *down,* every millimeter a glorious exploration of delight. And up again, and down again, until her breasts bounced in a sweet rhythm that tempted him to cup them in his hands. God, they felt amazing, so soft and warm, a sensual feast to his fingertips. He caressed them and moaned as she fucked him.

Gloriously ruthless.

Chapter Two

Blade felt huge inside Elyn, which was no surprise considering his girth, a luscious length of hard male heat. She wondered if a woman had conferred his nickname, talking about something other than a knife.

Gods, the sight of him lying sprawled beneath her. His dark eyes looked stunned, his mouth flushed and swollen from her hunger. The big vein pulsed hard in the strong column of his neck, and she eyed it with predatory intent, fangs aching.

Not yet. Not until she'd made him come. Not until *she'd* come. She rolled her hips and shuttered her eyes. Ahhhhhh, he felt incredible.

His fingers stroked her nipples, adding to her pleasure with each teasing pluck and twist. Elyn let her head roll back, closing her eyes as she savored each velvety sensation -- cock in cunt, fingers on breasts, sweet, rolling waves of pleasure.

He released his gentle grip on one nipple. She opened her eyes, about to protest, only to suck in a breath as he slid a thumb between her inner lips. He captured hot juice on his fingers and began to circle her clit. The instant raw jolt of pleasure startled a scream from her lips.

Blade grinned up at her. "Like that?"

"Whatever gave you that idea?" she managed, vaguely amazed she had the brainpower to joke.

Still she rode him, watching his handsome face as he hunched up to meet her, his hard abdomen flexing as he drove his cock deep. Her orgasm pulsed closer with every circle of his thumb on clit, pinch of fingers on nipple, stroke of velvet shaft in creamy cunt. Elyn shivered at the waves of molten pleasure and eyed the pounding vein in his throat.

Then he threw his head back and arched beneath her with a roar as his orgasm seized him and threw him high. The abrupt drive of his dick in her depths catapulted her into climax, and she gasped, coming in thrumming waves.

Falling forward, Elyn caught his hair in both her hands, tipping his head up so she could find that tormenting vein. She bit him, and he jerked, half in pain, half in pleasure, and then she was drinking, hot swallows of distilled delight.

His arms closed around her, and he held her tenderly as she drank. "Yesssss," he hissed. "God, that feels good. Take it. Take *me*..."

So she did. His blood was a crimson spill of raw male strength flavored with a fizzing rasp of nanotek.

Elyn had dreamed of his blood, of his cock, of his strong, skilled hands since the night they'd made love. Sometimes, true, she'd dreamed he'd killed her afterward -- she still wasn't entirely convinced he meant her no harm. But she'd still dreamed.

Now he filled her in reality, his cock pumping his orgasm, his heart pulsing his blood into her mouth.

And she was lost in him.

* * *

Stellar Gods, the feel of her fine inner muscles rippling around his cock, drawing deep the last pulses of his climax, her mouth sharp and busy on his throat. Her teeth inflicted a delicate sting of pain that somehow drove his delight higher, like a hot spice in sweet cream.

Until at last she collapsed atop him, sweating, silken limbs and velvet breasts pressed against him, and slid her fangs from his throat. He panted with her, listening to the hard thump of her heart echoing his own.

"I dreamed of you," she murmured, lips warm against his throat. "But it was never as sweet as this."

"I dreamed of you too." Some of those dreams had been as violent as they were erotic, and they'd troubled him on waking. But he felt no desire to hurt her now.

She'd been hurt enough.

He'd seen the scars in her eyes as she'd lain stretched across the bed in his stupidly cruel restraints. His wounded, broken Elyn.

His?

Now, wait a fucking minute. As delicious as she was -- and he'd never had better -- he didn't think he wanted to take on the shattered mess he'd glimpsed behind her tritanium facade. Her soul all but rattled.

He wanted a woman in fewer pieces, thank you. Not that he didn't have cracks of his own. Kruz had inflicted some of them when he'd killed every friend Blade had.

Blade had failed them all. He hadn't been there when Kruz and his vampire team had attacked; he'd been in bed with Elyn. Which was why Kruz had ordered her to seduce him at that particular time.

Joval, Borin, Ulo Mada, Adelia, and Charan. His comrades, all dead. Joval, who'd had such a way with a knife and a joke, Borin, slim as a rapier and loyal to the death. Ulo, the team's muscle, big and clever. Charan, braver than any man he'd ever met. And Adelia, sweet Adelia, who'd once held his heart before she and Charan found love.

And then there'd been Arden Galen, the man he'd sworn to protect. Arden's only sin had been to offer the winning bid on a space station construction contract worth trillions. Winning bids had been a specialty of Arden's, which was what got him killed. One of his rivals had decided to invest in Kruz's skills in order to discourage the habit.

Blade had slain the rival first. That was part of the service he offered. If he failed to protect you, he avenged you. Interplanetary law was a patchwork thing at best; sometimes one had to buy justice. And Blade provided it.

Which meant absolutely nothing in the end. Arden had left a widow and three small children to grieve for him. All so Kruz could add to his pile of blood money.

Assassination had apparently been a lucrative career for the vampire. All in all, no one Blade had ever killed deserved it more than Kruz.

* * *

"So," Elyn said into his sated, somewhat dazed silence. "What now?" She had slipped off his body to regard him with a wary intensity, her body still, ready for defense or attack.

And there was fear in her dark emerald eyes. Fear of him, because she knew as well as he did that her vampire strength was no match for a nanotekker's raw power.

Blade found her fear stung. It was far too similar to what he'd seen in her eyes when she'd thought Kruz was about to walk in. "I'm not going to hurt you," he snapped, irritated. "You've suffered enough."

"But I seduced you," Elyn observed, her tone quiet, supremely logical. Her eyes were just as darkly wary. "I made sure you weren't at Arden Galen's mansion to defend him and your fellow bodyguards. I kept you away until it was too late."

"I was the one who took the night off, Elyn," Blade said, his anger draining into weariness. "If it hadn't been you, it would have been somebody else at that bar. I'd been on duty for two months straight protecting Arden, working eighteen-hour days. I wanted a drink and a woman, in that order. So I wouldn't have been there regardless."

Kruz had jammed his team's distress calls to make sure Blade had no idea what had happened until he walked in on the gory scene. He shuddered at the memory of gleaming white marble splattered with blood, smears of brain crushed beneath a bootheel, bits of flesh and gore scattered here and there like confetti at some horrific celebration.

Stellar Gods.

Elyn studied him, her gaze level and sharp. "You thought I was guilty enough to chase me all these weeks."

"I was wrong."

"What about Urthar and Daven?"

He stiffened, wondering if she was going to argue that they, too, were Kruz's slaves. "They'll get no mercy from me." Blade had seen the postmortem recording from Adelia's internal computer, the only one Kruz hadn't found and erased. He'd heard the vampires laugh at Adelia's screams as Urthar used his knife.

No, they didn't deserve mercy.

"Good." Elyn's gaze went feral and flat. "I want to help you hunt them."

He blinked, not sure this broken creature was up to revenge. Or that it would be good for her even if she was. "I don't think…"

"I need this." Her lips shaped the next word with an obvious effort. "Please."

Stellar Gods help him, he couldn't resist those eyes. They slid right past all his psychic defenses, neat as a blade. He sighed. "Very well."

"Good." She sat up and scraped her blonde hair out of her face. "I'd have gone after them regardless.

Now we won't be getting in one another's way."

He snorted. "We wouldn't want that."

* * *

They talked after that, voices quiet in his dim quarters. Blade soon saw the advantages of teaming with her, broken or not. Elyn knew the two vampires' habits, their strengths and weaknesses, the way they fought, and the way they thought.

"Urthar is the older of the two, which makes him the most dangerous," she told him.

"Why?" Blade asked, interested. "He looks like a featherweight." Urthar was thin as a dagger blade, especially compared to his hulking partner. Stig Daven was a cyborg mercenary who weighed in at two hundred kilos, half of it tech and reinforced bone. Blade wasn't looking forward to tangling with him, given that all the tech was now enhanced by a vampire's strength.

"Age brings power to vampires," Elyn explained. "That's what made Kruz such a nightmare; he was over three hundred years old. Urthar is two hundred and twenty. By all rights he should have escaped Kruz a century ago, but he stayed because he and Kruz have the same revolting tastes. He's quick and experienced, and far, far stronger than he looks. He's going to be damned near as hard to take down as Kruz."

"Fighting style?"

"Likes blades. A lot. His favorite weapon is the sonic ripper, and he likes to take his time using it. He's quick as a snakecat. If you're not careful, he'll slip that blade right past your reinforced ribs."

Blade grunted. "What about Daven?"

She curled a lip. "He's younger than I am. Kruz was curious about how a vampire's power would be enhanced by a cyborg's tech. He's strictly muscle, but he's mean, and he's good hand-to-hand. Tends to drop his guard on his left, though. I broke three of his ribs when I escaped. He'll have undergone regeneration, but ribs heal slowly. Concentrate your blows there."

"Where do you think they'll go to ground?"

"Kruz had a safe house on Opolo. It's more fortress than anything else, and Urthar designed the defenses himself. He likes it there, so I suspect that's where we'll find them. If they're not out hunting you."

Blade was beginning to think he'd underestimated her. Wounded she might be, but she had a keen mind. "Why would they come after me?" he asked, though he knew the answer perfectly well.

"You killed Kruz. Urthar loved that psychotic fuck like a demon worships Satan. He's going to want revenge." She pursed her tempting lips thoughtfully, eyes going narrow. "Daven probably considers himself well rid of Kruz -- he didn't enjoy slavery any more than I did -- but he'll follow Urthar because he'd do better with him than without him. If I know Urthar, they'll go right back to the assassination business without missing a beat."

"If we don't kill them first."

"Which would be my preference." There was a diamond-cold gleam in her eyes. It occurred to Blade that for all her vulnerabilities, Elyn Castel would be a bad enemy to have. He was damned lucky she hadn't really wanted to kill him, just get the hell away.

Her psychic scars might be horrific, but she didn't let them stop her from kicking ass. He found he rather liked that.

* * *

They fell asleep, tangled together more like lovers than allies. Blade woke with his face buried in her tumble of bright hair, her clean female scent filling his nose. Elyn's head lay on his chest. When his hands cupped the warm, lithely muscled curve of her ass, her green eyes blinked open.

They made sleepy love, then wandered into his ship's sybaritic shower and did it again, her back braced against the curving wall as he pounded into her. She did not feed from him either time, much to his disappointment. Even his Tekker blood volume needed more time than that to recover, she told him, adding that she had no intention of giving him anemia right before a potential fight to the death.

Logically, he knew she was right, but he found himself missing the delicate sting of her teeth.

He wondered why the thought of feeding her filled him with such savage satisfaction.

* * *

Elyn started working the ripper's power bracer down over her hand to her wrist, then settled the attached silver rings into place on her fingers. A mental order made the ripper flicker into view -- a length of three-dimensional light, thin as a rapier blade and about the same length. The light blade itself was harmless, being basically a triddie projection; it served the same purpose as tracer rounds, letting the user know where the actual blade field was. Otherwise you could end up cutting your own hand off with the sonic vibrations the ripper projected.

Blade eyed the glowing weapon warily. "If you had a ripper, why didn't you use it on me?"

Her gaze flicked away from his. "Because I didn't get it for you. This is for Urthar." Elyn switched the ripper off and went to work attaching the shield bracer to her left arm. "Plus, I didn't want station security watching my every move. And they would have, it they'd picked up the ripper. I knew you were monitoring their comp system."

"Yet you're using it now." He watched as she tested the shield, its repulse field delineated by a glowing disc. It would let her own blade through, but nothing else.

She shrugged. "Urthar and Daven are probably after you, and I don't care to be unarmed when they show up. I'm good hand-to-hand, but not enough to fight a vampire Urthar's age." The twin bracers gleaming on her forearms, she moved to the hotel room's wide closet and got out a single suitcase. It was already packed and ready to go. Elyn gave him a curt nod. "I'm ready."

He studied her face, eyes narrow and too perceptive for her peace of mind. "It wasn't just Kruz. You're afraid of them. No -- you're afraid of Urthar."

She went still. "I have reason to be. He's a more creative monster than Kruz. Kruz wanted to break me so he could force me to do what he wanted. Urthar loved listening to me scream. He likes his ripper, but he *really* likes his whips." Elyn snapped her teeth closed, realizing too late that she'd said too much. The pity in Blade's black eyes burned like an acid bath.

He thought she was weak.

And worse, he had reason. Elyn gritted her teeth, remembering the raw terror she'd felt when she'd woken tied to his bunk. Shame scalded her. "Don't you pity me," she snarled. "I don't deserve it. I survived those bastards with my sanity intact."

"Yes." He said the word quietly, without condescension. "You did. How did you do it?"

There was enough genuine admiration in the question that she felt her protective rage die. "You. And the others he sent me to seduce." Her room door opened and whispered closed behind them as they walked out into the cool, soothing pastels of the hall.

"At first I couldn't stand to be touched. I hated our victims as much as I hated Kruz and Urthar. As much as I hated myself." Elyn raked her hair out of her eyes and shrugged. "But as the decades passed, those moments with men like you became a kind of twisted solace. They were going to die -- or suffer a horrific loss at the very least -- but I could give them *something,* a few minutes of peace and pleasure. And I could have the same."

He blinked. "But you were helping Kruz."

Elyn shot him a look, but there was no accusation in his eyes. He was simply trying to understand. She sighed. "I had no choice. Literally. That's what I was trying to explain to you. Those of us who are Kith -- like you are, like I was -- have a psychic immunity to a vampire's ability to control a mortal's mind. Unfortunately, we're also the only ones who can survive becoming vampires."

"And the psychic resistance breaks down when a vamp drains a Kith and infect him with the vampire virus." Seeing her brows rise, he smiled slightly. "I did do some research."

She gave him a grim nod of approval, then went on. "After the transformation, the master vampire controls the slave vamp as utterly as you control your nanoplant computer. It takes at least a century to gain the strength to break that control, and I'm nowhere near that old."

"So you were helpless."

"And I also knew that any part I played in what happened, I was going to pay for." Elyn's mouth tightened as she remembered just how she'd paid, and how often. "Kruz and Urthar were the only ones who didn't pay."

His eyes narrowed and went cold. "We're going to change that."

* * *

They entered the sprawling deck where the *Stiletto* waited among the other small private craft. Larger vessels orbited the station, with passengers and crew shuttling back and forth. It was late in the midwatch, and the deck was deserted except for the multiarmed servoids whispering between the ships, doing maintenance.

The *Stiletto*'s gangplank deployed at their approach, and Elyn strode toward it at Blade's side. "I'd suggest heading for Opolo first," she told him. "That's where the safe house is located, and that's where Urthar will want to go to ground."

"If the house is as much a fortress as you say..." Blade broke off as Elyn's head lifted. Ice skittered down her spine, and she flicked her fingers at him in a "Wait" gesture.

Which was when Daven hit him like a runaway shuttle in a hard crunch of muscle and bone that rammed him right off his feet.

Elyn swore as the two cyborgs tumbled across the deck, a blur of swinging fists and vicious kicks. They skidded apart, only to lunge at one another again with grunts of effort. Blade slammed a booted foot between Daven's third and fourth rib, right where the vampire had the healing break she'd described. Daven cursed and grabbed for his boot-top. Had to be a sheathed knife.

Just as she expected, a nanoknife shimmered in his fist as he came up swinging. Blade leaped back, avoiding the strike and flicking his own nanoknife out of a sleeve.

Mouth tightening, Elyn activated her ripper and

energy shield as she started toward them. The energy blade shimmered as she walked, emitting a low chime.

"Traitor bitch," a voice hissed, and she jerked aside by sheer instinct. A blade flashed past her cheekbone, and Urthar appeared as he dropped his stealth field.

She laughed in a bark. "Even you're not delusional enough to believe I owe you anything, you fucking rapist. You, and sure as hell not Kruz."

"He gave you immortality!" Urathar lunged. The ripper projection peeled a bell-like note from his fingers.

Elyn swung up her shield and drove her ripper through it. The two blades collided with a metallic ring entirely too damned pretty for anything so deadly. "He *tortured* me, and you helped him."

He whipped his weapon around hers and drove it toward her heart, but she caught it on her shield, knocking the strike skyward.

Simultaneously, Elyn flew into full extension, aiming the blade toward his right eye. He ducked and spun away, and their shields collided with a hiss and ozone reek.

Her heart pounded furiously, but her mind had gone white and calm, focused with a predator's intensity on his narrow hands, on the bunching muscles of forearm and leg. She sensed the next attack coming, a feint that flashed toward her ripper only to dance aside when she tried to knock it aside with her shield.

Elyn hissed as Urthar's ripper sliced her forearm, sending a crimson splatter flying upward. Twisting, she managed to throw up her shield and deflect it from her heart. Their bodies surged against one another, and the vampire's greater strength and weight bore her backward.

She slammed a leg back and caught herself before he could force her off-balance, then spun aside like a bullfighter.

Urthar's ice-white eyes blazed in his pale, narrow face, hate jerking his thin mouth. Their rippers danced, chiming as they tested each other's guard, seeking an opening, a path to heart or throat or hot, beating vein.

Pain bit her arm, but she thrust the sensation away and ordered her cyplant to take care of it. The pain faded and the bleeding slowed as the implant accelerated her vampire body's formidable healing abilities.

Enough wounds, however, would overwhelm it. She couldn't afford to let the vampire cut her again.

Urthar's cold smile told her he intended to do just that. "I'm going to butcher you, little sow."

Chapter Three

The nanoknife's thin blade scored Blade's cheek in a line of humming fire. He'd ordered his skin armored, but that kind of blade could still cut even nanobot-reinforced flesh. He grabbed Daven's wrist and jerked. The big cyborg flipped over his head, and he spun and let go, sending the fucker flying.

The cyborg vamp hit the ground rolling, bouncing to his feet to rush Blade again, a snarl lifting his lips. Fangs flashed and his blade hummed.

Blade twisted sideways, feeling his foe's weapon hiss past his flat belly. Daven dropped, sweeping one leg like a scythe. His reinforced boot toe rammed the back of Blade's knee, and Blade went down with a grunt of pain. If not for his cyborg joints, he'd have been crippled.

Daven pounced, blade drawn back. Blade caught the vampire on the soles of his boots and sent him flying, then bounced to his feet and leaped after him. His nanoknife hummed a high, vicious note that rose to a scream when he drove it downward.

Daven twisted in midair, cat quick, fangs bared. He landed on his feet with a solid thump, driving his nanoknife forward to catch Blade's as the Tekker landed with a *bang* of boot soles. Nanoknives hummed, screeched as blade hit blade again and again.

Strikes to the head, to the heart, to arms and legs -- so fast even Blade couldn't see them. He fought by instinct, his mind a cool, empty silence, aware of nothing except Daven's blade, Daven's eyes, the twist and leap of Daven's body. He couldn't afford anything else.

* * *

Elyn circled with Urthar, savagely intent on killing

her tormentor. But even as she fought, some part of her was acutely aware of Blade and the hum and scream of the nanoknives. The rhythm picked up, grew frantic, and Elyn made her mistake. Her eyes flicked sideways.

It was only for a split second, but Urthar saw it. A vicious grin split his narrow face, and his eyes lit with savage pleasure. "Ah, *there's* your empty heart!"

He whirled and darted, sword lifted, right at Blade's broad back.

Elyn acted without thought. Pure reflex sent her leaping with all her vampire strength. She was smaller than Urthar, lighter of bone and muscle, and she flew over the vampire's head to come down with a thud right by Blade's side. Driving her shield against his shoulder, she shoved. He fell, skidding across the floor on his slick combat armor.

Elyn got her blade up, catching Ulrich's vicious swing in a parry that jarred her teeth. She knew an instant of triumph.

And something hit her in the back with a solid thump that sent her stumbling forward. Her computer shrieked, "*Warning! Potentially fatal injury. Abort combat and retreat.*"

She looked down to see the tip of the nanoknife protruding from her chest, glowing softly as its vibrations ripped her flesh.

Daven had stabbed her from behind.

She heard Blade roar her name. Daven laughed and twisted the knife. Her momentary numbness vanished in an explosion of icy agony as the sonic blade tore her lungs, her flesh, her bones. Elyn tried to scream, but it emerged only as a bubbling gasp.

Urathar grinned. "Revenge is sweet, bitch." As if in slow motion, she saw his blade drop as he straightened, the better to enjoy her suffering at

Daven's hand.

That was her chance. She swung her blade up, vampire fast, gasping in anguish.

Urthar's eyes widened, and he went for the parry. He was too late. Her sword sliced right through his neck, and his head flew. His body hit its knees and toppled sideways.

Behind her Daven roared. "Bitch, you're --"

He never finished the sentence.

Elyn sensed a rush of air and rage, and suddenly the blade was gone as Daven tore it from her flesh to meet Blade's attack.

A high note sounded, falling to the familiar growling snarl of a nanoknife cutting bone. There was no scream, no gasp, but Elyn's vampire senses told her someone had just died.

Something bumped and rolled across the floor. Elyn looked down to see Daven's head tumble past her left foot. A meaty thud sounded behind her -- the rest of the cyborg vampire hitting the deck plates.

Her knees buckled, and she started to fall, hissing, bubbling as she fought to breathe.

A strong arm slid around her waist. "Elyn, what the fuck did you think you were doing?" Fear and temper sharpened Blade's voice to a bark.

"Saving your… ass," Ellen wheezed, though her voice was far fainter than she liked.

Blade lowered her to the deck, his arms careful and tender.

"I'm Tekker," he growled, frustration ringing in his voice. "My sensors would've warned me in time to jump out of the way. And my armored skin would have turned the blade…"

"Maybe… Or maybe Urthar would have shoved that ripper through your heart." Her voice fell to a gasping whisper as she stared blindly up at the ceiling. "I couldn't take the risk."

Ice rolled up her legs as her heartbeat began to slow. Elyn coughed, the sound deep and bubbling, and so damned painful it was all she could do not to shriek. Her mouth filled with the taste of copper. Another cough sent crimson spraying from her lips.

Distantly she heard Blade snarl, "Where's that regeneration unit?" Then, coldly, "Tell them to haul ass. I want them here ten minutes ago. She's in shock and coughing blood."

Elyn fought to keep her eyes open, but the ceiling spun sickeningly overhead.

Warning, her implant said. *Restarting your heart…*

The lights went out.

* * *

Blade paced the infirmary in long, restless strides, staring at the transparent tube that contained Elyn's regenerating body. Clouds of pink fog billowed in the tube, concealing her from view. Daven had damn near gutted her before Blade had managed to kill him.

She'd almost given her life for him. Never mind that he'd sensed the attack. Never mind that he'd been turning even as Urthar rushed him. Caught between two vampires, he could have easily ended up dead.

Elyn had saved him, and damn near died doing it.

He remembered the way she looked moving under him, all heat and passion. When he thought about how he'd have felt if she died, his stomach twisted. He felt hollowed out. A shell with a hole where his heart should be.

Why did she risk herself for me?

* * *

Elyn woke lying in an infirmary bed. Her body had that achy, logy feeling she associated with a session in regeneration. Which meant she'd come damn close to getting killed, as vampires healed most injuries just fine. Anything bad enough to put a vamp in regen would have killed a human outright.

A thought had her jolting upright despite her exhaustion. "Blade? Where's Blade?" They'd come so damned close to killing him. What if…

"I'm here." Blade rose from a chair beside the bed. She hadn't even seen him sitting there. His dark gaze was surprisingly tender. "How are you feeling?"

Elyn blew out a breath. "Much better now that Daven and Urthar are dead." A sudden thought made her frown. "They *are* dead, right?"

His smile was savage. "Oh, yeah. Between the two of us, they're most definitely dead."

"How did Station Security feel about us beheading a couple of vampires?"

Blade lifted on broad shoulder in a half-shrug. "I had death warrants on both of them, so Security didn't kick too hard."

Elyn considered that. He would have had to go to court to prove the two men were involved in the murders of Arden Galen and his team of bodyguards. Considering the amount of blood and DNA the vampires had left on the scene, she wasn't surprised he'd been able to get the warrants.

A new thought made her eye him warily. "Do you have a Death Warrant on me?"

"No," he said shortly. "I didn't seek one. You weren't involved in those killings. You were with me."

Elyn lifted a brow. "But I was still an accessory."

"Anything you did was not by choice." His gaze searched hers. "Are you ready to get out of here? Because I don't mind telling you, I hate infirmaries."

"Too much time in them?"

"Something like that."

"Then I'm ready to go."

* * *

They walked out of the infirmary a few minutes later. Elyn was still moving slowly. She felt weak as a fledgling before her first feeding, and her hands had a distressing tendency to shake.

Blade studied her. "You need blood."

She couldn't hold his gaze. "They gave me a transfusion."

"But you need more." His eyes blazed hot. "You need *me*. And I need *you*."

He was right, of course. There was psychic energy in feeding from a donor that you didn't get from a medical process. "Yes." She could barely get the word out through her tight throat. Her eyes flicked to the pulse in his throat, then across the width of his shoulders and down to his big hands.

Blade lifted his chin as if offering his throat.

Shame stung her. "You're not just a blood source to me."

His gaze didn't drop. "If I had been, you wouldn't have risked your life for me."

Elyn stiffened. "I don't want you out of duty."

"Duty has nothing to do with it." Heat sizzled in his stare. "This is about us." He reached out and took her hand. His fingers felt warm, alive -- and possessive.

* * *

They walked through the *Stiletto*'s airlock doors with their fingers still entwined.

Elyn found that her gaze kept sliding away from his, no matter how she tried to hold it. "I'm almost seventy years old. How do you make me feel sixteen?"

"What you feel is vulnerability." Blade pulled her around to face him. "I feel the same. It's tough to let someone in so close. They can hurt you." His dark eyes seemed to bore into hers, demanding her belief. Her faith. "But I'm not going to hurt you. How could I?" Pain flashed across his handsome face -- the expression of a man with a mortal wound. "When Daven stabbed you, I felt like he'd scooped out my guts. It hurt worse than when my team died, and I'd fought beside them for two decades." He shook his head. "How did you get so deep in me so fast?"

Elyn's heart was pounding so hard it thundered in her ears. "Infatuation?" But she didn't believe it.

"I'm forty-two years old. I know infatuation when I feel it. This is different. This is..." Blade tugged her full against him and threaded both hands through her hair. His mouth stormed hers in a delicious assault of lips and tongue and teeth. She moaned as he spun her around. Her back hit the airlock door, and he leaned into her, solid and male.

Elyn gasped at the feel of his cock pressing against her belly as he cradled her head between his hands and made love to her mouth. It was intoxicating as astral mead, a spill of fire that blazed like a fuse from her lips to her sex.

Her nipples hardened helplessly, and she instinctively grabbed the round, firm muscle of his ass so she could pull herself against him as close as skin. "I couldn't let you die," she gasped against his mouth. Rolling her hips, she savored the feeling of his hard length, his big body, his Tekker strength. "I need you too much."

Blade's mouth covered hers again, and they drank each other, desperate, drugging kisses that made her entire body tighten and her fangs throb in her upper jaw.

His big hands left her head to find the hem of her

top, and he stripped it off over her head with one hungry pull. It hit the floor with a soft thump. Her breasts bounced, bare nipples tightening. His hand cupped one, lifted the soft flesh. When his lips closed over her nipple, Elyn threw her head back with a throaty, helpless moan.

Blade dropped to his knees like a supplicant, his hands hooking the waistband of her skinpants. The fabric rolled down her hips, but only made it halfway to her knees before he yielded to temptation.

Blade's hands found her ass, dragging her forward to meet his hot and eager mouth. His tongue slipped between her folds, slick, a hard thrust over her clit, deliciously wet. She squirmed, panted, writhed. "Blade, Gods, Blade..."

Her hands found his hair, forked through the silken strands, held on tight as he sent her higher with each long lap.

* * *

Even as Blade savored her sweetness, his hands worked her skinpants the rest of the way down her long runner's legs. He paused only long enough to pop the seals on her boots. She stepped out of them like a dreamer, and he left off tonguing her. Rising to his feet, he tumbled her into his arms.

"Hi, there." Gloriously naked, she grinned up at him and looped her arms around his neck. His cheeks were flushed, her eyes bright, and her fangs gleamed white in her wicked smile.

"Hi, yourself." Blade had to grin back as he carried her down the corridor to his quarters.

It was all he could do to look where he was going. His eyes kept drifting down to the lush nudity cuddled in his arms. She felt delightfully warm and soft everywhere she should, and taut and muscled everywhere else. Her blonde hair lay in artful curls around her shoulders, and her nipples looked as rosy and fat as a pair of cherries. He knew from experience that they tasted just as sweet.

The door to his quarters whispered open at his approach, and he carried her inside, heading straight for his bunk. Tumbling her onto it, Blade followed her down, his cock throbbing against the fly of his skinpants. She grabbed the hem of his shirt and hauled it off over his head.

Elyn tossed the shirt aside without watching where it landed. She was too busy tracing her fingers delicately over the ridges of his ribs. She paused to flick her fingers over Blade's erect brown nipples. He inhaled sharply in delight.

Slipping one hand down his torso, she cupped the thick bulges of his balls. Blade's dark head fell back as she caressed him through his skinpants. "Stellar Gods," he groaned. "That feels incredible."

Elyn released his testicles and slowly traced one finger up the curving length of his cock. "*You're* incredible," she breathed, staring with absorbed fascination at its thick length. Grabbing his waistband, she hauled it down, freeing his hard flesh to spill into her hands. Unable to resist, she grabbed it and angled it up. Blade watched her, eyes glittering and hot as she leaned down and slid the broad shaft into her mouth.

The hot curve of its head felt slightly nubby in her mouth as she closed her lips and suckled, enjoying the feel of him, the heat, the intense masculinity. The way he jolted against her with every pull.

Big hands slid down to find her nipples, tugging and twisting with a gentle ruthlessness that made her quiver.

Elyn moaned softly as her need intensified. She

sucked harder, and he threaded one hand through her hair, gently urging her to take him deeper.

So she did, engulfing half the big shaft in one sudden swoop that tore a gasp from his lips.

"Elyn! Oh, Gods, Elyn!" The deep groan was impossibly arousing.

She smiled around her mouthful of hard cock. The hand on her hair suddenly tightened, and he gently drew her off him. "Blade, I'm not..."

"Neither am I." Flipping her onto her back, he rose over her, seized both of her ankles, and spread her wide. Releasing one leg, he grabbed his cock. His entry made her hiss in delight.

He started thrusting -- deep, grinding digs that stimulated every erogenous zone she had.

"Blade!"

"Elyn," he growled back, fucking her hard. Claiming her. The sensation of so much cock filling her so full sent rolling waves of fire surging through her body.

He shafted her without mercy until orgasm seized her in a wicked velvet trap that pulsed and gripped deep inside her. She tossed back her head and came. And came.

And came.

Somewhere above her head, he roared, an animal bellow of pleasure. He drove to his balls and held there, head flung back, every muscle of his big body in high relief. "Stellar Gods, Elyn!"

"Yesssss," she hissed. "Oh, yes!"

* * *

The storm released them at last, and Blade collapsed on top of her, a hot, deliciously satisfying weight. He wrapped his arms around her and rolled onto his back with a soft groan, taking her with him.

Sprawling across him, Elyn panted. Deliciously sated.

Her hunger instantly ignited again when his hands found her head and guided her to the pounding vein in his throat. With a desperate moan, she bit him there. Hot blood poured over her tongue.

"Mine," he growled.

She could only growl back -- an assent, a staking of her own claim. Intoxicating minutes passed as she fed, until she sensed from his heartbeat it was time to stop. Carefully, reluctantly, she eased her fangs from his throat and dropped her head to his chest.

"I love you." Blade said the words with a stark, simple honesty.

Elyn froze, her gaze flying to his. "What?"

"I love you." He sounded utterly calm, but his eyes flickered, and he winced just slightly.

She realized two things. The first was that he expected her to reject him. The second hit her in an explosion of joy that left no room for doubt. "Gods, Blade, I love you. *I love you*!"

He blinked, and she saw an echoing joy in his eyes. "Are you sure? We barely know each other."

"We know what counts." She wrapped arms and legs around him in a silent demonstration that she had no intention of letting go. "We know more about each other than people who've spent fifty years together." Her voice dropped to a hoarse whisper. "I know I'd die for you."

"I'd kill for you. And I know I have no desire to live without you."

"But I have..." She paused, searching for a word that communicated the depth of her suffering. "... some very bad memories."

"I know," he admitted. "And at first I thought

they'd broken you."

She winced. "Maybe they did."

"Oh, kakshit," Blade said impatiently. "A broken woman wouldn't have faced her worst enemy without blinking. A broken woman wouldn't have fought him even after someone drove a blade through her lungs." His gaze went fierce. "A broken woman wouldn't have taken his head."

Looking into those dark, certain eyes, Elyn felt the rise of pride. "I did what I had to do to save you."

"And you did. Which is why..." He broke off, as if gathering his nerve. "I want you to make me a vampire."

Her eyes flew wide, astonishment shooting through her. "But then you'd be bound to me for a century or more. I'd never enslave you, but what if you changed your mind?"

"I won't." His expression was serene with surety.

Her vampire senses told her he meant every word. But..."Let's just... wait. Let's just be together for a while." God, she wanted to say yes to him so badly her fangs ached, but she wanted him to be sure even more.

He simply looked at her. "I know what I want, Elyn. And I want you." Blowing out a breath, he added, "Enough to wait until *you're* sure of *me*. Because I love you."

"And I love you." Enough to deny her own desperate need for him. Enough to wait.

Somehow, deep in her heart, Elyn knew she wouldn't have to wait long.

Angela Knight

New York Times best-selling author Angela Knight has written and published more than sixty novels, novellas, and ebooks, including the Mageverse and Merlin's Legacy series. With a career spanning more than two decades, *Romantic Times Bookclub Magazine* has awarded her their Career Achievement award in Paranormal Romance, as well as two Reviewers' Choice awards for Best Erotic Romance and Best Werewolf Romance.

Angela is currently a writer, editor, and cover artist for Changeling Press LLC. She also teaches online writing courses. Besides her fiction work, Angela's writing career includes a decade as an award-winning South Carolina newspaper reporter. She lives in South Carolina with her husband, Michael, a thirty-year police veteran and detective with a local police department.

Angela on Changeling: changelingpress.com/ angela-knight-a-26

Changeling Press E-Books

More Sci-Fi, Fantasy, Paranormal, and BDSM adventures available in e-book format for immediate download at ChangelingPress.com -- Werewolves, Vampires, Dragons, Shapeshifters and more -- Erotic Tales from the edge of your imagination.

What are E-Books?

E-books, or electronic books, are books designed to be read in digital format -- on your desktop or laptop computer, notebook, tablet, Smart Phone, or any electronic e-book reader.

Where can I get Changeling Press E-Books?

Changeling Press e-books are available at ChangelingPress.com, Amazon, Apple Books, Barnes & Noble, and Kobo/Walmart.

ChangelingPress.com

www.ingramcontent.com/pod-product-compliance
Lightning Source LLC
La Vergne TN
LVHW020525100826
845148LV00010B/1342

9781605218083